Prince of the Lake

www.immanionpress.wox.org

Prince of the Lake

First Volume of the Saga of Beowulf Wagmunding,
Prince of the Goths

Roger Butters

IMMANION PRESS
Stafford, England

Prince of the Lake
By Roger Butters
© 2004

Cover Design Gabriel Strange
Cover Art (Winter) Anne Sudworth
Art Direction and Typesetting by Gabriel Strange

Set in Garamond, 12pt

10 9 8 7 6 5 4 3 2 1

An Immanion Press Edition
http://www.immanionpress.wox.org/
info@immanionpress.wox.org

The cover image *Winter* is available as a print from
www.annesudworth.co.uk

ISBN 1-9048-5306-4

Prince of the Lake

In Memory of the real Prince of the Lake
Whose life was all too short.

Also by Roger Butters

HIS EXCELLENCY
LOOK ABOUT AND DIE

Introduction

The story of a man who becomes a hero: based on the Norse epic which bears his name, this Saga deals with the early life of the Gothic prince Beowulf Wagmunding, Earl of Slane, and his cousin Athelstan of Karron Tha, called Hawkeye.

According to his half-sister, the mystic Ljani the Red, Beowulf is a reincarnation of the mightiest of all Gothic kings, Bjorn Longspear, the non-pareil Prince of the Lake, and destined for as glorious a future. But this seems unlikely. For Beowulf is a foolish. dreamy youth, scion of a family notorious for double-dealing, and himself the son of a murderer and a whore.

As Beowulf sets out on the journey which will make or break him, he survives the perils of outlaws, monsters and shipwreck before his greatest test of all: battle against the Hellian warriors of the demoniacal Ragnar of Torre, a Son of Muspelheim. Nor are Beowulf's adversaries confined to the forces of Evil; at the end destiny plays him a cruel trick by pitting him in battle against his kinsman and greatest friend, Hawkeye of Karron Tha.

Thus Beowulf begins his progress from amiable nonentity to the greatest of all Gothic warriors, whose name to this day remains synonymous with epic legend and the eternal conflict between Good and Evil.

I think Scandinavian Paganism, to us here, is more interesting than any other. It is ... the creed of our fathers; the men whose blood still runs in our veins, whom doubtless we still resemble in so many ways.'

Thomas Carlyle

Sixty leagues she had marched, and sixty leagues more,
Seven great lovers later, she meets him again.
At first in disguise; wrapt in the bearskin -
Another name, but the same name.
Seven leagues ere she knows him -

Prince of the Lake ...

Roger Butters

HARK!
A tale of timeless glory - northern lords of long ago.
In ancient time their deeds were told in the minstrel's lay,
Through song and legend in the feasting hall,
And by greybeard warriors in the firelight.
Living yet in the memories of the gods,
Written in the dusty chronicles of Midgard,
And in the runes, which never lie.
The Norns decide on life and death,
Joy or grief, which matter not.
A man must set his course
For good or ill. Nor god nor demon
Can take the choice
From him or for him -
Yea, though they slay him,
They cannot harm him.
Not the Chooser of the Slain,
Nor the Three who sit at the foot of Yggdrasill,
Nor yet the sons of Muspelheim, when they ride over Bifrost
On the last day, and Nine Worlds are destroyed by the sword of Surtur.
The High One himself, one-eyed who knows all,
Even he knows not what men think - man's heart is his own,
Where lie good and evil, faith or treason.
As he chooses, so is he remembered
In fame or infamy, or is forgotten. All else is dust.
So it was in the days of the great heroes,
Lords of Gothmark and the Sfear, northern lands of Midgard.
Death could claim them,
But not their honour. Greatest of all,
As I have heard, was one called Beowulf,
Son of Edgtyr, son of Wagmund.
Wagmund was the son of Eymor,
Son of Angjot, son of Offa, King of all Teutonic lands,
Who some say ruled the whole of Midgard -
Whether it was thus, I know not. Offa's sire was Garmund,
Son of Helm, the son of Witlag,
Heirs to that first mightiest king, Geat,
Founder of the Gothic race. Before him
Was so long since that of it no man can speak with certainty -
Yet Hark to the Saga of Beowulf Wagmunding,
Scion of the mighty: Son of Offa, Son of Geat,
Son of Thor,
Son of ODIN ...
HARK!

9

SHYLF

Jomfar
Delee

GHUL

Bakir

Scarlet-Town

SYRDAN

THE
TAIGA

EL

RON
HA

Lake
Fanora

Whitebear
Bay

town

R. Blood

SHADRON
MOR

'olf

TORRE

FANORA

Fanora City

Eaetern
Sea

Roger Butters

Prologue: Death of a King

RATHLECK WAS dying. For nine and twenty years he had ruled the Goths, and most of his subjects could remember no other king. Of those around his deathbed, only Naur, the aged priest, had lived through the troubled reign of the king's father, Swertan the Bastard. The rest were young, and Rathleck had always been their lord.

He would die lacking six weeks and a day of the fifty-ninth year of his life. There were some, perhaps most, who would not be sorry to see him go. In time of danger, Gothmark needed a new king, young, warlike and valiant. Rathleck had had his day.

He peered into the gathering darkness and saw by the flickering candle-light a half-circle of grave warriors' faces, their names part of Gothic history, no less than his: Falgard of Feldmark, Emund of Bor, Wylf of Hrosnaberg, Rigel, and Numa, and Wagmund of Slane. He could not read their thoughts, nor they his. And they wished to know his thoughts, for he had yet one task to perform, and not his least important. Three days after his death the Wittan, or Council of Elders, would meet to elect a new king. The dying voice of the old would count for much; indeed it was unlikely that any would dare speak against it.

Naur had ceased his incantations and now leaned forward to catch any word the dying man might utter. The hushed voices of those around fell silent. Tradition forbade their inviting the king to name his successor. He would know when his time had come, and would speak. If he should die without a word, that was his right, though an ill omen.

Rathleck's hand twitched toward his weapon of many years, *Kranting*, which lay beside him on the furs. A Gothic warrior must die sword in hand, or could not enter Falhal to sup with Odin and his men and fight for them at Doomsday. The king's younger son, Prince

Hyglack, reached out and placed a giant hand upon the hilt. It was as near as any dare come to an invitation to speak.

Amongst the shadows in the Chamber of Longspear, Rathleck could discern the face of his elder son; Athkyn, pale in the half-light. Yet Athkyn the Learned was always pale - pale and fair, with scarcely a stubble on his chin, despite having reached man's estate these fifteen years. Rathleck had never really understood Athkyn, nor cared much for him either, since that tragic elk-hunt eleven years ago, when by cruel mischance he had slain his brother Herbald. Herbald, vigorous, brave and cheerful, had been everything Rathleck had desired in a son, who he had hoped would succeed him. But the Fates had decided otherwise. It would be Athkyn or Hyglack.

Hyglack was his brother's opposite. Dark as Athkyn was fair, mighty of stature, quick to anger and fierce in combat. It was hard for the old warrior to believe that he and his long-dead queen could have produced two men so different. If Athkyn was a mystery, Rathleck understood Hyglack only too well. Were he king, the Goths and their neighbours the Sfear would be at war again within days. And maybe that would be for the best; a rash and boastful warrior might be preferable to a weakling. For months Hyglack had spoken for war, and had waged it too, in border skirmishing against Ottar and Ali, sons of the Sferian king, and both such men as he. Few liked Hyglack the Dark, but none could call him coward, and he was generous with booty for his henchmen. Furthermore he was married, with a son to secure the dynasty, whilst Athkyn at three-and-thirty was still single, and took no interest in women. Or much else either, save books and idle speculation.

A crash of thunder silenced the whispering amongst those keeping vigil. Odin had sent his son, Thor Redbeard, to summon his latest warrior.

If Rathleck chose Athkyn, Hyglack might rebel. Several times of late, the king and his younger son had quarrelled; only the closeness of the blood-tie had prevented matters being pursued further. Hyglack had refrained from taking arms against his father - against a feeble brother he might have less scruple. To be sure, such treachery doomed a man to Helheim, but many preferred a crown in this world to their speculative prospects in the next. Hyglack was amongst the increasing number of those who at times openly scoffed at the gods, and seemed none the worse for it. Truly the ways of Odin were strange. Maybe there was something to be said for a man like Hyglack, who feared neither god nor demon. Yet if he were chosen, many would consider Athkyn to have the better claim, and ambitious lords often preferred a weak king.

The thunder had given way to a steady hiss of rain. Rathleck's sons and their men were conversing once more, albeit in whispers. Naur, tedious old fool, began again to mutter prayers to Odin, begging him to

14

receive a valiant warrior, sword in hand, notwithstanding that he had not fallen in battle.

Few of those present had any doubt about that. Son of Longspear, his countrymen had called him - a title more exalted than that of king, granted only to those rulers who, like their greatest hero, Bjorn Longspear, had triumphed in battle over their country's enemies. In the five hundred year history of the Goths, of seven and twenty kings Rathleck had been but the sixth to earn that name. His father, Swertan, had been the fifth; never before had father and son, or two consecutive monarchs, won such an honour. Could he but be sure that one of his sons would do likewise, Rathleck would die happy. Hyglack might possibly achieve it: Athkyn never.

Rathleck felt a coolness upon his brow where Elfryth, his niece and Hyglack's wife, had placed a sponge. She would have made a good queen; and his quiet wife was one of the few with influence over the rash prince. Yet never in five hundred years had a younger son been preferred to an elder. And weak men sometimes survived where stronger fell. His beloved Herbald would have made a better king than either, but Odin had claimed him.

Two other men of the blood royal kept vigil in the gloomy chamber. Artur Emunding, brother to Elfryth, was a proven warrior, deliberate in counsel, and universally respected. But it would be impossible for the Goths to accept Rathleck's nephew before either of his sons.

Lastly, there was Beowulf.

Beowulf Wagmunding, Earl of Slane, only son of Rathleck's daughter. Almost as tall as Hyglack's seven feet, and saving him, the strongest man in Gothmark, so mighty in build that only the heaviest horse could bear him. But assuredly none of the Gothic lords would countenence a Wagmunding as king.

Neither did Beowulf himself inspire confidence. The only son of disgraced parents, he had shown little aptitude for anything save drinking, wenching, gaming and the hunt. The niceties of court life he held in contempt. Alone amongst the warrior caste he went clean-shaven like a churl; freedmen and thralls were permitted to share his table almost as equals. And whilst few of the Gothic lords made much pretence to culture, it was doubtful whether Beowulf could write his own name. A dull, foolish fellow, who wasted his massive strength in futile sport, and would have no part in fighting the Sfear. Wherefore he was despised by Prince Hyglack, who considered his nephew little better than a coward.

Yet Rathleck had always liked Beowulf better than either of his own sons. In drink, he never beat his slaves or horses, he could laugh, even at a jest against himself; Rathleck had never seen him angry. He treated all

15

men alike, and rarest of all qualities amongst the Northmen, he could forget an injury. Rathleck had occasionally imagined that in the youth who seemed an idle, careless wastrel, there lay some spark of greatness lacking in the older princes. In part it might have been his appearance, for he featured Herbald more than either of them. But if the Norns chose him, it would not be yet.

Rathleck noticed one other face before his eyes closed in death - that of a pale girl with fiery hair. Ljani the Red, Beowulf's half-sister, whose birth eighteen years ago had sparked the blood-feud that still lingered. Of all Rathleck's issue, the most enigmatic.

What would become of them all, when he was gone? As his strength ebbed, Rathleck cared less. He would dine with Odin tonight, with his father and eldest son. A flash of lightning cast the solemn faces around him into harsh relief, and the thunderclap followed instantly. Thor was very close.

All fell silent, save the old priest, who uttered a final prayer. The emaciated figure beneath the bear-skin stirred and opened his mouth. Naur leaned forward, and Hyglack turned his head in profile the better to hear. Several of the others exchanged glances. Prince Athkyn half-stood, then, aware that undue interest might seem out of place, hesitated and sat again. He was furthest from his father - if the dying man's words failed to carry, Hyglack might hear, but not his brother.

Again Rathleck stirred, and as the dark head of Hyglack bent over him, it seemed to some that the king might have breathed a name. With a sigh, he settled back into the furs and ceased to breathe. Rathleck the Wild, hero of the Fifth Sferian War, had departed.

Naur closed the dead man's eyes. The priest was deaf; if Rathleck had spoken, he had not heard. The Gothic lords looked around uneasily.

Hyglack stood and squared his massive shoulders. Of those present he alone seemed in command of himself and the situation. As he gathered his cloak around him, it appeared to them all that at that moment he was the man to whom they should look for leadership. He spoke, firmly but not loud, neither too forcefully nor with feigned reverence.

'Rathleck Swerting is dead. His dying voice he gave to Athkyn Rathlecking, my brother, King of the Goths and Sfear.' Hyglack drew the sword that none but him could wield, placed both hands on the hilt and knelt. Then he spoke the time-honoured words of the Gothic Ninefold Oath:

'I swear by the High One, by Thor, and Frey - by the Nine Worlds, by the Great Ash, and the Three Norns - by the Long Spear, by my sword, and by mine honour as a Goth and a warrior, that I will bear true fealty to my Sovereign Lord, Athkyn, King of the Goths and Sfear, and to his heirs and successors, until death. If in this I fail, let my name be forgotten, and Surtur claim my soul.'

He spoke in breach of Gothic custom, for the Wittan had yet to meet and approve the old king's choice. None the less, Hyglack thus acquired much esteem amongst his countrymen, even his enemies acknowledging that he had conducted himself with honour and dignity.

None doubted that Rathleck had been received into the Hall of the Slain, and at his funeral on the third day several of the priests avowed that they had seen his spirit ascend with the smoke to the abode of the gods in Asgard.

SO died Rathleck Swerting, of the House of Silverspur, Son of Longspear, twenty-seventh King of the Goths and Sfear, Earl of Geatburg and Fanora, Lord of the Gothic Isle and the Lands Between the Seas. He had reigned nine-and-twenty years, seven months and twenty days, and died on the second Odin's Day in the Month when the Stars Shine Brightest, in the 1496th year since the Creation of the World.

Roger Butters

One

THE LAKE blazed red and gold beneath the setting sun. A skein of waterfowl rippled the polished surface as they took wing in echelon, fluttering into reeds and branches to roost. From the battlements of Castle Slane, a lone sentry gazed out at the diminishing segment of the sun's disc. The rim dropped beneath the horizon; the sentry raised and lowered his arm. Behind him, the black chevron-banner came flapping and fluttering down the flagpole of the central tower. A squat elderly man, whose coarse dress proclaimed him a churl, scrupulously gathered it ere it touched the stones and folded it neatly into eight. Moments later, he was at the sentry's side, clearing his throat, and uncertain whether it was his place to speak.

'Horsemen,' he managed at last, jerking his head to the south, where a small patch of dust disturbed the glimmering plain.

'Seen them,' the sentry confirmed with equal brevity. 'No great number.'

'Twenty maybe,' agreed the other, encouraged by the civil reception of his warning. 'And at the canter. It must be a matter of some heat.' He squinted into the twilight haze. 'I cannot tell their colours.'

The sentry narrowed his eyes in concentration. 'Nor I, in this light. But a chevron-banner, methinks. The Earl of Hrosnaberg, it must be. If I am not mistook, they bear the royal banner too.'

'The king?'

'I think not; he would come in greater number. But royal business, no doubt. Pass the word to the gate below.'

Minutes later the drawbridge resounded to the thunder of a dozen sets of hoofs as the men of Hrosnaberg rode in.

BEOWULF twisted the iron ring and pushed open the heavy chamber door. 'We have visitors, Ljani.'

In the flickering torchlight the pale red-haired girl glanced up from the bench, where she sat burning some evil-smelling powder in a crucible.

'One moment, Brother Bear. I am not finished yet.'

She resumed her labours. Jars, phials and bottles were strewn in disorder across the worktop. To her right lay a roll of parchment, where she made the occasional note with her quill, peering intently through her spectacles - for Ljani was a shade long-sighted - as she formed the small neat runes setting out the results of her researches. She wore her favourite cloak of midnight blue, emblazoned with the runes and signs of the sun, moon, planets and the Gothic seasons, months and years. One wall of her chamber bore a chart of the heavens and earth, another a map of Gothmark, surrounded by the arms and pedigrees of the great lords. Another wall was her library, a case full of volumes of science, philosophy, history and ancient lore. Ljani possessed well over thirty books, whereas no-one else in Gothmark, not even the learned king, could boast more than a dozen. Beowulf, who could not read, had none, yet Ljani's room never ceased to fascinate him. Most interesting of all was an exquisitely engineered machine, of cogwheels and delicate metal spheres, whereby one could make the heavenly bodies rotate at differing speeds around the world of Midgard.

Everything here had belonged to the great wizard, Mintaka, who had died eight years before at a very advanced age. Some said he had lived over a hundred and fifty years, and could remember Ranulf Redbeard and other warriors of the Second War of Liberation, though Mintaka himself, so far as Beowulf could remember, had never made such a claim.

Mintaka had tried to interest the young Earl of Slane in his researches, but although as a boy Beowulf had been an enthusiastic pupil, he had become less diligent with age. Eventually the difficulties involved - for Beowulf had ever been a lazy youth - and other interests such as sport, drink and wenching, had caused him to abandon his study. At the time he had told himself that he had been too stupid to make further progress.

'Too idle, you mean,' the old fellow had retorted, shaking his head. But Ljani had remained with him, though the merest child, assiduously learning, enquiring, discussing and debating. And when the wizard died - upon the very day, and almost the hour, he had foretold - he had bequeathed to her, an eleven-year-old girl, all his books, machines and maps, orrery, chemicals, mathematical tables, notes and drawings.

'Knowledge is a trust, Ljani,' he had told her. 'And you must bear the torch for those who follow.' And the small thin girl with glasses and red hair had nodded earnestly and given her promise.

Beowulf had had to give consent to the arrangement, and had done so without hesitation. He had never regretted it, for since the death of old Mintaka there was no doubt in his mind that Ljani was the most learned and intelligent person in the whole world. She understood the motions of the stars, moons and planets, the structure of the nine worlds, and Midgard. She explained to him how the great furnace of Muspelheim beneath the earth kept the fire mountains hot, but that beyond the Northlands the sea was frozen over and the edge of the world sealed off by gigantic cliffs of ice, to prevent the ocean from draining off into the void. She knew the reasons for changes in the seasons and hours of daylight, and was familiar with the habits of all animals, birds, fish and insects. She could recite the history of Gothmark and the Sfear from the earliest times, and knew how to read and speak the curious runes of the language of the Southern Empire. She understood the prophecies of the great sorceress Fanora the Fey, and could even foretell the future, though she seldom consented to do so. Neither did she neglect her physical exercise, for she could ride and wield a sword and bow as well as most men. Only in the matter of love was she still a child, having known no man, but nursing a helpless passion for his cousin, Athelstan of Karron Tha, nine years her senior, and married.

Ljani completed the last of her entries, removed the spectacles from her long nose, and stood. 'Who is it?'

'Our kinsman, Ifar of Hrosnaberg.' More her kinsman than his, but that was a long story, and a long time ago. By now it probably meant as little to Ifar as himself.

'What does he want?'

'State business, as I understand. He bears the commission of king's messenger.'

'War with the Sfear?'

'In that case, I think he would have come with greater number, and told me straight away. As it is, he has promised to enlighten us over dinner, for which we seem a little late, Ljani. Let us go in.'

'AN EXCELLENT repast, my Lord of Slane,' observed Ifar, pushing his plate aside after a third helping. 'My compliments to your cooks and scullions.'

'Thank you, Ifar Wylfing. But why so formal? My name is Beowulf.'

The dark young lord smiled. 'Then, Beowulf, I thank you, on behalf of my henchmen and myself. Men,' he shouted, rising, 'we have dined well this evening, and I call upon you to show appreciation in the traditional manner. Salute to our host, Beowulf, Earl of Slane, and to our lovely hostess, Ljani the Red!'

The housekarls of Hrosnaberg stood, shouted and hammered with their flagons upon the long benches of the banqueting hall.

Ljani, a little flustered by this tribute, inclined her head in awkward acknowledgment.

Beowulf smiled and raised a hand in half-salute. 'More ale!' he called, 'for our friends of Hrosnaberg. And health to them, and all their tribe!'

The Goths shouted till the rafters shook. Not for a generation had a Wagmunding and a Wylfing lord shared a meal with their followers in such amity. True, Ifar was the most amenable of the lords of Hrosnaberg, not one to harbour a grievance like his father, nor so hot-headed as his younger brother. It was best to let old quarrels die; the men who had done wrong, and the woman too, had been in their graves these many years. Old Wylf himself, founder of their house, had expressed satisfaction with the wergild, so why could his descendants not let the matter rest?

'How is your grandfather, Ifar?' Beowulf enquired.

The Wylfing shook his head. 'Not well. He is very frail, and talks constantly of the day when he will join his lord Swertan and his warriors.'

'It must be a sad thing,' said Ljani, colouring slightly as she joined the conversation, 'to be the very last of a generation.'

'Indeed,' nodded Ifar, 'the last he is of those who fought in the Great War nigh on three score years ago. Methinks the Gothic host of Swertan will soon have their full muster in Falhal. But this is somewhat morbid; let us to the purpose of our visit.'

'Shall we adjourn, Ifar, or are you happy to conduct the business here?'

'Here, by all means, amongst our friends, from whom we have no secrets. Besides, our affairs, though of great moment, deal mainly with matters already common knowledge. You know, I think, how things stand at present with the Sfear?'

'I am not so near to court as you. But, I gather, indifferently.'

'Exceeding ill. The Sferian princes raid the western marches daily, despite our efforts to restrain them.'

This put matters somewhat favourably to the Goths, most of whose warriors, notably Prince Hyglack, were not averse to raid and plunder themselves. But Ifar had ever been Hyglack's man.

'Were it not for the g-good offices of our cousin A-athelstan,' Ljani pointed out, 'we should be at war already.'

As ever when she mentioned the name of the lord of Karron Tha, Ljani stumbled over her words, and her face turned as red as her hair.

Surprising, thought Beowulf, that the most complex woman in Gothmark could in this one thing be so transparent.

'True, red maiden,' agreed Ifar, nodding again. 'You know your kinsman - Beowulf' - he used the new appellation a little awkwardly at first - 'Will the Treaty of the Handshake hold?'

The so-called treaty was a verbal agreement between the Wagmunding lords that neither would allow his territory to be used for border raids upon the other. As a result, to the irritation of the war parties on either side, the central marches formed effectively a huge neutral state, into which neither dare venture for fear of pushing both Wagmundings into the enemy camp.

'Oh yes, I should think so,' replied Beowulf, in the vague tone he reserved for politics. 'Relations betwixt my kinsman and me remain excellent. Is that not so, Ljani?'

His sister took the bait, blushing furiously. 'Indeed, Lord Ifar, the Earl of Karron Tha is a most respected gentleman, with no mean influence at the Sferian court. It may well be that he can yet persuade them to peace.'

'Possibly.' From her right Dardo, Ifar's captain of guard, spoke for the first time. A warrior of middle years, even darker than his lord, sparing of speech amongst strangers. 'But the war party is strong. Sources in the Sferian court inform us that King Angantyr is increasingly influenced by his martial sons. The moderate voice of the Earl of Karron Tha is unlikely to defer war much longer.'

'The tide runs strongly for war,' agreed Ifar. 'Which brings me to the object of our visit. You are a friend, I believe, of Breck Bronding, Prince of the Isles?'

'Why yes,' Beowulf confirmed. 'Or rather, we were friends years ago, before he inherited the title. We would go drinking, dicing, wenching - the foolish pastimes of youth.'

'You are scarcely old now, brother,' Ljani reminded him. 'And still somewhat inclined to such pursuits, I fear.'

'Er, yes,' he admitted shamefacedly. 'To some extent, perhaps. However, for Breck Bronding, I have not seen or heard of him these four or five years.'

Ifar drained his flagon, and Beowulf nodded to a slave to refill it. 'Thank you, my - Beowulf. Health and Long Life. Well, as you know, in olden days the Princes of the Isles were valued allies in the Great War against the Sfear. So much so that Brond, the First Prince, was declared by Swertan the greatest subject in the kingdom, second in rank only to the king himself.'

'So is Breck Bronding, the Fourth Prince, now,' commented Ljani. 'In theory.'

'Exactly, red lady. In theory. For since the time of the Great War, the island princes have increasingly distanced themselves from the affairs of the mainland. Not that they have been positively hostile, but their assistance in the last war was purely nominal.'

'Obviously,' said Dardo, 'they no longer accept any form of Gothic suzerainty, preferring to pursue an independent policy. In peacetime that's no great matter, but in time of war ...'

Beowulf frowned. 'You are afraid Breck might align himself with the Sfear?'

'It's not impossible,' said Ifar. 'For the late prince was friendly with the Sferian king. His daughter is married to the Earl of Karron Tha, whilst one of Breck's sisters is – ' he hesitated momentarily, 'also a lady of the Sferian court.'

Beowulf laughed. 'You put the matter tactfully, Ifar Wylfing. She is my kinsman's whore.' He could not bring himself to look at Ljani, whose hopes, raised briefly by the disastrous state of his cousin's marriage, had been dashed again with the news of this latest liaison.

Ifar pulled an apologetic face. 'Er, as you say. She now shares the bed of Athelstan Wagmunding. Whether she maintains any contact with her brother in the Isles, our informants have been unable to discover. The fact remains, this double link with the Sfear, in the person of your distinguished kinsman, is worrying. Breck has been prince little more than a sixmonth, and his policy is yet unknown. The King would like you to make enquiry.'

'The King?'

'Ah.' Ifar gave an embarrassed smile. 'I see you realize the position.'

'My envoy at court advised me in his latest despatch.'

'Yes, well, as no doubt he told you, the King is ill. What ails him, no-one knows - the physicians and apothecaries are mystified. He shuts himself in his room all day and will see nobody. Some sickness of the spirit, no doubt.'

Beowulf nodded gloomily. Athkyn had not appeared in public these three months, and seldom before that. The Goths were tiring of a king they never saw, and already there was a hint - as yet scarcely whispered - that his future as monarch might be in doubt. So much Beowulf had learnt from his court representative, Hrothgar, who was a good man.

'There was even a rumour that the King was dead,' Ifar continued, 'but I can assure you that is false. Unless he has died this last week, for I spoke to him on Freyasday.'

'Your orders are from him, then?'

'Frankly no, not directly. It is most difficult to obtain instructions from him. The Wittan of course acts in his name.'

For the Wittan, Beowulf read Prince Hyglack, who had by far the strongest voice in the council. Aloud he said, 'I see. The idea of selecting me for the task was no doubt based on my old friendship with Breck

Bronding.'

'In part. It was also thought I should accompany you, for historical reasons.'

He referred to the fact that when Swertan and the Prince of the Isles had invaded Gothmark at the outbreak of the Great War, the first two mainland lords to declare for them had been Wylf of Hrosnaberg and Wagmund of Slane. It would do no harm to remind the new prince of old loyalties. Yet Beowulf felt the stirrings of unease. A lord of Hrosnaberg was not quite the companion he would have chosen for a long and hazardous journey. He let his eyes wander round the glittering mead-hall and observed his guests. They seemed sound enough fellows, quaffing ale, sharing jests with their counter-parts of Slane and ogling the serving-wenches like any other Northmen. Maybe he was worrying about nothing.

'The council emphasize the extreme delicacy of the affair,' said Dardo, breaking into his thoughts. 'There should not be the slightest hint of any threat, or we could drive the Isles straight into the enemy camp. Diplomacy of the lightest touch is called for.'

Beowulf was not remarkable for diplomacy or anything else, but it occurred to him that neither was he a man who made enemies, at least on personal grounds. Politics and inherited blood-feuds were beyond his control.

'The real object,' Dardo continued, 'is to ensure the Isles' neutrality. A firm promise of support would naturally be a welcome bonus, but that is probably too much to expect.'

'When am I commanded to depart?'

'Requested,' Ifar assured him earnestly. 'Requested as a favour to your friends and your country. The thing is not a direct order - that would be considered presumptuous.'

Evidently the Wittan had advised Ifar to handle him carefully too, for Wagmunding loyalties were hardly more certain than those of the Isles. Beowulf grinned. 'Requested, then.'

'As soon as possible. You will of course need time to prepare. How many men do you purpose to take?'

Beowulf paused for thought. 'A dozen, I should think. Less might seem discourteous, more threatening. And a few servants and slaves.' Ifar himself had brought that many; to outnumber them might likewise be regarded as less than tactful.

'Excellent,' said Ifar, seeming pleased. 'I too have brought a dozen, under Dardo here - a party of about thirty all told should be ideal. We shall have to put our backs into it, of course - no leaving all the rowing to the slaves - but that will not do us any harm.'

'Will you take the sea route, then?' enquired Ljani. 'The autumn gales are due. Might it not be better to use the overland route to Port

Targon, and take ship only for the last few miles?'

'It's not an easy decision,' said Ifar. 'Neither route is safe. There are strange rumours from the east. Travellers' tales, exaggerated no doubt by credulous fools.'

'There are always strange rumours from the east,' Beowulf pointed out.

'True. Yet there is one story that seems well authenticated. 'Tis said that something has happened in Targon.'

'Nothing would surprise me there.'

'Right you are. The place has always been a shambles. The story however is that things have changed. A foreign warlord from across the sea is thought to have deposed the Merchants' Council and seized power, ruling with a rod of iron.'

'Is that good news or bad?'

'Hard to say. The merchants of course were weak and corrupt; perhaps tyranny may prove better than anarchy.'

'What is the name of this new lord?'

'Eugen of Brabanne,' provided Dardo. 'A margrave of Teutonia. They say he has sworn to hang every cutthroat, thief and whoremaster in Targon.'

'Well,' observed Beowulf mildly, 'that should keep him busy for a while. What is his policy toward the Goths and Sfear?'

Ifar shook his head. 'We don't know. But as you say, his home-grown problems should keep him occupied some time.'

'You will proceed first to Rigel anyway, brother,' said Ljani. 'There should be further news available there before you make a decision.'

'Good idea,' agreed Ifar. 'The Earl of Rigel is a sound fellow, one of the few we can rely on nowadays. He will be sure to advise us of any recent news from the east.'

Beowulf said cheerfully, 'That's all settled, then. Tomorrow we prepare for the journey, and shall set out at sunrise on the aftermorrow. But for tonight, let us drink and be of good heart.'

Ꝺwo

THE LONG shadows had yielded to the grey sameness of dusk. A dozen of the brightest stars had already pierced the lambent sky; their lesser fellows would soon follow. Meanwhile, in the shadowy landscape beneath, a puny beacon of earthly light bobbed and flickered as it lit its bearer's steps along his hazardous route. Several times his feet slipped on the slimy rock of the causeway. Hroness, they called it, or Whale's Ness, the thin spur of land extending into Ironside Bay. Around the rocks at its foot lay the dark waters of the Western Sea. Far beyond the horizon, the Isles of the West, and far, far beyond them, the bleak, lost island of Ultima Thule, which stood on the very edge of the world. Even in summer the Ness was a desolate place, a promontory of sand and twitch-grass, deserted save for nesting sheerwaters, green divers and birds of passage. And it was summer no longer.

At the extremity, the highest point above the sea, stood a rectangular building in grey stone, weathered on the western side, moss-encrusted to leeward. The roof, steeply pointed to resist the northern snows, bore at its apex a thin spire as tall again as the building itself. A well-trodden path led to it through the grass. And along this path the torch-bearer, Prince Beowulf, walked alone.

There was no door but an entrance-arch. On one side, in bas-relief, was carved the figure of a warrior in coat of mail, six feet nine and a half inches tall. On the other, an inscription. Beowulf was neither a religious nor well-lettered man, but he knew some of the runes, which fuelled his memory of the whole.

'HERE LIE THE MORTAL REMAINS OF THE IMMORTAL: BJORN II, OF THE HOUSE OF IRONSIDE, WHOM MEN CALLED LONGSPEAR: THE EVERGREEN KING, SAVIOUR OF THE NORTH, CHIEF AMONG THE MIGHTY, PRINCE OF THE LAKE, THE NON-PAREIL. BORN THE 4TH TYR'S DAY IN THE MONTH OF THE DIAMOND STAR IN THE YEAR OF THE WORLD 1203. DIED ON THE LAST ODIN'S DAY IN THE MONTH OF THE BEAR IN THE YEAR 1232. KING OF THE GOTHS 1221-32. KING OR THRALL, BOW YOUR HEAD.'

The entrance was less than five feet high, so even the shortest man had to obey. Beowulf ensconced his torch in the wall, stood for a moment with head bowed, and stepped awkwardly across the threshold. It took some time to accustom his eyes to the darkness, but in the pale light from the slit windows he could just make out the device on the wall: a shield bearing a solitary star. On the opposite wall was a carving of the personal emblems of the great king, the Bear and Long Spear. Between them, the tombs.

The flagstones leading to the first were deeply worn. Despite its isolation and apparent neglect, the shrine was the most revered in Gothmark. Odin's temple at Geatburg was forbidden to all but the families of earls and housecarls; those of Thor and Frey were open to churls and freedmen - slaves had to obtain permission. But even the lowest serf was admitted to the tomb at Hronesness and, even more remarkably, pilgrims were admitted strictly in order of arrival. For in this spot, alone in all Gothmark, there was no distinction of rank; if a great lord, or the king himself, arrived and found a slave in prayer, he had to wait his turn. This curious custom was said to date from Longspear's time, and be by his express wish. As a result, among the common people, Bjorn was more loved than the gods.

Tonight Beowulf would be alone, for the last month had seen the annual celebration of Bjorn's victory over the forces of evil in the seven-day Battle of the Doomed. Pilgrims had come from far and wide, but had now departed, so that the next few days would be the quietest time of year. Beowulf knelt beside the tomb.

The warrior-image engraved on the casket was identical with that outside: 6 feet 9 and a half inches in height, clad in a coat of mail with open visor. In his right hand he held the great sword, *Fasling*; on his left arm, a shield emblazoned with the lone star. A pair of hunting-dogs lay at his feet. The runic inscription was simple: BJORN along one side of the tomb, LONGSPEAR the other. The spear itself, miraculously untarnished in almost three centuries, lay in a depression in the flags between the tombs, eight feet and half an inch.

Bjorn, alone of all Gothic kings, lay here. Of the others, not even the mightiest could aspire to the shrine at Hronesness. They lay in the Crypt of the Kings, beneath the great hall in Castle Longspear, beside their less distinguished brethren. When a King of Gothmark died, the Wittan decided the fate of his body; had he been a good or adequate king, he was admitted to the crypt. If they judged him evil, and no fewer than seven of their rulers had suffered this fate, he was thrown over the cliffs at Geatburg into the sea. In theory, by unanimous vote, they could decide that he was worthy to lie beside Longspear, but they never did.

The tomb next to Longspear's was empty, the warrior's figure on the lid heavily visored, so that his face could not be seen. This was the resting place of the king yet to come. For one day, according to the wise men of the Goths, there would be another perfect king, as great as Bjorn Longspear, and worthy to share his shrine. To lie, not amongst the kings at Geatburg, but half a league further north, where he could more readily defend Gothmark from her enemies.

Beowulf had not visited the shrine for months, and was not sure why he had come tonight. It was a twenty-mile ride from Sleinau, at a time when he should have been engaged in preparation for the journey tomorrow. He was anxious to succeed in the mission, for the amiable but useless Earl of Slane had never before been entrusted with a task of such importance. It was time to change, and show his countrymen what he could do.

Recently he had been troubled by disturbing thoughts. He did not find it easy to confide in anyone; priests would have talked superstitious nonsense, while his drinking companions would have laughed at him. Ljani might have understood, but he had not yet ventured to broach the matter. As for Bjorn Longspear, it seemed absurd to pray to a man two and a half centuries dead, though many did. Yet was Longspear totally dead? Maybe a man's spirit lingered in his native land so long as his countrymen kept his memory green.

'Lord Bjorn,' said Beowulf to himself, 'I know not whether you can hear me. May I have a sign?' He had some vague idea that priests asked for a sign when attempting converse with the dead.

'Talking to yourself, brother?' came a woman's voice, very calm and clear.

For some reason he was not surprised. He turned to see Ljani standing slim and cool in her dark outdoor cloak and riding boots, a half-mocking smile on her lips.

'I have tried to speak to Longspear,' he said awkwardly, getting to his feet. 'Can he hear me?'

'Ask him what you will.'

Beowulf knelt again. He had had some intention of asking for success in his mission, victory for the Goths over the Sfear, long life and happiness. Yet somehow this now seemed cheap and unworthy. He decided instead upon what he could remember of Longspear's own prayer to Thor on the eve of battle:

'Lord Thor, God of the Sea and Sky, grant that I may count courage greater than victory, prefer mercy to vengeance, and know that the only true victory is over myself.'

The last seven words were incomprehensible to Beowulf, as to most priests, who believed the passage corrupt and usually omitted it on formal occasions. Yet Beowulf had always had an obscure feeling that the heart of the prayer lay in those final words.

'I thought I should find you here,' said Ljani.

She had always known him better than any, just as occasionally he felt that he knew her. Between them there had always been an obscure bond, perhaps based in part on the mutual sympathy of two misfits. And that despite the fact that his father had slain hers.

It had been Ljani who had explained to him, so far as any could, the nature and design of the cosmos, and the meaning of life. How this world was fated to last four thousand years: it had been created a thousand years before the foundation of Gothmark, and Gothmark would survive another thousand. From the fall of Gothmark until Ragnarok would be a further thousand; and a thousand years would elapse before the world arose again, to follow the same cycle, time and again, for eternity. How the stars were fixed to the firmament, and circled the nine worlds once a day. That some stars lay too far south for the Goths to see, and that only from the centre of Midgard was it possible to see every star in the sky. Which of the stars were the gods themselves, and which the souls of heroes. And the purpose of it all ...

'Well,' said Beowulf, rising again, 'I have prayed, though I am not sure it has done any good. Do the gods exist? Does Longspear still live?'

'You need but look at the night sky to see the gods. And Bjorn Longspear is there too, amongst the Deathless Ones.'

They stood outside by now, in the cool breeze, silhouetted against the sky; giant prince and slim girl. High to the north the heavens were black, and silver stars sparkled clear and bright. 'You told me once,' he said. 'But I have forgotten.'

'The wandering stars are the gods,' said Ljani, 'and the fixed stars the souls of heroes. To the south are the heroes of foreign lands, who rise and set, even as their fortunes sometimes link with those of Gothmark, then pass on their way. Our heroes,' she said, pointing, 'the Deathless Ones, are the stars which never set. In the northern sky we see two bears holding off a dragon. The stars of the bears are brighter, by which is signified the ultimate triumph of good over evil. The five stars in the shape of the rune Sowelu are the five great kings of the Sfear, for we are not the only northern people with heroes.'

'Which stars are ours?' asked Beowulf. 'Tell me again.'

'The Little Bear,' Ljani explained, 'is the home of Bjorn Longspear, the constant northern star. Alone amongst the stars, he does not move. The two stars which guard him are his father and brother, Bjorn the Elder and Bjarki the Lame. Beyond them, the Great Bear, with the seven great kings of Gothmark; it is disputed who they are.'

'Who do you say they are?'

'According to the sorceress Fanora the Fey, four were dead, one living and two unborn. The four who lived before her time were Kjartan Kinslayer, Bolferk the Mad, Ranulf Redbeard and Finn the Valiant. So much I think is certain. The one who lived in Fanora's day was her husband, Swertan the Bastard, and the sixth star must have been their son, then unborn, now dead: Rathleck the Wild.'

'And the seventh king?'

'He is born, but not yet king.'

If he were alive, Beowulf did not see how his soul could also be in the heavens. For that matter, he knew the sixth star had been there long before the death of Rathleck, which had occurred but eight months ago. Indeed he suspected that the stars had always been there, long before the men they represented were born, much less dead.

'Past and future are all one,' said Ljani, answering his unspoken thoughts. 'And the thin line where they meet, which we call the present.'

'Who will the seventh king be? Do you know?'

'I believe it may be Prince Hyglack.'

Beowulf frowned, for the news was not altogether welcome. 'I see. So Prince Hyglack is to be the last great king. Is he my enemy?'

Ljani answered his statement, not the question. 'I did not say the last.'

'There are only seven stars in the Bear.'

'But many in the sky. Did not Fanora prophesy that Longspear should be followed by seven great kings before he came again?'

'I never heard the prophecy in that form. She made many, most of which cannot now be understood.'

'Seven. The first three have come to pass; this was her fourth.'

The notorious Fourth Prophecy was never repeated in public on the grounds of decency, though ribald versions of it were often sung by warriors in their cups.

'I do not know the original,' Beowulf confessed. 'Is it not indecent?'

'Only fools think like that,' said Ljani, tossing her mane impatiently. 'I have memorized it. It goes:

The northern queen in full armour
Has had many lovers, but one mistress.
Over fifty leagues she marched for her greatest love,
Him with the weapon longer than that of other men.'

31

'This stuff is not fit for a maid to repeat,' said Beowulf, shocked.

'It continues,' said Ljani, ignoring him,

'He slaughtered her ravishers, and enjoyed her himself,

At first in secret, then openly. Then he left.

Nigh on sixty leagues she had marched, and sixty leagues more,

Seven great lovers later, she meets him again.

At first in disguise; wrapt in the bearskin -

Another name, but the same name.

Seven leagues ere she knows him - Prince of the Lake -

Many times he enjoys her, then leaves again;

Her six-and-thirtieth conqueror lies with the twelfth.'

'I suppose,' said Beowulf thoughtfully, 'the northern queen is the realm of Gothmark.'

'Of course. So much is obvious.'

'But the talk of leagues and lovers is indecipherable.'

'You think so? The man with the long weapon, whose mention shocked you so deeply, is Longspear, surely.'

'In that case, by her lovers is meant the Kings of Gothmark.'

'You have it, Brother Bear. And her ravishers were the evil kings from the east, who invaded our land; the term conqueror includes both.'

'And the leagues?'

'How far is a league?'

'Why, four miles, even I know that. Oh, I see. By distance is represented time.'

'Quite so. Just over fifty leagues, or two hundred years, from the foundation of Gothmark, Longspear was born. And in sixty leagues from his death, he will come again.'

That would be two hundred and forty years. Every Goth knew that Longspear had died, of an unknown illness, in the late spring of 1232. Beowulf had been born on the fourth Tyr's Day in the Month of the Diamond Star in 1473, by coincidence sharing the same birthday as the mighty king. Of this he had naturally been very proud, and as a boy had formed a feeble determination to model his life on that of his great forebear. But it had come to nothing.

'He was only a young man,' he said, half to himself, 'even when he died.'

'Aye. The Evergreen King indeed. Maybe it is better thus, to live in men's memories, never more than nine and twenty. None knew Longspear as a greybeard, old and feeble. Nor yet as a middle-aged ruler, scheming to hold the crown and secure a dynasty. Death kept his honour bright.'

'I had never thought of it like that,' Beowulf admitted. 'And yet, methinks it somewhat sad.'

Ljani glanced at him quickly, then away. 'Fate gives some men a second chance,' she said vaguely. 'And maybe all men. Who knows?'

'I don't understand you.'

'Well, we will leave it. Tomorrow,' said Ljani, with a brisk change in her manner, 'you set out on your journey. This will aid you.'

From within the folds of her cloak she drew a piece of parchment wrapped around a stick, and unrolled it to its full extent. A map of the Northlands, carefully delineated in Ljani's neat hand, covered with runic letters and small figures of trees, mountains, castles, ships and monsters.

'I cannot read the runes.'

'Others may do so for you. Their meaning will appear. I have other gifts for you too.' She showed him a small earthenware jar, bearing the picture of a staff entwined by a serpent. 'This ointment is a salve mixed from Mintaka's secret formula. It will heal any wound, if the man be not already dead.'

'I hope I shall not need it.'

'Methinks you will, maybe for yourself, maybe another. And the runes.' Ljani handed him a bag in red leather, full of stones. 'You will have cause to consult them. Though you are not skilled in divination, yet they will speak. Respect the runes, but make your own decision. Finally,' she drew aside the cloak and unbuckled her belt, 'take this, Brother Bear. It is too heavy for me.'

'Your father's sword. I cannot take it. You know why.'

'I wish you to have it. It was wrought by the greatest swordsmith ever known in Midgard.'

'Weyland?'

'No, by the one from whom he learnt the craft. A man from the east, beyond Slavonia.'

'There are no lands beyond Slavonia. Only Jotunheim, and the cliffs of ice.'

'But there are. Examine it.'

The hilt was covered by exquisitely carved flowers, leaves and serpents, together with curious runes of a type unknown in Gothmark. 'Can you decipher these?'

'No, not even I. But on the other side a later hand has carved his Gothic name. *Nayling.*'

Beowulf wielded it. The balance was perfect. 'A fine sword.'

'The best in all the world, Prince Beowulf. No blade can stand against him. When *Nayling* fails you, your time will have come. So it was with my father, Prince Olaf. And his grandfather, Eymor. And the man from whom he took the sword.'

There was some legend about the House of Offa and a magic sword, but Beowulf had never known the details.

'I have no man, Brother Bear. You are the nearest I have to a champion.'

He nodded. Again the curious sense of kinship, closer than brother and sister. The cool night breeze drew the cloak away from her. He glimpsed the slim pale body beneath, and wondered guiltily what she would be like in love.

As ever she had read his thoughts, and coloured. 'I am your sister, Brother Bear.'

She often called him Brother Bear. Once she had told him that Bjorn and Beowulf were originally the same name, both meaning bear.

'The man in the prophecy,' he said suddenly. 'He in disguise, who wears a bearskin. Is he Longspear come again, or another?'

Ljani shot him an uncharacteristically direct glance, yet answered with another question. 'When a man be born again, is he the same man, or another?'

'The same, but not the same?'

'Exactly.'

'And he is the warrior who will lie at Hronesness?'

'Of course.'

'Which is his star?'

The cloak slipped from Ljani's shoulder as she raised an arm. 'Follow the tail of the Bear.'

He did so. A golden star shone low in the west, over the distant sea, brighter than any in the sky. 'It is a long way from the Bear. And does it not rise and set?'

'It sets very briefly, then rises again. The brightest star in the sky; greater than Longspear, but less constant.'

'And he will be the last great hero?'

'The greatest, but not the last. He will be followed by the King of the Winter Star, who is not yet born. After that, I cannot tell.'

'Many men,' he said, following Ljani's thoughts as she so often did his, 'must have been born about the same time as me.'

'Not many of royal descent, taller than Longspear, with a name that means Bear. And sharing the same birthday. Strange, is it not?'

Beowulf took back the torch from the wall beside the figure of the mighty king. 'It seems I have had a near miss,' he said lightly, 'being born 241 years after Longspear's death. A year too late.'

Ljani gave her crooked smile. 'Longspear died in the Month of the Bear; you were born in that of the Diamond Star.'

'Well then, two hundred and forty years, and ...'

'Exactly. And nine months.'

Again he glanced at the planes of the beautiful, gaunt face, twisted in the sidelong smile. She above all women interested him, with her mixture of youth and wisdom, knowledge and innocence. Of all those in Gothmark, her destiny would be most closely entwined with his. And she knew it too, better than he did.

In the orange halo of the torch, the two shadowy figures made their way back to the mainland, where their horses waited, placidly cropping the wet grass. Darkness closed on the shrine at Hronesness, and the tomb of the king yet to come.

Roger Butters

Three

NEXT DAY Beowulf, Ifar and their men launched their canoes in morning twilight. By land, the journey to Rigel would have occupied three days, but travelling downstream they could expect to reach their destination before sunset. The Slane was the only river in Gothmark navigable throughout its length, from Lake Longspear to Rigel Bay. Even the upper reaches were broad and placid; the least skilled canoeist had little difficulty, and if by rare mischance he should capsize, it was usually possible to wade ashore. As a boy, Beowulf had spent many a happy hour in these marshes, amongst the fish and wildfowl, with his old terrier, Tan, who chased but never caught the green spotted frogs unique to these parts, which poked their bulging eyes above the waterweed and croaked the whole year round. The frogs, fish and birds were still there, but not the old dog.

Beowulf pushed off and scrambled aboard, to the cheers and good wishes of the servants and villagers up at that hour to see him off. The previous night he had bid a passionate farewell to his favourite slave, Starlight, so there were two women waving to him from amongst the crowd on the landing-stage: one slim, red-haired, with a crooked half-smile as she saw her brother on his way, the other tiny, fair, and choking back her tears.

Rather vain and inclined to jealousy, was Starlight; no longer in her first youth, but still beautiful. 'Take care of yourself, my lord,' she had whispered as they kissed goodbye. 'Remember I love you alone.'

Beowulf was inclined to doubt this, for she had had several other lovers. Her latest fancy was for Kjartan, lieutenant of the guard, whose feelings had been equally apparent. So far Beowulf was fairly sure

37

nothing had come of it, for the young fellow combined an old-fashioned loyalty to him with hopeless shyness of women. For all that, he had been slightly relieved when Kjartan had volunteered for the mission, otherwise temptation combined with opportunity might have proved too strong. Not that he minded too much what Starlight got up to whilst he was away, for the Earl of Slane was an easy-going young man, and did not deceive himself by imagining he loved her. Kjartan was a nice fellow, and if half of Starlight's tears were for him, what of it?

Four other canoes snaked ahead of Beowulf, between the reeds and overhanging trees of the Slane, the prow of his own vessel cutting into their weed-free wake. Unnecessary to paddle here, for the river flowed steady, smooth and strong. From time to time he trailed a hand overboard and let the cool stream of water run up his arm.

Of all their strange, eventful journey, it was that first tranquil day that Beowulf later remembered most clearly. The small farms and homesteads near Sleinau; peasant women washing their clothes, whilst children splashed about in the shallows, waving to the travellers as they passed; the Emerald Forest, still green but wreathed in autumn mist, where deer and boar came to the river's edge to drink; bright-coloured jewel-birds flashing amidst the branches, and the grey spearbills, motionless for what seemed hours on end before making their sudden lethal stab for fish.

The sun climbed slowly through the pale cloudless sky until it stood low in the south, a heavenly beacon lighting their way to Rigel. In early afternoon they passed the crag of Sunset Castle, perched on a rock at the junction with Wolf River. This was the spot marking the most northerly point of the sun in midwinter; at Rigel alone of the great Gothic cities did the sun rise and set throughout the year. This too was the southernmost extent of Wagmunding lands, and here the travellers' heads turned left or right according to their allegiance. For as the men of Slane glanced east at the last outpost of their homeland, those of Hrosnaberg looked west to catch a glimpse of the curious rock, shaped like a horse's head, which gave their land its name. Young Tirl, Beowulf's minstrel, caught the prevailing mood, and played a couple of nostalgic airs. From now on, though still in Gothmark, they were not quite at home.

The Slane grew yet broader and slower, the forest thicker as the banks receded. It was rare to see an animal hereabouts, but bird, plant and insect life abounded. The banks blazed with the poison orchids of Fanora, the blue mangrove found nowhere else in Midgard, and the yellow-flowering lendrol trees. Five of the six types of kingfisher found in Gothmark were here, and the gauze-winged dragonflies, with bodies hooped in turquoise and green.

Evening brought them to the great delta, where for the first time they needed to work constantly. The mighty Slane, almost exhausted, oozed slow and sluggish as they drifted through its mudflats, using their paddles to fend themselves from the banks of silt obstructing its flow. In places the river split into narrow channels, scarcely navigable; elsewhere it became a choked tangle of weeds. Strange fish leapt from the stagnant water to gulp air; great eels and freshwater tarpon flopped about. And on the mudbanks, amongst the reeds and marshgrass, lay the giant toads and swamp-lizards of the delta, half fish and half reptile, gazing with sad, stupid eyes at the travellers as they drifted by.

'An easy trip,' said Kjartan, breaking a prolonged silence. 'We shall be in Rigel ere nightfall.'

'Well before then, I hope,' replied Beowulf. 'We must call upon the Earl for dinner. Not as a courtesy alone, but for advice.'

The sun was low by the time the first dwellings appeared on the banks. Upon a small hillock, all alone, they caught their first glimpse of the summer mansion of Rigel of Rigel, Lord of the Southern Shore.

THAT night Beowulf, Ifar and their captains dined with Rigel in his private chamber. Their host was a man of three and forty, whose genial manner concealed a shrewd brain and steely will. Governing as he did the furthest extremity of Gothmark proper, he had both need and opportunity to keep well informed. His spies, or envoys as he preferred to call them, kept him abreast of events far beyond the pale of his court.

'You did well to come to me, friends,' he said. 'The news from the east is not good. Outlaws and brigands abound in Silvermount.'

Silvermount, the highland region to the east, lay on the direct land route to Targon. Historically its difficult terrain and lack of roads had made it notorious as a haunt of bandits. Nor were the dwarfs who worked in the mines and quarries particularly well inclined towards outsiders. Swertan the Bastard, with fire and sword, had solved the bandit problem for a generation, but even he had despaired of bringing the dwarfs under control. 'Dwarfs' was actually a misnomer, for the men of Silvermount, although of low stature, were not abnormally so, and their sturdy build and skill in metalwork could make them formidable adversaries. Swertan had wisely not attempted to force the issue, simply obtaining a vague acknowledgment of Gothic supremacy in return for the benefits they derived from his firm hand against the bandits. Since then the dwarfs had been approachable if not friendly, meeting envoys and merchants from the west mainly for the purpose of trade in furs, beef and mules, all of which they lacked, against weapons, salt and jewellery.

'I thought Swertan had subdued them quite,' said Ifar, helping himself to another chicken-leg from the earl's generous table.

'Aye, that he did. For many years there was no trouble. But things have changed of late. Many travellers have been robbed, even slain. For myself, I should not care to venture the Greyshadow Pass with much less than fifty men.'

His guests, whose force numbered five-and-thirty all told, pondered this advice in silence. The sombre mood was broken by a couple of scullions bearing in the next course; deliciously spiced and steaming dishes of partridge and quail, well-basted and swimming in nutritious oils. Truly, thought Beowulf, in these warm and hospitable surroundings it was difficult to envisage the perils that might lie ahead. It was old Saward, his grizzled captain of guard, who next broached the matter on all their minds.

'What news from the Isles, my lord?'

Rigel shook his head. 'We know little more than you. So far as it goes, the news is bad.'

Beowulf had expected as much. 'How bad?'

The earl hesitated. 'I'm very sorry to have to tell you this, Beowulf, but rumour has it that your friend Breck Bronding is dead.'

'That is bad news indeed,' said Beowulf after a pause. 'He was only a young fellow, scarcely older than me. What grounds are there for the story?'

'I've tried to check, but you'll appreciate the difficulties. There's been no communication with the Isles this sixmonth or more. Of course navigation is never easy, but of four ships setting sail from Rigel during that time, none has yet returned.'

'Pirates?' enquired Ifar's man, Dardo.

'Or gales, perhaps.'

Beowulf looked doubtful. 'Have the authorities at Targon not investigated?'

'Ah, Targon,' said their host ruefully. 'That's another story.'

'We hear they have a new lord there.'

'Indeed. Eugen of Brabanne, a Teutonic lord of whom little is known. Some six months ago he invaded from the east with a handful of henchmen, and deposed the Merchants' Council. We are told he now hangs felons by the score in the Market Place every day. Many have fled the city to join the brigands in Silvermount.'

'Perhaps the sea route would be safer,' suggested Ifar.

Rigel nodded but pulled a dubious face. 'I've told you the fate of the ships, what with pirates and the autumn gales. Not to mention the Keys to Heaven.'

The latter were a notorious group of rocks off the coast of Silvermount, which had proved the ruin of many a good ship. 'Besides,' said Beowulf, 'to provision a ship for the Isles would take several days. The land route is shorter; we could start tomorrow and reprovision in Targon.'

'What sort of reception are we like to get in Targon?' asked Dardo.

Rigel shrugged. 'From the little I know, I should say your greeting would not be marked by any excess of cordiality. It is only fair to say that thus far Brabanne has not demonstrated any positive hostility toward Gothmark. Whether he would appreciate the arrival of five-and-thirty armed men is another matter. Some diplomatic skill on your part would seem to be required.'

'No doubt,' Beowulf agreed. 'What say you, Ifar? The brigands and the Lord of Brabanne, or the pirates and the Keys?'

'I am no sailor,' Ifar conceded, 'but on the whole I think I would take the Keys. And you?'

If anything Beowulf was inclined to the opposite opinion. It might be worth giving way for the sake of friendly relations, not that Ifar seemed to feel strongly either.

'I have it,' said Beowulf suddenly. 'Let us cast the runes.'

'Why not?' agreed Rigel. 'It might be of interest, though as a simple soldier myself, I tend to prefer commonsense to such things.'

'My sister Ljani,' Beowulf pointed out gravely, 'is the wisest woman in all Gothmark, and she swears by them.'

'In that case,' said their host with a touch of gentle irony, 'I would not dream of arguing. And it's true that men's lives are shaped by fate as much as choice.'

'For my part,' said Ifar, 'I think it an excellent idea. Were it an easy decision, we could make it unaided; harder, and it is no disgrace to ask the runes.'

Beowulf produced Ljani's bag from inside his jerkin, and poured them out on to the table: a jumble of four-and-twenty shiny polished stones, each bearing a sign of the futhark.

'Do you know the runes, my lord?' enquired Saward.

'Not to read them,' Beowulf confessed, 'as they are used for messages. But Ljani has taught me to use them for divination. There are several methods.'

'For a straight question and answer,' said Ifar, 'I always think the method of the High One is best.'

The High One was Odin, never referred to by name save in prayer or blasphemy. 'Explain,' said Rigel.

'The question is posed,' said Ifar, 'and a single stone drawn from the bag in answer.'

'That seems straightforward. Who will pose the question?'

'I had best put it,' said Beowulf. 'Since the runes are mine, they might perform better for me than a stranger.' Rather clumsily he scooped up the stones and returned them to the bag, which he shook thrice to allow the magic to work. Then he hesitated, slightly embarrassed. 'God of the Runes,' he began, 'Lord of the Gallows, Rider of Sleipnir, Bringer of Triumph and Disaster, Chooser of the Slain, One-eyed Lord of All Things, Prince of the Dead, God of Good and Evil, of What is and What is Not, Lord of the Ways, He who is Most High. Beowulf of Slane and Ifar of Hrosnaberg invoke thee: do we march by land, or sail by sea? As you advise, so will we elect. We charge thee, speak to us now, through the runes of wisdom.'

He paused and handed the bag to Ifar, who thrust in his left hand, stirred the stones and grasped one. All three exchanged glances and nodded; Odin had made known his will. Of a sudden Beowulf was seized with the conviction that the choice they were to make would determine not merely the way to the Isles, but the whole future course of his life. The flash of insight passed. Ifar withdrew his fist and pitched a stone on to the table.

It bore the device of a vertical line touched by a three-legged zigzag. 'Raido,' announced Beowulf, relieved that it was one of the runes whose names he was certain of.

'What means it?' enquired the Earl of Rigel.

'A journey,' replied Ifar. 'Do you not agree?'

Beowulf nodded. 'It is so. More precisely riding, or a journey on horseback.'

'So have I heard too,' confirmed Dardo.

'Mules, rather than horses, would be more practical,' suggested their down-to-earth host. 'If you intend the Greyshadow Pass, that is.'

Beowulf and Ifar nodded again. 'It is decided,' said Beowulf. 'The land route. Now that I consider it, the High One has advised us well. For it is undoubtedly quicker, and the gods of the sea are more to be feared than any ruffians of Silvermount.'

'Worthily spoken,' agreed Ifar. 'And are the warriors of Gothmark afraid of any dark lord?'

The others concurred. 'I am unfamiliar with the runes,' admitted Rigel again, 'but should we not thank the High One for his guidance?'

Beowulf and Ifar shook their heads. 'It is not customary to thank the High One,' Beowulf explained. 'He distributes good and ill fortune as he sees fit, and expects neither worship nor thanks.'

'Very true,' agreed Ifar. 'Often he shows favour to unbelievers, and betrays his followers, or gives victory to cowards who do not deserve it. It is all the same to him.'

Four

BEOWULF EDGTYRING, *of the House of Wagmund, Earl of Slane and March, Prince of the Lake, Lord Palatine of Sleinau and Castletown, to his kinsman Athelstan Alfarring, Prince of the Forest, Earl Palatine of Karron Tha, known as Hawkeye.*

Right trusty and well-beloved cousin, I greet you. Be advised that upon the fourth Sunday of the Month when the Stars are Like a Shield, I depart Slane for the Gothic Isle, and purpose to be hence some six weeks or more. Meanwhile my best-beloved sister, Ljani the Red, natural daughter of Olaf of the House of Wylf, is Lady of Slane and Castletown.

Now take note that during my absence as aforesaid, I hereby appoint and charge you to act as my Lieutenant and Attorney, Guardian of Slane and Castletown, Lord Palatine of the Great Lakes and all the Lands Between. And in pursuance of such appointment, I declare and confirm that you have full power on my behalf to act as Lord of my Court, levy arms and taxes, negotiate, complete and perform contracts of all description whatever, employ and discharge servants or agents, pay and enforce debts, buy, lease, rent and sell land, buy, sell and free slaves, purchase livestock, property and things of all description, pledge my credit without limit, delegate all or any powers conferred upon you hereunder as to you seems fit, and generally act as fully and effectually in all respects in relation to my affairs as I myself could do.

And I hereby instruct and charge all persons of whatever rank to whom this Power of Attorney shall be produced, to treat my Lord Athelstan of Karron Tha, known as Hawkeye, as possessed of all such powers set out above, until my return to Castletown or Sleinau and specific revocation of this document, or until proof of my death shall be received, whichever shall first occur.

In witness whereof I, Beowulf, Earl of Slane, have hereunto set my hand and seal at Castle Slane in the aforesaid province this third Freyasday in the Month when the Stars are like a Shield, in the year of the world one thousand four hundred fourscore and sixteen.'

THE DOCUMENT bore the signature 'BEOWULF' in the careful but awkward hand of the Earl of Slane, contrasting sharply with the flawless penmanship of Ljani, his scribe, and concluded with the small wolf's-head seal of the Wagmundings.

The dark lord whom men called Hawkeye read the paper through twice, scowling with concentration and mild annoyance, but spoke the messenger civilly enough. 'Thank you, my friend. You will join us for supper.'

Hawkeye was at the hunting lodge near his summer quarters at Bettany, on the Gothic border. His mistress this twelvemonth, Wanda the Fair, sat beside him on the grass. A newly-slaughtered boar turned on a spit above the campfire, the scent of roast pork sweetening the night air. It had been intended as a lazy and relaxed evening for the Earl, his friends, tenants and servants, to celebrate his birthday. For today the Lord of Karron Tha was twenty-eight.

'What does it import, my lord?' enquired Wanda.

He handed her the letter. 'Business for my kinsman of Slane. My attendance will be necessary.'

Hawkeye was at once flattered and slightly annoyed. His cousin had preferred to trust him, a Sferian, rather than his fellow Goths, yet it placed him in a difficult position. Gothmark and the Sfear were all but at war; to fulfil obligations both to kinsman and country might prove impossible. Typical of Beowulf, he mused in affectionate irritation, both to trust him implicitly and fail to appreciate the problems thereby created.

Wanda read the message slowly. He watched her, as he never tired of watching her, for his mistress was the loveliest woman in the Northlands. She finished and raised her dark-grey eyes to his. 'Will you comply?'

'I must.' Hawkeye sighed. 'First thing tomorrow.'

'Wherefore should Beowulf visit the Isles?'

'Royal business, I imagine. He is friendly with your brother; conceivably the Gothic king thinks Beowulf might persuade him to join Gothmark in the coming war.' And helping Beowulf, Hawkeye told himself grimly, could be construed by the less charitable of his countrymen as an act of disloyalty. But to the Wagmunding border lords such conflicts of interest were nothing new.

'There are strange tales from the Isles these days, my lord.'

'Do you ever hear aught of what passes there?'

She shook her dark-gold curls. 'Not for many a day, Hawkeye. I hardly liked to tell my brother of ... what had passed between us, besides which Breck and I ever had but little in common. Does Roslindis keep in touch?'

He flinched, if not outwardly, at least to himself. Roslindis was Wanda's cousin, and his wife. Originally betrothed to Wanda, Hawkeye had deferred to royal wishes to marry her cousin. Politically and materially this was the better match, for Roslindis was the king's niece and bore the richest dowry in Sfearland. Yet the marriage had been a disaster from the first. Had he not been a greedy, spineless fool, Hawkeye told himself for the thousandth time, he could have been the happiest man in the land, instead of tied to a woman he loathed.

'She never tells me anything,' he said aloud. 'But I think not. Her interests lie elsewhere.'

THE SOUNDS of revelry receded into the distance as Hawkeye left with a dozen henchmen for his quarters at Bettany to prepare for the journey. The affair would need prompt attention, for according to his letter Beowulf should already have set out. A couple of days in Slane should suffice, consulting with his cousin's sister and stewards, and dealing with any urgent business. Then he ought to return, for ever since the harvest the Goths and Sfear had been provisioned and ready to embark upon war.

Roslindis kept her own apartments in the east wing of the lodge, as far from his as possible in the same building. Hawkeye had long since ceased to trouble about her affairs, which had at first been a guilty secret, then a public scandal, then a dirty joke, and finally a bore. Before leaving he looked in at her room, having first ascertained that she was alone. A sulky, fair woman of thirty, originally plump, now running to fat, she was wearing a silk scarlet nightgown and preparing for bed.

'If it is of interest to you,' he said, 'I depart for Sleinau at first light, and plan to stay two or three days.'

She paused in brushing her hair, turned and gazed at him coldly. 'Does your slut accompany you?'

It was strange that she had remained jealous despite her own faithlessness, but she and Wanda had always detested one another. 'My slut, as you call her, will accompany me. No doubt Prince Ali will console you in your grief.'

Her cousin, younger son of the Sferian king, was the latest in her string of lovers. He had lasted longer than most, presumably on account of his exalted rank. Roslindis and Ali were well matched. A vain and dissolute youth, the prince fancied himself irresistible to women, and had a veritable harem of whores at his command.

A flash of anger crossed the plump, spoiled face. Then she said with some effort at civility, 'Will you divorce me, Hawkeye?'

Amongst the Sferian nobility divorce was fairly easy, if expensive. But the king would not take kindly to the idea, especially if his son were implicated, as could hardly be avoided.

'We have talked of this before, and got nowhere.'

'I will accept the blame if you wish. You may keep the dowry, so long as you leave the king's son out of it.'

Avarice, Hawkeye grudgingly conceded, was not one of his wife's failings. 'That is not unreasonable,' he admitted. 'But I shall have to see what the lawyers say. It might not be possible.'

'No doubt it will be if you pay them enough. Even then you should have plenty of change from the dowry.'

'You may have your dowry back if you share the cost. I am not really interested in such details.'

'It is agreed, then?'

'If the king raises no objection.'

'There will be no objection. Prince Ali will intercede with him.'

She was a fool if she thought that. The prince was treating her as a plaything. Once free and talking of marriage, she would see him no more. 'Where will you live?'

'Let me worry about that.'

No doubt she thought Ali would provide for her. If not him, she would soon batten on some other man.

'Wherefore does your cousin travel to the Isles?'

Evidently the servants had told her something of the matter. Hawkeye shrugged. 'He does not say. Perhaps to obtain alliance with the prince.'

'Some say the Bronding no longer rules.'

'Indeed? I had not heard that.'

She did not elaborate further, but simply said, 'Your kinsman should take care. I fear he might be in danger.'

She seemed genuinely concerned. It was an odd fact that Beowulf was well-liked even by the most disagreeable people. 'I am going to bed,' she announced, throwing aside the scarlet robe. 'You have been somewhat less objectionable tonight than usual. Do you wish to join me?'

What a slut she was. She claimed to be in love with Ali, but her need for men was like a disease. Otherwise why offer herself to the husband she hated? Yet he was tempted, for she still had a fine body, firm and full-breasted, with perfect skin. And if the curves of her rump and belly were now a little too generous, even that was erotic in a way. Occasionally, Hawkeye found himself troubled with savage desire for his wife, a desire borne not of love, but hate. He had nightmarish visions wherein he lured her to some isolated spot, enjoyed her brutally while she begged for mercy, and then put her to death by slow and hideous tortures. These evil thoughts came, he was sure, from Surtur, Lord of Muspelheim, Land of the Fire. Wherefore Hawkeye recently had as little to do with his wife as possible, lest one day his control should crack, and his soul be lost to the Prince of Evil. Not only was she vicious in herself, but provoked evil in him. Sometimes he thought she knew it, and enjoyed torturing him in this hellish way. He had grown to fear his wife, almost as much as he feared what he might do to her.

'Is Prince Ali not available tonight, then?'

'Thank you for spoiling things, dear husband.' She spat slightly as she spoke; he could almost see the poison on her full, moist lips. 'He, being a real man, is on a vicking raid in Gothmark, instead of dealing with his country's enemies. Anyway, I see you are determined to remain faithful to the Slut. How very admirable, if foolish. She will cuckold you as surely as I have done.'

Roslindis clambered through the draperies around the giant well-used bed, taking care to flaunt the full ripeness of her charms and turn the knife in the wound of his desire. Hawkeye tore his eyes from the sight and slammed the door behind him as he fled.

Roger Butters

ꝼive

HAWKEYE TOOK the forest road from Bettany to Sleinau. Beside him, upon a piebald mare, rode the Lady Wanda, adorned in the finest coloured silks from the lands of the south, accompanied by two of her women. His squire and groom, Leofric and Falco, kept a few paces to the rear. A dozen retainers and outriders bore aloft the sable chevron-banner of the Earl of Karron Tha.

Ravenswood Forest was still in full leaf, sunlight lancing through the canopy to create golden glades amidst the oak, ash and chestnut. Here the road became a mere path between the trees, curtained in green on either side. On the forest floor, an occasional rustling amongst the undergrowth told of small hunters and hunted disturbed by the intruders. Songbirds and crickets provided pleasant accompaniment to their journey, until after many a tranquil mile, Hawkeye and his companions emerged from the forest into a landscape of light woodland and spinney, and thence to the fields and hedgerows of Slane. By evening Sleinau was less than five miles distant. The odd farm wagon passed them; here and there a peasant gave them churlish greeting, or hurried by pretending not to have seen the visitors from the north.

'Your cousin's men want something in courtesy,' commented Wanda.

'I suppose armed men from the Land of the Sfear can hardly expect much welcome in Gothmark at present. Yet they know the Wagmunding banner well enough. I might have hoped for better.'

In fact it became worse, for upon rounding the next bend they found the road blocked by a force of peasant soldiers, mostly clad in leathern jerkins, and lightly armed with staves and pitchforks. Their leaders, two mounted warriors, wore hauberks and visorless helmets of a type now out of date.

'Not Wagmunding men,' said Wanda.

Hawkeye rode on impassively. At twenty yards distance one of the horsemen detached himself from the company and rode forth to meet him, raising a hand in mute order to stop. His surcoat bore the device of Hrosnaberg, a red chevron on white ground, with a horse-head badge.

'Your name and business,' said the man curtly.

'Athelstan of Karron Tha. My business, none of yours. By whose authority are we stopped on a public highway?'

'We serve the Earl of Hrosnaberg,' the horseman informed him. 'On whose behalf we demand to know your business.'

'Beowulf of Slane rules these lands. Your lord has no authority here.'

'More than you, Sferian.'

'Not so; I bear the commission of my kinsman, the Earl of Slane.'

'Let me see it.'

Hawkeye reached into his surcoat and handed the document over. The man appeared literate, though barely so, following the runes with his finger and speaking the words under his breath. Whilst waiting for him to finish, Hawkeye surveyed the man's followers. The setting sun glinted upon simple conical helmets and rustic weapons. If it came to a fight, not a very formidable enemy, although the women in Hawkeye's party might complicate matters. Besides, Hawkeye, if occasionally hot-tempered, was a man of peace. He would do his kinsman no good by exacerbating the feud with Hrosnaberg.

'This bears the Wagmunding seal,' admitted the man cautiously, 'and appears to be some kind of legal document; what exactly it imports I am not qualified to say. Edric!'

The other rider, a younger man, who had been fidgeting for some time as if uncertain whether to intervene, urged his mount forward beside the other.Hawkeye had a vague recollection of having seen him before, as a housekarl of Hrosnaberg, and so it proved.

'That is certainly the Earl of Karron Tha,' said the newcomer. 'I salute you, my lord,' he added uncertainly.

'And I you. Explain my business to your friend.'

'It is correct,' said the young man, 'that the Earl of Slane departed for the Isles yesterday morning with our Lord Ifar. 'Tis said, though I have no certain knowledge, that he appointed the Earl of Karron Tha his lieutenant meanwhile.' He read the paper in half the time of his colleague, nodded and handed it back. 'It appears to be in order.'

'Since I am Beowulf's lieutenant here,' said Hawkeye, 'I require of you an explanation.'

'You shall have it,' said the first man. 'Know, Sferian lord, that about the eighth hour this day, Wonred Wylfing, heir to the lands and title of Hrosnaberg, was slain by Sferian bandits under the command of that murderous braggart Ali of Scarlettown. It means war.'

There, Hawkeye reflected ruefully, he was almost certainly correct. Nor could he seriously quarrel with the description applied to Ali. 'As for that, I am sorry, but the affair is none of my making. We come in peace, about the lawful business of my kinsman, the Earl of Slane.'

'They are not equipped for war,' observed the younger horseman. 'Being but lightly armed, with their lance-tips covered.'

'True,' agreed his companion suspiciously. 'But before allowing you to proceed, we will search your train.'

'In Helheim you will. Where did the slaying of Wonred take place?'

'Seven miles east of Sleinau, near the Ashen Tarn.'

'That is not Wylfing land,' Hawkeye pointed out. 'Not by five leagues and more. Your lord must have been on a vicking raid too.'

'Not so, he was still in Gothmark.'

'What business had he in Slane?'

'For that, I know not,' said the man evasively. 'But certain it is that he was slaughtered by Sferian cutthroats under Prince Ali.'

'The matter will be looked into,' Hawkeye promised. 'You have my word on that. If any wrong was done, I will try to negotiate fair wergild; beyond that I cannot go.'

The Gothic horsemen muttered together briefly. 'Hawkeye was ever a just man,' he overheard the housekarl say.

'Very well,' said the senior man. 'You may pass.'

'Good,' Hawkeye replied. 'While for your part, you have twelve hours to clear Wagmunding lands, whereafter I shall send soldiers to evict you.'

'You presume too far, my lord.'

'Nonsense. I have said your complaints shall be investigated. Be off with you.'

'We shall return and report to Earl Wylf,' said the man, backing down with ill grace. 'He will not be pleased.'

'Tell him from me,' Hawkeye pursued, 'that I will not have Wagmunding lands used by warring earls, be they Goths or Sfear. That has ever been my cousin's policy, and mine. Now make way.'

As he rode through, Hawkeye spoke again. 'Where may I view the body? I wish to pay my respects.'

'It lies at Castle Slane for the present. Tomorrow it will be borne to Hrosnaberg.'

'I am bound for the castle in any event. My condolences to your lord and his family on the loss of his son.'

'Longspear and justice ride with you, my lord,' replied the horseman in a less hostile tone.

Hawkeye nodded in acknowledgment of the tacit truce. 'And with you and your lord.' He turned and raised a hand to his followers. 'Ride on.'

SLEINAU lay on the left bank of the river, a mile from the Western Lake. Youngest of the great towns of Gothmark, it had been founded by Hawkeye's great-grandfather, Eymor of Slane, but fourscore years ago. Modern and prosperous was Sleinau, if a little lacking in character. Yellow stone and tiled roofs replaced the thatch and timber of most Gothic towns. And the few burghers, tradesmen and wagoneers about - for it was the hour of the evening meal - greeted Hawkeye and his men with civility, if not enthusiasm. Sleinau, like Castletown, was less hostile to the Sfear than the towns of Old Gothmark. As a result of war, it had known both Gothic and Sferian rule from time to time, and the Wagmunding lords on both sides had ruled justly enough. Hawkeye was not well known to them personally, but his reputation stood high. Besides, though he little realized it, he made a good impression on those he met, raising a hand in greeting to warrior, churl and slave alike, with equal friendliness and courtesy, after the traditional manner of the Wagmundings.

The castle lay across the Slane, a motte and bailey defended to the west by the Great Lake, north and east by a loop in the river. Only to the south was there no natural defence, but a moat joined the lake and river, so that the earthworks, keep and bailey were entirely surrounded by water. In the absence of the earl, the black chevron-banner no longer flew from the central tower. The sentries on the gate saluted and gave signal for the portcullis to rise. Hawkeye and his followers clattered through into the courtyard.

LJANI sat at the head of the banquet table in the great hall, where less than fifty hours earlier she and Beowulf had entertained the men from Hrosnaberg. Today she presided alone, dressed in a light gown of yellow silk, without jewellery save for a gold amulet at her throat. Unfashionably she wore no covering for her head, allowing the red mane to fall around her shoulders. Beside her Hyglack of Geatburg, heir presumptive to the throne and mightiest of Gothic warriors, quaffed ale noisily. From the walls a score of torches cast warm flickering light upon the features of royal and Wagmunding henchmen alike. A herald entered and bowed.

'Athelstan Alfarring, Earl of Karron Tha.'

Ljani stood. 'Bid him enter.' Her voice, normally cool and clear, shook just a little, for the Lord of Karron Tha above all men had the power to disturb her. And Ljani, though a royal princess and the most learned woman in Gothmark, was but nineteen years of age and had never sat at the head of the feast before, certainly not with two such eminent guests.

Hawkeye entered with his henchmen, Wanda upon his arm. Ljani's face fell almost comically, for nineteen years is poor protection against disappointment in love. She recovered herself. 'You are welcome, my lord, with all your band.'

The room was quiet but not silent, the atmosphere tense rather than hostile. For the Earl of Karron Tha was both Wagmunding and Sferian; as the former at least he was welcome. 'Hyglack of Geatburg, my noble uncle, greets you also.'

Hyglack pushed back his chair and stood. Seven feet and half an inch, he was not a slim man. The heavy leathern epaulettes and padded shoulders gave him the appearance not so much of a giant as a sort of mighty troll, broad even in proportion to his massive height.

'I and my henchmen greet you, Karron Tha, albeit we have little love for your countrymen. You have heard the news?'

'Aye, my lord. It is a matter for regret that relations betwixt our countries should have come to this.'

'Aye,' repeated Hyglack ponderously. 'No doubt.' He proffered a hand, which Hawkeye took. The Earl of Karron Tha stood a foot shorter than the Goth, nor was he heavily built, yet to those present it seemed he was by no means dwarfed by the huge figure of the prince.

'May I see the body and pay my respects?' asked Hawkeye. 'Wonred of Hrosnaberg was a doughty warrior, and my father's cousin.'

'You may, my lord,' said Ljani. 'He lies in the Crypt of Odin; I will conduct you myself. Meanwhile your lady and your men will be provided for.'

Ljani and Wanda exchanged glances. For an instant Hawkeye imagined he saw something pass - a flash of recognition, or rivalry? - but then it was no more. Of course Ljani was commonly supposed to be infatuated with him. She was a mere girl, and would grow out of it. More woman trouble would have been as much use to him as a three-legged horse.

'I will accompany you,' said Hyglack. 'It will provide opportunity for private speech.'

Hawkeye nodded. 'I am at your service, my lord.'

THE THREE figures stood in silence beside the dead warrior, a bearded man in his fifties with a face calm and pale in the candlelight. The open casket was draped with the arms of Hrosnaberg, a silver field charged with the blood-red chevron and bay horse. On such occasions Hawkeye was ever troubled by the morbid speculation as to who would one day look down on him, or the body he had finished with, and pay the usual awkward tributes. Roslindis perhaps, or if he was lucky Wanda, by then grown old with him. Yet he had difficulty imagining either of them at the scene. It would be a Wagmunding occasion, he was sure of that. Young Beowulf would be there; he could see him clearly, yet no longer young, and perhaps ...

Ljani bowed her head to kiss the dead man's face. He had been her uncle, in blood if not in law. Hyglack drew his sword, reversed it with a flourish and resheathed it, in the traditional Gothic gesture of salute to a fallen warrior. Hawkeye did likewise, as Beowulf, he was sure, would one day do for him.

They filed out in silence. No word was spoken until their feet echoed again on the stone-flagged passage outside.

'I had no wish to quarrel in the presence of the dead, Karron Tha,' said Hyglack at length, 'but you will appreciate that this means war, as night follows day.'

'You judge too hastily, Prince Hyglack,' Hawkeye protested. 'I have sent messengers to the Sferian court enquiring into the matter, and reserve my position until I have heard their account. In these tragic circumstances I dislike to blame the dead, but it seems possible that the lord of Hrosnaberg and his men might also have been in some measure responsible for what took place.'

'How can you say so? They were despatched by the king and me to defend Slane against invasion from the north.'

'Were you with them, my lord?'

'Think you that if I were, your countrymen would have escaped unscathed, and myself lived to speak of it?'

His worst enemy could not have called Hyglack coward, as Hawkeye acknowledged. 'I suppose not, my lord. Yet to speak frankly, I see no reason for the presence of your lordship and his men in Slane just now.'

Hyglack flushed angrily. 'I have been patient in the face of wrong; do not try me too far. Though I need not explain myself, yet I choose to do so. I bore my own commission here, to advise my niece of my appointment as regent of the realm; in addition to supply any assistance she might require during the absence of the Earl of Slane.'

He had evidently heard of, and disapproved, Beowulf's decision to make Hawkeye his lieutenant. No doubt his intention had been to meet and form his own opinion of the Sferian. Alternatively he had invaded Slane along with Wonred, though he was not dressed for war, and on that point Hawkeye was inclined to give him the benefit of the doubt.

'You may be Regent of Gothmark, mighty prince, but in my kinsman's absence I am Lord of Slane. I will not have the province used for feuding; as for you and your men, you are welcome to remain my guests as long as you wish. But when you leave, ride west.'

Ljani seemed both proud and emboldened to hear him speak her warlike uncle so straight. 'Herein my cousin speaks for me too, my lord,' she said quietly.

Hyglack scowled. 'No doubt, for the Wagmundings have ever stuck together, regardless of Goth or Sfear.' Ljani was a Wagmunding in name only, a fact which seemed to occur to Hyglack as soon as the words were out of his mouth. He began to say something, thought better of it, and with bewildering change of mood laughed heartily and clapped Hawkeye on the shoulder. 'But enough of this - I had rather have a man speak his mind, though he be mine enemy, for I prefer to know where I stand.'

As indeed was the motto of the royal house of Gothmark: *Here I Stand.* Hawkeye felt a sudden liking for the bullying prince. 'I am not your enemy, my lord, and trust I never shall be.'

Hyglack looked doubtful, and it was Ljani who broke the ensuing silence. 'Some men's stars are born to be in conflict, my lords - neither side to blame.'

'It may be so,' Hyglack grumbled. 'Anyway, for myself, you will not long be burdened with my presence, for tomorrow we return to Geatburg.'

'For the council of war?'

Hyglack shrugged. 'Draw your own conclusion.'

'If that be so, my lord, I should like to accompany you, to plead the case, if not for peace, at least a truce for negotiation.'

'Noble blood has been shed. What honourable settlement can there be?'

'That is what I think might be explored.'

'As you wish. I can guarantee your safe conduct and a fair hearing, but will speak against you.'

'A fair hearing is all I ask.'

'Be it so, then.' They neared the hall, and heard again the sounds of drinking and laughter. 'Let the Fates decide the morrow,' said Hyglack with an expansive gesture. 'But for tonight, Sferian lord, we are your guests. Let good fellowship prevail.'

Roger Butters

Six

COVERED WAGONS creaked along the coastal road beneath a sky uniformly grey. Beowulf, Ifar and their housekarls walked alongside. Horses could not have scaled Greyshadow Pass, and no warrior would deign to ride a mule. Neither was the Earl of Slane prepared to lounge in a wagon and allow his men to walk; in the circumstances Ifar could hardly do differently. So it was that the wagons were occupied by churls and slaves, whilst their betters made their way on foot. An odd arrangement, but the Wagmundings were known for their unusual way of doing things.

The southern shore was bleak and rocky, and the weather, passable at their departure, soon deteriorated. The grey-green waves of Rigel Bay were topped with foam; a chill wind whipped sand and spray into their eyes. Tirl, cheerful as ever, attempted to raise their spirits with his songs and verses, varying from the traditional to the ribald. Though it was scarcely the third hour after noon, Beowulf ordered the torches lit. The same idea had occurred to others; a score of firebrands in the distance proved on closer approach to be a party of merchants and itinerant workers, a hundred strong and more, en route from Targon to Rigel for the autumn fairs.

'Any trouble from brigands?' Beowulf enquired from their leader, an alert greybeard.

The old man shook his head. 'We were lucky. Perhaps our numbers protected us. I wouldn't be in your shoes,' he added discouragingly, 'for all the gold in Silvermount.'

'Is it that bad?'

'In Targon they reckon the chance of being attacked is one in four.

We must have been one of the three Kovack decided to leave alone.'

'Kovack?'

'The outlaw chief. There are several, but he's the worst. They say he commands a thousand men or more, and puts all captives to death by torture.'

'No doubt they exaggerate,' observed Dardo drily.

'Maybe, but I shouldn't care to cross his path. The worst of it is, he and his men pose as liberators, and enjoy the support of many of the dwarfs. Gone are the days when a Gothic traveller could call at a tavern for a civilized drink, or obtain shelter for the night. Now, as like as not, he would finish up with a knife between his ribs.'

'We had heard something of the sort,' said Beowulf. 'But what of Targon? What sort of a man is Prince Eugen?'

'A hard man. Scarcely a brothel or gaming-house in Targon still operates. Half a hundred felons hanged daily is nothing; not a whore or usurer in the city but has felt the lash.'

That might be no bad thing, Beowulf reflected. In the event of delay in Port Targon he had not relished the prospect of having to dig his men out of taverns and houses of resort.

'Is he a just man, or simply a tyrant?'

The merchant paused for thought. 'I cannot say, in fairness, that he is unjust. No doubt there are cases of injustice, but they are not the rule. The place is certainly safer for the law-abiding; safer from criminals, that is. But if I were you I should watch my step there very carefully.'

'We will do so,' Beowulf assured him cheerfully. 'And thank you, friend, for your advice. Farewell.'

'Farewell to you, my lords.' The man concluded with the customary valediction to those setting out into danger. 'Ride with Longspear.' He and his men turned away; their torches became fainter as they receded toward Rigel, and safety.

The coastguard at South Rock gave similar counsel. 'Do not conceal your weapons as you enter Targon,' he advised. 'Disclose them at the city gates, and surrender them if ordered.'

'The hell with that,' grumbled Ifar. 'We are Gothic warriors, and will not submit to such indignity.'

'Well, we will think about it,' said Beowulf more temperately. 'And thank you, friend, for your advice.'

'Beware of outlaws too,' the coastguard continued. 'The one they call Kovack most of all. Ride with Longspear.'

Soon afterward, the windswept road turned from the shore into the stony foothills of Silvermount. Beowulf's party pitched camp that night at Bolferk's Cross, a tiny hamlet on the eastern tip of Rigel Province. Four-and-twenty hours later they were six leagues further on, encamped in a cheerless birch grove at the foot of the ascent to the pass. Autumn in Silvermount was a dismal season; mist rose from the nearby stream, and there was a halo round the gibbous moon. 'Greyshadow 7 Miles,' advised a rotting fingerpost.

The morrow would see their danger at its greatest. The last mile or two before midday, as they laboured to the summit of the pass, would be the most perilous of all. Beyond Lone Pine, a desolate spot five miles further on, the worst would be over; by this time tomorrow they could count themselves comparatively safe. For the first time Beowulf ordered his men to mount full guard.

'Do we douse torches tomorrow, my lord, crossing the pass?' enquired young Kjartan. 'It might be prudent.'

'Prudent,' agreed Beowulf, 'but scarcely valorous, methinks.'

'Well spoken, my lord,' said old Saward fiercely. 'Do we sneak across Greyshadow like thieves in the night, for fear of bandit scum?'

'Right enough,' concurred Ifar, amidst murmurs of assent from his men. 'Tomorrow we march in good order, in broad daylight or with torches. Let brigands come looking for us if they dare.'

Next morning, they broke fast early, and were on the march by dawn. Above and around them, the ever-snowy peaks of Silvermount gleamed and sparkled in the morning sun. Long blue shadows scarred the lower slopes, to fall across their path as the track before them narrowed. It became colder; the small clouds of their breath hung longer in the air before dispersing. The rocks on either side were sheer as they entered the dark cutting forged by the engineers and slaves of Swertan the Bastard half a century before. The sounds of their passage echoed eerily from wall to wall. Yet the first few miles had been easy. The Goths began to relax, and conversation became less subdued.

Soon after they emerged from the cutting the road narrowed further, and steepened as it became a gritty track no more than ten feet wide. Casual talk and bawdy jokes gave way to grunts and stifled curses as the Goths put their shoulders to the boards and wheels, scrabbling for a foothold on the gravel dislodged by their struggling beasts of burden. Axles groaned under the strain. An hour before noon the sky clouded, and a brief shower revived the sweating men and mules. Finally the ground levelled out to a tolerable gradient as they reached the entrance to the great pass of Greyshadow. Any relief was short-lived, for instantly the mountains closed in and shadows blotted out the sun. Here no trees grew, and no birds sang, nor were ever seen, except hawks and eagles circling in the bright narrow sky above the chimney of the mountain range.

'On, on!' cried Beowulf to his tired henchmen.

'Full speed, you idle buggers!' yelled Saward. 'Move it, no resting here!'

'Faster, faster!' bawled Dardo to the men of Hrosnaberg, as the

59

servants whipped up the mules. 'Any who fall behind will be left! On, on!'

The Goths struggled on as bidden, gasping, cursing and exchanging desperate jokes. For the next few miles every rock, gulley or shadow might hide an outlaw; every bend in the road might bring them face to face with a hundred of them. So the captains yelled 'On, on!' and drove their men relentlessly, and the men cursed the slaves, and the slaves cursed and drove the mules, until by the hour after midday, the exhausted travellers gained the highest point of Greyshadow, said to be no less than seven thousand feet above the sea. Here for a few minutes they emerged into sunlight, though the peaks around them reared another three thousand feet into the sky. Then came the descent into shadow again, less tiring but equally dangerous.

At last the mountains parted, as the Goths began the steep descent into the Targ Valley. At Lone Pine, the giant solitary tree, two hundred feet high and said to be as old as Gothmark herself, marked a broadening of the track as the peaks receded on either hand. Again the pale autumn sun shone out behind the travellers, more brightly now it seemed the danger was over. Fell, moorland and mountain streams replaced the naked rock of the pass. If the scenery was still bleak and wild, yet it was of a kind familiar to the Goths, much of whose country was similarly cheerless. With each small tributary of the Targ they splashed through their spirits rose.

'We have made excellent time, my lord,' said old Saward, falling into step alongside Beowulf. 'Think you we might make the Targ Bridge by close of day?'

For the umpteenth time Beowulf consulted Ljani's map. 'About five miles to go,' he said, placing a huge finger over the carefully-inscribed runes. 'But we need a rest. We should take time for a meal, and water the mules.'

'Aye,' agreed Saward. 'For all that, I should like to make the bridge tonight if possible. The men have had a hard day, and it would be fitting reward.'

'Indeed it would. First thing, I should have settled for getting as far as we have; anything from now on is a bonus.' Beowulf glanced at the sun, dipping behind a bank of cloud to the south-west, and gave the order to light torches. 'Perhaps we might continue the march for an extra hour if need be. Have you seen Targ Bridge before, Saward?'

'Not since I was a young fellow, campaigning with Rathleck. Places one knew in youth always have an attraction; I should like to see it again before I die.'

The Targ campaign had been one of the bloodiest of the Fifth Sferian War, and the Battle of the Bridge a famous Gothic victory. The last time Saward had seen it the river must have been running red and choked with corpses. 'It wasn't too pretty then,' said the old guardsman, reading Beowulf's thoughts.

'Was it true the dead were so many they blocked the Targon Ford, thirty miles downstream?'

'No,' replied Saward scornfully. 'That was a yarn, though there are many still believe it. But they were fishing the odd corpse out of the river at Targon for weeks. That much is true.'

To their right a dozen rooks took off from a crag, with raucous cries of alarm. Beowulf, quick to notice and query animal behaviour, narrowed his eyes, puzzled. In that instant, he heard beside him the vibrating thump of an arrow strike. Saward was no longer there, and the air was black with arrows from the rocks ahead and to either side. Men flung themselves under wagons, giving voice to the needless cry of 'Bandits!' or 'Outlaws!' and groping for weapons. Ahead a wagon had overturned, as stricken mules reared screaming in the shafts. And the bandits, thus encouraged, poured down the barren hillside to take advantage of the confusion they had wrought.

Therein the attackers made a fatal error. For the Goths, like ants disturbed, were a disciplined force whose apparent disorder was misleading.

'Hold fire!' shouted Beowulf, and not a Slanish archer moved, though in the torchlight the half-naked rabble flooded down the hill, waving swords and axes, and yelling encouragement to one another. At last Beowulf gave the word; bowmen loosed their shafts in a flight of whispering death, and brigands tumbled down the hill in a struggling mass, dead and living together. As the archers poured their volleys into the floundering foe, some turned to flee and were struck in the back, whilst others charged on to their death as they tried to scramble up on to the raised causeway of the road. Yet others splashed about in the shallow stream at the foot of the hill whilst further Gothic arrows decimated them. Less than a dozen exhausted outlaws succeeded in gaining the road, where the men of Slane cut them down without the loss of a man.

To the rear, the Hrosnabergers were having a sterner fight, for they had borne the main thrust of the attack. Indeed had their assailants managed to concentrate their effort they might have succeeded, but they reached the road piecemeal in twos and threes, so that many were killed as they surmounted the bank. Half of Beowulf's men continued to pour arrows into the rabble crossing the stream; the rest, including Beowulf himself, joined the fray. Ifar had engaged a great oaf of a fellow, as tall as Beowulf but running to fat, whose helmet, armour and gold ornaments proclaimed him a chief. As the giant missed aim with his broadsword, Ifar cut his hamstring to the bone with a fierce backhand sweep. The man bellowed with pain and tried to rise, but Ifar severed the arm he raised to protect his head, then hacked deep to the breastbone between neck and shoulder.

Seeing their leader fall, the remaining outlaws' courage deserted them. 'Kovack is slain!' they cried, as they turned to flee. Many would have escaped but for a quick-thinking Gothic muleteer, who slewed his wagon broadside across the road to block their flight. It cost him his life, for he was unarmed, and a dozen bandits swarmed into his wagon and butchered him. But the men of Hrosnaberg closed in from behind and did great slaughter to avenge him twentyfold.

The brigands' final attempt to escape was across the riverbed whence they had come. But in their panic they tumbled down the bank helter-skelter, some breaking arms and legs as their comrades fell on top of them. Hrosnabergers descended upon the resulting melee, smashing heads with axe and mace. 'No quarter!' was the cry, as the Goths wreaked savage vengeance.

The last round of the encounter, reflecting the first, belonged to the archers of Slane, who took target practice upon the remnants of the outlaw band as they tried to scramble back up the hillside. Some were brought down as they clawed their way toward safety, others, too exhausted or terrified to move, simply hung there motionless until their despatch. Yet others, mad with terror, flung themselves from the rocks and were killed by the fall. For nearly twenty minutes the silence was broken only by the twang of bowstrings, the thud of falling bodies and the screams and moans of the injured. Finally, the Goths moved in to finish the wounded, slaughtering them like cattle as they grovelled on smashed limbs and begged vainly for quarter. Beowulf, who lacked the stomach for such things, took no part. Bodies were heaved into gullies beside the road, dead and dying to be swept away by the swift-flowing stream. A couple of injured mules were despatched more humanely.

At last it was over. Beowulf, unscatched if breathless, felt slightly sick. Ifar approached, a gout of blood congealing on his left arm.

'All right?' Beowulf enquired.

'A scratch from that big fellow, that's all. What men have you lost?'

'Saward, I think, at least. And you?'

'Not a man,' said Dardo cheerfully. 'A couple wounded, but nothing serious.'

'Kjartan,' said Beowulf, 'as for that slave who blocked the road with his wagon. Inform him that he is a slave no longer.'

'He is dead, my lord. And the other slave in the same wagon.'

'In that case, their freedom is put back to the moment they moved it. They will be buried as freedmen, and their families compensated as such.'

'Quite right,' agreed Ifar. 'Do we bury our dead here, or at Targon?'

'As a rule,' said Dardo, 'Goths lie where they fall. That is the custom.'

'What,' said Ifar, 'amongst this murderous rabble? Besides, their graves would be desecrated.'

'We bury them at Targ Bridge,' announced Beowulf firmly, 'which Saward in his youth so valiantly defended. And the slaves have earned the right to lie beside him. We march forthwith; Saward wanted to gain the bridge tonight, and so he shall.'

'Aye, that he shall,' agreed Ifar, as Dardo and Kjartan nodded. 'As for these sweepings from the gaols of Targon' - he indicated the fallen outlaws - 'let them be heaved into ditches for the wolves and crows.'

'How many do you reckon we sent to their account?'

'Eight-and-thirty fell to the swords of Hrosnaberg,' provided Dardo. 'I had my men count them. And to Slane?'

'I made it but eleven,' Beowulf confessed, 'For few of them got through.'

'Indeed,' said Ifar hastily, as if anxious to dispel any notion that his henchmen were hogging the credit, 'your archers must have killed as many again as fell to sword and axe. Between us, I reckon we slew over a hundred of the rogues, including their chief.'

'I heard some call him Kovack,' said Dardo. 'The most feared outlaw of them all. You did well, my lord.'

Ifar blew contemptuously. 'Only as a hangman does well to despatch a felon. A ruffian like this is no match for a Goth.'

'True,' agreed Beowulf, 'but he was an ugly customer for all that. Let's have a look at him.'

It was indeed a harsh, brutal face, frozen by death into an expression of savage hate, and caked with blood and filth. 'Unquestionably he was their leader,' said Beowulf, 'for he is the only one wearing gold, or armour.'

'Look at that,' said Ifar, pointing to the bandit's severed arm. 'A curious device, is it not?'

He referred to a deep brand impressed into the hairy flesh, old yet still fiery red, in the shape of a cross formed by two interlocking doubly-curved lines.

'Do you know it?'

Ifar shook his head. 'Not I. Several of his fellows bore it too.'

'I fancy Ljani might recognize it,' Beowulf mused. 'Does it not strike you as evil?'

'Not so evil as the murder of harmless travellers. Ugly, I dare say, but how can a mere sign be evil?'

'No doubt you are right,' Beowulf agreed. 'The idea was a little fanciful, I dare say.'

'My lord! My lord!' A warrior of Slane came running up.

'What is it?'

'One of the brigands is taken.'

'Well, off with his head, then,' said Ifar briskly. 'No quarter is the rule with slaves like that - you know as well as I.'

'Er, yes,' said Beowulf unhappily. 'It has to be so, of course. They have brought it upon themselves.'

'That goes without saying,' said Ifar, doubtless thinking the Earl of Slane a strange fellow. 'I marvel you waste sympathy on such scum - you would have had none of them.'

'See to it, then,' said Beowulf. The man hesitated. 'What is it?'

'It is a woman, my lord.'

Ifar shrugged. 'That makes no difference, if she was taken under arms. Some of these bandits' whores do fight with their men.'

'She is not armed, my lord.'

'In that case,' said Beowulf, 'she may be entitled to a trial. Let her be bound and conveyed to Port Targon. Eugen of Brabanne can deal with her. Are the mules watered?'

'My lord, yes.'

'Then we march. Delay the meal. We still have two hours journey ahead. Saward shall lie at the Targ Bridge tonight.'

Seven

THE DEAD were buried by torchlight at the south end of Targ Bridge, which thirty years before a younger Saward had defended with his lord, Rathleck, against the forces of the mighty Sferian prince, now king, Angantyr. It was a simple ceremony, sombre but not morbid. Tirl sang an old Gothic lament, *Stilled are the Mighty.*

'Fitting, was it not?' enquired Beowulf of Kjartan on their way back to the tents.

'It was, my lord. Saward would have wished to lie amongst comrades and honourable foes, rather than with that vermin from Silvermount. And methinks he would not object to the company of former slaves, if they had conducted themselves valorously.'

'I am sure he would not.'

'I have observed that you have a soft spot for slaves, my lord,' said Kjartan thoughtfully. 'And of course you have been lucky to possess one so beautiful and talented as Starlight. But your luck has run out with the one we captured from the outlaws. She is as savage as a weasel.'

'Perhaps I had better try to talk some sense into her. I have little stomach for turning her over to the Lord of Targon. It might be better to keep her employed as a slave. We shall be short-handed now.'

Kjartan shook his head. 'I doubt whether you will get anywhere with her, my lord. For one thing she cannot speak Gothic - either that or pretends not to.'

'What a nuisance. Still, I'll see what I can do. Have her brought to my tent.'

*   *   *

65

A COUPLE of housekarls pushed aside the flap and dragged her in. She was a tiny creature, dressed in a dirty linen smock, and plastered from head to foot with mud. Her head was bald save for a half-inch of dark stubble, and the left side of her face was one enormous bruise, with a bloated slit for an eye. Blood was caked around the corner of her mouth. In any case she would not have been good looking, for her breasts sagged and her body was a stone too thin even for her modest height. It took both men to hold her, for she struggled constantly; silent but for gasps and snarls of rage. One of her captors had deep scratches on his cheek.

Beowulf indicated the state of the girl's face. 'Was that necessary, Hersir?'

'She is a hellcat, my lord,' replied the man with the scratches. 'She not only did my face, but nearly crippled Gamli with a kick to the balls. Stop struggling, damn you.' He struck the slave twice across the mouth with the back of his hand. Her head rocked, and blood burst from her teeth, but still she made no sound save for a small, savage hiss.

'Release her,' said Beowulf curtly, displeased.

'She will go for you, my lord.'

'Do you think I'm afraid of a creature her size? Let her go.'

They threw her to the ground at his feet. She remained kneeling, breathing heavily, her good eye turning from one of her captors to another, blazing with fury. Her body was shaking violently, whether from fear, cold, or simply rage, Beowulf could not tell.

'You will be hanged in Port Targon, hellcat,' said Hersir with relish. 'And I shall be there to see you do the neck-dance.'

'It may not come to that,' said Beowulf mildly. 'I have in mind to keep her as a slave. We are short-handed since the loss of those poor fellows this afternoon.'

'That would be of no use, my lord,' provided the other guard. 'She cannot understand Gothic - we have tried.'

'And she is not good-looking enough to provide the men with sport,' Hersir added.

At this the slave turned on him a scowl of such malevolence that Beowulf was fairly sure she must have understood. 'True, she is ugly,' he agreed. 'And a midget to boot.'

The slave scrambled to her feet and spat with fury. 'Who are you calling a midget, you great, fat, stinking pig?'

'He will have you flogged senseless for that,' said Hersir. 'May I carry out the beating, my lord? I will make her squirm.'

Beowulf had never much liked Hersir, and ignored him. 'They told me you could not speak Gothic, small slave,' he said, 'but your command of the colloquial language seems quite adequate to me. I have always regarded myself as muscular, or large-framed, rather than fat.'

The anger in her eyes died momentarily before returning, less certainly than before. 'And I am no midget. I am five feet four inches tall.'

'Nonsense. You are some way short of five feet, or I am mistaken. Bring a measuring-rod,' Beowulf ordered with a laugh. 'If she is not five feet four inches, she shall be punished for lying to us.'

'You pathetic lout,' she said. 'How I despise you, who sneer at a defenceless slave.'

'There is no limit to her insolence,' said Hersir.

'And courage,' Beowulf added with approval. Her voice had been a surprise. He had somehow expected it to be harsh and crude, but though shaking with rage, it was soft and low-pitched.

'Ah, good,' he said as Gimli returned. 'Now stand up against the rod, small one, and draw yourself up to your full height, for you will be beaten if you do not make good your boast.'

She moved reluctantly and stiffly. For the first time he realized she was lame. It must have been an old injury, for he could see no recent wound.

'Heels on the floor,' he ordered. 'No cheating.' He raised his eyebrows. 'Well, well. Five feet three and a half. What ill luck, to be beaten for half an inch.'

His fingers closed on her wrist an instant after she grabbed the knife from his belt. She was far stronger than he had expected, and it required effort to disarm her.

'Now you will be slain by torture, slave,' said Hersir with satisfaction.

'Pooh,' Beowulf scoffed. 'Could you not tell she meant to kill herself, not me? Leave us.' The guards hesitated. 'Leave us, I say.'

'As you wish, my lord,' said Gimli. 'But we will remain within earshot.'

Beowulf made a disgusted sound. 'She looks dangerous now, does she not?'

The slave had shot her bolt, and now knelt with her face buried in her hands. The guards shrugged and left.

'Well now, you seem a somewhat hot-headed slave, to say the least,' Beowulf said.

The girl remained silent.

'One of my oldest friends has been killed this day, slave, and two of my servants. If I thought you a brigand, I should have no choice but to convey you to Targon to be hanged as a felon. It is therefore important that you think carefully before answering my next question. Were you a brigand, or simply their slave?'

'Never mind what I am. Just hang me and have done.'

There was a long pause. 'Methinks no brigand would have answered me like that. Explain yourself.'

'Since my escape, I hung around their camp in the hope of stealing food. Food is scarce in the mountains.'

'So, you are a runaway. Whose slave are you - or were you?'

Across her face there flickered a haunted expression of revulsion and terror. At the same time she moved a hand involuntarily to her left shoulder. Beowulf pushed it gently aside. The flesh bore a deep brand in the shape of the evilly-designed cross he had observed on the bandit chief. It had been brutally done, the iron twisted and driven half an inch deep. Though old, the scar was still oozing and the flesh puffy and inflamed. 'Whose brand is that?'

'If you do not know, you are very lucky.'

'I dare say I am. Now answer me.'

She whispered so softly that he had to lean forward to catch the name. 'Ragnar of Torre.'

'That means nothing to me.'

'Evidently not. Ragnar of Torre' - the haunted look returned - 'is the worst man in the world.'

'He is certainly no hand with the branding iron.'

She sneered. 'You think that is all? Why do you think I have one leg two inches shorter than the other?' She turned her back and slipped the linen dress from her shoulder. Beowulf could hardly restrain a gasp. The whole of her back, from neck to waist, was a mass of lacerated flesh, some healed in great knotted scars, elsewhere still red and suppurating. The backs of her thighs were similarly marked.

'Odin's death,' he breathed. 'You have been cut to pieces, little slave. Did Ragnar of Torre do this to you?'

'His servants. What has been done to me is not one hundredth part of the evil he wreaks every day.'

'How long since this was done, and why?'

'A week. My head was shaved at the same time. Why, I refuse to say.'

'And if I return you to him, you will be treated the same again?'

'Not quite the same. This time my legs will be broken in a vice.'

Beowulf said nothing.

'From your expression, Gothic lord, it seems you are shocked. You have not looked upon the face of Evil, as I have done.'

'Apparently not,' he said slowly. 'Very well, small one, I am satisfied you are no brigand, but an escaped slave. You therefore have a choice. You may either become my slave, or be turned free and fend for yourself.'

'I will kill myself before I become a slave again.'

'Be sensible, small slave. If you are freed you will be dead of cold and hunger within the week. The mountains are inhospitable at this season, and your belly is rumbling like a wardrum already.'

'Stop calling me "small slave." I hate it.'

'What else should I call you? What is your name?'

'I have no name. In the House of Torre I was called by an obscene name, which I refuse to repeat.'

'If you have no name, you are poor indeed. I can assure you that if you become my slave, you will at least be given a name.'

'Thank you. I would rather remain a slave without a name.'

Beowulf sighed and shook his head. 'Well, if you are determined to leave, I cannot stop you.'

'Of course you can. And no doubt will do if need be.'

'No. If you decide to leave, I have no right to prevent you.'

She seemed puzzled for a moment, then regained her former hostility. 'Better the bleak wilderness than the beds of men who will use me as they will.'

'You are quite mistaken,' said Beowulf, shocked. 'According to the laws of Gothmark, even a slave has the right to give or withhold her favours as she wishes. I am appalled that you should misjudge us thus.'

Again she hesitated. 'If you speak true, your men an improvement on most. Certainly upon those I have met.'

'Perhaps you have not fully understood the terms of my offer. If you become my slave, I shall expect you to work hard and cheerfully.'

The girl laughed bitterly.

'Should you call me a pig again in front of my men, or refuse to obey reasonable orders, I shall have you beaten, because I cannot allow a slave to defy me in public. On my side, you will be decently treated, given three square meals a day, and proper clothing and shelter. You will not be beaten without good cause, and will be entitled to my protection.'

'Will you have me beaten now?'

Beowulf frowned. 'What for?'

'The measuring-rod.'

'Of course not; that was just a halfwit jest. Anyway you were much nearer the mark than I was. Funny, you looked smaller.'

'May I have time to consider?'

'Of course. But try to let me have your decision by tomorrow, when we strike camp. Meanwhile you are free to go, of course. If you are not here for breakfast, I shall know you have decided to leave us.'

'I shall not need that long, my lord.' She paused and frowned. 'That is the first time I have addressed to you as "my lord." I had not intended to; the words had simply slipped out. Perhaps some part of me has already decided ...' She raised her head to meet his gaze. 'I accept your offer, my lord. From this moment I am your slave.'

'Good. You will need livery, for it displeases me to see you in those filthy rags. There should be a spare tunic with Hort, the storekeeper in the end wagon. Wash yourself thoroughly in the river, put on your new clothes, and report to me again.'

'There is one more thing, my lord. When I grabbed your knife, you were mistaken. I do not well know what I intended, but I think it may have been to attack you, not kill myself. I cannot allow you to own me without knowing that.'

'Oh, I realized that, of course. Let us speak no more of it - you were desperate, and I had taunted you thoughtlessly.'

Her jaw dropped, and it was some seconds before she found her voice. 'What manner of man are you, my lord?'

'You speak in riddles, slave. Be off with you, and next time I see you let it be in the livery of the Wagmundings.'

WITHIN a quarter of an hour, the girl returned. She now wore the white linen livery of a Wagmunding slave; kneelength, with a light belt, a black and silver stripe at the left breast.

'Why did they not provide you with boots?' he asked.

'There were none to fit me, my lord. Even the smallest were far too big. But I am used to going barefoot.'

'Turn around.'

She obeyed. Cleaned up and without the scowl, she was not as ill-favoured as he had at first thought, though far from pretty. 'It suits you,' he said truthfully. She flushed. 'You are however still purple with cold.' He picked up one of his cloaks. 'Here, wrap yourself in this. It will be far too big for you, of course, but that is all to the good.'

It looked as if a tent had collapsed upon her, and they both laughed. It was the first time she had even smiled. She had oddly protruding teeth, which he rather liked.

'That's better. But I am forgetting essentials. You say you have no name, but that is not true of me, and I should have introduced myself earlier. I am Beowulf of Slane. As for you, I cannot continue calling you "small slave," especially since it annoys you so much. I shall have to think of one for you. What was your rank?'

'An unranked serf, of course. The lowest of the low.'

'That will not do at all. None of my slaves are without rank, however humble. Henceforward you are a slave of the third rank, which is the most junior. If you perform your duties well, you will be promoted.' He smiled. 'And let me say that I am very glad you have decided to stay with us. Despite certain oddities of behaviour, I cannot recall meeting anyone, slave or free, to whom I have taken such an immediate liking.'

The slave uttered a few speechless noises. Finally she regained her voice. 'Thank you, my lord. And let me say that I never heard any free man address a slave as you do. Almost as if ... as if you were talking to

70

an equal.'

Beowulf shrugged. 'Who is to say who is equal to whom in the eyes of the gods? But it's strange you should say that.'

'How so, my lord?'

He paused. 'I have little memory of my father. But as I recall, the very last time I saw him he gave me some advice. He said I should remember the Wagmunding tradition, to treat all men as important, but none as very important. Being a child of five at the time, I did not understand him, but I never forgot it, and as I have grown older I have come to realize what he meant.' Beowulf gave a short self-conscious laugh. 'And I have never told anyone about it before. Anyway, enough of that. Another thing I should like to know is your age. How old are you?'

'I am not absolutely sure, my lord, but I believe I was born in the Year of the Dragon.'

That made her three-and-twenty. Unless ...

She smiled. 'Three-and-twenty, my lord, not five-and-thirty. I know I look older.'

'Three-and-twenty of course, I never thought otherwise. Quite a coincidence, little slave, for that is my age too. In what month were you born?'

'Early in the Month without a Star.'

'Then you are barely three weeks my junior, for I was born on the fourth Tyrsday in the Month of the Diamond Star. The same day as Longspear,' he added proudly. 'Can you cook?'

She seemed slightly bewildered by the sudden change of subject. 'Why, yes, my lord.'

'Good. The men have lit their campfire and are preparing a meal. You will tell the cooks I have sent you, and obey their instructions. I shall dine by the fire, with my friends Ifar and Kjartan, and you will serve me. For yourself, you will obtain a large mug of broth, two pieces of black bread, a chicken wing, and two tuber roots. If you really need more, tell me. Eat slowly at first, or you will make yourself ill.'

'Thank you, my lord. You are very kind.'

'Nonsense. And send Kjartan to me. He is the slim, beardless young fellow with short hair, who wears the Wagmunding livery.'

'It shall be done, my lord.'

'AH, Kjartan. I had wanted a word with you, following the loss of Saward.'

'A sad blow, my lord.'

'Indeed. Acting captaincy of the guard is now yours.'

The young man gave a start. 'There are several senior to me, my lord.'

71

'But none better.'

'I thank you most heartily, my lord. I had not expected it.'

'Mind, I say acting. When we are returned to Slane, it may be that you will be relieved of the post. There are several senior members of my household there.'

'That is understood, my lord. Meanwhile, I shall do my best to justify your confidence.'

'I'm sure you will. Your first order will be to Hersir, who brought the little slave to me.'

'Yes, my lord?'

'Yes. He is to be rewarded with a spell of latrine duty.'

'Latrine duty, my lord?'

'Exactly. Until we reach Targon, it will be his job to dig and fill in the latrine holes every time we pitch and strike camp.'

'That is slaves' work, my lord.'

'Quite so. It is my hope that after a day or two performing tasks normally undertaken by slaves, he may acquire more insight into their lot. It will be an instructive experience for him, I'm sure.'

Kjartan grinned. 'I understand, my lord.'

'Good. I shall carry out personal inspection of his work, and if it is not satisfactory, I shall require it to be done again. And give orders to the slaves that they are forbidden to advise or help him, upon pain of beating.'

THE SLAVE ate and drank slowly as he had advised, shuddering with sensuous pleasure as the food and warmth entered her body. She huddled beneath the cloak, and as the meal wore on moved tentatively nearer to Beowulf. Once, while talking to Ifar, he put an arm round her shoulders in a careless, friendly way. Instantly the tiny body stiffened with fear, but he pretended not to notice. A little later she relaxed again, and even moved closer.

The fire burned low, and the stars were cold. 'Go and prepare my bed, little one,' he said, yawning. 'Take a couple of cloaks and make one for yourself.'

She sprang to her feet. 'Yes, my lord. I ... er ... My lord ...'

'What is it?'

'You wish me to share your tent?'

'Of course, silly slave, otherwise you will freeze to death. Get along with you.'

She inclined her head to him and left.

'Your slave improves upon acquaintance,' observed Ifar. 'I was told she was a hellcat.'

'She will be all right,' said Beowulf. 'She has been brutally used.'

Ifar nodded. 'One can tell a lot about a man,' he remarked, half to himself, 'from the way he treats his slaves.'

'You're right, Ifar. This Ragnar, of whom she spoke - if she fell into his hands again, I dread to think what he might do.'

Ifar looked at him in amusement. 'And if Ragnar fell into yours, Beowulf, I should not care to be in his shoes either. It'd be more than a spell of latrine duty for him, I'll warrant.'

Beowulf laughed and stood, stretching. 'Aye, true enough.' A shadow fell across his face. 'I'm not entirely happy about Hersir, you know.'

Ifar shrugged. 'As my grandfather always says, it wouldn't do for us all to be alike.'

'Indeed not. But one man like Hersir is more than enough, methinks.'

'Not the most amiable of individuals, it's true. But neither is Dardo, and he's the best man I've got. You can't expect them all to be like Gamli.'

Gamli, the other victim of Suth's spirited resistance to capture, was one of Ifar's senior housekarls and a man of perpetual good humour, who got on with everyone except his immediate superior, Dardo. 'No, true. How is Gamli, by the way?'

Ifar laughed. 'Takes more than a kick in the rocks to bother him.'

Beowulf laughed in turn and raised a hand briefly in valediction. 'Right. He's a good fellow. Good night, Ifar.'

Ifar stood likewise, and kicked dirt into the fire before retiring. 'Good night, my lord.'

THE GIRL had prepared Beowulf's bed. He found her kneeling beside it, head lowered.

'Now what is the matter?'

'I wish to say something, my lord.'

Beowulf shook his head. 'You do not have to ask permission every time you speak. You have gone from one extreme to the other; not two hours since you were calling me a fat pig.'

'It is that of which I wish to speak. You have treated me with great kindness, my lord, whereas I have been foul-tempered and insolent. I apologize most humbly, and promise that such a thing will not occur again.'

'Handsomely spoken, little one. But I must ask you to exchange forgiveness with me. For whilst you were indeed outspoken to the point of folly, I must admit that at times I spoke unfeelingly myself, and with less excuse. Life has been unkind to you, I fancy - from now on I hope to offer you something better.'

She stood, trembling. 'Oh, my lord...'

It seemed quite natural to take her in his arms. She began to cry;

harsh, ugly sobs shaking her thin body.

'Let it all come out, little one,' he said softly. 'All the pain and fear and misery. You will feel much better. There. Are you all right now?'

'Yes, my lord.' She stepped back from him and tossed her head. 'Apart from having made a complete fool of myself.'

'There is nothing to be ashamed of in a few tears between friends. And we are friends, are we not? Oh, but I forgot, oaf that I am. Your back has been dreadfully marked, and I have been holding you too tight.'

'No, my lord, you were very gentle.'

'Well, anyway,' he said after an awkward pause, 'I think I may have the thing for you. Before my departure, my sister Ljani gave me an ointment she claimed would cure any wound, however grave. She is the wisest woman in Gothmark, with great knowledge of many things, including healing. Perhaps it might help your eye and back.'

'Please try it, my lord, if you think it might do good.'

Beowulf dug the jar out of his travelling-chest and removed the lid. It was a curious dark purple colour, with a pungent but not displeasing smell.

'Funny-looking stuff,' he said. 'Smear some on your face to start with.'

The girl scooped a little unguent from the jar and rubbed her eye gently. 'It is very soothing, my lord. Methinks it feels better already.'

'Good. Now let us try your back. Perhaps if you pull the tunic over your shoulders.'

Instead she removed her dress altogether and lay on the bed face down. She was trembling again. The wounds were cleaner now, but still gaped hideously. He paid particular attention to the obscene brand on her shoulder. She flinched.

'I'm sorry, little one. Did it sting?'

'Just a little, my lord. That must mean it is doing good.'

He applied the salve smoothly and with great care. Caressing a woman's naked body, even one as thin as the little slave's, could hardly fail to provide sensuous pleasure. There was not an ounce of fat on her, but the small muscles were surprisingly well-formed. Skinny she might be, but her little rump was trimly curved ...

'I have been thinking about your name, little one,' he said, hoping the topic might distract him.

'Have you chosen one, my lord?'

'I have. You must approve it, of course; if it is not to your liking I will change it.'

'It can hardly please me less than "small slave" or "little one." What is the name, my lord?'

'Well, as you have just demonstrated once more, it seems to me that you always make a practice of speaking the truth - a rare quality, especially among slaves. So I propose to call you Suth, which in the old language of the Goths means truth.'

She turned her head, and he could see her lashes wet with tears. Beneath a thin arm he caught a quick view of her left breast, fuller than he had first thought. 'That is a very lovely name, my lord. Thank you. I shall try to deserve it.'

'I'm glad it pleases you.' He touched her shorn head briefly. 'Your hair. What colour is it?'

She half rose from the bed again, granting him another tantalizing glimpse. 'My hair, my lord? Why, very dark. Black, in fact.'

'Good. I like black hair. You will wear it shoulder length, which I think should suit you. There now, your back is finished.'

Following his remarks about her hair, the little slave seemed uncharacteristically pleased with herself. 'I do not think it is quite finished yet, my lord,' she contradicted, rather smugly he thought. 'Methinks a little more might still do good.'

'Very well,' he said, puzzled.

He had been rather slow on the uptake, but the small creature was breathing deeply and making little grumbling noises of physical pleasure. 'You have very strong hands, my lord,' she purred. 'Strong, but gentle.'

'Not all that gentle,' he said sternly, giving her a smart slap on the curved little rump.

'Oh!' she squealed in mock anger, then laughed.

'Now get dressed again, baggage, before you get yourself into serious trouble. And go to bed.'

She grabbed her livery and stumbled over to the cloaks, half covering herself, blushing but still laughing. 'Yes, my lord. Good night, my lord.'

'Good night, Suth.'

'MY lord! My lord!'

'What is the matter now, Suth? It is the middle of the night.'

'I think, the fourth hour after midnight, my lord.'

'I will take your word for it. Go back to sleep.'

'No, no, my lord. Look!'

Beowulf peered out from under the furs. The candle he used as a nightlight was still burning, so it was not completely dark. 'Look at what?'

'My back, my lord. Look at my back!'

She turned away from him, a thin, excited, naked girl. The candle he used as a nightlight was still buring, so it was not completely dark. She covered herself awkwardly with her hands and knelt beside him.

'Are you a wizard, my lord?' she asked in awe.

'Of course not, Suth, I am a very simple fellow. Ljani's medicine must have done the trick. I told you she was the wisest woman in Gothmark.'

'No, no, my lord, it was you. I am sure it was. And my face is better, and even ...'

The dreadful brand was still there, but a thin white scar, no longer poisoned or swollen.

'Much better,' said Beowulf in satisfaction. 'I am very pleased for you, Suth.'

She grabbed one of his hands and covered it in kisses. 'I love you, my lord, I love you with all my heart. Forgive a grateful slave such insolence, but I must speak what I feel.'

'There is nothing to forgive, Suth. You have simply become over-emotional - a fault of yours, if I may say so. I am very pleased, but now go back to bed.'

'Yes, my lord, I am sorry. Have I displeased you with my foolishness?'

'Of course not, Suth. As a matter of fact I rather like it. But now let us get some sleep.'

Eight

AN HOUR after dawn, the Goths stood ready to leave. Since the events of the previous day, the wagons had been moved to the middle of the convoy for protection, preceded by the warriors of Slane, those of Hrosnaberg bringing up the rear. In the van, a brawny housekarl held aloft Beowulf's personal standard of the Black Bear; amongst the mailed retinue waved the silver chevron-banners of the Wagmundings and the Wylfings, and the Lone Star of Gothmark. Ifar and Dardo, bearing the Red Horse of Hrosnaberg, brought up the rear. A couple of mules lifted their heads and brayed; harness jangled and glinted red in the torchlight, for the sky was dull and overcast.

'Are we ready?' demanded Beowulf in the invariable daily ritual.

'Ready, my lord,' Kjartan confirmed.

Beowulf raised his sword arm and pointed ahead. 'March.'

Their route lay along the south bank of the Targ, past the great stone bridge which gave the spot its name. Two armoured knights on leaden horses were crossing from the north. At the approach of the Goths they emerged from the bridge and turned broadside to block the road. The shields thus presented bore the device of a sable tower marked with the twisted cross which Beowulf now knew to be the badge of Torre. Their helmets were of a design unfamiliar to him, like masks with slits for eyes and mouth. One was black, the other red, and their lowered lances were trimmed in the same colours.

'Have the men in readiness,' murmured Beowulf to Kjartan. 'But make no move for the time being. It may be they intend no harm.'

At twenty yards distance Beowulf called a halt and raised an arm with the conventional Gothic greeting: 'We salute your soul.'

The black rider gave voice in the Teutonic language of the south. It differed a little from Gothic, but gave Beowulf no difficulty, for the Wagmundings had originally been a Teutonic tribe.

'You are the Gothic lord of the Black Bear.'

'Aye,' Beowulf acknowledged. 'A servant of Athkyn, King of Gothmark. Beowulf is my name. You have the advantage of me.'

'We serve Ragnar Rolanding, Count of Brabanne and Torre. You have amongst you a runaway slave.' The rider took a parchment scroll from within his hauberk and read: ' "Item: One female serf of no name, born in the Year of the Dragon, height five feet three inches, thin build, black shaven hair, blue eyes. Lame in the left leg, and branded with the mark of Torre." '

Suth, looking sick with terror, had appeared at Beowulf's side. 'I am here, my lords.' She made to step forward, but Beowulf grabbed her wrist.

'Stay where you are.'

'Let her go,' said the horseman in red. 'She is to be returned for punishment.'

'Well,' said Beowulf in a friendly tone, 'perhaps that need not arise. I have taken a fancy to the slave, and will buy her from your master.'

'Our orders do not permit it. She is to be returned.'

'I ought to go with them, my lord,' whispered Suth, though shaking in every limb. 'Otherwise it will be the worse for you.'

'The slave speaks truly,' said Black-helmet, who must have had very acute hearing. 'Thus far, we may be disposed to believe you have acted in ignorance of our lord's claim. Any further delay, however, is at your peril.'

'Kjartan,' said Beowulf, 'this slave is being obstinate. Convey her to the rear under guard.'

Kjartan jerked his head at a couple of housekarls, who did as instructed, Suth putting up little more than token resistance.

'Now, my friends,' Beowulf continued cheerfully, 'name your master's price. You will not find me ungenerous.'

'We have said she is not for sale,' repeated Red-helmet. 'Come, no more of this. Yield the slave to us at once, or we will ride you down.'

At a nod from Dardo the men of Hrosnaberg formed square and drew their swords. Those of Slane looked to Beowulf for a similar sign, but he remained unruffled.

'Dear me,' he said mildly. 'You seem a rather aggressive pair of fellows, but there is no need to be unfriendly. I am no robber. What is the going rate for an unranked slave? A quarter of a thaler? I will double that, which is generous for a slave who is lame and puny.'

'Look to defend yourself against the wrath of the Lord of Torre,' said Black-helmet harshly, levelling his lance.

'Lower your weapon, fierce horseman,' said Beowulf. 'I will make you an offer you cannot refuse. Two thalers, nay twice that if you insist.'

A silver thaler was the price of a good horse, more than that of any slave except perhaps the loveliest courtesan.

'You could offer us gold,' said the man impatiently. 'It would make no difference.'

'You misunderstand me; I am offering gold. Four gold thalers; well, as I am feeling generous, say five. Five gold thalers is my offer, no more, no less.'

Ifar gaped in astonishment, and the horsemen themselves seemed nonplussed. A gold thaler, or mark, was twelve score times the value of a silver one. Upon half a gold mark, a man of the middle station in life could live in style for many years.

'Art mad, Gothic lord?' demanded the black horseman. 'Five *gold* thalers?'

Beowulf raised a hand. 'Bring the treasure-chest.'

Hort, his storeman and treasurer, departed shaking his head. The men of Slane were used to Wagmunding eccentricities, but this was akin to madness.

'Here you are, my lord.'

'Good. And here is the price: five gold thalers for one female slave. Draw up the bill of sale.'

The horsemen exchanged glances. 'We have not decided yet,' said the red one. 'It needs thought.'

'Surely not. Come, sign the paper; it is all prepared.'

'Ten,' said Black-helmet, after consulting again with his fellow. 'Ten gold marks.'

'By day and night, you drive a hard bargain. Ten it is, then; sign the bill. Ifar, bear witness.'

They signed the document without reading it, grabbed the precious coins and rode off - not whence they had come, but east to Targon.

'I am glad she will not be leaving,' said Tirl. 'For I had composed a little song in her honour. Without her it would have lost its point.'

'Was that the one I heard you regaling some of the men with last night?' enquired Ifar in disapproval.

'Oh no, that was merely a ditty about the problems associated with latrine duty.' Hersir was not popular with either churls or slaves. 'Has it occurred to you, my lord,' continued the minstrel unabashed, 'that those fellows intend to misappropriate the money?'

'I know I have a reputation for stupidity,' said Beowulf, 'but I am not, as you seem to imagine, a complete simpleton. However, I remind you they are Ragnar's men, and claimed to act in his behalf, so property in the slave has legally passed to me. If they now steal the money, Ragnar of Torre must sort it out with them. It is naught to do with me.'

'Your grasp of legal niceties,' commented Ifar, impressed, 'is matched only by your financial imbecility.'

'YOU should have let them take me, my lord,' said Suth miserably. 'They will return with greater power.'

'Not at all. The transaction was concluded amicably - or if not amicably, at least to the satisfaction of all concerned. You are now legally mine, bought and paid for. So mind you behave yourself in future.'

She shook her head. 'Please do not lie to me, my lord. Ragnar of Torre cares not for money, but for power and vengeance.'

'Here is the bill of sale. I assure you it is perfectly valid. I will get Hort to read it to you.'

'I can read, my lord.'

'Really? That is more than I can do. Here you are, then.'

She read it carefully as she stumbled along beside him, her bare feet scurrying through the dust to keep pace with his giant strides. As she returned the document to him her eyes were full of relief and joy.

'It is far more than I am worth, my lord. Far more.'

'I do not think so. Had I known you could read, I might have been tempted to pay even more.'

'Oh, my lord,' she laughed, 'ten thalers is forty times my value at least. But there is an error in the document. I hope it does not invalidate it.'

'Why, so do I,' said Beowulf earnestly. 'Hort drew it up for me, and I shall be cross if he made a mistake. What's wrong with it?'

'The price, my lord, is stated to be ten gold thalers. Silver is of course correct.'

'Is it?' he enquired, smiling.

Suth stopped in her tracks. She tried to speak, but at first could only make incoherent noises. 'Are you mad, my lord? Forgive me … No words ...' Again, she shook her head. '... No words.'

'Oh, cheer up, little one,' said Beowulf. 'Ten gold marks might be somewhat above the market price, but I still think I have a bargain.'

'Above the market price?' she repeated. 'Only ten thousand times, that's all.'

'I see you have a head for figures as well.'

'Be serious, my lord, and listen. It is well known that the highest price ever paid for a slave was but half a gold mark by the King of Drakonia for Mircalla, the most beautiful and talented courtesan in the harem of the King of Parthia. Even then the price was considered excessive, and paid by way of ostentation.'

'Well, well. And I have paid twenty times as much for a skinny slave of uncertain temper.'

'My lord,' she said, laughing, 'I know why you have done this. You intend to save me from the vengeance of the Count of Torre, rather as some good men are said to buy caged birds to set them free. In a thousand lives, I could never repay you.'

'You make too much of things,' said Beowulf, embarrassed. 'Hurry along now; the others will be leaving us behind.'

'Yes, my lord.' Suth hastened into step beside him. 'But even for a thousand marks, or all the money in the world, Ragnar of Torre would not have sold me. His men must have betrayed him and made off with your money.'

'If they have, I care not. I have my slave and my bill of sale, which is all that concerns me.'

'My lord, you are such a good man, but I fear that all you have done is bring the vengeance of Torre upon yourself and your men.'

'Perhaps,' said Beowulf. 'But if so, I think the count might find that Gothic warriors are not quite such easy meat as you seem to imagine.'

'SUTH,' said Beowulf in his tent that night. 'I wonder if you could help me.'

'What is it, my lord?'

'It concerns the futhark,' he continued, in slight embarrassment. 'You are obviously a very learned slave. I should like you to teach me.'

'Certainly, my lord,' said Suth, seeming pleased. 'It is not difficult.'

He shook his head. 'I have always found it so. Several times, I have tried to learn, but Ljani always became impatient with my slowness and stupidity'

Suth frowned. 'You are not at all slow or stupid, my lord. That is merely a foolish pose you have adopted, and ought to abandon, otherwise you will drift into a life of idleness and missed opportunity. Forgive a slave for speaking so bluntly.'

'Hmm,' murmured Beowulf thoughtfully. 'Well, that is telling me, Suth. And to be frank it accords with my own recent thoughts on the matter. So as not to waste any more time, I suggest you start teaching me now, whilst the cooks are preparing dinner.'

'Should I not be helping them, my lord?'

'No, this is more important. We have no pen or paper to hand, but can use the rune-stones Ljani gave me. Light some candles and drop the tent-flap, for it is getting cold.'

As she obeyed, Beowulf pulled the rune purse from his jerkin and emptied the stones on to the lid of his treasure-chest.

Suth came to squat beside him. 'Do you know any of them, my lord?'

He ran his fingers through the stones. 'The first six, and those of my own name. Most of the others I am not sure of.'

'Very well, we will start with the first six. Arrange them in the correct order, please, and recite their names.'

He achieved this without much difficulty. 'Fehu, Uruz, Thurisaz, Anzus, Raido, Kano. That spells futhark.'

'Very good, my lord. Now what comes next?'

'Is it Gebo?' he asked uncertainly.

'Gebo it is, my lord, very good. Place it next to Kano. And now ...'

'Wunjo is next. I know that because it occurs in my name.'

'Quite right, so place it alongside Gebo. Those are the first eight letters, my lord - since you know them already, I think we could do another four tonight, making twelve.' Her quick fingers picked out a rune consisting of two upright strokes and a sloping cross-piece. 'Next comes Hagalaz, and then Nauthiz, which is similar, with but one downstroke. Then Isa, without the cross-piece. Notice how each helps remind you of the next. And we will finish with Jera. He is more difficult, a square on his tip, with two of the sides extended. So. Repeat them, please.'

Beowulf did so, pointing to each in turn. Then she mixed them in with the rest and asked him to pick them out and place them in order. He managed it with only slight prompting.

'Good, my lord. Now just one thing more before we dine. Dealing with the runes one by one can become monotonous, so we will try spelling your name, as you claimed to be able to do.'

'I will try,' said Beowulf. 'Though Ljani usually has to help me. If I get it wrong, you must give me the stick.'

'Oh, you great fool,' she said, laughing. 'Forgive me, my lord, I forgot myself. But I am not afraid of you. Strange, is it not?'

'Not really. No-one is ever afraid of me.'

She looked at him closely. 'I had noticed that, my lord. And yet you are such a huge and powerful man ... It is most strange. Well, anyway, back to the runes. Please spell your name.'

He noticed that again she avoided speaking his name directly, lest she be thought presumptuous. This time he picked the letters out quickly: Berkana, Ehwaz, Othuz, Wunjo, Uruz, Laguz, Fehu.

'Excellent, my lord. Now, I hear them call dinner, but immediately after, I think you should obtain pen and paper and copy out the twelve runes you know; nay, sixteen including those in your name. Then tomorrow we will learn four more, and on the aftermorrow the last four, which will complete the futhark. The next step will be combining them into words, which is less difficult than you might think.'

'You are indeed a very learned slave,' Beowulf repeated. 'I had no idea you possessed such skill.'

'It is not difficult, my lord. You had mastered much of it yourself already, and knew it not, and have made further progress this evening. But you must apply yourself to it every day, repeating the futhark whenever you have a moment, and visualizing the runes as you do so. That will be far better than a long tiring session once a week.'

'Very well,' he agreed. 'I will write out and recite the futhark as far as I know it, every day. There is one more thing.'

'Yes, my lord?'

'I should like to learn one other rune tonight.'

'If you wish, my lord. Perth is next.'

'No.' He was suddenly embarrassed. 'It is a particular one I have in mind. The hissing sound - sss, thus.'

'That is Sowelu, my lord. Here he is.'

The rune consisted of a zigzag line with three angles. 'Ah, thank you.' He placed it in front of him, seized the runes Uruz and Thurisaz, and pointed to it proudly. 'There. I have spelt your name: Suth. Is it right? Or have I made a mistake?'

She seemed to have difficulty in replying. 'No, my lord,' she said in a shaky voice, blinking rapidly. 'That is absolutely correct. Well done. Now let us go to dine.'

Roger Butters

Nine

'YOU HAVE recalled and written all the runes correctly, my lord,' said Suth the following evening. 'But I think you would find it easier to hold the crayon thus, between thumb and the first two fingers, rather than like the haft of a spear.'

'That is what Ljani said. But it feels awkward to me.'

'No doubt it will at first, my lord. But if you do not try it, you will never get any better.'

'She said that too. Very well, Suth, I will try doing it your way in future.'

'I am sure you will soon manage it. But that is enough for tonight, or you will get stale.'

'Good. It was beginning to make my head ache. Well, good night, little slave, and thank you.'

'My lord,' she said diffidently, 'I wonder if I might ask a question.'

'Why, of course,' he said, sitting heavily on the furs of his bed and sticking out his boots towards her. She pulled them off without trouble. The first time she had tried she had tumbled backwards on to her behind, which had caused them both much merriment.

'It concerns your rank, my lord. When we first met, you introduced yourself as Beowulf of Slane, as if you were a private gentleman. Your followers, however, call you by various titles, Earl, Margrave and even Prince. Evidently you are a man of great distinction. Could you please enlighten me as to your exact position?'

'Certainly, Suth, it is a little complicated. Strictly speaking, I am Beowulf Edgtyring, of the House of Wagmund, third Earl of Slane and various other places. My lands border those of my kinsman, the Earl of Karron Tha, a subject of the King of the Sfear. I am accordingly sometimes called Margrave, or border lord, although that is not part of my formal title.'

'And prince, my lord? Are you the son of a king?'

Beowulf laughed. 'Nothing so eminent, little one. My father, Edgtyr Wagmunding, was just an earl like me. I am, however, the grandson of a king; possibly it might interest you to learn something of the history of my people, the Goths, and their royal house.'

'Very much, my lord, if it would be no trouble.'

'None at all, I am glad you are interested. But it may take some time, so change the candles and bring me a small flagon of ale. Help yourself at the same time, if you wish.

'Thank you, Suth,' he continued as she complied. 'Now squat down beside me, and I will begin.'

Suth sat with legs tucked beneath her amongst the furs piled at the foot of the bed. In the soft candlelight, she looked surprisingly well-favoured. And when her hair grew shoulder-length, she would look better still. It was really rather cosy being with her like this. He had never felt cosy with Starlight.

'I am ready, my lord,' she prompted.

'Ah, yes. But to start with, I should make it plain that I am by no means well versed in Gothic history. All I know comes from my sister Ljani, who is the brainy one of the family. If therefore she should ever tell you anything different from me, it will doubtless be her version which is correct. However, I think I have remembered most of it with tolerable accuracy.

'The Goths are an ancient people, whose history is reputed to go back several hundreds of years, though many of the early tales are legendary. It seems clear, however, that by the time of the mediaeval period - that is, the two hundred years or so before the present century - the Goths were ruled by a valiant and noble tribe of princes, the House of Ironside. As with all such dynasties, some kings were good, some bad, some just and warlike, others treacherous and ignoble. But until the last hundred years or so, it is probably fair to say that the good outweighed the bad, all things considered.

'Then, alas, the House of Ironside fell upon evil times, as more and more kings tended to abuse the trust placed in them by their people. Until eventually the crown descended to one Guthmund the Vile, a man of savage temper and perverted sexual appetite, fawned on by vicious favourites who plundered his subjects, great and small. Though mercifully he was king for only a short time, his name is still a watchword for tyranny and misrule.'

Suth frowned. 'Did none attempt to depose this evil king, my lord?'

'Indeed they did, small one, which brings me to the substance of my story. For the king had a cousin on his mother's side, one Finn of the

House of Falgard, a man as generous, bold and popular, as Guthmund was vicious, cowardly and detested. Many were they who urged Finn to rebel and seize the crown, yet such was his loyalty that his reply was ever the same, that the king was still young, and would learn to mend his ways. Finally, however, his hand was forced. The king, fearful of Finn's popularity, despatched some henchmen with orders to arrest him upon a trumped-up charge of treason. At this, Finn's patience finally snapped. He raised the standard of revolt at Thorn, in the province of Feldmark, upon the last Freyasday in the Month of Ten Thousand Stars, in the year of the world 1382. Men flocked to his banner, Guthmund's followers deserted him, and Finn was proclaimed king amidst universal rejoicing. The former king's evil counsellors were publicly executed, and Guthmund himself was thrown into the dungeons at Castle Longspear, where soon after it was given out that he had died of chagrin, melancholy and despair.'

'Is it not more likely, my lord,' ventured Suth, 'that he was murdered by adherents of the new king?'

'Not only likely, but near-certain. Be that as it may, Finn Falgarding, or Finn the Valiant as he became known, ruled Gothmark with distinction for twenty years. During that time there were but two clouds on his horizon. The first, naturally, was the somewhat dubious manner by which he had achieved the crown. As you pointed out, disillusioned little slave, Finn and his henchmen were doubtless responsible for removing his predecessor not only from the throne, but from the world. Few were inclined to hold this very seriously to his account; nevertheless it would have been preferable for Guthmund to be tried for his crimes before the Council of Elders and sentenced in accordance with law, rather than secretly and squalidly murdered.

'More to the point, Finn was not, according to descent and primogeniture, next in line to the throne. For the old king had a brother, Asmund the Simple, in whom the degenerate blood of the Ironsides had run, not to depravity, but foolish simple-mindedness. Finn accordingly did not have him put to death, but permitted him to live as a private gentleman on his estates near Hrosnaberg. Asmund showed no interest in politics, indeed upon electing Finn, the Wittan had expressly debarred him and his heirs from the succession. Despite his supposed idiocy, however, he married, and produced two children: a son, Sigmund, and a daughter, Renate. These three, the last of the Ironsides, served as a constant reminder to Finn of the fragility of his claim to the throne.

'I now turn to the history of our northern neighbours, the Sfear. They are a less ancient people than the Goths, yet it is generally believed closely related. In olden days, the Kings of the Sfear had been vassals of those of Gothmark, and liable to pay them tribute. The power of the Sfear seldom approached that of the Goths, for even today their numbers are scarcely a third of ours, besides which it chanced that many of their kings died young, leaving children of tender age. Sferian history is thus littered with dynastic squabbles, ambitious nobles, corrupt regents and infant kings. At the time of which I speak, such a dynastic struggle, indeed civil war, was in progress in the Land of the Sfear. From this war, Finn and the Goths wisely held aloof.

'Eventually the conflict resolved itself in favour of the sole surviving contender for the crown, a young warrior named Saur Silverspur, of the House of the Chariot. At his coronation, held with great pomp in the Sferian capital of Bakir, he caused a proclamation to be read. This stated, first, that the payment of tribute to the Goths was unlawful and would be discontinued. Second, that certain border territories historically in dispute were the property of the Sfear, and would be occupied forthwith; finally, that Finn Falgarding was an usurper and a murderer, and that Asmund the Simple was rightful King of Gothmark.'

'Surely, my lord, that must have meant war?'

'Naturally. Silverspur, still a very young man, was apparently so puffed up with pride in his victory that he imagined he could conquer Gothmark with equal ease if need be. The Goths, as you say, had no alternative to an immediate declaration of war. To be sure, the question of tribute was not important - indeed by the time in question it was purely nominal and rarely paid. And the border provinces had not been in serious dispute for years; methinks any outstanding points could have been settled by negotiation. But it was Silverspur's third claim, disputing Finn's title to the throne, which of course made war inevitable. Three great battles were fought that year - in all of them the Goths were victorious. And in the last great battle, before the gates of Bakir, the whole flower of Sferian nobility, and Silverspur himself, were slain. The Sfear were compelled to sue for peace, which by the Treaty of Bakir, signed within the week, provided that the payment of tribute should recommence, the disputed provinces be yielded to Gothmark, and the absolute right of Finn and his heirs to the Gothic throne was confirmed. The terms imposed were lenient, in part because the Goths too had suffered severely in the war, indeed Finn the Valiant himself had fallen in the moment of victory.

'The peace did not last. Silverspur was unmarried, and the crown of the Sfear therefore devolved upon his younger brother, Ulf, a boy of twelve. Ulf, like Silverspur, was proud and vainglorious, but possessed of more military and diplomatic skill. Immediately upon attaining his majority, he renounced the Treaty of Bakir as having been imposed upon him by duress, and thus began the Second Sferian War.

'The result was as disastrous for Gothmark as the previous conflict had been for the Sfear. For Finn's only son, now King of Gothmark, proved as incompetent and luckless a warrior as his father had been bold and fortunate. Finbar the Craven, he was called, in derisive contrast to his father's nickname of the Valiant. In the final battle, at the Hrosnaberg Gap, Finbar the Craven, belying his name, refused to flee, saying, according to legend, that if he had not lived like a king, at least he could die like one. And so he fell, and all the mighty power of Gothmark with him.'

'How sad,' commented Suth.

'It was indeed. Truly, Finbar's nickname did him scant justice, for he seems to have been unfortunate rather than ignoble. The consequences of his overthrow for the Goths were however catastrophic, the terms meted out to them being by no means as lenient as those previously imposed upon the Sfear. Under the Treaty of Geatburg, tribute was now payable by the Goths at more than forty times that formerly levied upon the Sfear: the border provinces, and much of Gothmark proper, were seized and incorporated into Sfearland: all the old Gothic nobility were dispossessed and their estates transferred to Ulf's henchmen: Sferian became the official language of the Gothic court, and the Goths were treated in all respects as a subject people. Asmund the Simple was dumped on the throne as a mere puppet, whilst Ulf secured the ultimate succession by marrying his only daughter. Such were the dire consequences of Gothic subjugation to the Sferian yoke. These things happened right at the extremest distance of time that the very oldest men now living can remember, that is, upwards of fourscore years ago. In course of time the Goths became cowed and servile, as befitted a nation of thralls. One small object none the less lay in Ulf's path to absolute power in Gothmark.'

'Did you not mention earlier, my lord, that Asmund the Simple had a son?'

Beowulf was a little taken aback. 'It is disconcerting,' he confessed, 'for a fool like me to own a slave so much his intellectual superior.'

'Please do not talk about yourself in that silly way, my lord, or I shall get quite cross with you.'

'Well anyway, with your usual perceptivity you have hit the nail on the head. Asmund's only son, Sigmund, was indeed the problem. He grew up into a strange, dreamy youth, apparently hardly more in touch with reality than his father. Yet, as the last of the male line of Ironside, he must have appeared a threat to Ulf, who however took no action against him. Perhaps he deemed it inadvisable to alienate his wife and father-in-law; maybe even the Goths, demoralized though they were, would not have countenanced the murder of the last of the Ironsides. I prefer to think that Ulf, though harsh and ruthless, was not at heart an evil man. At any rate he did nothing, and when Sigmund attained his majority the inevitable happened. He declared the Treaty of Gothmark null and void, claimed to be the rightful heir to the throne, and raised his standard against the Sferian king. His claim was strengthened by his marriage to the only daughter of Finbar the Craven, whereby he united the two royal houses of Gothmark.

'Regrettably his action stood no chance of success, being ill-prepared and lacking either noble or popular support. All his life Sigmund remained a moody, eccentric fellow with no grasp of practical affairs. The Goths had become docile and subservient to Sferian rule, Asmund himself was obliged to declare his own son outlaw and traitor, and the rebellious forces were defeated with ease after the merest skirmish. Sigmund, his wife, and their handful of remaining followers were forced into exile. This pathetic episode has been dignified by Gothic historians with the title of the Third Sferian War, though at the time it was simply called the Sigmund Rebellion.

'Sigmund and his men took refuge in a bleak, rocky island south-east of the mainland, since known as the Isle of the Goths. There they managed to eke out an existence of sorts, with the help of the tiny local population, whilst still claiming dominion over the whole of Gothmark.'

'I know the Isle of the Goths, my lord,' said Suth. 'It is not far offshore. Would it not have been possible for Ulf to invade and put them all to the sword?'

'No doubt, bloodthirsty little slave. In fact for the first few years the exiles lived in constant fear of such an attempt. But he never did. Various reasons have been advanced. The island is protected by strong and treacherous currents, the Sfear are not a seafaring people, and to equip and arm a fleet would have been a costly process. Victory would have been certain, but at heavy price. Ulf's vindictiveness seems to have spent itself by this time. Indeed, it is even possible he had a perverse liking for Sigmund. Besides, the exiles were no possible threat. Anyway, for whatever reason, Ulf refrained from making their plight any worse.

'Thus matters continued until the death of Asmund the Simple, whereupon Ulf abandoned all pretence, and mounted the throne as King of the Goths and Sfear. The Wittan, which alone had legal power to elect the Gothic kings, had been disbanded years before. At the same time Ulf offered amnesty to Sigmund, saying that if he and his men acknowledged Ulf their rightful lord, they might return to Gothmark with the honours of war, and be granted lands and pensions. The response of the exiles was to elect and proclaim Sigmund the Exile their king. His coronation was held soon after - a pitiful, threadbare business; the crowning of a king of shreds and patches by a handful of penniless fugitives. And yet, methinks there was something rather fine about the way they kept faith with a hopeless cause, and closed ranks around the pathetic creature who was their king.

'Seven years later Sigmund the Exile died, and at this point the fortunes of the island Goths reached their very lowest ebb. He left no male heir, and but one daughter, a girl of thirteen called Fanora the Fey, who was duly crowned Queen of the Goths. Old men can just remember Sigmund, for he died little over threescore years ago.

'Fanora was the last of the Ironsides, and of course many of the dispossessed Gothic nobility paid court to her, urging her to marry and continue the royal line. She was a strange girl, not unlike her father in temperament, and refused them all, saying that it had been revealed to her in a dream that one day a prince would come from across the sea to claim her, and that Gothmark would be saved by an enemy. These prophecies appeared meaningless at the time, yet curiously, it turned out exactly as she had foretold. You may remember, Suth, that when I began my story - now, I fear, grown overlong - I mentioned a man called Saur Silverspur.'

'King of the Sfear,' provided Suth, 'and elder brother of Ulf. Defeated and killed by Finn the Valiant at the Battle of Bakir.'

'Very good, little one - forgive me, I mean Suth. I am glad you continue to pay attention. Well, as I said, Saur died unmarried and thus without lawful issue. He had, however, a favourite slave, one Thalia the Serf, who some six months after his death gave birth to a male child as like to Saur Silverspur as it had been his twin brother rather than his son. Swertan, she called him, and none doubted that he was the issue of the dead king. Ulf acknowledged him as such, and he grew to manhood surrounded by the panoply of royalty but without power, treated with that mixture of deference and contempt peculiarly reserved for royal bastards.

'Until early middle age, Swertan showed no interest in anything but the usual pastimes of the idle nobility - the hunt, drinking, dicing and wenching. He also ventured abroad, in pointless military campaigns against the Great Cassar and his empire. When he had attained the age of three-and-thirty, Thalia the Serf died. Soon after, Swertan called his henchmen together and announced that upon her deathbed his mother had revealed to him that in a secret ceremony on the eve of the the Battle of Bakir, she and Silverspur had married, and that he was therefore not the natural, but the lawful son of Silverspur, and rightful King of the Sfear.'

Suth looked dubious. 'Did any believe that, my lord?'

Beowulf smiled. 'The story was of course highly improbable. All witnesses to the alleged ceremony were long dead, and even if Swertan were telling the truth, his claim rested solely upon the testimony of a dead slave. In three-and-thirty years, no-one had even hinted at the possibility of such a marriage, which bearing in mind the comparative rank of the parties was excessively unlikely. It is doubtful indeed whether such a thing would even have been lawful.'

'And surely, my lord, the throne of the Sfear is elective?'

'Swertan's answer to that was that upon electing Ulf, their nobles had been in ignorance of a material fact. Even had they known it, however, I cannot see that it would have made much difference, for they could hardly have elected an unborn child their king. However, Swertan's henchmen believed him, or said they did, as a result of which, needless to say, he and they were proclaimed traitor. He tried to rally support against his uncle, but few believed him. Anyway Ulf was popular with the Sfear, not only having defeated and subjugated their enemies the Goths, but being a wise and firm ruler. Swertan by contrast was but a soldier of fortune, a brash, hard-drinking, hard-swearing aristocratic ruffian. To a man, the Sfear sided with their king, and Swertan was obliged to flee. He and his followers took sail for the Isle of the Goths, where he wooed and won Fanora the Fey, thereby fulfilling the first part of her prophecy.

'Having failed to secure the support of his own people, Swertan now gambled all on an appeal to the Goths. He landed on the southern shore, near Rigel, with his wife and a handful of warriors, whence he travelled throughout Gothmark, promising that if he acceded to the crown, he would accord his wife, last of the Ironsides, equal status with himself, that he would restore all the ancient lands and privileges of the Goths, use Gothic as the language of the court, discontinue tribute to the Sfear, and rule in all respects as a Gothic prince. All this, and more, he promised.

'It is not clear why Swertan and Fanora should have succeeded where her father had failed. Yet there was something about the pair - the tough, hard-bitten soldier with a vulnerable seventeen-year-old girl at his side - which won men's hearts and minds as Sigmund the Exile had never done. Of the mainland princes, Wylf of Hrosnaberg was first to declare for him, followed by Wagmund of Slane. Others followed, and the outcome was the Fourth Sferian War.

'It lasted three years, and was the most terrible conflict of all. Casualties on both sides are said to have been twice as many as in all the other Sferian Wars put together. Ulf was the greatest warrior of his day, supported by all the Sferian lords. In theory the Gothic party should have stood no chance, being fragmented, unused to war, and led by a soldier of fortune. Yet perhaps I have given a misleading impression of Swertan, who was far more than the drunken ruffian portrayed by his enemies. He had distinguished himself during the Teutonic wars with the Great Empire, he feared neither man nor devil, and as the war progressed more and more of the Goths came to see their country's destiny as being linked to his.'

'I have heard of Swertan, my lord. Did he not retain the title of Bastard?'

'Aye, that he did, despite his claim, and thought it no disgrace; neither was it, really. At any rate, seven great battles were fought during those fateful years, besides many minor engagements. At Wolf Valley and Haggar's Cross, the forces of Swertan the Bastard emerged victorious; at Bettany and Rigel Mount, those of Ulf the Avenger. At Four Ash and Dapple Heath, both sides claimed the victory, and at the Siege of Sleinau, neither. But in the summer of the third year, Ulf died suddenly at Rainbow Falls of the red fever, and the Sfear were forced to concede that they could hold Gothmark no longer. By the Treaty of Castletown, it was agreed that Swertan the Bastard, Fanora the Fey and their issue should thenceforth rule in Gothmark, whereas Ulf and his heirs were rightful Kings of the Sfear. Most of the border lands were to remain with the Sfear, but payment of tribute would be discontinued. And finally, a truce was agreed between Goth and Sfear to last for one generation, that is, according to the Gothic method of reckoning, for seven-and-twenty years.

'The truce was scrupulously observed on both sides, but the question of territory remained in dispute, and at its expiration skirmishing broke out again on the Gothic-Sferian border. Possibly matters might still have been resolved peaceably, but for the fact that in a minor engagement near Bettany, Swertan the Bastard was slain by a stray arrow from Sferian lines.

'Fanora the Fey had died a few years before, so the crown devolved upon their only son, Rathleck the Wild. Three battles were fought that summer in the Fifth Sferian War, and the forces of Rathleck were totally triumphant. The Crown Prince of the Sfear, Aslack Goldspur, was slain by Rathleck, some say in single combat, and the Sfear had to sue for peace. The terms granted were again lenient, indeed generous, consisting simply of the secession to the Goths of some, but not all, of the border lands in dispute, and another truce was arranged for a further seven-and-twenty years. By these terms, remarkable, as I have said, for their moderation, Rathleck hoped to bring the Sferian dispute to a final conclusion. And in this for a time he succeeded, for the Sferian king, Aun, was a man of peace. Five years ago, however, Aun died, and was succeeded by his warlike son Angantyr, whose own sons, Ottar and Ali, were similarly keen to try their luck in battle. The truce expired upon the final day of last year, and Rathleck the Wild died in his bed ten days later.'

'So the scene is set for another war.'

'It is not certain, but the odds favour it, I fear. Ottar and Ali have begun storming our northern borders, and Rathleck's younger son, Hyglack, another warlike prince, has responded in kind.'

'Is not the present King of the Goths called Athkyn, my lord? What manner of man is he?'

'Hyglack's elder brother, and methinks a man of peace. Some thought Rathleck might prefer Hyglack as his successor, for all that Athkyn was the elder son. Upon his deathbed, however, Rathleck duly named Athkyn, and the Wittan respected his choice. Curiously, only one of those present at his death actually heard the words he spoke. Hyglack was that man.'

"Twas generous of him to admit it, then.'

'Aye, yet those who dislike Hyglack say he did so to curry favour with the nobles, realizing that he would gain repute as a man of honour, whilst Athkyn would prove a failure as a king in any case.'

'And what think you, my lord?'

Beowulf frowned. 'I was there. And it seemed to me that in that moment Hyglack showed himself not merely an honourable man, but in some measure a great one. Besides, it seems ungenerous to me, when a man does what is right, to attribute evil motive.'

'You always think the best of people, don't you, my lord?'

'I suppose I do. It had not occurred to me.'

'Do they not take advantage of your trust in them?'

'Very seldom. And surely it is better to be made a fool of now and then, rather than be constantly hostile and suspicious towards others?'

Suth shook her head, and seemed near to tears.. 'Oh, my lord. You are such a good man. I think perhaps it is I who am the fool, and you wise. But what of you personally? You said you were the grandson of a king, by which I suppose you must have meant Rathleck the Wild. Is the present king your uncle?'

'Quite right. Hyglack and the King are both my uncles. It is through my mother, Rathleck's only daughter, that I trace my royal descent. Which brings me to another story, and a painful one. Some other time for that.'

'If you wish, my lord. But I would know more about you, if I could. With war apparently imminent, should not a great prince like you be armed and levying soldiers? This small band of yours - forgive me, my lord - is no war party, for all that you put a rabble of outlaws to flight.'

'True, little one,' he agreed. 'We travel to the Isles on a mission of peace. The Princes of the Isles have long been allies of the Goths, and their present ruler, Breck Bronding, was a friend of mine in younger days. It was thought that his allegiance, or at least neutrality, should be secured before dealing with the Sfear.'

'That seems prudent, my lord. But there are rumours from the Isles that Breck is dead, and others have seized power.'

'So have I heard also, but reports are conflicting. We may learn more in Targon. But I have talked too much, Suth, and it is past your bedtime. Snuff the candles, and let us say goodnight.'

'Goodnight, my lord.'

94

ᴔen

THE LAST day of the journey dawned overcast and windy. Striking camp later than usual, the Goths soon left the foothills of Silvermount behind, and the sheep-speckled moors gave way to arable land of rye and barley. Small farms and homesteads made their appearance; here and there a horse and ploughman cut their furrows. Cattle grazed in the fields.

'Things become decidedly more civilized,' observed Ifar.

Beowulf nodded. 'Busy road,' he said, pointing to the well-trodden mud around them. 'Many horsemen have used it this morning already. It rained last night, and these prints are fresh.'

'Strange that we have not met any. But no doubt at this time of day there are more entering the city than leaving.'

Beowulf was conscious of the first stirrings of unease. 'No wagons either, but horses alone.'

'If they intended any harm, my lord, I doubt they would choose a spot so close to Targon. It is but a mile to the gates.'

This was confirmed by the next milestone, which, allowing for measurements being taken from the city centre, said, 'Targon, 2 miles.'

The line of mules ahead came to a halt. 'What is it?' asked Ifar.

Beowulf shrugged. 'Let's see.'

Reaching the head of the line, they discovered the truth. Many of the Goths, hardened warriors though they were, winced and turned away. A cook and one of the slaves were vomiting.

'Human offal,' said Ifar unnecessarily. 'Ye gods, the stink.'

The remains were strewn so widely over the road that at first it was not clear how many men had met their deaths. Eventually it became apparent that no more than two individuals had been involved, but the quantity of blood, smashed bone, entrails and excrement gave the impression of a far greater number.

'Rockenwolves?' suggested one man foolishly. He referred to the enormous legendary creatures commonly supposed to haunt ryefields by night.

Ifar shook his head. 'They would not mutilate a carcass to that extent. Some unknown monster.'

'In human form,' grunted Dardo. 'No beast rips its prey to shreds like that.'

'Or places its head on a pole,' said Beowulf, returning from a brief foray round the next corner. 'Don't look if you have a weak stomach.'

This ensured that they all steeled themselves to do so. Two mutilated human heads, features contorted with agony, gazed sightlessly from the pair of ash-staves, upon which they had been impaled.

'Oh, by the gods,' breathed Kjartan. 'Their eyes have been gouged out.'

'And teeth smashed. Other tortures inflicted on them too, no doubt.'

Suth, so light on her feet that she was wont to materialize without warning, said quietly, 'The work of Ragnar of Torre, my lord.'

'You think so?'

'Are these not the men who accosted us foryesterday?'

'I suppose they might be, but they were visored. Even had we seen their faces, I doubt we could recognize them now.'

'Here's a note,' said a sharp-eyed Hrosnaberger, removing a paper nailed beneath one of the heads. He handed it to Ifar, who passed it to Beowulf.

'Suth,' he said sheepishly, giving her the note.

'Certainly, my lord.' She looked at it and shuddered.

' "To the large Goth who bears the standard of the Black Bear, calling himself Beowulf.

' "You have stolen my slave and corrupted my servants. Observe and ponder the fate of those who betray me. If you would live, take the gold and leave the slave bound to this post. Smash her teeth, but leave her eyes for me." '

There was an appalled silence, from which Ifar was first to recover. 'There speaks the Lord of Evil himself.'

'He has many guises,' agreed Beowulf, nodding. 'Some in human form. Mark how he wishes us to yield our souls to him by committing acts of evil.'

'Very true,' said Ifar. 'The three dread sins whereby men betray themselves: greed, which we are to commit by taking back the gold; cowardice, by abandoning the slave to his mercy; and cruelty, by inflicting tortures upon her.'

'Truly this Ragnar is one of the Sons of Muspelheim, if not, as you say, the Prince of the Fire himself.'

The down-to-earth Dardo shrugged. 'To my mind, he's flesh and blood like us.'

'Yes,' agreed Beowulf, recovering himself. 'Yes, of course, you're right. Is the money there?'

'It is, my lord,' confirmed the finder. 'Ten pieces of gold, at the foot of the stake.'

'Don't touch it,' said Ifar sharply. 'It is the property of Ragnar of Torre.'

'My lord,' said the man, 'I have obeyed you all my life, yet would not touch it were you to order me on pain of death.'

'You are wise,' Ifar confirmed, 'for what is death compared with eternal blackening of one's soul?'

'It is in any case the Lord of Torre's by right,' Beowulf pointed out. 'The money is his; let no man take it up.'

THE FREE city of Targon, chief of the seven ports forming the League of the Eastern Sea, was a vast, sprawling metropolis, with a population estimated at not less than thirty thousand free adult males. With women, children and slaves, it must have contained well over a hundred thousand souls, making it by far the largest city in the Northlands, and, as some believed, in the whole of Midgard. The heart of the city was the great dock area attracting the dregs of the Eastern Sea: Goth, Sferian, Dan, Teuton and Slav, even a few from the distant Empire of the South. Taverns, brothels, and gaming-houses relieved the newpaid sailor of his earnings more or less legally, whilst in its dingy alleys cutpurses - and cutthroats - made no such pretence. Drug traffickers and whores plied their trade openly. The indoor slave market in the Citadel was thought the largest in the world, a gallery of three thousand cages in which the wretched merchandise was kept in conditions of indescribable squalor. Meanwhile, in the low hills beyond the city gates lived the rich merchants who profited from the trade, legal and illicit - in Targon there was no clear distinction - in furs, livestock, arms and jewellery from Gothmark and Silvermount, silks, spices and ivory from the south and east, and human flesh worldwide. They lived in uneasy luxury, with private armies of variable quality to guard them from the less fortunate denizens within the city walls.

Supposedly Targon was governed by the Merchants' Council, a corrupt cabal who had long given up the struggle to enforce any effective system of authority. For years there had been in Targon no true civil or criminal law, no city administration, no proper tax collection, no water supply but the filthiest public wells, nor any roads much less than a century old. Disease was rampant. Law enforcement and debt-collection were in the hands not of the courts, but thieves and extortioners. Yet somehow, the place and its inhabitants survived. Thus, corrupt, squalid, vital and unconquered, was the great free city of the North, Port Targon.

At least it had been so last time Beowulf had visited, some four years earlier. Yet as the mule train passed through the huts, stables and taverns on the outskirts of the city, he sensed that the atmosphere had changed. There were no beggars, pedlars or whores; the populace hurried about their business with downcast eyes, seldom stopping to speak or look around. And on each street corner, sometimes directing wagoneers, sometimes giving orders or enquiring the business of young or suspicious-looking men, were soldiers in black leather jerkins, observing, counting and signalling to one another.

'Melikes this not,' grunted Ifar. 'In the Targon of old at least you knew where you were.'

'We are still outside the city walls. Once inside it might be different.'

The Great West Gate, formerly just a fifty-yard gap between decaying walls of yellow stone, was now fully restored, with twin sentry-towers, and thirty-foot gates open to wagon traffic, checked by a dozen guards. On either side was a narrow passage for foot-travellers, and a sentry-box. Beowulf and Ifar marched up to the main gate at the head of their men, flying the banners of Slane and Hrosnaberg alongside. A few of the curious stopped to observe them, but were quickly moved on. Meanwhile a dozen soldiers stood to arms and barred their way, as reinforcements moved unobtrusively down from the walls.

'Hold,' said their leader, darkly clad like his men, distinguished only by the device of a black tower on his grey tunic. 'In the name of the Lord of Targon.' He spoke with a heavy Teutonic accent.

Beowulf raised a hand in signal to his men to comply. The mule-wagons jangled to a halt. 'And who is that?'

'Eugen, Duke of Brabanne. You know little, stranger, if you know not that. And who are you?'

'We are Goths,' said Beowulf mildly, 'from the court of King Athkyn, and my name is Beowulf.'

'We know not Athkyn. Rathleck the Wild is King of Gothmark.'

'It seems news travels slowly hereabouts. Rathleck has been dead these eight months and more. His son Athkyn rules in Gothmark.'

'I was testing you,' said the guard sourly. 'We are well aware of that.' Whether this was true, or he was saving face in front of his men, Beowulf could not determine. 'Your business?'

'To obtain ship for the Isles.'

This seemed to take the man by surprise, for he conferred with a couple of colleagues before replying. 'An unusual mission, lawful if injudicious. Advance and declare yourselves individually, and leave your arms.'

'We need to defend ourselves from the rabble within your city,' said Ifar hotly. 'Who made these new laws?'

'Eugen of Brabanne is Lord of Targon, and all who enter are answerable to him. A respectable warrior of rank may bear a sword, but that is all. Spears, shields, clubs and missiles must be surrendered. They will be returned when you leave.'

'We will consult,' Beowulf informed him.

'Move to one side then, for you are obstructing others.'

At Beowulf's signal the muleteers complied. 'Odd business this,' he continued softly to Ifar. 'What do you think?'

'We can't take ship anywhere else. But I am not happy.'

'Nor I.' Beowulf turned back to the guard. 'May we see the Lord of Targon to discuss the matter?'

'If you wish. I should advise against it. Laws cannot be changed to suit a band of armed foreigners, and the Duke is a bad man to cross.'

'He has hanged an hundred felons this week already,' volunteered one of his companions.

'More than that,' supplied another. 'For I saw another couple of dozen kicking their heels in the Market Square this morning.'

'Are we to be given receipts for our weapons?' Beowulf enquired.

'Why, of course,' said the guard. 'Otherwise there would be endless disputes. You will be given a full list of the items surrendered; I advise you to check it carefully, as errors cannot be rectified later.'

'Very well,' sighed Beowulf. 'We will surrender our weapons, to be returned as we take ship. Is that right?'

'Right enough.'

'Give the word to the men,' said Beowulf to Kjartan, 'that they are to surrender weapons in exchange for receipts. Any who cannot read must get you or Suth to help them.' Ifar gave similar orders to a grumbling Dardo.

Beowulf handed over his bow, arrows, quiver and dirk. One of the sentries made to search him. 'I object to being searched,' he said firmly. 'You have my word as a warrior.'

Again the black guards consulted. 'So be it. Those who give their words will not be searched, except for churls and slaves.'

This seemed not unreasonable, although somehow Beowulf did not relish the idea of Suth being pawed by a sentry. Matters proceeded without incident until she came to pass through.

'What is this?' demanded the chief guard, voice thick with suspicion.

'Why, but a small slave,' said Beowulf. 'I wonder you make so great a matter of it.'

The man pointed to her arm-brand. 'Whose slave?'

'Mine.'

The guards stood to arms immediately. 'Who are you?'

'I have told you. Beowulf of Slane, nephew to Athkyn, King of Gothmark.'

'Whose is that brand?'

'Oh, that is the brand of Ragnar of Torre, I believe.'

There came a long pause. 'Aye,' said the man, 'that it is. Ragnar of Torre, kinsman to our lord, Eugen.'

'I did not know that,' confessed Beowulf, hoping his voice did not betray his alarm.

'Well, you know now. How came you by this slave?'

'She is not stolen, if that is what you mean. I paid good money for her. Hort, show him the bill of sale.'

They perused it at length, the two or three men able to read explaining it to their colleagues. All the time, Beowulf noticed, further soldiers were arriving and taking position.

'There is a manifest error in the amount said to have been paid,' commented the guard. 'But that is no great matter. Dealt you with the Count of Torre in person?'

'No. With his servants.'

'It may be so,' said the guard suspiciously. 'Well, you have bought this slave, it seems, but we are not satisfied. You come under arms, over thirty strong, with a slave whose brand proclaims her the property of the Count of Torre. You must see our lord - he will deal with you.'

'This is practice,' said Ifar angrily. 'We have surrendered our arms upon the understanding that we be allowed to pass.'

'There is no practice, Gothic lord,' said the guard. 'If you feel we have misled you, by all means have your weapons back. You may then leave the way you came, or fight us, as you wish.'

'We have gone too far to turn back now,' said Beowulf as mildly as ever. 'And I see no reason to fight. We will meet the Lord of Targon.'

AN ESCORT fifty strong led the Goths along the broad Treppian Way from the Great Gate to the Market Square. The side streets were cleaner than Beowulf remembered, though still far from fragrant. He commented on this to Kjartan.

'It is forbidden to throw offal or excrement into the street,' volunteered the chief guard, 'although vegetable matter is permitted. Offenders are heavily fined.'

'Much has changed,' Beowulf commented.

'For the better.'

'So it would seem,' agreed Beowulf cautiously. 'Last time I was here the way was lined with the bodies of butchered slaves and brigands.'

'That would have been at the time of the disturbances four years ago, no doubt,' said the guard, and Beowulf nodded. 'All malefactors are now hanged in the main square. You will see.'

They did. The stalls and awnings in the produce market were as colourful and noisy as ever, and the pigeons still stalked and fluttered about, but the part of the square formerly given over to the sale of slaves was now a giant gallows-forest, or so it seemed to the shaken Goths. Chained corpses with blotched and bloated faces and protruding tongues hung from every scaffold. Beowulf counted seventeen. 'Do they hang here all day?' he enquired.

'But till the midday hour. The squeamish may visit the market after that.'

'What of the slave market?'

'Abolished,' said the man shortly. 'Slave trading now may take place only by private contract, for which permission must be obtained from the Duke.'

'Most strange,' observed Ifar. 'What was the reason for this new law?'

'I know not. We do not query our lord's decisions, but obey.'

Ifar jerked his head at a squat ugly building of yellow brick on the corner of the square. 'The slave quarters are still there.'

'That is now the House of Correction for debtors, whores, and other minor offenders. Whippings and judicial mutilations are also carried out there.'

Soon they stood before the stone-columned court-house which fronted the east side of the square, hung with the black, white and red banners of the duke, beside the Triple Anchor of Targon. The guardsman at the gate exchanged salutes with their escort.

'The Goths for examination by the Duke,' said their captain.

'How many?'

'Seven-and-twenty men at arms, three churls and three slaves.'

News of their arrival had apparently gone before, for the court guard said, 'Our orders are to admit the most senior men only into the presence of the Duke. He who calls himself Beowulf, his chief captains, and the female slave. The rest will wait in an anteroom.'

'Why should he want to see the slave?' asked Beowulf.

'As I understand it, she is the main cause of your being here. Anyway, I am not employed to answer questions. Make your enquiry of the Duke.'

101

Roger Butters

Eleven

EUGEN SAT in the seat of justice in the Tower Chamber, three black-robed men of law occupying the bench on either side. Each of the four doors was guarded by a warrior with drawn sword. The windows, small and low, admitted but little daylight. From the domed roof depended a chandelier, which cast its flickering beams upon the tiles of a great circular mosaic in the centre of the floor, its design a black tower on a white ground, flanked by a pair of red swords. Behind the tribunal hung a tapestry in the traditional form for the courts of the Northlands: a sword of justice, above the mailed fist of power and the open hand of mercy. Beowulf and his men were marched in under escort, Ifar alongside him, with Dardo and Kjartan two paces behind. Suth brought up the rear.

'On your knees,' ordered the officer accompanying them.

Beowulf remained standing. 'Gothic warriors kneel to none but Longspear.'

The guard looked to Eugen for guidance. 'The slave will kneel,' said the Duke. 'The others are excused.' Unlike the guard, he spoke Gothic with little perceptible accent, but rather formally, as if not totally at home in the tongue.

He stood. In stature he was on the border between tall and middle height, sturdily built rather than heavy. His age was perhaps five-and-thirty, or a little more. He wore the same uniform as his judicial colleagues, without adornment. The overriding impression he gave was that of darkness; his face was in shadow, and his hair, beard and gown were alike jet black.

Beowulf raised a hand in greeting. 'I salute your soul, Lord of

Targon.'

'And I yours, Gothic lord, if such you be.' The Duke evidently had little time for such niceties, for he turned to business with a brusqueness verging on discourtesy. 'What is your business in Targon?'

'We seek ship for the Isles.'

'So I have been told. And your business there?'

'Our affair,' said Ifar crossly, but Beowulf smiled and answered. 'A diplomatic mission to the Prince. I am sure your lordship will appreciate that confidentiality prevents my giving further detail.'

'Hm,' grunted Eugen. 'Well, so far as diplomacy is concerned, you appear to have the edge on your colleague, at least. Why do you go fully armed?'

'In part for defence from brigands, in part out of courtesy. Our king could scarcely send us looking like a party of churls. Do you think we could take Targon with thirty men?'

'I took it with a couple of dozen. Admittedly the circumstances then were rather different. As for the Isles, your mission is vain, for Breck Bronding is dead.'

'So we have heard,' said Beowulf, heart sinking. 'But if so, we still intend to travel to the Isles to treat with his successor. Presumably he has one.'

'Indeed he has. I now rule the Isles, or would do if every man had his right. And make no mistake, it shall be so within the year.'

'But for the present?'

'For the present, no man knows, for storms have cut the Isles off for weeks. Before then, no travellers returned since the Month without a Star, and then but one, who said that the Bronding is dead, reputedly poisoned.'

'Travellers' tales,' said Ifar uncertainly.

Eugen shrugged. 'I only speak as I hear. And why do you purpose to deal with the present Prince of the Isles? Remember, in right, I am he.'

'Very well,' said Beowulf, after a pause for thought. 'You may be aware that the Lords of the Isles were historically allied to our countrymen, since the First Prince, Brond of the Eastern Sea, gave his support to Swertan the Bastard in the War of Liberation from the Sfear.'

'I have heard something of the sort.'

'My purpose was to confirm and strengthen the old alliance.'

'Then you have failed in your mission, for your squabbles with the Sfear are of not the slightest interest to me, so long as you both keep your hands off Targon.'

'We are assured, then, of your neutrality?'

'By all means. Brabanne has no interest west of Targon.'

'I never heard of any claim to Targon either, or the Isles.'

'Fortunately your approval of my design, though doubtless desirable, is not absolutely essential to its performance. Suffice it to say that we have.'

So far as Beowulf knew, the Duke of Brabanne made no pretension to royalty. He queried the pronoun. 'We?'

'My elder brother, Rikhard, is likewise a Duke of Brabanne, and rules there. To me has fallen the task of asserting our ancient rights in the north.'

The Gothic system of primogeniture did not invariably apply throughout Teutonia, so that it was possible for there to be several men using the same title; a confusing practice which led to much discord.

'You act, then, on behalf of your brother?'

Eugen smiled crookedly. 'I perceive your drift, and though I need not answer, I will. My brother is content to rule Brabanne, and leave the north to me. A better arrangement for all concerned than the usual strife and dissention between brothers over their inheritance at home. And far better than a younger son inheriting the throne by killing the elder.'

Beowulf frowned. 'I hope I do not understand you.'

'Come now, has that not happened in Gothmark?'

'By Odin's death,' said Ifar furiously, 'had I my sword, you should not live to speak such insult to our king.'

'I spoke naught but the truth. Did he not slay his brother whilst hunting?'

'Aye,' said Beowulf indignantly, 'but in tragic accident. You suggest the damnable lie that ...'

'I suggest nothing. Did I say it was deliberate?'

'No,' said Ifar, somewhat mollified. 'If you accept that, as Prince Beowulf says, it was but evil mischance, I am content to let the matter drop.'

'I did not say that either. I spoke but as I knew, no more, no less. As to what passes in a man's heart, who knows?'

'Our lord Athkyn,' Beowulf persisted, 'is a most honourable and learned gentleman.'

'Really? I was advised that he is a deranged weakling. No doubt my information is at fault.'

'It certainly is. Why ...'

'Well, let us speak of it no more. We disagree, and that is all there is to it. As for your trip to the Isles, do you still intend it?'

'It is our duty; we have no choice. Unless you stop us. Thanks to the practice of your guards, we are in your power.'

'I have acted perfectly within the law. If you intend no harm to Targon, you may proceed; in fact I have no right to stop you. Your reason for visiting the Isles appears plausible, if misguided. It might conceivably assist me.'

'In what way?'

'If the Bronding is still alive, which I gravely doubt, you will so advise me on your return.'

'And then?'

'And then, nothing. I not deny he is Prince of the Isles. If he is dead, that is a different matter, for the Isles revert to Brabanne. In that case, however' - again Eugen gave a crooked smile - 'no friend of the Bronding would be likely to return to tell the tale.'

'You believe the present ruler, whoever he is, hostile to Breck Bronding?'

'Since he presumably arranged for him to be poisoned, it seems a reasonable assumption .'

'Who is the present ruler? Ragnar of Torre?'

A draught caught the lights of the great chandelier, and the Tower Chamber was momentarily darkened. After a brief pause, the Duke replied, 'Ah yes, my kinsman, Ragnar of Torre. Interesting that you have had dealings with him. As to who rules the Isles, I have already said I know not. Let the slave step forward.'

Upon mention of the name of Torre, a stifled gasp had escaped Suth, who however stood and walked up to the Duke bravely enough.

'She is lawfully mine,' said Beowulf, 'as evidenced by the bill of sale.'

'We have seen it,' said Eugen, snapping his fingers at one of his fellow-judges, who handed it to him. 'And confess that it appears to be in order. The price indicates that you are either a complete imbecile or so rich that you can afford to indulge any whim, but I suppose that is none of my concern.'

'May we leave?' demanded Ifar, with barely suppressed anger.

'Not so fast. In the normal course, ownership of a slave would not concern me in the absence of a legal dispute ...'

'Has Ragnar put in a claim for her?' asked Beowulf.

The Duke seemed to find this amusing, and for the first time laughed out loud. 'So far as I am aware, no. That is not his way.'

'He is your kinsman. Do you speak for him?'

'Of course not. None speak for Ragnar but his servants. You have had dealings with him, and should know.'

'My only dealing with him has been through his servants, as you say.'

'Quite. That is the normal procedure.'

'Slightly less normal is the fact that their mutilated corpses now disfigure the Treppian Way.'

'No longer. They have been removed on my orders, and burnt. What were your dealings with him?'

'I told you. I purchased this slave. They purported to act for him, and accepted payment.'

'Purported,' murmured the Duke. 'A good word, purported. Ragnar is not wont to sell his slaves. It occurs to me, as doubtless it has to you, that his servants might have abused his trust by purporting, as you put it, to sell, and making off with your money. A supposition strengthened by the subsequent rather drastic indication of his disapproval.'

'That is no concern of mine. They were his servants, with power, so they alleged, to transact business on his behalf. I cannot be held responsible for their behaviour after that.'

'For a simple soldier-man you appear to have a nice grasp of the law.'

'Well then, are you satisfied?'

'Not altogether. The price. Explain it.'

'I do not see that I have to.'

'You are probably right,' the Duke admitted, 'in law. Let us say then, answer as a favour to me, to satisfy my curiosity. In order to acquire what is frankly a not very well-favoured female slave, you have apparently parted with enough money to purchase a medium-sized kingdom.'

At this Suth turned on him one of her scowls so black that despite his apprehension Beowulf was tempted to burst out laughing. 'If you must know, the slave had been cruelly ill-used. I bought her to spare her further suffering.'

'That is perfectly true,' Suth confirmed, eyes flashing. 'But I do not suppose the Lord of Targon is capable of understanding such a thing.'

'You speak out of turn, slave,' said Eugen calmly.

One of the guards stepped forward. 'Is she to be flogged, my lord?'

'No-one beats my slaves save on my orders,' said Beowulf. 'And then only if they deserve it.'

'It will not be necessary,' said the Duke to his guard. 'If this slave has belonged to Ragnar of Torre, no doubt she has had previous experience of flogging.' He paused, as if inviting Suth to speak. 'Is that not so, slave?'

'It is so,' said Suth fiercely. 'Your kinsman's whips cut me to the bone, and things were done to me of which I cannot speak. His soul is as black as your garb. He is a son of Muspelheim, and a creature of him whom men dare not name.'

'Surtur,' said the Duke, even he hesitating before mouthing the word. 'Lord of the Fire. Indeed he is. Yet your body, though thin and undernourished, is unmarked. Explain that.'

'These lords took me in when I was a starving fugitive, and showed me every kindness. Prince Beowulf is a wizard, who owns a magic potion that cures all ills. He treated my wounds and they recovered overnight. He is the best man in the world,' continued Suth, 'and if you spare him you may return me to your kinsman of Torre.'

'Never!' cried Beowulf hotly, stepping forward, but two armed men barred his way.

Eugen however relaxed and smiled. 'I begin to perceive, Gothic lord, why you have paid ten pieces of gold for this slave. She is indeed one in ten thousand. As for the Count of Torre, I would not give him care of a mad dog, let alone a slave. He is my kinsman, but also my enemy, who hates and fears me above all men in the world.' He extended a hand. 'Any enemy of Ragnar of Torre is right welcome.'

Twelve

HAWKEYE'S MISSION to the Gothic court had gone better than he had dared hope. Hyglack had spoken, and Wylf, old Earl of Hrosnaberg, father of the murdered man, along with Wulfgar, his fiery son, and others of the war party. Despite which, the voice of peace had won the day, at least for the time being.

It had not been his eloquence, for Hawkeye was a man sparing of speech and unskilled in the diplomatic arts. Nor yet was it his evident sincerity. The reason indeed had lain not on the Sferian side at all, but that of the Goths.

For Athkyn, their king, had behaved most strangely. Upon the day of Hawkeye's arrival, he had claimed to be too ill to meet him. Hawkeye had construed this as a ploy, or deliberate discourtesy. Next day Athkyn had attended, though over an hour late, and granted Hawkeye twenty minutes, during which time he had spoken in so odd and abstracted a manner, so little to the point, that Hawkeye had begun to doubt his sanity. Stories of the king's mysterious illness had not been exaggerated; if anything they had fallen short of the truth. Upon the third day Athkyn had again been deemed unfit to meet Hawkeye, no doubt because of the embarrassment by now affecting his courtiers and henchmen. He had however attended a meeting of the Wittan, and from Beowulf's trusty envoy, Hrothgar, Hawkeye had learnt something of what had passed.

It had been quite impossible to obtain a decision from the king. He had said nothing save when spoken to, and had then simply agreed, in a strange and vacant manner, with the last speaker, whether for peace or war. Begged to express his own opinion, he had rambled on about wars of the past, now long forgotten, and the death of his brother Herbald, in his grave these eleven years.

In the resulting embarrassment, even the forceful Hyglack had been somewhat at a loss. It was clear to everyone that the king was out of his wits; presumably elevation to the highest rank of all had turned his brain. The electoral system of monarchy ensured that no lunatic was ever made king; if any thereafter showed signs of violent madness he could be deposed or slain. But a harmlessly deranged monarch, living in a world of his own, was a different problem, and in some ways a harder one. Wise men and lawyers searched books of precedent without success. The one certainty was that war could not be declared without the royal assent. This Athkyn could not or would not give.

Eventually Hyglack, appointed regent by the Wittan, had seen Hawkeye to advise him of the decision, namely that talks with a view to peace might not be entirely out of the question. The delicacy of the king's health, however, necessitated a modest delay.

Hawkeye, seizing the initiative, had suggested a meeting in ten days' time at Castletown, traditional site for Gothic-Sferian negotiations. At the same time, he continued, why not a joust and martial sports to enable warriors on either side to test their skills in friendly contest?

This idea was an inspiration. For Hyglack, mightiest warrior in Gothmark, adored the joust, in which he had never been unhorsed. Nothing would be more welcome to him than the opportunity to add to his reputation against the Sferian princes. He agreed with alacrity, parting from Hawkeye upon terms which three days earlier would have seemed impossibly cordial.

As Hawkeye had guessed, the same tactic worked with his own countrymen. At the prospect of the joust, the royal princes had fallen over themselves in their eagerness to measure arms against Hyglack in particular. Ottar was similarly unbeaten, and looked forward to the prospect with relish. Ali, thus far bested only by his elder brother, was equally keen. Hawkeye's pleasure in his diplomatic success was tempered by the reflection that in manipulating three rather naive princes for his own - though not dishonourable - ends, he had acted in true Wagmunding tradition.

The following week was spent in a frenzy of preparation, but between them Hawkeye, Ljani and their men managed to achieve their aims. The harvest had been good, so food was plentiful. Lists were constructed on the lakeside fields, stands and bunting run up, and summonses sent out to the best warriors, bowmen and charioteers in Gothmark and the Land of the Sfear, not forgetting wrestlers, pugilists, experts at quarter-staff, falconers, acrobats, jugglers, minstrels and actors.

Fortune had smiled on them too; for suddenly, the day before the tournament, Athkyn had appeared much improved. He spoke little, was still prone to long moody silences, and muttered conversation with himself, but the worst of his irrationality seemed a thing of the past. Peace talks were to commence tomorrow; it was unlikely that he would be able to attend - better in a way if he did not - but at least he should be fit to approve the outcome. So the Goths hoped, though the future under such a king seemed likely to be bleak. Maybe in time the lawyers could devise some sort of permanent regency, similar to that obtaining under a boy king. Or Athkyn might recover. The third possibility for the present men pushed hastily out of their minds.

EVEN after a week of perfect weather, the lists at the lakeside field were green, for the lands between the lakes were never dry. But for the low sun and trees of sparse multi-coloured leaves, it might have been midsummer. All ranks of Gothic and Sferian society were represented; housekarls and their squires rubbed shoulders with yeomen and falconers, merchants, craftsmen, grooms, labourers, servants and slaves. Sport and national rivalry united all men, from king to serf.

At mid-morning the three-and-fifty glittering horsemen who were to compete in the joust paraded in their finery before the royal stand. Amidst them, a single riderless horse was led round by a servant in the livery of the Wylfings. For Wulfgar of Hrosnaberg alone, in mourning for his father, had declined to compete, a decision accepted by all. For him to have contended with Prince Ali in friendly sport would have been a mockery.

His part in the ceremony completed, Hawkeye dismounted from Dandy, his favourite bay, handed him over to the grooms, and made for the Sferian tent to change. For he, being amongst the elite of the warrior caste, would not be required to ride until the end of the first day's sport.

Meanwhile, upon the high dais of the royal stand sat the rival kings, Athkyn and Angantyr, surrounded by the panoply befitting their rank; knights and courtiers in attendance, thrones backed by the flags and banners of their ancestors and chief subjects, the lords of Gothmark and the Sfear. Angantyr, a hatchet-faced elderly man, whose every word and gesture betokened one accustomed to the exercise of power and obedience from others; the King of Gothmark, a mere youth by comparison, nervously fiddling with his cloak or gloves, alternately staring straight ahead, or glancing uncomfortably from side to side. Prince Hyglack, accompanied by his wife and children, was taking his seat, brash and boisterous as ever. Of the Sferian princes, Ottar had not yet returned from the parade, but would likewise sit with his wife and family. Roslindis shamed herself and Hawkeye by accompanying Ali, who wore her favour. As always when he saw them together, Hawkeye experienced a fierce stab of jealousy. Unreasonable, no doubt, yet surely it was not too much to expect a little more discretion, less blatant flaunting of her adulterous passion.

He turned away in disgust. A walk around the arena, he decided, would do more good than sitting near them in the stand and seething. He preferred to stretch his legs anyway, wandering amongst the stalls, occasionally stopping to bargain for trinkets, or throw away a few pence to the tricksters who came to every fair, for the Wagmunding lords were notoriously tolerant of minor roguery. Some of the crowd recognized him, greeting him in cheerful, informal fashion, as was the custom in the Lands between the Lakes, where lords and churls alike were often careless about niceties of rank.

At length the attention of all turned to the lists, pristine and new-swept for the start of the premier event of the tournament, the individual joust. The bell-tent at the Sferian end, decked in blue and silver bunting, opened to reveal a young horseman in plate armour, bearing lance and shield. His mount was a sturdy bay, caparisoned in black and gold. The same colours marked his shield.

Opposite, his opponent was in position too; a heavily-built man of middle age, similarly clad and mounted, before the pavilion of the Goths. His shield bore the arms of Rigel, a green serpent rimmed silver, upon a red ground. Each man dropped his visor and lowered his lance.

At a signal from Bluemantle, Marshal of the Lists, the warriors advanced, slowly at first, but as they reached the central barrier they spurred their mounts to the canter. A crash, a shout, and the horseman in black and gold was bundled from the saddle, whilst Rigel thundered on, raising a gauntleted fist in triumphal salute. The vanquished one grovelled momentarily before regaining his feet, and staggered away unaided to the obscure ignominy of his tent. Rigel had demonstrated fair skill, thought Hawkeye, his opponent little. Yet the victor's performance had not been without flaw - he had wielded the lance a shade clumsily, and gathered speed too late.

The ineptitude of the next two warriors was apparent even to the common herd, who indeed were no mean judge. The victor should provide someone with easy opposition in his next joust.

Of course, great skill was not to be expected. Not every housekarl, or even every earl, had the wealth and leisure to obtain a powerful, fiery yet disciplined horse, plate armour and endless practice. The first day would see the end of the road for most; they would have had the honour of competing in the Great Joust, and their moment of glory. Of the three-and-fifty eager horsemen who had paraded in gleaming armour and heraldic colour before the kings that daybreak, eight only would survive to contest the supreme honour, the Golden Lance, on the final day.

Favourite for the title was Ottar. Never had he been defeated in combat; his thanes and housekarls acknowledged themselves no match

for him. He had even ridden in the lists abroad, against the might of
Teutonia and the Empire, and brought the garland of victory back to the
Sfear. His brother Ali enjoyed a reputation second only to his own. The
Goths to a man supported Hyglack, like Ottar undefeated, possibly a
shade less finished in technique, but physically immensely strong. Of the
rest, only Hawkeye was reckoned in the same class. He competed but
rarely, and then only in small local events, for the Lord of Karron Tha
was known to dislike the pomp and ceremony of great tournaments, yet
for what it was worth, he too had never been unhorsed.

After another dozen passages of arms, with modest skill displayed,
the barriers were cleared away. Wagoneers and slaves heaved bales of
straw into the arena for barricades, supported by poles and wooden
hoarding. Trumpeters and heralds entered, and after a fanfare
announced the first of the chariot races.

Of all events, Hawkeye liked racing least. The drivers were all
madmen, it was cruel to the horses, and there was no little risk to
spectators. Seldom did a tournament take place without a broken limb
or two, and deaths were not uncommon. These scruples, needless to say,
were not shared by the majority of his countrymen, it being the greatest
betting event of all.

Six teams were involved, bearing the colours red, green, gold, silver,
purple and blue. The first three were from Gothmark, blue and silver
from the Sfear, whilst the purple was a rare entry from a traveller
representing Port Targon. The race took a dozen laps of the track, and
the teams lined up in rows of three, according to the numbers they had
drawn. Red, green and blue had the favoured positions.

The marshal cracked his whip, and they charged off full tilt, wheels
grating and juddering against those of their rivals, whilst drivers
exchanged curses and obscene gestures. At the first bend the leading
Sferian was smashed crudely into the bales by the Goths on his inside,
overturning in a flurry of straw, spinning wheels and screaming horses.
'Foul! Foul! Shame!' and catcalls came from the Sferian section of the
crowd; hoots of glee and derision from the Goths. No doubt there
would be an objection; inevitably it would be overruled. The rules were
vague; half the judges were Sferian, half Goth, and if they disagreed the
result stood. Amongst the royal party, old Angantyr's face was black
with rage, whilst Prince Hyglack bellowed with laughter.

The drivers continued crazy as ever, cutting each other up on the
bends, ripping the turf into shreds and throwing great clods of earth into
the crowd. By the eighth lap another two had departed the race, as a
Goth and Sferian became entangled on the far side of the track in a heap
of splintered wheels and terrified horses. Their drivers came to blows, at
first with whips, then at close quarters with fists and boots. Mounted
marshals raced across to separate them.

The Sferians were thus out of the race, which now lay between the leading Goth and the man from Targon. The other Goth was a lap behind and destined for third place, unless one of those ahead came to grief, which seemed quite possible, for the Tarragonian in particular was in a frenzy, lashing his sable team as the foaming creatures plunged alongside his rival with nine laps complete and three to go. Their own men being out of it, most of the Sfear had transferred their allegiance to him, and fights broke out in the crowd.

The chariots came round again, abreast, the Goth on the inside, drivers lashing one another as often as their teams. Neck and neck they thundered towards the bend where Hawkeye stood.

The black horses plunged straight for him. There was a splintering noise as the rustic barriers gave way, and sudden panic: 'Ye gods! Look out! Freya's tits!' and cruder expressions. Hawkeye flung himself to the turf, as a five-foot iron-rimmed wheel bounced inches past his head.

'Seize the horses there! Ho!'

A bold fellow nearby did just that, as the one-wheeled chariot slewed around in a lethal swathe. Hawkeye scrambled to his feet, shaken but unhurt. Around the ring, gasps and cries of horror gave way to muted cheers as the surviving Goths came home in first and second places, thus securing qualification for the next round. The Northmen were not a squeamish people.

Hawkeye's squire, Leofric, pushed his way through the crowd towards him. 'What happened, my lord? Was the Tarragonian fouled?'

'Not that I saw. He made no attempt to take the bend. Perhaps he lost a wheel on the approach, but it happened so quickly. Let's hear what he has to say for himself.'

'He is dead, my lord,' said one of a group leaning over the wrecked chariot. 'Killed in the smash, no doubt.'

'Nay,' said another. 'There is no mark on him. A seizure, methinks.'

'I'm not surprised,' grumbled Hawkeye. 'All these drivers are madmen.'

'A near thing for you, my Lord Hawkeye,' said Leofric. 'Another six inches and we should have been pulling you out of the wreckage with those yonder. Better to have been born lucky than rich.'

Thirteen

AN HOUR'S chaotic rescue work later, the jousting recommenced. The final toll was two dead, including the driver, four maimed, and several with minor injuries. It seemed clear that the Tarragonian had died instantly of a seizure, just as his team approached the bend. They had careered straight on, smashed through the barriers and lost a wheel. But for the quick thinking of the experienced horseman who had grabbed and calmed them, more lives might have been lost. It was written off by one and all as a regrettable but inevitable hazard of racing.

Hawkeye was due for one joust this day; if he came through he would ride against the elite of his peers on the aftermorrow. A token offer was made by Bluemantle to postpone his ride if he needed time to recover from his escape. Hawkeye refused, as was expected of him.

So it was that early that evening he sat, mounted on Dandy, beside the blue and silver bedecked tent of the Sfear. The jousts had been arranged so that as far as possible Goth and Sferian rode against one another rather than their own countrymen. Exceptions might have to be made as one side or the other became depleted, but thus far it had worked well.

This, Hawkeye's first contest, would be hardest on his nerves. He and seven other great warriors, four Goths and three Sfear, had been selected by their countrymen and excused participation in the early jousts. Each of them now had to ride against one of the eight qualifiers, and would be expected to justify the confidence placed in him. To lose subsequently could be excused; to fail in this round might be deemed not far short of a disgrace.

Hawkeye would be fifth to ride; the first three jousts had all proceeded as expected. In the fourth young Numa, eldest son of the

Gothic earl of that name, and his black-clad opponent were presenting arms in the traditional salute to the kings and their courts. Hawkeye drew a deep breath. The next few minutes would be the most nerve-racking of all.

The contestants parted, Numa in red and gold, to the far pavilion, that of the Goths. The all-black knight was to ride from the Sferian end. He was not of the Sfear, but one of the handful of outsiders, mostly from Targon, who had accepted the challenge. Alone among the contestants, this knight had given no name. Or rather, since some name had to be given, he had called himself Sable of Shadron, which was patently false, for none lived in the mountains of Shadron Mor, and sable was a colour, not a name. Whoever he was, he had ridden well thus far, and Hawkeye had been a little relieved to avoid him in the draw.

They took position, Numa in the distance, shield tucked into his breast as he snapped his visor shut. The marshal threw down the mace, and they advanced at increasing speed, Numa if anything a little the faster. They neared one another and spurred; young Numa faltered before crashing from his mount into the well-worn muddy track beside the barrier. A groan of despair broke from the Goths as his riderless horse cantered on to be grabbed by the grooms near the Sferian tent. The dark rider, omitting the usual courtesy of a salute to the crowd, thundered on out of the ring.

Hawkeye, a little less nervous now, trotted forth to parade before the stand, raising a mailed hand in acknowledgment of the crowd's support. At the dais Dandy behaved perfectly, kneeling in momentary salute as Hawkeye dipped his lance. Old Angantyr allowed his leading warrior a grim smile of support; Athkyn was gazing apathetically ahead. Hyglack was absent, being due to ride next. Wanda waved enthusiastically, causing Hawkeye to check that her favour was still in his helm. It did not occur to him to look for Roslindis.

His opponent was a young Gothic yeoman called Manfred, who had done well to get this far, and probably would not expect to proceed further. Hawkeye dropped his visor as a sign that he was ready. His adversary did likewise. The mace fell.

Hawkeye trotted his mount slowly at first, eyes on the red lion on his opponent's shield. The crowd noise receded as he concentrated on the task ahead. The shield grew larger; his own was in position, braced well forward to absorb the shock of the impact. They were spurring their mounts now - Hawkeye lowered his lance, moved it quick and late to the edge of the shield, felt the jolt but remained secure in the saddle. A triumphant shout from the Sfear, and he cantered on. His gallant adversary stumbled to his feet and saluted his conqueror. A wave of relief flooded over Hawkeye, but on returning he did not forget to touch hands with his successor, a young and inexperienced countryman, and wish him well against Prince Hyglack. It availed the lad little, for a minute later the giant Goth unhorsed him with ease.

TABLE positions for the banquet that night had caused Hawkeye and Ljani some difficulty. Ultimately they had decided that the order of precedence should be Angantyr, Athkyn, Ottar, Ali, Hyglack, each accompanied by their respective wives, Ljani having the unenviable task of pairing off with Athkyn. The only point which might have been disputed was the placing of Hyglack, heir presumptive to the Gothic throne, below Ali, second son of the Sferian king. Hawkeye had been inclined to favour giving precedence to the Goth, but Ljani had assured him that Hyglack was neither well informed nor fussy about matters of etiquette. This proved to be the case, so that nothing occurred to mar the evening, save for Hawkeye the sight of Roslindis fawning upon Prince Ali. She looked like what she was, with her breasts practically falling out of her bodice. Something about his sluttish wife still touched Hawkeye on the raw.

Otherwise all went well. Wherever he looked lords, churls and even slaves glowed in the aftermath of good food and wine. Minstrels, tumblers and jesters plied their trade in the square between the mead benches, rewarded by coin and acclamation, occasionally barracked in good-humoured excess of drunken high spirits. At midnight would come the draw for the final jousts, which would take place on the aftermorrow, thereby allowing a whole day for speculation and debate about the outcome, and the placing of wagers.

Cupbearers entered with a fanfare, to deposit a pair of golden chalices on the high table, one before each of the kings. Before Athkyn were four coloured discs, each about the size of a mark piece, representing the warriors of the Sfear. Angantyr's cup similarly contained four, three coloured and one black, who would be their opponents. Bluemantle announced the making of the draw, and explained the procedure. Each king would draw alternately, Angantyr the Gothic names, Athkyn those of the Sfear.

The Sferian king placed a hand in his cup, stirred the discs round, and paused with a smile to savour the drama of the situation. He withdrew his hand and opened it. Green and gold.

'Artur Emunding,' announced Bluemantle.

Saving Hyglack, Emunding was the leading warrior of the Goths, tough and experienced, though still a youngish man.

'Rides against ...'

Hawkeye tensed in anticipation. Unfortunately the critical moment was slightly marred by Athkyn, who had to be prompted both to make the draw and open his hand. Silver and blue.

'Ottar, Prince of Wendel.'

A deep murmur of interest, for the mightiest warrior of the Sfear had come first out of the cup. Unlucky for the Emunding, who gave a wry smile.

Angantyr had drawn again, the black disc.

'He who calls himself Sable, of Shadron Mor.'

A silence, indeed a shadow, fell across the feast, a curious phenomenon, thought Hawkeye, for the black knight's name had to be uttered sooner or later. Yet even in the bright-lit hall, it served to dampen men's spirits, for none supported him, and alone amongst the contestants in the joust, he was not present. Matters were not helped by Athkyn's repeated slowness in drawing the next disc. Hawkeye felt the muscles of his belly contract. For some reason he did not want the black knight. Better Prince Hyglack, even. The king's hand opened, and luck was with him.

'Magnus of Syrdan.'

A good man, as were they all by now, but probably the weakest Sferian left. The sinister black knight might well progress further. Two names now remained in the Gothic cup: Hyglack and Rigel. And in the Sferian, Hawkeye and Ali. Next time the old king's hand opened it bore the multi-coloured device of the southern lord.

'Earl Rigel of Rigel.'

The next name out of the cup would determine the whole remaining draw. Hyglack gave a broad grin of satisfaction, and his eyes challenged each possible opponent in turn. Surprisingly, he turned his gaze first not upon the vain, flamboyant Ali, but the quiet Hawkeye, who acknowledged with a twisted smile. This time Athkyn's slowness was an advantage in allowing tension to mount. Hawkeye permitted himself a rare glance at Roslindis, who together with Ali was placed as far from him on the top table as courtesy would permit. The Norns would now decide which of her two men would ride against Hyglack, and which would have the decidedly easier task against Rigel. It was done, and again luck was with him.

'Athelstan, Earl of Karron Tha, called Hawkeye.'

A great buzz of interest and appreciation, not so much in the last pairing as the next, which would be the joust of the round. Though fixed, it was drawn as a matter of course. Hyglack, Prince of Gothmark, would ride against Prince Ali of Scarlettown.

'Your luck has held again, my lord,' said Wanda happily.

'Aye, that it has. My lucky day indeed,' he added, musing on his narrow escape that afternoon.

Last thing before the feast broke up, he exchanged a few brief words with Roslindis, who excused herself from Ali and came over to him.

'Good luck against Rigel, Hawkeye.'

'Thank you. I hope Ali defeats Prince Hyglack.' Up to a point this was true, for he judged the Goth the more formidable adversary later.

She nodded. 'I will pass on your good wishes.' He could not determine whether she spoke ironically or not. She continued awkwardly, 'I saw what happened this afternoon from the stand. I am glad you were not hurt.'

'It was nothing, as it happened. I was lucky.'

There had been no need for Roslindis to seek him out and speak, indeed he had been trying to avoid her eye. Maybe he still held some power over her, as she did over him, despite everything. Truly, as the saying of the Northmen had it, it was easier to know a woman's body than her soul.

Roger Butters

Fourteen

THE FINAL arrow thumped softly into the round straw target, missing the red-painted central circle by three inches. Amidst a murmur of approval from the crowd, Hawkeye lowered his bow and awaited the tellers' call.

'Three-and-forty.'

The onlookers cheered, and Hawkeye was pleased. Of the thirty-six arrows he had fired, all but four had struck the target, eleven of them the red, which scored double. He saluted the kings, acknowledged the plaudits of the crowd, and returned to his tent.

'Good shooting, my lord,' said Leofric. 'You are in the lead thus far, methinks.'

Hawkeye smiled and nodded. He would probably miss the Golden Arrow, awarded to the greatest archer of all, but the silver might lie within his grasp. That morning, target-shooting at various distances, he had finished in third place with a score of forty-nine. Now, in rapid-fire, a further forty-three should keep him amongst the leaders.

The men of Karron Tha expected their lord to do well, and he had determined not to disappoint them. A place in the first dozen was desirable; to win would have been an unexpected bonus. In the latter case Hawkeye would have been gratified, but not elated. To the martial skills, as to most things, the Earl of Karron Tha attached neither more nor less importance than they warranted, neither did he over- or underestimate himself.

Outside in the sunshine, Wanda embraced him. 'Well done, my lord. The Sfear are claiming you will win.'

'I think not. Some of the best are still to shoot.'

121

The tellers announced the score of another competitor, followed by muted applause for an adequate performance. Wanda indicated the gaily-decked stand beside the butts. 'Will you sit amongst the gentry?'

'No, no, I'll stroll around for a while.'

'Then I'll wait for you in the stand, Hawkeye.'

He kissed her again and watched the statuesque young figure in white silk pass beneath the awning to the royal dais. For his own part, despite yesterday's disaster, he preferred mixing with the common people. At the moment, Hawkeye found himself the most popular man in the north. This surprised him, for the Earl of Karron Tha was a man of dark, and, he fancied, somewhat dour appearance, without the charm or ready wit of his cousin Beowulf. Yet he seemed to be well-liked, and in true Wagmunding style felt more at ease amongst the masses than with his peers.

'Well done, my lord!'

'Will you win the joust, Hawkeye?'

'I have half a thaler riding on you, my lord!'

'And I a whole one!'

'Give the Goths what for, Hawkeye!'

He passed among them with an embarrassed grin, but deeply gratified. Some clapped him on the shoulder, or insisted on shaking him by the hand. A serving girl with lowcut blouse and extraordinarily large breasts hung a garland round his neck and kissed him, to the accompaniment of whistles and ribald comment. It pleased him that so many called him Hawkeye; they would have dared address few other nobles by their nickname. He preferred to regard it as a sign of friendship rather than presumption. Not only Sferian folk, either; he knew several of them for Goths, who would rather a Wagmunding win the tournament than one of their own countrymen.

'Five-and-twenty.' Another indifferent shot, and the last of the session. Heralds and scoretellers conferred busily.

'You are in the lead, my lord,' called one of the churls nearby.

'I don't know about that,' he replied, though he knew he would be disappointed if it were not so.

'True, my lord,' said another. 'Egbert here has been keeping count.' A spotty earnest boy of about twelve grinned awkwardly and confirmed.

'Fourscore and twelve, my lord. There is no-one else exceeds threescore and eighteen.'

A fanfare, and the herald advanced. 'My lords, ladies and gentlemen: scores for the Golden Arrow thus far, eight and forty competitors having shot, twelve remaining.

'First, Athelstan Wagmunding, Earl of Karron Tha' - The herald had to break off as his announcement was drowned in cheering - 'with fourscore and twelve. Second, Cadmon of Thorn, with threescore and eighteen. Third ...'

'You will win, my lord,' several assured him.

Hawkeye shook his head. 'There are some good men yet to shoot. A couple were ahead of my first-round score.'

His modest denial was swamped in dissent, and unflattering comment about the prowess of those remaining. This confidence soon began to appear justified; the next two archers performed but moderately, the third, one of Hawkeye's main rivals, shot a thoroughly bad round. There followed a useful score, eight-and-thirty, by a competitor too far in arrear to stand a chance.

'Anselm of Ghul,' announced the herald, amidst murmurs of interest and Sferian suport. A tall blond youth stepped forward.

Most of the archers were churls or yeomen, a few minor aristocrats. Of the great lords, only the Wagmundings professed much skill with the bow, for despite its success in war it still retained a somewhat plebeian reputation. Anselm, younger son of the Earl of Ghul, was an exception. Hawkeye regarded him with uncharacteristic ill-will; if he were beaten, he would prefer it not to be by Anselm, one of those he suspected of having shared Roslindis' bed.

The teller enquired whether the archer was ready. Anselm, clad in the usual bowman's garb of leather jerkin and leggings, fitted an arrow to his bow, pointed it to the ground, and indicated assent. The time-teller beside the target placed a hand on the giant hour-glass and turned it over, whilst a slave tolled a bell. From now until the glass was empty would elapse a period during which a man might slowly count to about two hundred. Anselm raised his bow and fired; the arrow found the target near its outer edge. The next shot was well wide, causing the crowd behind the target to scatter. The third found the red section, but to Hawkeye the rate of fire seemed reassuringly slow. He kept the score in his head, and when time was called knew that Anselm was several arrows short.

'Five-and-thirty.'

In the first round he had scored fifty, only one more than Hawkeye, so this effort put him into second place. He did not look too disappointed. For the first time, Hawkeye allowed himself to imagine what it would be like to win the Golden Arrow. If it was not this year, it would probably be never, for his cousin Beowulf, though careless of most martial sport, was acknowledged supreme in archery.

Two more competitors came and went without distinction, before:

'Ljani of Slane.'

This should be interesting, he thought. At the end of the first round she had stood ninth, an outstanding achievement from the only girl to compete. The targets had been threefold: at seventy, a hundred, and a hundred and twenty yards. At the furthest, a light bow and comparative lack of muscle had cost her dear, but at a hundred she had scored well, at seventy outstandingly. In rapid fire, at the shortest distance, he thought she should do well if not too nervous. After her there would be but four archers left, including Rollo of Bakir, leader after the first round, and Hawkeye's only serious remaining rival.

Ljani stepped forward, slim and pale as ever, pushing aside a lock of hair. Unlike most bowmen she was clad not in a jerkin but light body armour, though her legs were bare save for deerskin boots. She wore a rakish little archer's cap, inadequate to control her tempestuous mane, and a short cloak in the red, green and gold colours she favoured for sport. For Ljani, by birth neither a true Wagmunding nor Wylfing, nor yet a member of the royal house, went her own way, and wore colours of her own choice. She carried three full quivers. Most used four, yet none had yet succeeded in discharging all forty-eight arrows they contained. Some experienced bowmen preferred to overfill their quivers, with up to twenty arrows in each, reckoning the overcrowding less costly in time than the extra changeover. For all but the most nimble-fingered, this was not so.

The red-haired girl moved up to the line. She stood about medium height for a woman, well below that for a man. A light breeze had sprung up, which was unlucky for her, but should not cost too many points if she kept her head. To Hawkeye's sympathetic gaze she seemed a little nervous, which might be all to the good, and rather frail. She adjusted the goose-feather in her cap, then fitted the first arrow to her bow, as was allowed before the bell. She drew a breath and nodded gravely to indicate that she was ready.

The bell sounded. She raised her bow, and after momentary delay to sight the range, the first arrow sped on its way, to land with a soft thud in the outer target. So did the next two, the fourth missed, but the fifth and sixth found the red. She was very lithe and graceful; her action could not be faulted, though it might be she was a little slower than the men.

Three or four shots later, Hawkeye became aware that something strange was happening. Ljani was not fumbling for arrows like most, but finding them more quickly as the quiver emptied; her movements, far from slowing through fatigue, gathered speed as her action found its rhythm. Belatedly Hawkeye remembered a conversation with Beowulf two or three years ago, when his cousin had told him that whilst he could beat Ljani at target, at rapid-fire she had no peer. Hawkeye had not believed him, and subsequent enquiry of the awkward fifteen-year-old had led to her turning crimson, mumbling incoherently and running away. He had forgotten that until now.

Ljani tossed the quiver aside and slung another on to her shoulder in a single easy movement. Twelve arrows already was quicker than any had managed thus far, and the crowd had begun to react with gasps of astonishment and appreciation. The glass was still three-parts full, and it was Hawkeye's turn to catch his breath as he realized that in the first quiver there had been not twelve arrows, but twenty.

By now, there was no doubt. Shots fell on the target like heavy rain, and it seemed that even before an arrow had struck home the next was on its way. Yet the girl with red hair did not hurry, but fitted arrow after arrow to the bow, and loosed the string, time and time again, in a succession of easy flowing movements. And she seemed no longer frail, but whipcord, as the soft twang of the bow and hiss of arrows, and plop of the target were first heard in stunned silence, then gradually drowned as the crowd murmured, here and their cried out in appreciation, and finally were moved to massive and continuous applause.

The second quiver was thrown aside and the third emptied with movements swift but unhurried, graceful yet full of power. And those who had been watching the wrestling or the falconry, or buying at the stalls of the fair, or watching the jugglers or the men on stilts, now came running across to the archery butts, pushing people aside or jumping up and down in an attempt to see. They were shouting, smiling and laughing foolishly, or gaping in awed silence. And still the arrows fell upon the target, as regular and rapid as if they came from the bows of an army instead of a single slim girl.

The slaves tending the quivers had realized that she would exhaust her supply of arrows before the time expired, a thing never known before. They borrowed one from the next competitor and placed it at her side. The glass was three-parts empty now, as Ljani discarded the third quiver and picked up the fourth. At last she seemed a little tired, but not exhausted; her movements were as lithe as ever, and the arrows struck home just the same, but the soft pitter-patter sounded a shade less quickly, and the sands were running out. The centre of the target was jammed so thick with arrows there seemed no room for more, yet they continued to find their way through, pushing their fellows aside to form a thick hedgehog of red, green and gold.

The last grains sped through the glass, and the bell sounded for time. Ljani lowered her bow; the arrow in flight found its mark. There was no applause now, but an expectant hush, broken only by a few ruffians banging on the trestle-boards containing the lower elements of the crowd. The tellers met and conferred, nodding and gesticulating as they checked and rechecked the score. The crowd were becoming increasingly restive. Finally, the tellers agreed. The herald stepped forward.

'One hundred and three.'

The hubbub climaxed into a great crash of applause and cheering from Goth and Sferian alike. No man there could recall an archer in rapid fire registering threescore and ten; the magic figure of a hundred had never been dreamt of. Angantyr, that fierce old king, was on his feet, yelling 'Bravo!' and pounding Athkyn on the back. Even the Gothic king seemed shaken from his lethargy, and was smiling and nodding at all and sundry. Prince Hyglack was clapping hands above his head, bellowing madly, and all the fine ladies in the stand, even Roslindis, were on their feet in tribute to the heroine who had vanquished all the men. Amongst the commons, it was pandemonium. Everyone, Goth and Sferian alike, was shouting or laughing insanely, as if they had won a great victory. No two men could have equalled Ljani's score that day, even if they had been as skilled as Hawkeye. For himself, Hawkeye suddenly realized that his sight was blurred with tears of joy, and he was shouting 'Well done, little girl! Bravo, Ljani!'

Yet the victory belonged to the slight but strong figure in green, who saluted the kings, acknowledged the tribute of the crowd, and left the stage. Like a leading actor she was compelled to return several times, being reluctantly dragged back by fellow-competitors to accept and acknowledge further frenzied applause. A pity, thought Hawkeye, she could not have shot last, for what followed would be an anticlimax.

It was only now that he recalled he had lost the Golden Arrow, but he would not have exchanged the last few moments for a dozen arrows. For what it was worth, the remaining archers predictably let their concentration lapse, and Hawkeye duly secured the silver.

THE PRIZE-GIVING, performed by old Angantyr, took place half an hour later. Instead of shaking hands with Ljani, Hawkeye put an arm around her shoulders and kissed her. The crowd gave this incident a huge cheer, and Ljani, a moment before so cool and poised, changed back on the instant to an awkward nineteen-year-old, blushing furiously and uncertain where to look. For his part, Hawkeye would have liked Ljani's feat, and his own more modest achievement, to be his last memories of the day, but it was not to be.

Wanda was not familiar with Castletown, so that evening, after the dinnerfeast, she insisted he accompany her on a tour of the old part of the city. During the tournament, traders stayed open all hours, and the narrow streets were alive and bustling in the glow of torches and oil-lamps. Every little shop- and stallholder knew Hawkeye, by sight at least, and congratulated or commiserated with him, chatting casually, almost as if they were equals. As indeed they might be for all he knew, for Hawkeye never troubled to compare himself with others. Wanda soon disappeared in search of dress materials, while he stood outside a saddlers to examine leather goods.

The proprietor a plump, middle-aged man, hurried out. 'Interested in a new saddle, my lord Hawkeye? We have a large selection, and methinks you may find our prices a little more to your taste than those of Bakir.'

Hawkeye did not doubt this, for not only was the Sferian capital notoriously expensive, but nearly a week's ride from his home in Bettany. He had a local saddler, but though reliable his choice was rather limited. Hawkeye was in the mood to treat himself to something a little more elaborate. 'Let's see, then.'

The words were scarcely out of his mouth before he found himself grovelling on the pavement in a state of confusion. He must have grabbed at the stall for support, because reins, boots and splintered woodwork had toppled down on to him. Struggling free of the debris, he identified the fault as that of a ruffian who had shoved him crudely to the ground, apparently on purpose. Regaining his feet, Hawkeye made to strike the man, who however grabbed his arm and pointed. There in the doorframe, precisely in the spot he had been standing a moment before, a bolt from a crossbow was embedded six inches deep.

'What ...?'

'Up there, my lord!'

Across the way tiles were crashing into the street, causing passers-by to look up in consternation. Belatedly Hawkeye realized what must have happened. 'On the roof!' he cried. 'Stop him!'

He had not seen the man, but further commotion from the rear of the houses opposite suggested he was still nearby. There came a crash, a cry of alarm, and a thud as of a heavy object falling. Hawkeye and his new companion dashed across the street, under a stable-arch to the ill-lit courtyard of the tavern whence the sounds had come.

They were too late, or nearly so. A man dressed as a groom lay on the cobbles with smashed legs, blood trickling from his ear. Near his left hand lay the guilty weapon.

'I saw it clearly, my lord,' said another man. 'The slave loosed a bolt at you from the eaves yonder, then fled in panic. He slipped on the tiles, and ...'

'Well,' said Hawkeye wryly, noting the would-be assassin's glazed eyes and stertorous breathing, 'he has paid for all now, or soon will.'

Half of them were claiming to have seen it by now, except for his saviour, a big bearded Goth in rough sheepskin, who was making off unobtrusively. 'You, my friend,' said Hawkeye, stopping him. 'I owe you my life. If ever the Earl of Karron Tha can show you favour, name it.'

'I may one day, my lord,' said the man, with a sturdy independence, 'should I fall upon hard times. But for the present, your thanks is enough.'

'Your name?'

The man smiled. 'You will remember me, my lord, if I mistake not.' At this, he disappeared into the crowd, and in the longstanding tradition of anonymous heroes could not be persuaded to stay or claim reward.

Wanda had appeared on the scene. 'Are you all right, my lord?' she enquired anxiously.

Hawkeye shrugged. 'Perfectly. Which is more than can be said for him. Stop that,' he ordered, as several of the crowd looked likely to execute summary justice upon the offender. 'It will be all the same in a minute, anyway.'

He had just recognized the man. It was a shock. One of Roslindis's servants, who had waited on her, and if he knew his wife, lain with her too, for he was, or had been, a handsome enough young fellow. 'Who put thee up to this, sirrah?' hissed Hawkeye fiercely, lips to the man's ear. 'Thy mistress?'

At first there was no response. Then the man's eyes cleared momentarily as he gathered his scattered wits together for the last time. 'Aye, it was ... she.' His eyes slipped out of focus, rolled up into his head, and he died.

Wanda, unused to the sight of violent death, was shaken. 'Did he speak, my lord?'

Hawkeye stood and shrugged again. 'The ramblings of a dying slave,' he said harshly. 'I understood him not. Let his body be buried without honour in the felon's plot at the city gaol.'

Fifteen

HAWKEYE WAS armed and ready early; too early, for it had given him time to become nervous. Again he checked the straps securing his breastplate, and removed the helmet to take the weight from his shoulders and breathe freely. The trumpets were sounding, and heralds announced the pairings for the last eight. Magnus, due to ride next, was flustered and wandered about, searching for some leg armour. Hawkeye walked awkwardly up and down, mailed joints clanking as he tried to shake the tension from his limbs. Ottar and the Emunding had been announced, and once more a fanfare rang out. Hawkeye decided to watch. It would get him used to the light, besides which observation of the winner could be useful if they met later.

He was too late for the first bout, for the crash and commotion came just as he reached the tent flap. Narrowing his eyes in the glare of sunlight, he heard and caught a glimpse of the Goth's riderless horse pounding by. At the far end of the lists, Ottar had drawn to a halt, acknowledging the cheers. His opponent was stumbling to his feet. Around the ring, the blue and silver banners of the Sfear waved in jubiliation.

'One for us,' announced Falco the groom with satisfaction, holding Dandy's head as Hawkeye mounted.

Hawkeye lowered the helmet carefully on to his shoulders and fumbled with the catches. 'Aye. Good luck, Syrdan,' he added to the departing Sferian, who was riding to the stand to pay his respects. Hawkeye shuffled himself firmly into the saddle and moved his feet in the stirrups. The tension was abating a little.

'All in order, my lord?' asked Falco.

He smiled. 'Perfectly. Don't worry.'

Leofric brought his lance. Syrdan rode back at the canter. Watching any joust, Hawkeye reckoned himself able to pick the winner by his demeanour more often than not. Something about Syrdan seemed to suggest lack of confidence.

They had drawn up, turned and closed visors as the mace went down. The last instant before the collision Hawkeye knew the result - Syrdan had flinched, drawn back and was lost. The black rider galloped on victorious, unmoved by the admittedly lukewarm applause. Hawkeye was not mistaken; the normally resolute Syrdan had lost heart and pulled his mount, hoping to ride the impact instead of going through with his challenge. He wondered if any other had noticed.

'By day and night,' drawled a scornful aristocratic voice behind him. 'He drew. He drew a mile. Nay, a league.'

Hawkeye knew the voice, but turned just the same. Ali of Scarlettown lounged by the tent, fully armed save for his helmet, a disdainful expression on his thin superior face. 'Ye gods, and he calls himself a Sferian. What say you, Karron Tha?'

'I did not observe,' said Hawkeye coldly. He closed his visor and rode off.

AT the dais, Hawkeye looked first for Wanda, who was just taking her seat. She smiled and waved. Then he searched amongst the Sferian royal party for Roslindis, who to his surprise was staring at him intently, and gave what could have been the tiniest indication of support. He in turn acknowledged her, with a motion of the head so slight it was almost imperceptible.

The combatants returned to their stations and dropped their visors, first Hawkeye, then Rigel. In theory, the green-clad Gothic knight was the least formidable of the survivors; an experienced middle-aged warrior who seldom lost to those he should defeat, or overcame his superiors. Yet Hawkeye never underestimated an adversary, and took care to do everything right, yet not too right, combining boldness and aggression with control, concentrating at the critical moment ... He took the Goth's point in the centre of his shield, whilst his own lance found his opponent's breast and tipped him off as neat as a dummy on the practice lists. For the second time the Sferian shouts rang out for him, as a Gothic lord sprawled in the mud. Hawkeye turned in the saddle to see his adversary, chivalrous as ever, raising a mailed fist in salute. Riding back, acknowledging the cheers, Hawkeye remembered to touch gloves with Ali.

'Good luck.'

Ali nodded. 'Well done.'

Evidently his performance had passed muster with the prince. In fairness, Ali had observed the civilities, and that at a time when the encounter with Hyglack must have been foremost in his mind. Hawkeye returned to the tent and dismounted. Falco grabbed and patted the neck of his mount.

'Well done, my lord. A flawless ride.'

'Thanks.' He tucked the helmet under his arm and entered the tent to general acclaim. He must have been a little slow in getting changed, for a crash and shout indicated that the next joust had already taken place.

'Who won?' he enquired, hurrying to the tent-flap.

'Neither, my lord,' said the guard there. 'They ride again.'

Each man checked his lance briefly for damage, and prepared for the second passage of arms. This time, there was no doubt. To the huge relief of the Goths, Hyglack, their last survivor, unhorsed the Sferian prince, who returned to the tent in the worst of humours. Hawkeye deemed it advisable to depart for the stand, to be greeted by Wanda, who flung herself into his arms and kissed him passionately in view of all. He caught sight of Roslindis, her face wet with tears. She had taken her hero's defeat hard, it seemed. Hawkeye felt a pang of savage triumph. He was glad Ali had lost, and she had been hurt.

'You seem less than delighted, my lord,' Wanda reproved him as she detached herself.

'No,' he said lamely, 'I'm very pleased. Just a gloomy thought.'

More like a shameful one. For gloating over the misfortune of others was not the conduct of a Sferian, or a Wagmunding.

MINOR events occupied the rest of the morning, whilst all the talk was of the semi-finals to come. Three of the four survivors had never been unhorsed in combat - as for the black knight of Shadron, no man knew. Yet now, for the first time, all but one must taste defeat. The winner of the contest would take not only the Golden Lance, but the gold chalice awarded to the Supreme Champion of the tournament. In two hundred years, no-one had won two of the three main events; lance, archery and chariot. When they went to different winners, whoever had done best in the other events was champion. And if that too failed to decide, the champion was him who had won the joust.

For the midday meal all, even the kings, stood informally around long benches stacked with food and drink. Most ate sparingly, for tonight would be the great feast of the whole meeting, at which the Supreme Champion would sit between the kings as guest of honour. If, as he now dared to hope, it were Hawkeye himself, it would present a problem in that host and chief guest would be one and the same. More likely though, it would be Ottar or Hyglack. The prospect of the obscure and sinister black knight sitting there was simply bizarre.

131

Amongst those who came to offer congratulations were Ali and Roslindis, very cold and formal, and a highly embarrassed Ljani, who still showed a tendency to flush and mumble when addressing Hawkeye about anything but the most routine matters.

'You should have entered the joust as well, red maiden,' said Ottar good-humouredly, rescuing them from embarrassment. 'Shown us all how to do it.'

They laughed and relaxed. Hawkeye liked the crown prince, who lacked the condescending manner of his younger brother. If he were not to win the joust personally, he would prefer it to go to Ottar.

'Well,' agreed Hawkeye, 'you showed us all how to use the bow yesterday, and no mistake. Beowulf's hand was there, or I am mistaken.'

Ljani nodded seriously. 'Brother Bear was a great help indeed.' She started to say something else, then paused and looked beyond Hawkeye, so intently that he turned his head, expecting to see something behind him, but there was naught.

'What's the matter?' asked Ottar.

'Nothing, my lord,' said Ljani, collecting herself. 'Yet ... All is perhaps not well with my brother. I have these premonitions sometimes when we are apart.'

Hawkeye knew of the curious bond between her and Beowulf. 'Where is he, Ljani? Can you tell?'

'Out east, many leagues distant.'

'I had heard he was up to some mischief in the Isles,' said Ottar with his amiable smile. 'But seriously, I am sorry if he is in danger.'

'Can I help?' asked Hawkeye. 'Maybe we could ride out tonight with some of my men.'

'I hardly liked to ask, Lord Hawkeye. We have duties to our guests, however. They would hardly take kindly to being abandoned upon a whim.'

'First thing tomorrow morning then. That is a promise.'

A herald called for silence, as the kings made the pairings for the semi-finals. Hawkeye was no longer apprehensive. Already he had fulfilled the expectations of his men. Further success would exceed them, whilst gallant failure would be excused. The one certainty was that he would not fight Ottar, for the two Sferians would be kept apart.

Hyglack's name was first out of the Gothic cup, Ottar's from that of the Sfear. Hawkeye would ride last, against the black knight.

'YOUR armour, my lord.'

Hawkeye raised his arms to allow Leofric to fasten the straps. 'How is Dandy?'

'Well enough, my lord, to help unhorse the black knight.'

'I hope so.' Hawkeye frowned. 'Is naught known about this black knight at all? It's most strange.'

'Nothing, my lord. I have made enquiry of friends amongst the Goths, but they are as mystified as we are. Be of good cheer. Both Numa and Syrdan fought ill against him.'

That was what Hawkeye was afraid of. In both bouts, normally bold horseman had flinched as they neared their adversary, as if seized with sudden fear. Should he do the same, he could imagine Prince Ali elaborating with relish upon his shortcomings of valour. 'He drew a mile,' he could still hear his rival's superior tones. 'Nay, a league.'

Outside the tent, the groom helped him to mount. Dandy was as good as gold, unmoved, yet ears pricked and alert. Hawkeye slapped his neck in appreciation before donning his gauntlets.

Ottar and Hyglack were making their salutes. Hyglack bore the green and gold favour of his wife, Elfryth; Ottar that of his, Tanara. Ottar was a big man, Hyglack huge. Excitement amongst the crowd was at fever pitch, despite the feeling that the Fates had sold them short. The two greatest warriors in the north should surely not have met before the final. As it was, the winner would be strongly tipped to beat Hawkeye - for Hawkeye it would presumably be; the black knight's run of luck had got to end. A pity, yet neither Goth nor Sfear would have considered interfering with the verdict of the Norns; they had decided that Ottar and Hyglack should meet at this stage, so it would be.

'Good luck, Ottar,' called Hawkeye, as his countryman stood ready to depart. The prince smiled acknowledgment and dropped his visor. The giant Goth at the far end of the lists did the same, and the crowd was hushed. For the Goths this was their last chance of glory; if Hyglack fell, the championship would fall with him. And for the Sfear it was almost as important, for few believed that Hawkeye could prevail should Ottar fall.

They lowered their lances, the marshal gave the sign, and they moved off, gathering speed every second. Within moments, the crowd would see one or other defeated for the first time. They met and clashed; neither made any mistake that Hawkeye could detect, moving their lances late, shields held firm and high. Yet Ottar's weapon found the middle of Hyglack's shield, that of Hyglack the edge, whence it glanced off to strike the Sferian champion full tilt, and pitch him from the saddle to the turf. Mad yells of delight came from the Goths, whilst a stifled groan escaped the Sfear. Ottar, their mightiest warrior, had fallen. Hyglack pounded on past the Sferian tent, arm raised in triumph.

'Fair and square,' said Hawkeye ruefully.

His squire nodded. 'It rests with you now, my lord.'

'Aye, so it does,' came a woman's calm voice. 'Be of good heart, Hawkeye.'

He looked down in surprise to see Ljani the Red gazing at him intently. 'Why, think you that I am not?'

She betrayed none of her usual confusion when talking to him. 'This black knight has powers, you think.'

'It had occurred to me ... Numa and Syrdan ...'

'They drew,' she said impatiently, 'like nervous novices. Surely you noticed that.'

'Aye, that they did.'

'It is the gaze of the black knight, like that of the stoat to the hare. Do not meet his gaze, Lord Hawkeye. Look away. Numa and Syrdan fell victim to their own fear. Conquer yourself, my lord, and you will overcome the black knight.'

He had no time to reply before the trumpets sounded for the last joust but one. Hawkeye urged his mount forward and knelt alongside the black knight before the kings, dipping his lance in salute. He glanced at the women - Wanda cheerful and apparently confident of his success, Roslindis withdrawn and nervous-looking. Scheming against him, no doubt. The murderous slut. He would have to consider what to do about that; she might well try again. The most drastic solution of all might not be out of the question. But Hawkeye had never killed a woman ...

On the way to the start he remembered that he had omitted Wanda's favour, which until now he had always worn in his helm. It was too late to do anything about it, which worried him obscurely.

They were opposite each other, the all-black figure staring at him intently. Hawkeye, who dropped his gaze to no man, stared back.

As his name suggested, Hawkeye had better vision than any man in the north. At that distance most would have seen no more than a blur for their adversary's face, but he could still make out detail. And he could have sworn, at the moment before his enemy dropped his visor, that in the dark hollow of his helm, the black knight had no face at all. An illusion, of course, he told himself impatiently. But he was not convinced. In the shapeless blackness he had seen, nay rather sensed, something so dreadful, of such obscene horror, something beyond the grave, he knew not what ... Yet an illusion it must have been, for now he could see two bright yellow eyes shining out of the darkness, and felt a sudden chill descend upon him. For in the black knight's gaze he saw defeat, despair and death, the hopelessness and futility of his life, all that he had ever failed in, every humiliating and unworthy thing that he had ever done. And above all he felt fear - blind panic that bid him throw down his lance and flee the field.

They were trotting now, Hawkeye's mind fluttering back and forth like a trapped bird in feeble attempt to escape. At last, with defeat staring him in the face, it lighted upon the voice of a girl: 'Conquer yourself, my lord ...'

Ljani had been right. Whether he triumphed or fell, he would not flinch. His countrymen expected better of him; so did his cousin's men, even his enemies the Goths. And, which was more, and most of all, so he did of himself. Hawkeye was no longer afraid of defeat, or death, or anything but dishonour, and urged Dandy on, impatient for the fray, concentrating his attention on the dark figure of his enemy with the featureless shield. As the horses neared each other, he moved his lance slightly, as was his wont, and went through manfully with the attack. And in that last half-instant of time before the clash of steel, it was the black knight who faltered, and flinched, and drew from the fight. The lance of the Sferian took him in the breast and toppled him over in defeat, to a tumult of triumphant sound from the ranks of his countrymen.

Hawkeye raised an arm in salute and turned to ride back. All around the ring, the blue and silver Sferian-banners were waving in triumph. Nor was the tribute confined to his countrymen alone. The banners of the Goths were waving too: the Lone Star of the royal house, the arms of the Emundings, of the Southern lords Falgard, Numa and Rigel, and of course the Black Chevron of Slane. Before Hawkeye's tent, Leofric and Faldo were jumping up and down, slapping and embracing each other. Prince Ottar, stifling his own disappointment, was cheering too, as were his wife and children. Both kings were on their feet, applauding wildly. Even Ali, with no trace for once of his superior manner, was clapping and cheering his countryman. Roslindis was tossing her head and laughing. Wanda was in tears of joy, and the girl with red hair who had reminded him of himself ...

'Well done, Sferian!' boomed Prince Hyglack, knocking the breath out of him with a hammer-blow on the back. 'Well done! I had a thousand times rather you win than that black knave!' He raised Hawkeye's mailed fist once more in victory salute, and together they rode the length of the lists, acknowledging the cheers of Goth and Sferian alike.

So the mysterious black knight was defeated with ignominy, and quit the field never to be seen again, either in Wagmunding lands or those of the Goths or Sfear.

Roger Butters

Sixteen

THE EARLY evening sun cast the shadow of the stand to the edge of the lists, still green, but now with a well-worn track along each side of the central barrier. At the south end, the mighty figure of Prince Hyglack sat on a heavy chestnut stallion, the Lone Star of Gothmark on his breast, whilst his shield bore the complex royal quartering of red, blue, silver and gold. North, beside the tent of the Sfear, Athelstan Wagmunding, mounted on a bay, armed black and silver, the chevron and wolf's-head displayed on his shield. A small man by comparison, but he sat well in the saddle.

Hawkeye dropped his visor, and the crowd were still. Nothing moved but the two chargers, Hyglack's pawing the ground impatiently, Dandy contenting himself with a shake of the head. A light evening breeze fluttered the flags and bunting round the arena. After his experience against the black knight, Hawkeye felt almost friendly toward his great rival. Yet for his countrymen it was important that he win; both archery and chariot had fallen to the Goths, and he alone could prevent its becoming a clean sweep.

After what seemed an eternity, Bluemantle threw down the mace, and the final encounter and climax of the three-day tournament was to hand. Soon would be decided whether Hyglack or Hawkeye would win the title Champion of the Lists, and more impor-tant, whether Goth or Sferian would secure the greater honour.

The mighty figure in silver, plumed green and gold, drew near, shield perfectly positioned for cover, lance lowered at just the right angle. For Hyglack, brute force was not enough; he knew the skills of the lists as well as any. To defeat him would require a combination of flawless technique, concentration, flair and nerve, plus more than a little luck. Hawkeye lowered his lance late; they spurred their mounts. There came the crash, as Hawkeye took the Gothic lance on his shield, braced himself, jolted in the saddle, but survived. At the same moment his own lance shattered to pieces against the shield of his adversary. He glanced back. Hyglack was still in place. Massive cheers and counter-cheers proclaimed the fact that both champions remained undefeated.

A fanfare sounded, and Bluemantle announced unnecessarily that neither warrior had been unhorsed. Slaves cleared the splintered lances from the lists, as Hawkeye threw the stump of his weapon aside.

'Unusual, for both to break a lance,' commented the armourer beside the Gothic tent, throwing Hawkeye a replacement. 'Good luck to both of you, my lord,' he added courteously.

Hawkeye acknowledged, weighed the new lance in his hand, and made ready, heart pounding from his exertions and sudden release of tension. During the second passage of arms, he knew from experience that both he and his adversary would be vulnerable. Slightly out of breath, with an unfamiliar lance, half their minds still on the previous encounter, with difficulty keying themselves up again. He must concentrate extra hard, wipe the last couple of minutes from his mind, and approach the affair afresh.

Hyglack was ready again, lance and shield positioned as before. For the second time, Bluemantle's arm fell. The horsemen closed. Hawkeye levelled his gaze at the target, the top left-hand quarter of Hyglack's shield. If he could place his lance there, it should spin off and take his opponent in the body.

Suddenly he was aware of a blurred vision of light and colour, a crash, and great confusion. At first, he thought he must have unhorsed Hyglack, then came a sharp pain in his right shoulder, and a sudden thump. In the instant before he hit the ground and darkness closed in, he realized that for the first time in his life he had been defeated in the joust.

AS always, hearing returned first. 'Practice,' Hawkeye heard an angry Sferian voice. 'Nonsense, fair and square,' 'Dirty fighting,' and much foul language.

He opened his eyes.

'Are you all right, my lord?' enquired an anxious face above him. Leofric, his squire.

Hawkeye felt the back of his head. 'A little sore, that's all. Disappointed. Ah!' He caught his breath as pain stabbed through his shoulder.

'Take care, my lord,' Leofric advised. 'I pulled the lance out while you were senseless, and padded the wound as best I could. Move slowly.'

138

'Was I unhorsed?' he enquired foolishly.

'By practice, my lord,' his squire assured him. 'The lances were not of equal weight or size. The Goth used a battle lance, several inches too long.'

Jousting lances were lightweight, to avoid causing injury. 'Were they not checked?' asked Hawkeye, forcing the fog from his brain.

'Aye, the first pair. But if you remember, my lord, they shattered. Replacements are not checked - a flaw in the procedures of the lists, no doubt, but they are required so seldom.'

Hawkeye struggled to his feet, aided by Leofric. 'Is this true?'

'Of course it is not true,' came Hyglack's angry reply. 'Do you think I would not have noticed such a thing?'

'I'm sure you would.' Hawkeye recognized the light superior tones of Prince Ali.

Hyglack laid a hand on his sword. 'Say that again.'

'Part them!' cried a dozen voices, as their blades clashed.

'Hold!' sounded one of more authority. Bluemantle, Marshal of the Lists, strode forward. He was an elderly man, who feared no-one. 'Put up your weapons, while we enquire into matters calmly. Let the lances be produced.'

'Here they are,' said Ali. 'Ours within the regulation size and weight, I think you will find.'

'Lay it on the ground, with the other.'

Hyglack complied with very ill grace. 'A foot or more overlong,' announced Bluemantle. 'Indeed, almost fifteen inches.' He weighed it in his hand. 'And much overweight, as is apparent from the thickness alone. A battle lance. You were not vanquished, Wagmunding, but cheated and traduced.'

'Make your decision then,' invited Ali, who seemed to have appointed himself spokesman for the Sfear.

'It grieves me to do so,' said the Marshal, 'but I have no choice. By virtue of the powers invested in me by the Kings of Gothmark and the Sfear, I here proclaim Athelstan Wagmunding, Earl of Karron Tha, Champion of the Lists, upon a foul.'

Hyglack, face black with rage, had to be restrained from striking him. 'A Wagmunding servant declares in favour of his own lord. I should have expected no other.'

'Wagmunding housekarl he may be,' agreed one of the Sfear, 'but your countryman, not ours. Even he is convinced.'

'You talk nonsense, Hyglack,' said Bluemantle. 'Your guilt is plain for all to see. If you have any explanation, let us have it.'

'What, find me guilty first, then call for my defence? You shall not have it.'

'In that case, Prince Hyglack, you admit your guilt. I confirm my decision.'

'Stay a bit,' came a new voice, calmer and slower than most. Rigel of Rigel, a man greatly respected, whom none had ever known to lose his temper, had appeared on the scene. 'I am most loath to believe ill of my friend and lord, Prince Hyglack, ever a most valiant champion. Let us hear what he has to say.'

Hyglack looked sulky.

'I implore you, my lord,' urged Rigel. 'If you speak not, dishonour will fall upon us all.'

'Very well,' said Hyglack, a shade placated. 'In truth, I admit I did not check the lance before the second passage of arms. Does anyone ever do so?'

Bluemantle was adamant. 'Could you not tell by the weight? An experienced warrior like you.'

'No, I could not,' shouted Hyglack, losing his temper again. 'Nor could anyone in the middle of a fight. Beforehand is a different matter. Come, Karron Tha, I concede the business betwixt us is not settled. We will ride tomorrow.'

Hawkeye shook his head dizzily and staggered. 'He is not fit, my lord,' he heard Leofric say. 'Nor will be this week or more. That should be obvious.'

'I have been thinking,' observed Rigel quietly. 'At the second passage of arms, the combatants had changed ends. Prince Hyglack would have been rearmed not by his own man, but by the Sfear.'

In their rage and confusion, all but him had overlooked this. 'Why, that proves I am free of guilt,' said Hyglack inaccurately. 'Look amongst your own countrymen, Wagmunding, for him who has betrayed you.'

Leofric was almost apoplectic with fury. 'Do you believe this of me, my lord?' he managed to Hawkeye at last.

'Of course not,' Hawkeye assured him wearily. 'No-one accuses you.'

'Prince Hyglack does. Am I the man, my lord? Am I the man?'

In different circumstances, thought Hawkeye, the spectacle of his short fat servant jumping up and down to challenge the mighty prince could have been comic.

'I know not,' said Hyglack impatiently. 'Do you expect me to tell one slave from another in the middle of a fight?'

'Slave! You call me slave, my lord?'

'Calm yourself, my good fellow,' said Bluemantle. 'This was not the man; he stood aside from the lists once he had armed the Earl of Karron Tha.'

Hyglack nodded reluctantly. 'I admit, it does not look like the man to me.'

'I take that as an apology, my lord,' said Leofric stiffly.

'Who would have rearmed Prince Hyglack?' enquired Bluemantle. 'Does anyone know?'

Hawkeye was feeling a little better, and thought it time he contributed. 'Faldo, I expect, one of my grooms. Also a most decent fellow.'

'Let him come forth,' said the marshal, 'and explain himself.'

'My lords! My lords! Murder!'

'Ye gods,' groaned Hawkeye. 'What now?'

A couple of servants ran up in heat, followed by a steward of the lists. 'The Sferian groom is slain. A dagger in the throat.'

'When was this done?'

'But a few minutes since, my lord. The blood is scarcely dry.'

'Here is treachery indeed,' said Bluemantle. 'A most vile and murderous plot. Who threw you the lance, Hyglack? Him or another?'

'I told you, I know not. I never knew the fellow who was slain, so how can I tell?'

'It seems to me,' said Rigel, 'that this is a deep-laid scheme indeed; with what object is difficult to say. Some vicious knave slew your servant, Hawkeye, and stood in for him with the illegal lance.'

'That may be so,' agreed the marshal. 'Indeed it seems most likely. But my decision is unchanged. The Earl of Karron Tha was unhorsed illegally, and is clearly unfit to continue. Responsibility for checking the lance lay with Prince Hyglack, who therefore loses. As to whether he has done anything morally disgraceful, it is not necessary for me to make a decision.'

There were noises of angry dissent from the Goths. 'How do we know,' demanded one of Hyglack's henchmen, 'that this is not some Sferian plot to discredit our lord?'

'Aye, true,' agreed another. 'They well knew he could not be unhorsed in fair fight.'

A Sferian knocked him down, and within seconds a dozen had joined the melee. In the confusion someone stumbled into Hawkeye, and the pain flooded back. He must have passed out again, for the next thing he was conscious of was a harsh voice of unquestioned authority. King Angantyr, who had not been present before.

'Clear away this rabble. Hyglack, your guilt is admitted even by Bluemantle, your own countryman. The honours of the tournament therefore belong to us.'

'Never!' he heard Hyglack shout.

'And further note, Prince Hyglack, if no man else dare speak it: I here call thee coward, traitor, and nything - a man without honour.'

Angantyr, though an old man, had ever been rash to a fault. The dread word 'nything' was an insult to a slave. To a warrior it could only be wiped out in blood.

Hawkeye raised his glance at the instant of the blow. The fierce old king fell backward into the arms of his henchmen. A trickle of blood ran from the corner of his mouth into the silvery beard. Both Goth and Sferian fell silent.

'Put up your swords,' he ordered his men. 'They shall have work enough to do another day. For that blow, Gothic slave, ten thousand men shall fall. It means war.'

Seventeen

'HAGALAZ, NAUTHIZ, Isa, Jera, Perth, Ywaz, Algiz, Sowelu, Teiwaz, Berkana, Ehwaz, Mannaz, Laguz, Inguz, Othila, Daguz.'

'Very good, my lord,' said Suth. 'That is the fourth day running that you have recited the futhark perfectly without help from me. There is little danger of your ever forgetting it now.'

Beowulf shook his head. 'That is all very well, but I still cannot read or write as quickly as I would wish.'

'Speed is entirely a matter of practice, my lord. It is important that you try to read something every day, and preferably writing too, even if it is only copying something out.'

'Finding time may be difficult from now on. But I prefer having something to do.'

The last week had been frustrating for the Goths, detained in Targon by persistent storms. Even now the sea was far from calm, but they had decided to embark. The imminence of war with the Sfear meant that every day was precious. So it was that Beowulf now sat with Suth at the tiller of the longship *Freya*, watching the foam of the wake fan out towards the receding waterfront. Before them, a dozen pairs of oars cleft the grey, choppy waters of the Gothic Strait. The Isles were less than five leagues distant, but even with fair weather they would be lucky to make land before nightfall.

'You will indeed be kept busy today, my lord.'

'All of us will. Navigating the strait in autumn is no task for the idle.'

'Starboard one point!' cried Ifar from the bow, continuing 'Steady as she goes!' as Beowulf and the oarsmen complied. Within a mile of Targon, the East Current already flowed at five knots, and by midstream

143

it could reach a dozen. To make straight course for the Isles the *Freya* would have to steer further and further to starboard, so that by the time she was halfway her silver serpent-head would be pointing south-east by south. Finally, if they were lucky, the current would slacken to form small but treacherous eddies near the coast of the Gothic Isle. Not a trip for the faint-hearted, especially as there was doubt about their ultimate reception.

'I think we have made the right decision,' Beowulf continued, half to himself. 'The runes advised it, and to have returned without attempting the journey, on the strength of a mere rumour, might have been regarded as irresolute.'

'At least I am glad to see the back of Port Targon.'

'It's not to everyone's taste,' he admitted, 'but funnily enough I have always liked the place. And the Duke seems to have done more good than harm.'

'Most certainly he has,' agreed Suth with some warmth. 'But I cannot agree with you about the way it was. A vile and loathsome place, stinking of corruption.'

'It never seemed quite that bad to me. But no doubt you know it better, for you lived here at one time, did you not?'

Though reluctant to talk about her early life, Suth had told him that much. 'Yes, my lord, I was born there. My mother was a slave employed at one of the waterfront taverns.'

'And your father?'

'I never knew him.' She seemed readier to talk than usual. 'My mother died when I was ten, after which I did menial work in the tavern for a year or two, before being ordered to dance for the entertainment of customers.'

'I thought you might have been a dancing slave,' said Beowulf. 'You have dancer's legs.'

'Dancer's legs, my lord?'

'Lean and muscular. Also you are very light on your feet.'

At this compliment Suth flushed with pleasure and turned her gaze upon the dark waters rushing past the stern. 'Be that as it may, my lord, it must have been an amusing spectacle for the customers: a skinny, frightened little thing hopping clumsily about for their entertainment.'

'I should not have found it so.'

'Needless to say, I soon became a whore. I tried to pretend to myself that I was not, but it was expected of me ...'

'Speak no more of it if it distresses you. I'm sure it must have been unpleasant.'

'Unpleasant,' she repeated bitterly. 'Yes, mostly it was. But sometimes, if a man was young and healthy, and did not treat me badly, I took pleasure in it. You see, my lord, what a low, degraded creature I was, and still am.'

'Nonsense. You take things far too seriously.'

She kept her gaze on the water. 'One evening, during the disturbances four years ago, some servants of Ragnar of Torre visited the tavern. Filthy, foul-mouthed ruffians, as are they all. They bought me from the tavern-keeper, and conveyed me to the castle of the Lord of Torre.' She shuddered. 'I will not speak of what was done to me there.'

'This Lord of Torre,' said Beowulf, 'of whom all men seem afraid. We have seen some of his handiwork for ourselves, but what else is known of him? When I enquired of Duke Eugen, he was as vague as you.'

'Few have seen Ragnar, my lord, but dreadful tales are told. 'tis said he keeps a dungeon, deep in the heart of his kingdom, where prisoners are daily tortured for his amusement. Female, and even male slaves, are forced to slake his bestial desires. His servants, vicious, perverted wretches that they are, boast that one day he will rule the whole world. For he well knows the hearts of men, how to corrupt and enslave them by pandering to their secret vices. A man of insane ambition and foully diseased mind.'

Beowulf raised his eyebrows. 'How old is this dread lord?'

'Not an old man. It is thought, about five-and-twenty. Son of the previous count, himself a monster, who died long ago.'

'It cannot be all that long.'

'Five-and-thirty years.'

Beowulf laughed. 'I allow you certain liberties, little slave, because I am a tolerant man and have taken a fancy to you. But even I cannot allow you to pull my leg. It stands to reason that if the Count of Torre numbers no more years than five-and-twenty, his father cannot have been dead much longer than that. Unless you suggest that he rose from the grave to get him.'

'That is one of the stories, my lord. Another is that he was ten years in the womb.'

Beowulf smiled and shook his head. 'I am afraid I have doubts about the whole story. Now, do not scowl at me, little one - I know full well that you have been brutally used by evil men, and doubt not that they serve a savage warlord called Ragnar of Torre. But these stories of his insane perversions and supernatural origin are evidently fables, or at least gross exaggerations, such as are often related of brutal and powerful men.'

'You saw what he did to his servants. Was that a fable?'

'No,' replied Beowulf slowly. 'That was indeed a vile and hideous act of cruelty, yet I have heard of men capable of such things. I not deny, the Lord of Evil may act through mortal men. In that, Ragnar is not unique.'

'If he be not unique, my lord, there is small hope for Middle Earth. I have told you a couple of versions of his conception.'

'And I did not believe either of them.'

'On the whole, my lord, neither do I. An alternative account seems to me more likely, yet if anything even worse.'

'Go on.'

'It is said that the old count, himself as I said a vicious and dissolute man, fathered but two legitimate children, twins, a boy and girl, hideously deformed in both mind and body. These creatures were mercifully dead before the age of twenty, but Ragnar of Torre is their son. A monstrous progeny, got by the boy upon the body of his own sister.'

'How very unpleasant. No doubt, being the incestuous offspring of two creatures themselves deformed, he is warped in body as well as mind.'

'No, my lord, strangely not. For all agree that Ragnar of Torre is a man of goodly stature, fair of face, whose countenance betrays nothing of the filth and corruption of his soul.'

'None of the tales seems very likely to me.'

'I know another, my lord, most terrifying of all. Some say, he is not the issue of humankind at all, but one of the Sons of Muspelheim, spawn of the Lord of the Fire, whom men dare not name ... They who will ride over Bifrost on the last day ...'

'Where is this land called Torre, anyway?' he demanded brusquely. Mention of the Last Day was not popular amongst the Northmen, even to a man as cheerful and easygoing as Beowulf. For no man knew when it would be, whether ten thousand years hence, or tomorrow.

'In the east,' said Suth vaguely. 'But the Lord of Torre in recent times has extended his power. He now lives, 'tis said, in Yflon, where the weird beasts dwell.'

Yflon was the old name for the Lost Land of Fanora. There had always been strange tales about it. 'Hm,' said Beowulf doubtfully. 'Well, Suth, you have scared me silly with your tales of horror, so I now propose to take a hand at the oars and drive such morbid fancies out of my head. Being short-handed we must all take a turn. Except for you, of course.'

'Why not me?' demanded Suth indignantly.

Beowulf laughed. 'Because, tiny one, you are so small and weakly that if you were to take an oar the boat would go round in circles.'

She stood and stamped her foot like a child. 'You are unbearably condescending, my lord. I can pull an oar as well as any man.'

'Right, silly slave,' he said. 'Just for that, I shall give you an oar. When you flake out, which will happen before the time it takes to tell a hundred, I shall first of all say I told you so, then as punishment I shall make you carry on for another dozen pulls. After that I expect to hear no more nonsense about your being the equal of a man.'

'And if I am right?'

'If you are right, which is impossible, I will personally apologize to you, and prepare your meal for you this evening, instead of the other way round.'

'Good,' said Suth. 'I shall not let you off either, you smug brute. Now lead me to the oar.'

SHE was far stronger than Beowulf had expected, with hard little muscles beneath her soft skin. She knew how to wield an oar, and would not admit defeat. For the first half-hour, she stuck to the task with little sign of fatigue, keeping pace with the others in deep, even strokes. After that the limitations of her slight frame began to tell, but she gritted her teeth and pulled as strongly as ever. Beowulf became worried. The normal shift for a man was an hour, followed by half an hour's rest. Suth would not be up to that; on the other hand she would not thank him for stopping her.

In the event he was saved from a decision, though not in the way he would have wished. Clouds to the south and west had been gathering for some time, blotting out the setting moon, and a cold breeze was followed by a few spots of rain. The whales and other monsters often seen in the strait were absent, having sought the calm and safety of the depths. White horses split the dark-grey waves, and bitter spray splashed up to douse the sweating oarsmen. They set course further and further south, but the wind and current would not be denied. Though Beowulf pulled as strongly as ever, many flagged, and the struggle was unavailing. The black coastline of the Gothic Isle, faintly visible on the horizon, slipped gradually from beam to larboard bow, and thence to the serpenthead. Kjartan lashed the tiller and scrambled forward, soaked and shivering despite his furs. Beowulf bent his head to hear.

'We shan't make it, my lord!'

By now, that was obvious. The isle was but a single point to larboard, and within minutes would disappear behind the great curve of the prow. Wind and current were bearing them north-east, beyond the Isles, into the vast emptiness of the Great Eastern Sea, whence none had ever returned. Some said that the ocean continued for ever, with tides so strong it was impossible to turn back; others that ships fell off the world into the Great Void. Ljani however had explained to Beowulf that round the edge of Midgard the sea became frozen into great mountains of ice which crushed the strongest ship to fragments. He had no doubt that this explanation was correct.

'Change course!' he yelled. 'Four points to starboard!'

Kjartan passed the order to the bow. They headed straight into the

storm, but dared not do otherwise. To run before it would be to risk the
Eastern Sea, the ice or the Great Void. Yet the course they had chosen
was almost as hazardous, into the blackness of the lightning-shattered
sky. Mountains of water loomed behind the prow, hidden from the
oarsmen until the waves broke over them. Gasping and spluttering, they
battled helplessly against wind and tide. Every man not rowing was
baling, with waterjars, helmets, jugs, even bare hands. The useless mast
had long since snapped.

'Overboard with sail and tent!' Beowulf ordered. 'Cargo too!
Anything to lighten her!'

The sail and unfurled tent for sleeping-quarters were heaved into
the sea, with many a stout weapon and shield, ruined food and ale-kegs,
furs and treasury. Their goal was no longer the Isles, but survival.

'We could do with coming further to larboard, my lord,' gasped
Kjartan, hair plastered in strands over his forehead as water streamed
down his face. 'What say you?'

'One point only. It's as much as we dare.'

If a wave took them abeam, it would roll them over like a log
downhill. The full fury of the storm now struck the starboard bow,
swamping the desperate oarsmen in a tidal deluge.

'Ship oars! Every man to bale!'

In an instant the *Freya* spun stern to wind and was tossed like a
cork, running before the storm at a score of knots or more. The rain was
a thick curtain, a wall of water, more solid than liquid. Beowulf baled for
his life. Water was in his eyes, his neck, nose and mouth. Up to his
ankles, now his knees. Yet still the sturdy *Freya* kept afloat. When the
end came, it would be sudden.

Beowulf paid little attention to the others, yet occasionally
glimpsing those nearest: Kjartan, grimly baling, now turning to bellow
orders: Dardo urging on the Hrosnabergers with earthy language: and
Suth, scrambling about in the bilge-water, baling, throwing things
overboard, or helping a man who had tripped and fallen. Alone of all of
them, she was smiling through the rain and wind, the deafening tumult
of the waves and thunder, crash of lightning, the curses and the groans
of timber. She seemed not the least afraid, rather invigorated by the
activity and danger. This quality was rare in men; he had never before
observed it in a woman. He also noticed that never in his whole life had
he seen anyone so wet. They were all soaked, but Suth, in the
transparent linen of her livery, was absolutely saturated. In different
circumstances the effect might have been erotic, for all that she had such
a skinny little body. As it was he felt moved to insane laughter.

'What ails you, my lord?' she asked in concern.

'Nothing,' he shouted foolishly, 'save that you are rather wet.'

She pulled a face and threw a bucket of water over him - a mad act, yet in the chaos none noticed. And what did it matter? They were in the hands of the gods; one bucketful could make no difference.

'Think you we should pray, my lord?' asked Kjartan.

Beowulf shook his head. 'If Thor and Njord be angry with us, so be it. Do Gothic warriors need fawn on them for favours?'

'Well spoken, my lord,' said Dardo heartily, in the intervals between baling. 'I have no time for toadying, whether to men or gods. Trust in ourselves alone. Are we not the heirs of Longspear?'

Longspear, Beowulf remembered, had prayed not for success, but for courage. And curiously enough, from the moment that thought crossed his mind, it seemed the tempest abated; though the wind still blew strongly, thunderbolts still split the sky, and waters piled up on either side, he felt no fear. Waves broke over the decks of the *Freya*, but her timbers were sound, and held firm as smoothly and swiftly she ran before the tide. At long last the stars peeped through again as the clouds drifted away to the north-east. The Goths continued to bale as long as they could, cleared all but a few inches, and one by one collapsed in exhaustion.

Ifar crawled to the stern through the bilgewater. 'Where the hell are we?'

Beowulf shrugged. 'The gods alone know. Too far north, that's certain. Give everyone a quarter of an hour's rest, then to the oars again. Row west.'

That was their only hope. With luck they might fetch up somewhere on the coast of Fanora. North and east lay the endless sea, and they could never make headway against the tide to the south.

'Couple of casks of fresh water left,' grunted Ifar, reading Beowulf's thoughts. 'And one man lost: Ingeld, your farrier.'

At the height of the storm, he had stood upright, with fatal results. 'Be of good cheer, my lord,' advised Suth, detecting his mood. 'Thor and Njord have spared us; they will not change their minds now.'

'Land ho! Land ho! Land off the larboard bow!'

The Goths almost capsized the boat in their scramble to see. The lookout, Anselm, was right - the blurred outline of low cliffs poked above the pale horizon.

'Oars!' Beowulf yelled. 'Hard a-starboard! The twelve strongest pairs of men! Give it everything you've got!'

The exhausted warriors grabbed the oars and heaved. Kjartan jammed the tiller starboard and lashed it. If the tide bore them beyond the headland, they would be in the Great Eastern Sea, and as good as dead men. The prow came round, but the current bore them almost broadside.

'Two more points to larboard!'

The oarsmen groaned and cursed as they took the full force of the current on the bow. The *Freya* scarcely seemed to move as the black waves slid past at five leagues an hour, yet bit by bit she edged toward their goal. Slowly and painfully, the coast drew nearer, but all too soon the headland appeared on the starboard quarter.

'Rocks! Freya's tits, look at them!'

A hundred reared their heads like jagged teeth.

'Hold course!' cried Beowulf. 'Beach her if you can!'

The beach, black grit and gravel, was no more than a cable length distant, but astern the rocks of the headland drew nearer. The *Freya* was driven on to them willy-nilly. For every yard gained by a stroke of the oars, the tide bore them north five times as far. They braced themselves for the impact.

'When we strike,' Beowulf ordered, 'hold on to everything you can - oars, driftwood. It'll be every man for himself.'

There came the grating sound he had been dreading. He had expected some warning while the ship settled, but instead the bottom opened up as if sheared by a giant sword.

'Abandon ship!' cried Ifar needlessly, as the water rose to their armpits. Beowulf committed himself to the sea, little afraid for himself, for the strongest swimmer in Gothmark rashly fancied himself a match for even the mighty Eastern Current. Around him, heads were bobbing like corks. Some men grabbed oars to give themselves buoyancy; elsewhere shattered timber littered the surface of the flood. The serpenthead reared for the last time, and with a sudden plunge took to the depths. Any still on board would be lost, but most seemed to have got off. The poorer swimmers were trusting to their oars as the current pushed them northward into danger. With sudden panic Beowulf realized he could not see Suth.

Thirty yards from shore, the current died as if turned off by a giant tap. With ten yards to go his feet touched bottom, and he waded on to the shingle, frozen and dripping, but safe at last. A couple of Hrosnabergers had beaten him to it; Ifar and Kjartan were close behind. For the next few minutes the growing band of survivors endured the agonizing sight of their comrades drifting past while they remained powerless to help, save by shouting and waving encouragement. Those swept beyond the headland would be doomed, but the majority were going to make it. Though sick at heart, Beowulf kept count. A dozen, fifteen, now twenty. And others were floundering amongst the shallow waters of the headland. If they did not panic, or succumb suddenly to fatigue or cold, they should be all right. As each man stopped swimming and began to wade, his countrymen ashore gave him a cheer and rushed to his assistance. Three-and-twenty.

'You look sorrowful, my lord,' said Kjartan. 'But surely our chances are much improved. Nearly all have made it.'

The pain was almost more than he could bear. Fortunately the wind and rain had covered his face with water anyway. 'Aye. But I was thinking of one who has not. Such a brave little creature, too.'

'As to that,' said Tirl, 'the last I saw of her she was clinging to an oar and paddling strongly for the headland. I expect she is amongst those who have fetched up there.'

Bewoulf had not run fifty yards before he saw the tiny dark figure scrambling ashore through the rocks. Despite his fatigue he plunged into the breakers and dragged her out. She was soaked and frozen, but far from exhausted.

'I am really quite able to manage unaided, my lord,' she scolded, though not to his way of thinking too displeased.

He was kissing her all over her wet, happy little face, and she was kissing him back. 'Come here,' he said harshly, and crushed her to him. This time his kiss was fierce, even brutal.

She responded at first, then struggled and tore her mouth away. 'No, no, my lord! No!'

He let her go, expecting her to run away, but she knelt before him in the waves, shaking with cold and humiliation.

'Forgive me, my lord,' she stammered. 'Slut that I am to lead you on and change my mind.'

'Stand up, little one,' he said kindly. 'You make too much of things, as usual. I had thought you dead, and was overcome by my feelings for the moment. Next time I shall be more considerate. If there is a next time.'

'Please let there be a next time, my lord. It is just that I do not feel ready yet. I do not understand myself.'

'Well, I understand you perfectly, Suth. You have oft been abused in the past, and now need more sensitive treatment than you have just received from a thoughtless oaf like me. Let's make our way back. If we stand here like this much longer, we shall begin to make ourselves conspicuous.'

Roger Butters

Eighteen

A ROLL-CALL revealed that in addition to Ingeld, three Hrosnabergers had been lost, swept beyond the headland whilst clinging to an oar. Their party now numbered twenty-nine. There was not a scrap of food between them, and ironically less than five gallons in their waterbags. A chill wind blew in from the sea, but a brief search enabled the shivering band to find a cave where they huddled together in groups of two or three for warmth. Beowulf, Kjartan and Anselm formed one such group, together with Suth, who snuggled into the crook of Beowulf's huge arm and was asleep within seconds.

For his part, Beowulf slept little, wedged uncomfortably between damp rocks, watching moisture running down the walls. He was also more than a little disturbed by Suth nestling against him. She looked younger when asleep, indeed she was really not at all ill-favoured. Even within a week she had begun to fill out, and it was not surprising that he had forgotten himself with her just now. She was a funny little thing, always veering from one mood to another, and incapable of the least disguise of her feelings. A couple of days ago she had asked him if he was married, and when he said no she had wandered about with a smile on her face for the rest of the day.

A pity that she did not take more care of her appearance. Perhaps the ordeals she had suffered at the hands of men meant that she was afraid of looking too attractive, and her rejection of him might somehow be connected with that. Like the odd habit she had of washing herself several times a day, as if she felt permanently dirty. He was still trying to puzzle it out as he fell asleep.

At dawn the sky began to lighten over the sea, confirming that they had been cast up on the east coast of the mainland. The day was clear and the air fresh, but less cold than the previous day.

The travellers were assembled outside the cave. 'We march south for Targon,' announced Beowulf briskly. 'The water ration is two mouthfuls each, until the midday rest.' Fortunately the atmosphere was damp and the day would not be warm.

A Hrosnaberger raised a hand. 'Do we know where we are, my lord?'

The leaders had discussed this the previous night. 'No idea,' confessed Beowulf frankly. 'At a guess, four or five days' march.'

They scaled the low cliffs and set off to the south-west. Wet and hungry, most went bare-headed, and scarcely a dozen had managed to retain their swords. But Beowulf and his captains had insisted that they march like soldiers, rather than shamble along as they pleased. This, and the morning sun, helped raise their spirits. Tirl had lost his rebec in the storm but undeterred, led them in the singing of the one song known to all in the Lands between the Lakes, *The March of the Wagmundings:*

> 'Silver is the banner
> > Sable is the bend;
> Dreadful to a foe, but
> > Ever faithful to a friend ...
> Archer and swordsman,
> > Housekarl and thane,
> We march in the cause
> > Of Wagmunding of Slane ...'

The Hrosnabergers responded with another traditional Gothic air, *The Song of the Sword.* Both songs had coarse parodies, but with their leaders present the men confined themselves to the original versions.

For mile upon mile they marched through scrub and marram-grass, then down on to the beach between the dunes, and up once more to what seemed to be a roughly trodden coastal path atop the cliff. This, the first sign of human agency, cheered them still further. They were a fine race, thought Beowulf. No grumbling over the fact that their mission thus far had been an abject failure; no sign of depression at the daunting prospect ahead, just a calm acceptance of their fate, and the will of the gods.

Strange sea-birds kept them company, of a type unknown in Gothmark. Now and again a whale-serpent broke the surface of the sea, as the marine giants returned with the advent of calmer weather. Anselm was the first to point out a great bat-lizard, likewise indigenous to Fanora, hovering motionless a hundred yards offshore. Opinion differed, but it was widely believed they lived on fish. This was confirmed soon after, as the marine flyer closed its leathery wings and plummeted into the water, to emerge moments later with a snake-fish in its beak.

'Wish it was as easy as that for us,' commented Ifar.

Beowulf nodded. 'Crabs and shellfish might be the answer for the time being. One or two of us could try our luck during the midday break.'

In fact shortly afterwards the featureless land ahead began to fall away steeply. 'Could be the approach to a river mouth,' Kjartan suggested.

'Targon?' asked an optimistic Hrosnaberger, immediately ridiculed by his more experienced fellows.

'No such luck, I'm afraid,' Beowulf explained kindly. 'Unless my navigation be much at fault, we are many leagues too far north for that.'

It was a sizable river for all that, broadening into a muddy estuary. As they descended the slippery incline, too steep to be called a hillside, too gentle for a cliff, they were delighted to glimpse a medium-sized town on the far bank.

'Steady, men,' Ifar warned, restraining their enthusiasm. 'We know not whether the inhabitants be friendly. Halt for the present. What say you, Beowulf Wagmunding?'

'Most strange,' he agreed, as the little band came to a stop and perched amidst the bracken and bushes on the slope. 'I know of no town on the east coast save Targon.'

The Goths were vague about anything lying north of the Isles. Even Ljani's map, saved from the sea by being strapped to Beowulf's bodybelt, was of little help. The damp and blotted parchment showed no town in Fanora, but simply pictures of mountain, swamp and dragons.

'Nor I,' confessed Kjartan. 'Could it be that we have somehow or other circumnavigated the whole of the Northlands, and fetched up at one of the northern ports of the Sfear, say Janfar Delee?'

'I doubt it,' said Beowulf. 'No-one has ever made the north-east passage before, in fact the map shows it blocked off by ice. Besides, in that case the sun would surely have risen over the land.'

'I know Janfar, anyway,' said Dardo, putting the matter beyond doubt. 'Nothing like it.'

'Yet it seems a fine-looking town,' said Ifar, noting its golden temples and public buildings, spacious walks and town houses. 'Funny that there are no farmsteads or villages about. Nor any sign of life. And somehow foreign, don't you think?'

'Exactly what I was going to say. Of course, I've never seen the Great Empire of the south, but ...'

The truth struck both of them at once, and they groaned in unison. 'Fanora,' said Beowulf, pointing to the map, where the name had been obscured by a blotted crease. 'The abandoned city.'

And so on closer inspection it proved. Fanora City had been the most grandiose conception, and signal failure, in the whole distinguished reign of Swertan the Bastard. Designed originally as a tribute, later a monument, to his wife Fanora the Fey, the city named after her had been part of a grand design to bring the benefits of Gothic civilization to Yflon, Lost Land of the East. Stone from the quarries of Rigel and Silvermount had been shipped to the mouth of the river Yflon, renamed Fanora, and architects, sculptors, masons, carpenters and builders brought in from all over the Northlands. And beyond; Eusebius and Vannius, chief designers of the Great Empire of the Cassars, had been employed to plan a city intended as the showpiece of the northern world. But surrounded by mountains, swamp and forest by land, and treacherous currents by sea, Fanora had been doomed from the start. Swertan had been loath to admit defeat, so that it had taken over twenty years for the money to run out and work to grind to a halt. A handful of Goths had remained for a while, relying on hunting and simple agriculture, but the soil was poor, and after a time the survivors had departed. The shell of a great city had been left, a monument indeed, not to success, but failure.

'We are even further north than we feared,' grunted Ifar. 'How far to Targon?'

'According to tradition,' said Beowulf, 'one-and-fifty leagues, not that I suppose anyone has ever counted it.'

Ifar pulled a resigned face. 'Ye gods, ten days' march. Well, let's have a look at the place. It might be possible to do some foraging, though most of the food will be older than we are.'

THE GOTHS wandered awhile amidst the overgrown ruins. Fanora City was unlike anywhere else in the Northlands; planned as a rival to the cities of the Great Empire, yet fallen as soon as built. A marble column lay in segments across the moss-encrusted slabs of the main thoroughfare; statues of the southern gods and goddesses and the Cassar emperors mingled with those of Gothic leaders such as Swertan and his queen. Some lacked arms or heads, others still stood intact, though scarred and weathered, pitted with dirt and frost-cracked. Near the market square, or Forum of Ironside as it had been called, lay the scattered bones of a long-dead horse, bleached and picked clean by crows. Nowhere was there any sign of life save insects, a few bright-coloured birds, and the occasional lizard scuttling from one sunny rock to another amidst the grass and weeds.

On the north side of the forum, up a broad flight of shallow stone steps, stood the Panthyr, or Hall of the Gods. The southern sculptors had demonstrated a strong tendency to equate the Gothic gods and heroes with their own, so that Odin, Thor, Frey and their kin - seldom depicted by the Goths in any case - appeared in unfamiliar guises, alongside statues of the Great Cassar, whom the citizens of the Empire worshipped as divine. Most disconcerting of all was the fact that most statues, particularly those of the gods, were unclothed.

'I am surprised that Swertan permitted such indecency,' said Kjartan.

'Shocking,' Beowulf agreed. 'Why, look at that one - no detail of his person has been left to the imagination.'

'The Rombergers must indeed be a decadent people,' opined Ifar. 'No wonder their empire is on the point of collapse. There must be no limit to their depravity in private matters.'

Suth giggled.

'Naughty slave,' said Beowulf, smiling in spite of himself. 'You really should not be looking at such things.'

'I never knew you were a prude, my lord. There is nothing indecent about the human body.'

'Well, maybe not,' he conceded reluctantly, 'But amongst the Goths it is not the custom to portray it so blatantly. Take that goddess yonder - Freya, I assume her to be ...'

'She's a big girl,' agreed the grinning Gamli.

'Do you not consider such things wrong, Gamli?' enquired Kjartan seriously.

The Hrosnaberger laughed. For once his superior Dardo supported him, with a wry grin. 'Not really. When you've knocked about as much as I have, you get used to it. None of us are seeing anything we haven't seen before, anyway.'

'No doubt travel has broadened your mind,' said Beowulf, 'but for my part I still find these things difficult to get used to.'

And indeed most of the Goths were of the same opinion. Far from prudish in most respects, they nevertheless tended to avert their eyes from the more explicit statues, or made jokes to cover their embarrassment.

Amongst the strange, indecent, or sinister deities occupying the shadowy marble halls stood one alone who was familiar. Somewhat shorter than the rest, though still taller by far than the average man, a life-size warrior in coat of mail; the lone star on his shield, a long spear in his right hand. Thus far the Goths had surveyed the marble figures with curiosity or embarrassment, but no enthusiasm. Upon sight of their hero and friend, however, every man in the party came to attention and saluted.

'Lord Bjorn looks a little out of place,' commented Ifar.

Beowulf shook his head. 'The Lord of the Goths is at home anywhere. See here, Suth, the greatest man ever born in Gothmark, or, as we believe, in the whole world.'

'Aye,' agreed Ifar, and the others nodded.

'I have heard of Longspear, my lord,' said Suth. 'Strange that such a great man should be accorded but a small statue.'

'Longspear is always depicted life-size,' Beowulf explained. 'It is the custom. And whatever his size, does he not look more of a warrior than any of them?'

'Aye, aye,' agreed his comrades.

'Stand beside him, my lord,' said Suth.

Beowulf cast her a puzzled glance, and complied. To a man the others caught their breath.

'What is it?' Beowulf asked.

Dardo was first to recover. 'The damnedest thing, my lord. Were you to grow a beard ...'

Ifar shook his head. 'My lord,' he said simply, 'you *are* Longspear.'

Nineteen

THE MOMENT passed, and the Goths, if they subsequently referred to it at all, were inclined to treat it as a coincidence, or even a joke. Yet looking back on it in years to come, it seemed to Beowulf that from that time on, a subtle change took place in his companions' attitude toward him. Nothing that he could define, yet maybe a little more respect, and a little less familiarity, as if he were, not a better man than them, but somehow different. But at the time he thought little of it.

'No southern hand carved him, I'll be bound,' said Kjartan. 'None but a Goth could have understood him so well. And he is better maintained than the others. Methinks our countrymen lacked enthusiasm for these foreign gods.'

'The Great Cassar certainly seems to have seen better days,' grinned Beowulf, pointing to the headless statue lying beside its plinth, which bore a pair of feet but nothing else. 'Well, this is all very interesting, but more to the point would be to search the city granaries for food.'

Ifar pulled a face. 'Will any be fit to eat?'

'We shall never know if we don't look. Four parties, seven men to each, can search the four quarters of the city. Anything not positively rotten, however unappetising, must be considered. Also clothing, fabrics, pottery, weapons, anything likely to be of use. We can't afford to be choosy. And be back here within the hour.'

AT mid-morning, the Goths surveyed their booty, amidst much derision for the less wholesome items. Among the finds were some fungus-infested bread, weevil-ridden grain, windfall apples and several dead rodents. On the whole however they had done better than expected. A quantity of flour and salt, stored in tightly-sealed bins, was still edible, as was some wild corn from the fields. Kjartan and his men had done best, in the northern orchards. Wild apples, plums and pears had become smaller and harder than their cultivated ancestors, but accepted gratefully. The haul of fresh meat consisted of two hares, two squirrels, a magpie and a large rat. There was no shortage of wine, cooking utensils, furs or draperies. Most men sat or squatted close to the statue of Longspear, amusing themselves by throwing scraps of inedible food at the foreign deities, to most of whom they had taken a strong dislike.

'That meal was really not too bad,' said Beowulf, wiping his mouth with a forearm. 'Thank you, Suth. That reminds me - I still owe you a meal for your performance with the oar.'

'I have not forgotten, my lord. But as for this meal, it was not only me. Everyone has helped.'

That was true. To leave all cooking and baking to the churls and slaves would have been absurd in the circumstances, and Beowulf had insisted that every man find some employment, skinning food, baking, tent-making or cleaning fruit and tuber-roots. As a result they were well supplied for the time being.

'We could eke out an existence here indefinitely,' Ifar pointed out. 'But of course we must press on.'

'Ten days' march,' sighed Kjartan, 'to reach the place we set out from yesterday. And then what are our plans, my lord?'

Beowulf and Ifar exchanged troubled glances. 'The prospects in Targon are none too good,' Beowulf admitted. 'Last time we were wealthy, and able to purchase and equip a vessel. I am not sure the Duke's tolerance will extend to granting us credit for another.'

'The mules are still ours,' said Ifar. 'We could sell them for what they would fetch - not much after eleven days livery charges, I suppose - but at least we could then make our way back to Rigel.'

'And abandon our mission?'

Ifar shrugged. 'Have we any choice?'

'I suppose not. We have tried, but the gods were against us.'

'Methinks,' said Ifar slowly, 'the gods served us well, for all that we cursed them at the time. It was not meant that we should reach the Isles - had we done so, of a surety we should never have returned.'

'Certainly the Duke thought us foolhardy even to attempt it. He dared not undertake it himself, even with an army at his back.'

'There is no doubt,' agreed Kjartan, 'that some evil has overtaken the Isles; what it is we have no means of knowing. It is well that we abandon this mission. None can fairly criticize us; as you say, my lord, we tried, and that against the odds.'

Now that they had finally decided to abandon the ill-fated enterprise, all felt much relieved. No-one had much wanted to be the first to suggest it; once agreed, however, reasons justifying the decision flowed thick and fast. The Isles had already fallen, so much seemed certain; the venture was rash, probably impossible; the gods had been against them, and yet for all that, they had tried. If they were to be criticized, surely it should be upon the grounds of recklessness rather than cowardice. And yet ...

Dardo swigged the last of his wine and threw an over-ripe pear at a well-developed female statue. It splattered on one of her ample protuberances. 'Got you, my beauty. Right in the titty. For all that, my lords,' he continued, 'it seems to me our journey could fairly be said to have turned out somewhat ingloriously.'

The others looked uncomfortable, and made vague noises of dissent.

'Nay, my lords, you know it as well as I. The Goths are not a tolerant people. If we return bootless, but with our force mainly intact, there will be those who call us dastard, behind our backs if not to our face. I have been thinking, and I have a plan.'

The others fell silent. Since setting out, Beowulf and the men of Slane had learnt a great respect for Dardo. A year or two short of forty, since Saward's death he was the oldest warrior, and the most experienced. He spoke little, and was not an immediately likable man, yet what he did say was usually worth hearing. From Ifar Beowulf had heard that Dardo was widely travelled, having visited not only Targon and the Land of the Sfear, but the Dannish and Teuton domains of the south. As a soldier of fortune, he had taken part in the great slaughter of Forestmount, when the Teutonic lords had destroyed three whole legions of the mighty Cassar. His reputation in Hrosnaberg as a fighting man and survivor was second to none.

'We are listening, Dardo,' Ifar prompted.

'Very well. My idea is thus - may I see your map, my lord?' he asked Beowulf.

'Of course.'

'It is as I thought,' said Dardo. 'We must be nigh on ten days' march yet from Targon. Say the best part of another week overland to Rigel, and a three or four-day journey upstream to Slane. Even if all went well, we should not see much change out of a month, by which time for aught we know the Goths and Sfear could have fought another war.'

'Very likely,' agreed Ifar, 'since by then we shall have been out of touch a month and a half. But what is your alternative?'

Dardo spread the map on the ground between them, and pointed south-west. 'To Slane, as the crow flies, is no more than thirty leagues, all told. With luck, five days.'

The others sat back, at once impressed and daunted. Ifar whistled through his teeth but said nothing. It was Beowulf who finally broke the silence. 'Straight through the Lost Land of Fanora. I must confess that never occurred to me.'

161

'Nor to any of us, my lord,' said Ifar, 'except Dardo here. Continue, Dardo, I see you have something more to say.'

'My lords, consider the advantages. No man has ever been known to cross the Lost Land and emerge alive. Some travellers have claimed it, but their tales have never been confirmed. What a noble venture it would be if we were to do so. Who could call us coward then?'

'He has some reason there, my lord,' agreed Kjartan enthusiastically. 'Why, what a tale we will have to tell our friends and women. You will be able to boast to Starlight of having succeeded where no man went before ...'

Kjartan's propensity for referring gratuitously to Starlight was a standing joke amongst his comrades, who exchanged grins at his expense. Suth alone seemed less than amused.

'Better than slinking back to Targon with our tails between our legs, anyway,' said Ifar bluntly. 'I admit I am three-parts convinced. But what say you, Prince Beowulf?'

Beowulf nodded slowly. 'It seems a very admirable scheme. I am only sorry I did not think of it myself. If it succeeds, we shall knock three weeks off our travelling time, and who then can suggest that we lack stomach for the fight against the Sfear? All agreed?'

The others nodded.

'Then it is decided. And I thank you, Dardo. Now no man can now say that we return without honour.'

AFTER a brief rest, the Goths set out in marching order from the North Gate, along the broad stone road called Swertan's Way. Originally it had been intended to connect Fanora with the Slanish city of Castletown by means of a mighty road, forty feet wide and thirty leagues in length, thus opening up the Lost Land to Gothic agriculture and trade. A grand design, which had taken little account of practical difficulties. To be sure, the western section, from Castletown to Kreb's Bridge, had posed few problems. Westward from Fanora was another matter. Men, horses, bullocks and materials had been lost in great numbers in the battle against the wilderness. Though Swertan had never formally admitted defeat, for years before his death work on the scheme had become merely token. It had been left for Rathleck to call a halt officially, which he had done early in his reign, leaving the imperial city and its road to the mercy of the elements.

Yet so far as it went, it was still a good road. Though the slabs were cracked and clogged with weeds, it remained a firm and level track, easy to follow, its tawny scar leading up into the lightly wooded hills beyond the city walls. There the travellers had further opportunity to plunder gardens and orchards for fruit.

Spirits were high, for it was a mild, sunny day, and easy to forget the hardships which lay ahead. As man after man returned laden with pears and plums, many were the earthy jokes about the absence of bowel problems. Like many jokes, thought Beowulf, they contained much truth. Old Seward had told him that the churls and slaves, who walked much and had to survive on fruit and vegetables, never suffered from piles or constipation, unlike the warrior horsemen who ate the choicest cuts of meat. So fruit, vegetables and foot-marching had become the regime of the eccentric young Wagmunding lord.

At the highest point of the Fanoran Hills, Beowulf turned for a last look at the golden city by the sea; the sun shining on the great domes and columns as its mighty roads gleamed white amidst the mansions and brightly-coloured villas on its borders. A city of gods, but without men. Beautiful, bright, strange, and sinister. He took a dagger from his belt and tossed it in the air, end over end. Several men did the same. According to Gothic belief, if the point fell facing the city, he would be back some day; if it pointed away, he would never return.

'You will be back, my lord,' Kjartan assured him cheerfully.

Ifar clapped him on the shoulder. 'Nay, Beowulf, never look back. Ever onwards.' For amongst the Goths it was believed that to stand looking back for long was bad luck.

'You're right,' he agreed. 'Onward, to our goal.'

The road descended through thickening woods of oak, ash, beech and chestnut. Within a few miles the northern trees had begun to give way to others less familiar, with dark shiny leaves, and abundant ferns and creepers. Eventually the forest closed in, and the strange trees met overhead. But still the Swertan Way was broad enough to give easy passage, and the Goths marched on in gathering gloom at a steady three miles an hour. There was little sign of life beyond the tramping of their feet and the murmur of insects, mostly large fire-flies with humming wings. The travellers became subdued and talked less. No birds sang, and they missed the small scurrying animals of Gothic forests. The road became tougher, with thorns and brambles to break their stride. Sometimes they had to resort to swords to clear a path, but mostly the gloomy trees ahead opened up around the flagstones of the Swertan Way, even as behind they closed in.

Yet the trees were winning. The road was no longer forty feet wide, but twenty, now ten, as it yielded to the forest. Gamli spotted a milestone hidden amidst the vegetation, and a halt was called while he and Dardo went to investigate. They scrubbed off the moss, peered closely and returned.

'Fanora twelve miles,' reported the captain. 'Castletown thirty leagues: Kreb's Bridge three and twenty.'

The bridge, though a dozen miles inside Fanora, was generally reckoned the furthest outpost of civilization. A desolate moorland hamlet, but every man would have given half his worldly goods to be there at that moment.

'I never thought the words Kreb's Bridge would sound so much like home,' remarked Ifar, speaking for them all.

'Nor me,' Beowulf agreed. 'But let's look on the bright side. It's warmer here.'

It was common knowledge that the climate of Fanora was in places anomalously mild. In Gothmark, a thick sunless forest would have been decidedly chilly, yet most of them were sweating in the humid atmosphere, and moisture dripped from the trees. The reason for this was not known, but some held that Fanora was perilously close to Muspelheim, Land of the Fire. Others, including Beowulf, scoffed at this as mere superstition. Yet it was one thing to scoff from the safety of Wagmunding Castle, another matter out here.

'There should be eight more miles of Swertan's Way,' he said to Ifar. 'The end of it should be a convenient place to pitch camp.'

'If it lasts that far. The forest might bring it to an end before then.'

Ifar's pessimism proved unfounded. Within a mile it seemed to Beowulf that there was more light from above, and a mile after that there could be no doubt. The forest was thinning, but if anything it became warmer and wetter still, as shallow pools began to appear in the sodden pockets between tree-roots. Soon afterward the forest broke, and trees gave way to a featureless expanse of ochre-coloured mud, with no vegetation save a few patches of moss and lichen. Here the road had been built up into a causeway, twenty feet or more above the surrounding oily pools. The stones of the road were warm to the touch; below them the greasy mud ponds boiled and spat, blowing great bubbles which either subsided silently or burst with an obscene plop.

'This is a foul place,' grumbled Ifar. 'I'm not sure I didn't prefer the forest.'

'No wonder work was abandoned,' said Kjartan. 'Imagine what a job it must have been building this.'

A couple of miles further on they saw their first sign of life for some time, in the shape of a large brightly-coloured insect sunning itself on one of the flagstones. At their approach it flew away to the west, where it soon proved to be the first of many of such flies, yellow-bodied and scarlet-eyed, with sparkling glaucous wings. Some specimens were colossal, measuring nearly two feet across. These creatures were the heralds of other forms of life, as the ponds lost their foul stench and no longer bubbled. Plants began to appear, green slime and waterweed at first, then ferns and mosses, and finally substantial trees. Many resembled common horsetails grown to monstrous size, with boles that must have measured thirty feet across or more, and tall in proportion. Others were like no trees Beowulf had ever seen but like the horsetails reminded him of small weeds enormously enlarged. Occasionally a disturbance in the stagnant waters suggested the presence of fish. And as the size of the pools increased to ponds, and ponds to small lakes, the Goths saw many a pair of protruding eyes watching from amidst the weed.

'Swamp toads,' said Ifar briefly. 'Twice the size of those in Rigel.'

'More than twice,' replied Beowulf. 'Ye gods, look at that monster.'

A huge creature, in shape more lizard than toad, but with moist skin and pop eyes, was lying on a distant bank, At their approach it stirred itself, waddled awkwardly to the water and flopped in.

'Twenty feet, do you think?' asked Ifar.

'At least,' Beowulf agreed. 'With a tail on him like no toad I've ever seen. A lot handier in water than on land.'

The immense creature, ungainly and sluggish out of water, indeed swam with great power and even a curious kind of grace. There were several different types, some having long thin snouts, the others, especially the larger sort, squat heavy heads and massive jaws.

'Perhaps the thin-snouted ones eat fish,' Beowulf suggested. 'And I expect the big ones prey on the smaller.'

This speculation was halted by a loud splash from the rear, accompanied by a yelp of alarm. Beowulf and Ifar ran back to the site of the trouble. A slave had missed his footing on the slippery road and slid into the ooze. He floundered desperately until a rope was thrown to him, whereupon, with great effort and at no small risk of joining him, the others hauled him to safety. He remained lying for a while, gasping like a landed fish, and retching from time to time, for he had swallowed several mouthfuls of the foul mud. Otherwise he seemed not badly hurt and was soon fit to continue.

The route grew darker still, as a curtain of horsetails and giant ferns closed around them to form a canopy overhead. The rays of the low sun slanted through the trunks to illuminate pools of silver fish, dragonflies and the great solemn swamp toads, waddling on the mossy banks, or lying below the surface with bulging eyes. No flowers or birds disturbed the varied pattern of dark and light green, brown or yellow.

About now Beowulf looked for Suth. She was lagging behind a little, and limping. As a rule she was so active he was inclined to forget that she was lame.

'Does your leg hurt, little one?' he asked.

She looked up stoically. 'It is nothing, my lord. I can manage.'

'No, I can see it is causing you pain. I will carry you.'

'Nonsense, my lord. I can make it perfectly well alone.'

'I expect you can, silly slave, but it will hurt your leg unnecessarily, and you will hold the rest of us up.' Beowulf bent over. 'Up you get. Piggy-back.'

'Very well. But don't call me "silly slave." '

She was as light as a feather, and the sensation of carrying her was decidedly pleasant. Suth seemed to find it so too, for after a brief period of silence, she said, 'This is not at all a bad way to travel, my lord.'

'What did I tell you? Mind you, this must not get to be a habit. I have noticed you are now walking much better.'

'I still limp, my lord, as you observed.'

'A little, but I did not mean that. You have begun to carry yourself properly, as a woman, instead of slinking about like a slave.'

'Really?'

'Indeed. Your posture is much improved. A good thing too. Slouching, with shoulders hunched can make a woman's breasts droop.'

'You say the rudest things, my lord,' she protested.

'Evidently your outspokenness is catching. Anyway, I am anxious that you should not think me a prude. It surprises me that one who can take indecent statues in her stride should be so shocked by a harmless compliment.'

Suth gave a wicked chuckle. This was the nearest approach to horseplay between them since the first evening. Beowulf found it lifted his spirits.

A less pleasing incident occurred soon after. Careless wielding of a sword by Hersir whilst cutting his way through the undergrowth resulted in injury to Anselm, whose left arm bled profusely.

'What's up?' asked Beowulf, arriving on the scene at once.

'My fault,' grunted Hersir sourly.

'It's nothing much, my lord,' said Anselm with a shrug.

'Be all right by tomorrow, I dare say,' said Beowulf after brief inspection. 'I'll have Hort fit you up with a sling meanwhile.' He turned to the culprit. 'Till then it'll mean you have to do two men's work. Understood?'

Hersir apologized in graceless fashion, and took himself off grumbling. Beowulf sighed.

'He could be a problem,' said Ifar, appearing at his side.

'Oh, I doubt it. There's always one.'

'I'm not so sure about that. Gamli, who's no tale-bearer as a rule, mentioned to me yesterday that he caught Hersir trying to stir up disaffection amongst the Hrosnabergers. Nothing you could really put your finger on, not to challenge our authority directly, but ...'

'Gamli's a trustworthy man?'

'Splendid fellow. I'd stake my life on him. Excellent family, too. Son of a war hero. His father fell at Dannenberg against the Great Cassar.'

Beowulf nodded. 'I'll keep my eye on Hersir.'

'It might be an idea for you to have a word with him.'

'Maybe. But I'll leave it for the time being. There's no sense in looking for trouble. Let's hope it blows over.'

IN late afternoon, the Goths had a stroke of luck. A section of the road ahead had subsided almost to the level of the surrounding water, and one of the toads had decided to treat it as a mudbank, lying half asleep with its huge head on the flags between its front legs. It was slow to observe the travellers, and began too late to waddle away. Ifar and his men descended on it with savage cries of triumph, and hacked it to pieces with swords and axes.

'Fresh meat for tonight, Suth,' said Beowulf. 'Well done, men. Nothing to be wasted, remember.'

The creature was eviscerated, the meat chopped into convenient lumps and conveyed in hides strapped to poles. Whatever remained from their meal could be salted down for a couple of days' rations.

'If things were different,' mused Beowulf, 'with proper provisions and experienced guides, which of course do not exist, I would not mind an expedition to these swamps. Good hunting, methinks.'

Yet it was not only the hunting, rather the glint of sunlight on the water, the beauty of the giant trees and dragonflies, even in a sense the great toads themselves. In fact, for hunting itself Beowulf no longer greatly cared, for it meant killing things. And he offered a silent prayer, thanking the gods and the great foolish creature that had strayed across their path and given his life so that they could eat.

The light had faded, and it was time to halt. Besides, rest was essential before they embarked on the next stage of their journey. Just before pitching camp, they came across the very last sign of any inroad made by their countrymen upon the great green forest. A moss-covered stone, set up in the middle of the causeway, covered with runes; both those of Gothmark and the south.

'You had better read it for me, Suth,' said Beowulf, lowering her to the ground.

' "This stone," ' she quoted, ' "marks the furthest distance attained by the engineers and labourers of Gothmark, in the construction of the great road from Fanora to Slane, work whereon was finally abandoned on the last Freyasday in the Month of Ten Thousand Stars, in the fifth year of the reign of Rathleck the Wild." ' She pointed. 'Below are the distances: Fanora, twenty miles: Kreb's Bridge one-and-twenty leagues, Castletown eight-and-twenty.'

'So now we are really on our own,' said Beowulf, 'though there is a path ahead of sorts, which will give us a start tomorrow. Here we pitch our tents for now, with thanks to the gods for having brought us safe thus far.'

'More to Longspear than the gods,' said Ifar. 'For Longspear gives men courage to succeed by their own efforts, the gods simply luck.'

'Aye, right enough,' agreed Beowulf. 'Thanks to Longspear it is. Lord Bjorn, we salute you.'

Twenty

THE GOTHS pitched camp upon the last few yards of Swertan's Way, hammering their pegs into the muddy cracks between the flags. There were four tents, and the leaders had one to themselves, together with Suth, who by now was constantly at Beowulf's side. They had dined well. Wrapped in furs and with Fanoran draperies for shelter, they were warm and comfortable.

'Well, Suth,' said Beowulf, as they returned to the tent after the meal, 'tonight might be our last comfortable one for some time, so I shall take advantage of it to tell you a story.'

'I should like that, my lord, very much.'

'Good. You will remember that soon after we met I told you of the manner of my descent from the royal house of Gothmark.'

'Indeed, my lord, I remember well.'

'You may now like to hear the story of my father's family, the Wagmundings. They are not quite so eminent, but their tale is not without interest.'

They and their companions entered the tent and arranged themselves amongst the furs. 'I hope my friends will not be too bored to hear me speak of matters they already know,' he continued.

'As a matter of fact, Beowulf,' said Ifar, 'the tale would interest me too. The history of the Wagmundings is less well known than that of many of our noble houses, besides which I confess myself less well up in such matters than I should be.'

Dardo and Kjartan nodded. The question of the Wylfing feud would need careful handling, but Ifar seemed friendly, and genuinely interested.

169

'Then come and sit beside me, little one, while I begin.'

Suth squeezed in alongside him and leaned her dark head on his breast. 'Your hair is growing nicely now,' he said.

'Yes, my lord. I am no longer quite so ugly.'

'If you belonged to me, small slave,' said Ifar with a grin, 'I should soon show you whether you were ugly or not.'

This was the wrong thing to say, as Beowulf at once inferred from the coldness of Suth's reaction. He caught the eye of the Hrosnaberger lord and shook his head in mute rebuke.

Ifar shrugged, abashed. 'Well, anyway. You are a lucky man, Beowulf.'

'Hear that, Suth,' Beowulf said. 'And not a man in this band but agrees with him, so let us hear no more nonsense about your being ugly. Now, being not only beautiful but highly intelligent and learned, I am sure you must have heard of a great King of Teutonia in bygone days called Offa the Angle.'

'There can be few have not heard of Offa, my lord. Some say, he ruled the whole of Middle Earth, and no king so mighty but had to pay him homage.'

'Aye, so have I heard too,' said Beowulf seriously. 'Yet for my part, I do not think it can be right that he ruled the whole world, for there is no record of him in the annals of the Goths. Nor, so far as I know, did he ever penetrate the Empire of the Cassars. Be that as it may, he was certainly a very great king, and ruled the Teuton Empire many years.

'Eventually, however, Offa grew old, and as death approached, as it must for all men, he was much troubled as to how he should divide the empire between his two sons. If he left it all to the first-born, Angjot, the younger, Dan, - a fierce and haughty youth - might well revolt. Yet Offa was loath to fragment his realms and territories, besides which, if he did, Angjot might justly complain of being deprived of his birthright.

'Offa finally decided upon a compromise, which in the circumstances was probably the best solution. He called his sons together, and obtained their consent to an arrangement whereby the elder, Angjot, would receive the bulk of the Teutonic lands, whilst Dan would become king of the nation that now bears his name, besides inheriting certain border territories, such as the Isles of the West.

'This just solution came to naught, for six weeks before Offa's own death, his elder son, Angjot, died suddenly of an unknown illness, leaving two sons of tender age, Ikalon and Eymor. Offa accordingly entrusted the whole empire to Dan, upon his promise that when the boys attained full age, they should inherit; Dan retaining for himself only those lands originally devised to him. To all this Dan solemnly promised; and Offa died. I dare say, being both a wise and disillusioned slave, you will guess what happened next.'

Suth nodded. 'In fact I know, my lord. Dan became King of the Teutons, and the sons of Angjot, to my knowledge, were never heard of again.'

'That may be the story in some places, Suth, but as Ljani told me, matters were as follows. Dan duly ruled the empire ten years, until the elder of his brother's sons, Ikalon, came of age. By now of course Dan held the reins of power, all the great nobles having sworn fealty to him, not to an untried boy. Accordingly, a few days before Ikalon attained full age, Dan sent for him and offered him lordship of the Isles of the West - which you will remember were Dan's own property under his father's will - in exchange for the rest of the empire. Evidently considering that something was better than nothing, Ikalon agreed to this lop-sided bargain. He therefore departed for the Isles, where his descendants rule to this day.'

'How very unfair,' commented Suth.

'Deplorable,' Beowulf agreed, 'but such is the manner of princes when corrupted by ambition. And many, I dare say, would have behaved worse than Dan, for at least he let his nephews live. As you know, he profited little from his breach of faith, for rebellion and insurrection were soon to tear his empire apart. But that is another story. Anyway, some four years later, Eymor in turn attained the age of eighteen years. You may be sure that Dan, having so cheaply disposed of the claim of the elder boy, saw no reason to be more generous with the younger, whom he attempted to buy off with a mere pittance. Eymor, however, proved less amenable than his brother, and raised the standard of revolt.

'His rebellion was a predictable failure. The Teutons knew and feared Dan, whilst his young nephew had neither experience of power nor influential friends. His forces were soon routed, followers slain or dispersed, and Eymor himself was captured and brought before his uncle in chains. Dan, no doubt prompted by pangs of conscience, did not have him put to death, but passed upon him and his heirs sentence of exile until the fourth generation. If within such time Eymor or his seed set foot in any Teutonic land, that moment was their death. So Dan decreed, and Eymor was banished.

'He made his way north, to present himself at the court of Gothmark. There the King treated him with every kindness and generosity, granting him much fertile land in the Slane Valley, upon the strict condition that Eymor refrain from taking any action to assert his claim to the Teuton throne. This Eymor promised, and kept his word until his death, which occurred over twenty years later. These things happened some three or fourscore years ago.'

'Forgive me, my lord,' Suth interposed, 'but at that time was not Gothmark subject to the rule of the Sfear?'

'Quite right, Suth, you have an excellent memory. Ulf the Avenger

171

then ruled in the land of Gothmark, and it was to him the Eymor swore allegiance. It happened however that Eymor died shortly before the outbreak of the fourth Sferian War, leaving two sons, Wagmund and Wylf, who were not of his mind. He had married a Gothic woman, so his sons doubtless considered themselves part Teuton and part Goth, but Sferian not at all. They were in fact the first two Gothic lords to declare for Swertan the Bastard, whom they served loyally and with distinction throughout the war. At its conclusion, both were handsomely rewarded with riches, lands and titles; Wagmund and Wylf being created respectively Earls of Slane and Hrosnaberg. Swertan for his part never forgot the debt he owed the sons of Eymor, and repaid it generously, so that they became the most powerful men in Gothmark save the king. Wylf of Hrosnaberg still lives, a very aged man, and Ifar here is his grandson.

'Similarly, Wagmund of Slane was my grandfather, though I never knew him, and a complex and devious man. Whilst never failing to advance his personal fortune and that of his kinsmen, yet neither, so far as I know, could he truly be accused of ever behaving dishonourably.'

Beowulf paused, a little fearful that Ifar might dissent, but all the Hrosnaberger said was, 'My grandfather often speaks of Wagmund. It is as you say.'

'Yet men distrusted him,' Beowulf conceded, 'perhaps because of his foreign ancestry, or his too rapid rise to power. Maybe again, his smile was a little too ready with all men, or his wit a little too keen. It was said his financial dealings were not invariably honest, but he was never accused of anything specific. He manipulated the strings of power, but never won men's hearts. And yet, not a bad man really, for like most men he preferred justice and mercy to vengeance and cruelty, nor was he always guided by self-interest alone, for he cast in his lot with Swertan long before the outcome of the war could have been predicted. For this, maybe he deserved to prosper, and prosper he did.

'Between the wars, Wagmund and Wylf were the king's chief counsellors, and always belonged to the peace party. Had it not been for them, indeed, it is likely the Fifth Sferian War would have begun long before it did. Peace suited them, of course, especially Wagmund, for marcher lords have much to lose in time of war.

'But marcher lords also have the opportunity to treat with the enemy, and here Wagmund's behaviour, though in my view falling far short of treason, was certainly open to question. For, strange to say, besides being Swertan's chief henchman, he was also a close friend of Aun, King of the Sfear, who gave him his only sister in marriage. Upon both kings Wagmund constantly urged the virtues of peace, and tried always to preserve the friendliest relations betwixt them, telling each - albeit not with strict accuracy - how much he was admired and respected by his rival. By this, both kings were much pleased, and further honours were heaped upon Wagmund, nor, strange to relate, did either king appear to resent the favours shown him by the other. For Wagmund somehow managed to convey to Aun of the Sfear, no less than to Swertan the Bastard, the impression that if despite his efforts war should ultimately ensue, Wagmund of Slane would side with him. As signs of war grew, wagers were struck amongst the nobility of the Goths and Sfear as to whom Wagmund would eventually support: whether he would still serve his old friend and benefactor Swertan, or revert to his father's allegiance to the Sfear. Odin himself, it was said, did not know what lay in his heart; and in the event no man ever knew, for Wagmund of Slane died some three months before the outbreak of the Fifth Sferian War.

'He left two sons, Edgtyr and Alfar, who were with him at the end. What arrangement they reached between themselves may be surmised; for whilst Edgtyr, like his father and uncle, fought for the Goths in the ensuing war, his brother Alfar returned to his grandfather's allegiance to the Sfear. Thus it was said that whoever lost the Fifth Sferian War, it would not be the Wagmundings of Slane.

'Yet neither king had cause for complaint about the loyalty of his respective henchman. For while Edgtyr fought with skill and courage beside Rathleck the Wild, Alfar was no less ardent and valorous in the cause of the Sfear. However, men noted that the two brothers were never called upon to contend against one another directly. Somehow, it always chanced that if Edgtyr was besieging Scarlettown, Alfar was engaged in the defence of Bettany; and when Alfar was ravaging the Gothic march, his brother was engaging the Sfear at Wendel, and so forth. So it transpired that the Wagmundings, though the loudest spokesmen for peace, profited above all men from the war; for upon the Gothic victory Edgtyr was rewarded by Rathleck with most of the land ceded by the Sfear, and much more besides. And Alfar was compensated tenfold for anything he had lost, Aun granting him the whole land of Karron Tha, whose former lordship had become extinct through the fortune of war. Alfar was thus created First Earl of Karron Tha, with lands and riches little inferior to those enjoyed by his elder brother. So the Wagmunding lords between them held dominion over lands totalling more than a thousand square leagues, and their realms and territories became called by many the Third Kingdom.

'I now come to a part of my story which is most painful to me, namely the fall of my father, Edgtyr, from royal favour, and the dishonour of both my parents.'

'There is no need to tell of it, my lord, if it distresses you.'

'Indeed not,' agreed Ifar. 'It may be you consider such things best not spoken of. There is no sense in reminding us of old enmities.'

Beowulf shook his head. 'I will tell you, my friends, for it is to some extent common knowledge, and insofar as it is not, maybe I have kept it to myself too long.'

'As you wish, my lord,' said Ifar. 'Of course it will go no further.'

'Of course not, nor did it occur to me otherwise. Well, in brief, at the time of the war Edgtyr of Slane was unmarried. Indeed he remained so until early middle age, when dynastic considerations obliged him to take a wife. Rathleck the Wild gave him in marriage his only daughter, Ragnhild, a girl of fifteen years. Edgtyr was then thirty.

'This is the unhappiest part of my story, so I will pass over it quickly. In short, it appears that my mother did not love my father - perhaps the difference in their ages was too great. Also I have heard that despite his fame and valour, Edgtyr was a somewhat secretive and unemotional man, not well suited as husband to a young, high-spirited girl. For her part, my mother had wished to be betrothed to his cousin Olaf, the son of Wylf of Hrosnaberg, a young and dashing prince.

'When I was four years old, my mother gave birth to a girl-child, Ljani, of very singular appearance, with red hair and brown eyes. Neither of my parents had this colouring, and amongst the Northmen brown eyes are excessively rare. Olaf of Hrosnaberg, however, had red hair and brown eyes. When taxed, my mother admitted her shame, that she had indeed formed a criminal liaison with Prince Olaf, and my sister was the fruit of their adulterous passion.'

'The ways of the high-born are strange,' mused Suth. 'Is human frailty of that sort such a terrible thing?'

'Funnily enough, little one, I have sometimes thought on similar lines myself, but considered that I must be wrong, since no-one else agreed with me. However, to continue, the outcome was a tragedy for all concerned. I have said that Edgtyr was a secretive man.'

'Unemotional too, I think you said, my lord.'

'Aye, that I did, yet there methinks I did him an injustice. Rather, he seems to have been one of those whose feelings lie well-hidden beneath a cold exterior. For when he learnt the truth, Edgtyr slew Prince Olaf in jealous rage, not after challenge in fair fight, but in secret, by stealth and ignobly.

'When his guilt came to light, the Wylfings clamoured for revenge, claiming the life of Edgtyr under the law of bloodfeud. To this Rathleck the Wild would not agree. Yet even he was bound to concede the justice of their case, and banished Edgtyr the realm for a period of ten years. The Wylfings were dissatisfied, and swore vengeance on his return. Meanwhile Edgtyr sought sanctuary in the court of Rothgar, King of the Dan, where he survived several attempts on his life; it is said by agents of the Wylfings.'

'No "it is said" about it,' said Ifar, his face darkening. 'It was indeed my kinsmen, who thereby made their guilt as great as his. To call a man out in single combat is one thing; to plot his death by stealth quite another.'

'You put things most fairly and honourably, Ifar,' said Beowulf in relief. 'Rothgar of the Dan, a wise and moderate king, finally arranged settlement of the feud through payment of wergild, though some say the Wylfings were but partly appeased even then.'

Ifar shook his head. 'There may be some feel thus, but for my part, death cancels all debts. Let the hatreds and enmities of the dead vanish with those who harboured them.'

'Well spoken,' agreed Beowulf, to murmurs of assent from Dardo and Kjartan. 'As you may have guessed, Suth, the tragedy did not end there. Within a year my unhappy mother, disgraced and having brought about the death of the man she loved, was dead by her own hand. As for my father, he never saw his native land again, but died a few months before his term of exile was complete.'

'Oh, my lord,' said Suth tearfully, 'what a pitiful tale. But I am glad and honoured that you have chosen to confide not only in your highborn friends, but also in me. Did you inherit the Slanish lands after all?'

'I did, for Rathleck could not bring himself to forfeit the lands of one who, whatever his dishonour over a private matter, had ever been his most loyal henchman. The lands of Slane were held by my grandfather the king upon trust for me, and I came into my own three years ago. Similarly, my cousin Athelstan, whom men call Hawkeye, had inherited the province of Karron Tha from his father Alfar some years before.'

'Is he married, my lord?'

'He is, Suth, yet - it is common knowledge, so I break no confidence - relations between him and his wife are but indifferent. They live apart, and have no child.'

'I asked, my lord, because it occurred to me that if, which the gods forbid, you or he were to die without issue, then ...'

'In that case, Suth, all the Lands Between the Lakes, from the Purple Mountains to the River Slane, would pass to the survivor, who would possess a power scarcely inferior to that of the Gothic and Sferian kings. The consequences would be grave indeed.' He saw another question in Suth's eyes, which even she, outspoken as she was, dared not ask. 'I know what you are thinking,' he said. 'As soon as I was of an age to understand such matters, it oft occurred to me to wonder whether my mother's infidelity with Prince Olaf had been responsible for my sister's birth alone.'

'My lord,' Suth protested, amidst murmurs of dissent from the others, 'I never suspected any such thing.'

'Well, however that may be, I, like Ljani, resembled Edgtyr of Slane but little. He, like most of the Wagmundings, was a man of middle height and stature, dark of countenance, whereas even as a child I was far above the average size for my age, and in those days fairer than I am now. Fortunately I bore no great resemblance to Olaf Wylfing either, besides which I have been told that my mother, whilst freely confessing her guilt so far as Ljani was concerned, always insisted that I was the lawful son of Edgtyr Wagmunding. Some say I tend to feature his father, Wagmund, but although a portrait of him hangs in Wagmunding Castle, I cannot see it. And there is in Gothic law a presumption that all men are legitimate unless the contrary be proved. Nevertheless, upon my cousin Hawkeye coming into his inheritance, certain of his court, seeking to curry favour with their new lord, put into his head a suspicion regarding my legitimacy, which, had it been true, would have resulted in all the Wagmunding lands being forfeit to him.

'At this time, some nine years ago, I was a boy of fourteen. At his request, I came to see my kinsman who was himself no more than nineteen. And here I was lucky. You might have observed, Suth, a small birthmark on my left arm, just inside the wrist, resembling in shape a wolf's head.'

'I have indeed, my lord. And a small speck alongside it, which you explained your parents fancifully thought to resemble a bee, hence the derivation of your name.'

'In part, yes. That and the fact that Beo-Wulf, or enemy of the bee, also means Bear. But I digress. This birthmark, called by some the Wolf of the Wagmundings, was borne by my grandfather and some of his ancestors, but seems to have missed the Hrosnaberg branch of the family. Not all the Wagmundings have it - my cousin's father bore the mark, but not Hawkeye himself, or indeed Edgtyr of Slane. None but the Wagmundings bear it it, however, and upon first meeting me, and seeing the mark, Hawkeye grasped me by the hand, swore by the Ninefold Oath that I was his cousin in sooth, that he would always acknowledge me as such, and would listen no more to those who sought to turn him against me. And so it has been between us ever since; for Hawkeye of Karron Tha is not alone my cousin, but the man whom above all others I am proud to call my friend. And that is really the end of my story.'

'Not quite. But let us end it now.' Ifar stood and extended a hand. 'The feud is over, Beowulf, at least so far as I am concerned. For my father and brother, they speak of the matter but seldom, and when I tell them of the dangers we have faced together, they will feel the same as I. The Lord of the Fire claim my soul if ever I hate you or your house.'

Beowulf also stood, and the men seized forearms and upper arms in the two-handed Gothic grip of eternal friendship. Dardo, Kjartan and

Suth cried 'Bravo!' and clapped their hands.

That night, though he knew it not, Ifar became Earl of Hrosnaberg, as his grandfather Wylf died peacefully in his sleep at Wagmunding Castle.

Roger Butters

Twenty-one

NEXT DAY brought news that Lars, the slave who had fallen into the swamp, had been taken ill during the night.

Beowulf went to see him immediately along with his storeman Hort, an old soldier who was as near as they could come to a physician.. 'How do you feel, old chap?'

'Fair, my lord,' said the slave gamely, his yellow skin and profuse sweat belying his words. 'A little cold.'

'More blankets,' Beowulf ordered. 'Use the tent material, and pile it on thick. Obviously you won't be able to walk yet awhile, but we can rig you up a litter from a couple of tent-poles.'

'Thank you, my lord,' breathed Lars. 'But I will delay you.'

'Nonsense,' Beowulf replied briskly. 'Anyway these swamp fevers seldom last long. I dare say you will be as right as rain tomorrow.'

'What are his chances?' he asked Hort softly, once they had left the tent.

The storeman shook his head and sighed. 'Swamp fever, my lord. He swallowed half the pond. No-one knows what poisons it might have contained. We must be prepared for the worst.'

Beowulf nodded. 'A pity I lost Ljani's mixture in the wreck. Still, so far as I know, it only worked for wounds, not fever. See what you can do for him, Hort. And let's strike camp. No man is to leave the track in any circumstances.'

At first, the going was easier than expected. Preliminary work had been done on the next stage of the road, and even after the causeway petered out it was possible to wade without great risk. The huge mossy roots of the horsetails served as natural stepping-stones, and the water became shallower as the land rose.

'Methinks the terrain is improving,' observed Ifar. 'The air is clearer as well.'

'Yes, I'd noticed that. Let's hope it continues.'

The drier conditions soon led to more varied vegetation; the swamp-dwelling mosses and horsetails being increasingly replaced by tree-ferns and curious tufted plants, about twice the height of a man, like giant land anemones. Wading became unnecessary, the water being confined to plentiful streams, lakes and woodland pools.

'This is really quite pleasant,' said Beowulf to Kjartan. 'Thus far Fanora's evil reputation seems a little harsh.'

'You might speak too soon, my lord. Still, we must profit from conditions while they are still tolerable. Hurry along, men, no sightseeing.'

'Why, look,' said Beowulf, disregarding his advice at once. 'A pine tree.'

This familiar sight proved the first of many, as the ground rose and the flora became less exotic. Fir and pine now mingled with the tree-ferns and land anemones, while the horsetails eventually disappeared. Dragonflies became less common, and the swamp toads were accompanied by a variety of lizards, smaller than their giant cousins, but more active.

The last few miles would have been amongst the most pleasant of their journey, but for the worry about the sick slave, who had lapsed into delirium, broken by uneasy slumber.

'How is he?' Beowulf asked Hort.

'Very ill, my lord. The next two or three hours should see the crisis.'

Soon afterward the ravings ceased and the man drifted into coma. It was clear that the end was not far off.

The land continued to rise as their route emerged into upland country, lightly forested with conifers and bracken. Meanwhile a mountain range to their right drew nearer every mile. The weather was still warm, with a cloudless sky, but something struck Beowulf as wrong. 'Have you noticed,' he asked Ifar, 'the absence of birds and their songs?'

Ifar frowned. 'It had not occurred to me. But something did seem wrong. Now you mention it, I cannot remember seeing or hearing a bird since we left the city. Odd.'

'Most strange. You take over the lead for a while, Ifar. I'll go and see how Lars is.'

No sooner had Beowulf arrived at the litter of the unfortunate slave than a commotion broke out up front. He ran back to discover that Ifar and his men had disturbed a huge reptile, crouched over the remains of its prey, a smaller but still sizable creature. The predator was a fearsome beast, with massive head and protruding canine teeth. Its slate-green body was adorned with a webbed structure along the spine like the sail of a longship. As Beowulf arrived, the monster roused itself from its torpor and rushed fearlessly amongst the Goths, knocking several of them from their feet with lashes of its powerful tail. One luckless warrior fell prey to the mighty jaws, which crushed his skull and shoulders like an apple.

Recovering from the first shock of the engagement, the Goths rallied and struck back: half a dozen spears were driven into the dragon's flanks and throat. The decisive blow was struck by Dardo, who with mad courage flung himself at the creature's shoulder and cut deep into its neck with his axe. He was swamped by a torrent of blood from the wound, after which the monster's movements became increasingly sluggish. The Goths fell to with swords and despatched it swiftly.

Amazingly, only one man had been lost; he who had been half-devoured by the dragon's dreadful jaws. A few others were nursing minor injuries. Dardo was unhurt. By tradition, Goths lay where they fell, so after a brief respectful ceremony their comrade's body was laid to rest.

'By yea and no, a real monster,' said Ifar, examining the dragon closely. 'Twenty feet, if an inch. Well, seventeen or eighteen, anyway.'

'A little less, I fancy,' said Beowulf sceptically. 'Still, the question can soon be settled. I am the tallest here - let me be our measuring-stick.'

The result was a slight disappointment. During the fight the creature had seemed truly colossal, but even including its tail it was not quite long enough to reach the top of Beowulf's head a second time.

'Nearly two beowulfs long,' admitted Ifar sadly. 'Less than fourteen feet. Funny, I could have sworn it was bigger.'

'Never mind,' said Beowulf wryly. 'I'm sure it will have grown again by the time we return to tell the tale. Let's push on, anyway. There may be more such dragons hereabouts.'

The next halt was depressingly predictable. After a brief return to consciousness, Lars the slave died, and was buried at the foot of a giant pine. Soon after, the forest cover broke up into woodland and scrub, where the land seemed hospitable enough for them to halt for a meal, after six hours hard marching.

'Five leagues, methinks,' opined Kjartan, munching his bread.

'Yes,' agreed Beowulf, 'but there'll be no mileposts from now on, I fear. I doubt if any Goth has ever penetrated this far before.'

A cloud passed over the face of the sun, and it grew momentarily colder. Suth shuddered.

'Is anything wrong, little one?' Beowulf asked.

'Fanora, my lord, is part of the domain of Ragnar of Torre.'

'What, all of it?'

She looked doubtful. 'Perhaps not all of it, but none knows exactly when and where he could manifest himself. His creatures are everywhere.'

'The monsters, you mean?'

'I do not think so. The monsters are indeed bizarre and terrifying, but methinks they have been here much longer than him. Indeed, the wilderness and monsters might have prevented him from expanding his realm. There are limits to his power, no doubt.'

'I should damned well hope so,' said Ifar cheerfully. 'No more of your terrifying tales, small slave, or my men will hide beneath their blankets all night and refuse to get up tomorrow. If we are all finished, let's away.'

Soon afterward, they joined, if not a road, at least what seemed to be a trodden path. 'Some kind of animal?' Beowulf suggested.

Ifar shook his head, in a manner indicating doubt rather than disagreement. 'Maybe. The ground is too dry for tracks. Let's hope it's not the usual walk for those dragons, anyway.'

The track wound upward into increasingly mountainous terrain, scrub and moorland giving way eventually to a rocky escarpment skirted by a hewn mountain path. To their left the land fell away into a dark and thickly forested valley, with swamp and lakes in the distance. Beyond the farthest lake, on the blue horizon, rose a mountain range with plumes of smoke issuing from a dozen peaks.

'I have heard of the mountains that burn,' said Beowulf, 'but always had my doubts about them till now. We are well out of that valley, methinks. I expect dragons of the sort we encountered are common there.'

'No doubt,' agreed Ifar. 'And look at yon great flying beasts, leatherwings such as that we saw near the sea. I reckon they could pick a man up and carry him off, they are so huge.' The creatures he spoke of were fortunately far off, circling the lakes and swamps, wings silhouetted against the dark orange sky.

'Our course should really lie more in that direction, though,' said Beowulf, worried. 'By the sun it seems that we are bearing a little north of the best route.'

Ifar shrugged. 'We can't very well turn back, and to attempt a descent of these cliffs would be rash. Let's hope for a chance to change direction soon.'

In fact, little more than a mile further on, the track forked; the left-hand route leading steeply down into the valley of the dragons. A few minutes earlier there had been a brief but heavy shower, and Kjartan pointed out some hoofprints in the moist earth. They led straight ahead, into the mountains.

'No more than one horseman,' said Ifar. 'But recent, no doubt of that.'

Further evidence of human activity came in the shape of a fingerpost a few yards ahead. It bore no more than seven runes, which with his new-found knowledge Beowulf was easily able to interpret. 'Atrofon,' he said awkwardly. 'Is that right, Suth?'

'It is, my lord.' She shuddered. 'I like it not.'

'Why, what does it mean?'

'Methinks it must be the name of this place, or the next one we come to. I have not heard the word before.'

'Nor I,' said Ifar. 'But we seem to have little choice. I'm none too keen on wading through more dragon-infested swamps. Besides, the light should last longer in the mountains.'

'Yes, and there seems to be some sort of civilization there too. What do you think, Suth?'

'Both ways are unpropitious, my lord. These are the lands of Ragnar of Torre.'

Dardo was inclined to favour taking a chance with the dragons, on the grounds that the valley seemed the more direct route. Kjartan was undecided. Beowulf was about to suggest consulting the runes, when a lake amidst the forest beneath parted to reveal a creature of monstrous bulk with serpentine neck and tiny head.

'Freya's tits,' breathed Ifar. 'What a monster.'

'Grotesque,' agreed Beowulf. 'Perhaps the gods intended it as a warning. Let's try straight ahead.'

For a while they tramped along the cliff path three abreast, before catching sight of the owner of the mysterious footprints; a single knight on a white horse, clad in black coat of mail and proceeding in the same direction as themselves. Upon hearing their approach, he turned and raised a hand in greeting.

'I salute your souls, strangers,' he said in a friendly tone. 'Who are you, and whither bound?'

'We are Goths,' said Beowulf, 'from the court of King Athkyn, and bound for Kreb's Bridge.'

'You have more than fifteen leagues to go,' said the knight, 'through hard terrain, beset with many dangers. But the City of the Sky will offer you hospitality tonight to refresh you for your journey.'

'Many thanks. How far is this city? And what is the name of your lord?'

The knight fell into step with them, chatting pleasantly, the failing light reflecting on a frank, ruddy-complexioned face beneath an old-fashioned conical helmet with no visor. 'Our city is called Atrofon, City of the Sky, being the highest of the cities of Shadron Mor.'

'We have heard of Shadron Mor,' said Ifar, 'but thought it was a barren mountain range.'

'Aye, so outsiders seem to think. They visit but rarely, of course, the way being rugged and full of danger. When they do, they are made right welcome, and many elect to stay.'

'And your lord?'

'We have none at present, but are governed by our lady, Helga of the Isles.'

'Why, that is most pleasing to hear,' said Beowulf in surprise. 'Is she not sister to Breck Bronding, their prince?'

'That she is, lately expelled from her homeland, alas, by the forces of evil. But that is a long story, of which our lady may tell you more this evening if you wish.'

'We should be most pleased to hear it,' said Ifar, 'for the original purpose of our journey was to see her brother.'

'You have not visited the Isles recently, I'll wager.'

'No,' said Beowulf, 'being driven off course by a tempest and wrecked. 'But tell me of my friend Breck Bronding. Is he dead? For so we have heard.'

'Dead?' repeated the knight vaguely. 'Aye, dead, so he is, I believe, poor fellow. Our lady can give you details, no doubt. From here you may see our city.'

They rounded a bend in the road and caught their breath. Beneath them, in the last rays of the dying sun, lay a fair city of marble, glass and steel, with spacious streets and squares, imposing colonnaded walks, baths and temples. In the distance, the silver torrent of a mountain river was spanned by a shining bridge of steel. In all their lives, none of the Goths had ever seen a steel bridge. Compared with this, Fanora itself was a collection of hovels.

'Beautiful, is she not?' said the knight with pride. 'Of all the cities of the mountain, Atrofon is said to be the fairest, as our queen is the fairest of all women. She and her court dwell in the Palace of the Rock, yonder.'

It was the most glorious building of all, perched high on a crag above the city. The twilight glinted on its domes, spires and parapets of crystal and marble. Gates of pearl and gilded metal surrounded the courtyard, approached by a broad, curved avenue lined with statues and terminating in a triumphal arch. There seemed few ordinary citizens about at this hour, but many knights, squires and men-at-arms saluted the visitors as they passed. Truly, thought Beowulf, the fairest and mightiest city he had seen. No wonder so many elected to stay. The humblest buildings were palaces themselves, with windows of plate glass, in giant sheets far clearer than any that could be fashioned by the craftsmen of the north. And yet perhaps, the city was a little too perfect in its geometry and cleanliness, with plane trees planted in straight lines, and never a weed or fallen leaf be seen. He would not have changed it for his own simple residence in Castletown, and the fields and lakes of Slane.

'Welcome to Atrofon,' said their companion as they entered the gate. 'And the land of Shadron Mor.'

Roger Butters

Twenty-two

A YOUNG and amiable lord hurried into the courtyard beyond the gate to meet the visitors. 'Greetings, brave warriors,' he said. From his dress, bearing and attendants he was evidently a man of importance. 'My name is Magavell, grand steward of our lady, Helga, Queen of the Isles. Such poor hospitality as we possess is at your service. We have already begun our meal, and must apologize for being unprepared to receive you as your rank and valour deserve. No doubt you are tired after your journey; I will show you where you may wash and change clothes.'

The great hall was not low-beamed like those of the Northmen, but airy and high-vaulted, lit by half a dozen chandeliers, with many braziers ensconsed in the walls. Long tables filled three sides of the room, and warriors quaffed ale from horns, dining from choice meals and exotic fruits on golden dishes. All were young, cheerful and fair of face. Tumblers and jugglers performed in the centre of the great room. There was a brisk hum of conversation, whilst servants and slaves, dressed like lords themselves, passed about bearing drinks and further dishes. From the ceiling and minstrels' gallery the banners of the nations hung down in cheerful array. Amongst them Beowulf was pleased to see those of Gothmark and the Sfear, besides those of Teutonia, the Dan, Targon, the Isles of the West, the Empire of the Cassars, and others unfamiliar to him.

At the head of the table sat a woman dressed in a close-fitting gown of white samite trimmed with gold, a circlet around her light brown hair. Beowulf judged her age to be about five-and-twenty. Breck had once told him of his sister back in the Isles, but Beowulf had never previously met her. At that moment she appeared the most beautiful woman he

187

had ever seen.

'We greet you, Beowulf of Slane,' she said in a clear voice, 'friend of my brother. You and your warriors are doubly welcome. Be seated as our most honoured guests.'

It was strange that the number of places available corresponded exactly with the number of visitors, but so it proved. Apart from the queen and a few serving wenches, there were no women present, but custom varied in such matters. In Gothmark, the women always dined with the men. At her invitation, Beowulf sat at the lady's right.

'As travellers from the east,' she said, 'you must have many a tale to tell.'

'One or two, my lady.' He and Ifar outlined their story since leaving Targon.

'You have done well to get this far,' she said. 'Many never get beyond the end of Swertan's Way.'

'How came you here, madam?'

'Oh, the seven cities of Shadron Mor are very old. They have been here, 'tis said, since the time of the first Gothic settlements some five hundred years ago, or even before then.'

Beowulf did not see how this could be, or there would surely be some record, or at least rumours of the place, but it would have been discourteous to argue.

She continued, 'The gods were good to you in bringing the storm. Had you reached the Isles, you could scarcely have escaped with your lives.'

'How so?'

'The Isles have fallen,' said the Queen sadly. 'Since my brother died this last twelvemonth.'

'We had heard rumours of his death,' replied Ifar, 'but nothing for certain.'

'Is it true he was slain?' asked Beowulf.

The Queen nodded.

'And by whom? Ragnar of Torre?'

An enigmatical expression flickered across the lady's beautiful face. 'Aye, Ragnar of Torre, that Son of Muspelheim. He it was who slew my brother and has enslaved the Isles.'

'Has his power spread to the mainland?'

'That it has. Until recently, his sway was confined to the east, whence comes all evil things. Now his henchmen have invaded Fanora, whilst his kinsman, Eugen of Brabanne, rules in Targon.'

'Is Eugen not his enemy?'

'That may be so,' she replied vaguely. 'Report is variable. Some say they are in league together.'

'The Northlands then stand in great danger.'

The lady nodded. 'Very great. Yet so long as Shadron Mor still stands, right shall prevail. As you can see, we are a mighty people.'

Splendid if not mighty, for the hall was ornamented with carvings, tapestries and paintings far richer than any in the Northlands, and of a style unfamiliar to the Goths. The meal over, a minstrel sang a lay, and a mime and jollification followed. Finally, in tribute to the guests, the minstrel and harpist played the most beautiful of Gothic airs, *The Song of Tears*. Beowulf by now was a little confused by wine, and very happy. Young Kjartan, a place or two to his right, was in earnest conversation with one of his men. He nodded gravely, and the man withdrew again to sit with his comrades lower down the hall. A few moments later the captain was at Beowulf's side.

'An incomparable feast, my lady,' he said. 'Magnificent indeed.'

The Queen smiled sweetly. 'Nothing. Had we known of your coming in advance, a far more fitting reception would have been prepared.'

Kjartan hung around for a while, making rather vapid conversation. At length he murmured, 'I wonder if I might speak to you apart, my lord. A small personal matter.'

'Forgive me, lady,' said Beowulf. 'I will be but a moment.'

'Of course.' The Queen smiled as he stood and removed himself a few feet away.

'What is it?' he asked.

'Probably nothing, my lord. I hesitate to trouble you with it, yet for what it is worth, one of our men, Hugo ...'

'I saw him talking to you just now.'

'Quite. He claims, absurd though it is, to have met Breck Bronding.'

'Not absurd. He met him several years back, when Breck visited me. Got to know him fairly well, in fact.'

'You misunderstand, my lord. He claims to have met the Bronding this very night.'

'Tonight?' Beowulf shook his head slowly, a little troubled by the wine. 'Nay, that is indeed impossible. Poor Breck is dead - not only his sister confirms it, but many here. Indeed, we were almost sure of it before we arrived. The man has partaken of too much wine. As have we all, I fear.'

'Hugo does not drink overmuch as a rule, my lord. He appears as sober as I am, although perhaps that does not say a great deal.'

Kjartan drank as little as any man in their party. Beowulf thought it over again, then said, 'A spectre? Such things are spoken of, though I have never seen one myself.'

Kjartan nodded. 'Possibly, my lord. Or a simple mistake. Some men do look like others, of course.'

'Strange if that is so, for Hugo knew Breck quite well. They became friends and often went hunting together. He should not have been mistaken. Where did he see him?'

'Upon the way to the jakes, my lord, just down the passage. Breck Bronding, he says, was emerging from the latrine, glanced up, saw him, and hurried away.'

'So they never spoke?'

'No, my lord.'

'How near were they to one another?'

'Not much more distant than we from the Queen at this moment; say fifteen feet. He did not seem like a spectre, Hugo said, albeit somewhat distracted in his gaze.'

'In the circumstances, a spectre seems unlikely,' said Beowulf with a grin. 'Ghosts seldom feel the need to relieve themselves, I fancy.'

Kjartan smiled. 'That had occurred to me too. Hugo must have been in error, I suppose, but it is odd. Would you like to speak to him yourself?'

'Nay, not tonight. It would seem to make too much of a slight thing. A trick of the light, I dare say. I will ask him about it in the morning when we are sober; it will seem different then.'

'You are tired, my lord,' said the Queen, as Beowulf returned to her side. 'Thoughtlessly, we have kept you and your men overlong. Servants will show you to your quarters.'

Beowulf had lost track of night and day, which was easily done in the Northlands, especially in winter, when it was dark much of the time. He nodded assent and drained his goblet. The wine, like all else here, was sweeter than anything in Gothmark. He replaced the vessel, and stiffened. Upon the base it bore the curious twisted cross he had come to associate with evil.

'The mark of Ragnar,' said the Queen, biting her lip. 'Our people and his have long been enemies, and this goblet must be amongst the spoils recovered from them.' She frowned. 'This brand of evil must be removed. It should have been done already. I apologize, my lord, and hope the sight has not offended you.'

'Not at all,' he assured her. 'It was just a little startling, that's all.'

As the Goths trooped out of the banqueting hall, weary and slightly befuddled, it occurred to Beowulf that he had not seen Suth all evening, since soon after their arrival. For some reason she had seemed to have one of her moods, and no doubt had slunk off to sulk on her own. A pity. He was more regretful than annoyed. Meeting the Queen had quite driven her out of his head.

One other disturbing thought had crossed his mind briefly. Of those at the banquest not one had apparently been aged more than thirty. He mentioned as much to Dardo as they said goodnight.'

'Aye,' said the Hrosnaberger. 'Funny, that. But everything here seems a bit too good to be true. I noticed something else in the city, as we made our way in here. Or rather, didn't notice.'

'What?'

'Horse-shit,' said Dardo simply. 'There was no horse-shit in the streets.'

THE GOTHIC captains, as befitted their rank, had each been accorded a chamber of their own. Beowulf's was magnificent; the great postered bed was caparisoned in black and gold, whilst rich tapestries and paintings adorned the marble walls.

'Why,' he said to the attendant who admitted him, 'This is too fine for a simple warrior.'

'Not nearly fine enough, my lord, for a Prince of the Goths,' the man replied suavely. 'Our lady wishes to apologize for its inadequacy. If there be aught else you require, there is a bell beside you.'

He bowed and withdrew. Beowulf sat on the bed, removed his jerkin and heaved off his boots. They would not be making an early start tomorrow. The best plan would be to stay an extra day - one day should make no difference - and set out fresh on the aftermorrow. Again it occurred to him to wonder where Suth was. No doubt the servants and slaves had been allotted separate quarters. He lay on the bed and closed his eyes. By yea and no, he was tired. And the bed so soft ...

Half-opening his eyes again, Beowulf tried to make sense of the multi-coloured mural on the opposite wall. A battle scene, evidently depicting conflict between good and evil. Indeed, now he came to look more carefully, it was that of the greatest of all Gothic victories, the Battle of the Doomed. There was the mighty Bjorn Longspear, and there his brother, Bjarki the Lame. Against them, the whole army of the East: hideous trolls and monsters, mounted on dragons, led by Dmitri the Damned, one of the Sons of Muspelheim. Something was wrong with the picture, though; he could not tell what. In the candle-light, the colours were indistinct, shadowy and dream-like. It blurred into a distorted pattern of good and evil, inextricably confused. The wine must be affecting his wits. Breck Bronding - was he there, and if so, on which side? Illusion, all was illusion ... Too tired even to douse the candles, Beowulf drifted into a fitful slumber.

BEOWULF dreamed a dream. He stood on a wild and desolate heathland, similar to parts of Gothmark, though if it was in Gothmark it was a region he did not know. There was grass and scrub beneath his feet, yet the whole seemed dead and sterile. It was night-time, and the world the monochrome of those dreams that are disturbing, not refreshing. It was cold. He could never remember having felt cold in a dream before. And whilst he knew that it was a dream, that made it none the less demoralizing.

Over the heathland there lingered a mist, through which he could distinguish giant half-human shapes, immobile like massive standing stones. He was hopelessly lost, and did not know in which direction to proceed. There was a thin cold wind.

The sky was neither clear nor cloudy, but like the landscape, hazy with light mist. No stars could be seen, but a gibbous moon was haloed near the horizon. Beyond the stones the land sloped gradually upward, and it was in this direction that Beowulf made his way, through the cold giant standing stones, using the waning moon as his guide. The phase and altitude of the moon should have enabled him to determine the direction in which he was travelling, but in his confused state he could not remember the correct method of reckoning. Very likely the calculation would not work; it was but a dream anyway. And a dream from which he was uncertain that he would ever awake.

Upon the blurred horizon rose a dark hill; the only hill on an otherwise featureless expanse of terrain. He made for the hill. The land remained dead. There was no indication of the life that in his waking world would have abounded - the small creatures amongst the grass, the trickling of springs and streams, the sight and sound of a night-hawk above the plain. And, as ever in dreams, it was impossible to distinguish detail. When one examined things closely in a dream one woke up. Maybe he should try doing that. Yet he knew that this time he would not wake up. Perhaps this was what it was like being dead. Very likely he was dead. Death might be no more than a dream from which one never awoke. Was this indeed Helheim, the dismal Land of the Dead? Or Niflheim, the Land of Mist?

Maybe it was one of those dreams in which one could never achieve one's object; it was some time since he had begun walking, yet the hill seemed as far away as ever.

And yet it was not. Little by little, the hill was getting closer. And it was his destination, he knew it now. The very summit of the hill. And upon that summit he could discern, albeit indistinctly, a dark inchoate shape. A shape that filled him with dread. A greater dread than he had ever known. And yet he had to make for it. It occurred to him to wonder whether that shape was Death, the ultimate goal that none could avoid, and for which all men were unwillingly destined.

Now he was climbing the hill. It was barren and stony, with stunted tufts of heather and twitch-grass the only sign of life. Maybe, he thought, they represented tiny evidence for the ultimate triumph of life over death. And for the first time it occurred to him that this cold and desolate land had a beauty of its own, harsh and terrible though it might be.

The shape upon the hilltop began to take a more evident form.

Albeit still nebulous, it now appeared as a horseman, black against the cloudy sky, half-lit by the cold dead moon. For some reason Beowulf was not surprised. Nor, now that he could discern the shape, was he quite as fearful as before. Though sinister and ill-omened, no longer was it so terrifyingly alien.

He climbed yet further, feet slipping and sliding upon the gravelled slope. On the steeper stretches, he needed to grasp the woody shoots of heather to haul himself up. At last he could see the horse and rider clearly.

The horse was very tall, one of the largest Beowulf had ever seen. Seventeen hands high at least, yet wiry as a warhorse, not heavily-muscled for the plough. With the light behind it it looked dark, yet somehow he sensed that it was grey. As he approached, instead of tossing its head in the manner of most horses, it remained altogether still. And he observed that, despite the cold and damp, there was no breath steaming from its nostrils.

The rider wore a long dark cloak. He was a very tall old man, with a conical helmet of a type from long ago. Within the cloak Beowulf could discern the dull gleam of chain-mail. The rider wore a patch over one eye. And Beowulf knew him, as any Northman would have known him.

With a screech, a huge black bird flew across the face of the moon and landed upon the rider's shoulder. A raven. Truly it was him. And now he spoke.

'You think you know me, Prince of the Lake. Yet you know me but through a glass, darkly. In sooth, even the wisest know me not.' His voice was very deep, slow and calm.

'To the Northmen I am called the High One. In the West, I am known as the Great Spirit. In the Empire of the South, they know me as Lord of the Ways. In the East, they say that I am immortal life, and death; I am what is, and what is not. As the sage of the Great Empire said, where is God to be found, if not in earth, in air, in sea, in sky, in courage? Never seek for me beyond. Whatever you see, whatever you touch, that is the High One.

'Remember, Prince of the Lake, that things are seldom as they seem. What seems harsh and frightful may wreak no harm, and what appears most fair may at heart be evil beyond measure.

'There are three women in your life, Prince of the Lake. One is fair and fickle; another is dark and true, and your future in this life lies with her. The third you have always known, and always will, even to the last day. Long ago, you knew her as Zana Flamehair. And in lives to come, you will know her again. As I told an Indian ruler countless ages since, you have been born many times, Prince Beowulf, and many times have I been born. I remember my previous lives, but thou hast forgotten thine. As when you wake, as shortly you will, you will have forgotten me. And yet not entirely forgotten, for I am always there.'

A phrase came into Beowulf's head. A phrase he dared not utter. Yet the rider spoke it for him. 'The Northmen call me Odin, the foul and untrue. They alone dare argue with the gods. It does not matter. Whether they worship or revile me, I am the same. I am the charioteer to princes, the slave in the triumph of the Cassars. When celebrating conquest, remember thou art mortal. In moments of despair, remember thou art a man.

'Again I say, I am the lord of life, and death. Soon you shall realize that death is not the worst that may befall a man, and may sometimes come as a friend. Yet your time is not yet come, Prince Beowulf. The sun shall cross the sky ten thousand times, and then ten thousand more, before you die. I say to you, as I said to the Spartans at Delphi: If you fight with all your might, with all your heart and courage, you shall have victory, and I, the High One, will help you, both when you call on me for aid, and when you do not.

'Men shall call you hero, Prince of the Lake. In the eyes of the gods there is no such thing, but there is such a thing as a man. And in being a man there lies the greatest achievement of all, and the greatest tragedy.'

And Beowulf woke.

Twenty-three

BEOWULF HAD woken from a disturbing dream, but could not remember the details. It had not been pleasant, but something about it gave him courage. All he could remember was that it had occurred in a place as different from Atrofon as anywhere could possibly be.

It appeared to be day. Appeared, because the light seemed different from normal daylight, as if the inhabitants of Atrofon had discovered a method of bright illumination not dependent upon the sun. Like much else in the city, it was at once both beautiful and disturbing.

At the far end of his chamber, he could see a large transparent door, in some respects more like a window, extending almost the entire length of the wall. It was strange that however much fatigue and wine had dulled his senses, he had not noticed it the previous night. Neither had he realized that it was possible to forge such a large expanse of plate glass. And it was so clear. Perhaps it was not glass at all, but some extraordinary form of crystal. Magic, perhaps, if one believed in such a thing.

Beyond the transparent door lay a spacious terrace, the surface patterned in highly-polished tiles of scarlet, silver, black and gold. Beowulf pushed open the door and stepped through.

The terrace was bordered by a low parapet constructed of another substance with which Beowulf was unfamiliar. Dardo had told him of the building materials he had encountered in the Empire of the Cassars, made of sand and limestone mixed with water. Yet he did not think it was that. More than anything, it resembled some form of olive-green translucent stone, gleaming darkly in the morning sun. Or rather the morning light, for although the sky was shining, there seemed no source

195

of illumination.

From the parapet to the north-west, Beowulf could view the whole of the shining city laid out before him - domes and minarets of sparkling stone, glass and metal, spacious terraces and bridges linking mighty constructions built high in the air, and other buildings which piled storey upon storey, hundreds of windows piercing constructions higher than any he had ever seen, so that he could imagine that they almost touched the sky. Faraway, carriages crawled along straight roads built with geometic precision. Carriages rendered tiny, and their detail indistinguishable, by distance; but allowing for that distance he realized that they must be travelling, not at snail's pace as he had first thought, but almost inconceivably fast. It occurred to him to wonder whether this vision presaged the remote future. Would the whole world be like this one day?

And now he could see even beyond the glittering city, to the icy blue mountains of Shadron Mor on the horizon to the north-east, and the thickly forested valleys to the south and west. In the south-east there should have been the morning sun, yet although the sky was bright and cloudless he could not see it.

'My lord.'

He turned. The Queen stood beside him, clad in a cloak of dark green over a gown of gold. Around her head, she still wore the golden circlet confining her light bronze hair.

'Madam.'

She waved a hand. 'Will you break fast with me, my lord?'

He had not noticed that upon the terrace a table had been prepared, bearing eating and drinking vessels of china and glass. Amongst the Northmen the first meal of the day was usually bread and cheese, or at best some form of grain mixed into a gruel. And generally, it was the only meal of the day to be unaccompanied by strong drink. But this was far finer; finer indeed than any northern dinner, with choice cuts of meat and poultry garnished with honey and spices, accompanied by sweetmeats of a type unknown in Gothmark. Beowulf's only misgiving, faced with this delicious fare, was that it would prove a trifle rich for the first meal of the day.

Again his glance strayed beyond the meal, the terrace, and the city, even to the farthest horizons. Directly ahead the land fell away to form a deep valley, which must be that of Yflon, where the strange beasts dwelt. Beyond, hazy mountain-tops thrust their peaks into the lambent sky. And upon the horizon, in the saddle between two of the peaks, there stood a horseman, in armour of red and gold, the device of a black eagle upon his shield. His mount was a well-muscled chestnut, polished coat shining in the morning light, and caparisoned in the finest multi-coloured silks. It was armoured too; both head and breast, with a silver spike between its eyes giving it the appearance of a unicorn. It was not clear to Beowulf how he could determine so much detail of a figure afar off, but it was so.

He glanced to the left. Within a densely wooded valley lay a broad mountain lake, wavelets glistening in the morning light. Upon the far shore, he could see another horse; grey this time, and apparently an old animal, for the grey tended towards white. Likewise armed for war, less gloriously but more heavily, with plate armour upon its withers and haunches, beneath which a coat of mail hung down to protect its flanks. The rider was armoured in silver-grey, and upon his shield he bore a red cross.

Beowulf turned again. Behind him, the mountains were highest of all, great jagged peaks rearing many thousand feet into the sky. And again, upon the horizon, a horseman. Clear as ever, upon a bay or brown horse, the rider armed all in black. Lightly armed compared with the others, yet of the three he seemed to Beowulf the most terrible. Even at the first sight of the rider, fear gripped his heart. Irrational fear; for what it was about the rider that thus terrified him he could not say. A fear the more terrible for being of the unknown. Upon his shield, the rider bore the device of a saltire.

Beowulf thought that that was all; but then, as he turned his head to the right, beyond the great city, upon the farthest horizon, standing in a cleft between the mountains to the north-west, he glimpsed the fourth horseman. Unlike the others he was not caparisoned in splendour, but clad as a simple warrior, in battered armour and leather. Upon his head he bore a conical helmet of a type from long ago. He was a very tall old man, with a grizzled beard and a patch over one eye. In his right hand he held a spear. His horse was tall and lean, and pale in colour.

Beowulf should have known him, and had the feeling that indeed he did know him; that he had met him not long ago, maybe in a dream. Strange that his mind did not seem to be working with its usual facility. Perhaps he had met the man in real life, and this was the dream. That would explain why his reasoning powers were less acute than normal. Which was the dream, and which reality? What happened when one awoke from a dream? Perhaps the people one had met in the dream, being products of one's own imagination, died upon the instant. But from their point of view, it could be that he was the one who had died, while they continued to live. What happened to the man one had been in a dream, when one awoke? Maybe life was nothing but a dream, a magic show or chimaera, a phantasy, from which one was woken at the moment of death ...

'They are the horsemen of Shadron Mor,' the Queen explained. 'Perennial scouts and guardians against the forces of evil. To the south-west, upon the red horse, you see Armin of Teutonia, Guardian against

197

the Empire of the Great Cassars, whose power is waning. To the south-east, upon the white horse, stands Crusad of Torqueman, Guardian against the forces of the Crescent Moon, whose fortunes are waxing. Whilst to the north-east, upon the black horse, stands the Rider without a Name, Guardian against the forces of the Lord of the East, the eternal source of evil.'

Beowulf frowned. 'And what of the fourth horseman?'

'The fourth?'

'Him upon the pale horse, guarding the north-west.'

The Queen shook her head, puzzled. 'There is no fourth horseman.'

Beowulf looked again, but the horseman had vanished. He had glimpsed him only momentarily, yet he was sure that he had seen him. Once again, he remembered something from afar off, as it were a distant dream. And he was seized by an irrational conviction that of the four horsemen, this one, despite his humble attire and sudden disappearance, was the mightiest of them all. He was both life and death. He had always existed, and always would.

'Methinks you are tired, my lord,' said the Queen kindly. 'It is time you took your rest.'

That seemed strange too, because it seemed to Beowulf that he had only just risen. But time was so confused in this bright city that it was possible many hours had passed without his being conscious of them. And certainly the sky was darker than before. Glancing down at the table, he noticed to his surprise that he had almost finished the meal. Indeed, he had apparently dined most handsomely. The whole of a chicken lay before him, picked clean to the bones, and the last remains of vegetables covered with rich sauces. A half-eaten loaf of bread lay beside his plate, and a final morsel smeared with honey. His wine-glass was empty, but not clean. Yet he could not remember eating or drinking anything. And he did feel so tired ...

"Most gracious of you, my lady,' he said. 'It's true that I feel a trifle tired. With your permission, I think I will turn in.'

IT seemed to be night when Beowulf awoke once more. His head was clearer, though he felt lethargic and unrefreshed. He could not tell how long he had been asleep, but from the state of the candle beside his bed, he estimated about two hours. Several hours more before he need rise, so he could catch up further on his sleep. Not without effort, he removed his shirt and breeches, and blew out the candle.

He was drifting into the state between sleep and consciousness when he was disturbed by a soft sound like a footfall, and opened his eyes. He rubbed them to make sure that what he saw was the truth.

The Queen stood by his bedside, bearing a candle which she placed upon the table. She held a finger to her lips for silence.

Beowulf could not have spoken had he wished. In the candlelight the silken transparency of her gown was more sweetly erotic than if she had been naked. She was exquisitely slender, save for the fullness of her breasts. Sweet perfume arose from her body as she leant forward to kiss him softly. The gown opened to reveal her superb breasts to full view.

It was the first time he had realized that the Queen had intended any hospitality beyond that normally expected from a gracious hostess. Although she had seemed a remarkably beautiful woman, there had been other things to think about, and the possibility of dalliance had never seriously occurred to him. Besides, she had seemed ethereal and above such things somehow. It was all dreamlike, unreal. Yet now he realized that he had never wanted a woman so much. He reached out to drag the flimsy gown from her, whilst she began talking in a low voice, murmuring of her need for him. In the morning he might wonder if it had all been a dream, as indeed perhaps it was ...

Of a sudden the dream took a different turn. In the wall beyond, he saw a clear vision of a woman's face; a face, not fair and smiling like the Queen's, but dark as night, and scowling furiously. Not beautiful, but plain, with funny protruding teeth. The face of a moody slave, flawed and vulnerable.

The Queen, completely naked by now, looked troubled as she observed the shadow cross his face. Even in the heat of his passion, as he kissed the smooth creamy breasts, it occurred to him to wonder whether the Queen offered all her guests the same delicious extra feast. And he was conscious that he felt a little disappointed in her. In his mind's eye, he could still see Suth, dark and scowling as ever.

The mural was becoming clearer now. Something was indeed wrong, very wrong. Longspear was trying to warn him of something. And, horror of horrors! Longspear was about to fall! Dmitri, the Son of Muspelheim, was riding in triumph! And amongst his ghastly retinue was the figure of a woman. It was wrong, wrong ... for this woman was ...

'Enjoy me, my lord,' purred the Queen, opening her mouth.

In that moment, Beowulf knew. Knew even before his lips and tongue reached the mark at the base of her left breast. The dark red mark in the shape of a twisted cross. He knew it at last, and to his shame and horror realized that in a sense a part of him had always known. Suth was his woman, and the Queen a vicious slut. Nay, far worse, a creature of Hel and Muspelheim ...

As he pushed her away, she opened her mouth again with a hiss. The enigmatic smile of the evening before had been concealing two rows of pointed, sharp-filed teeth. Most dreadful sight of all, the creature's eyes changed as he watched, from blue to deep violet, and finally to burning red. She flung herself upon him, screaming, biting and spitting with rage, clawing with her nails and abusing him in the foulest language, whilst the beautiful face contorted with insane savagery into the likeness of a fiend.

'Guards! Guards!' she screamed. 'Seize him! Seize him!' Beast-like slobber dripped from her jaws. 'Should he escape, you die by torture!'

There was no chance of that, for a dozen warriors piled into the room upon the instant, armed with pikes and axes, which they held to Beowulf's breast as he rose. He glanced helplessly from side to side.

'You are taken, Gothic lord,' said the Queen, her voice a hiss of hellish joy. 'You fool. Did you not know? Ragnar of Torre promised you to me. Would that I could have enjoyed you first, for you have a splendid body, but some other time for that. You have spurned the Queen of Helheim - for that, your death shall be even more exquisitely agonizing.' She turned to the guards and nodded. 'Proceed.'

Beowulf braced himself for the sensation of steel entering his vitals. But instead, it was a blow to the ribs with a mailed fist. He struggled and fought, but to no avail, as four of them brought him down like mastiffs on a bear. There were more blows, from boots and clubs. He heard and felt a rib go. A delay as always, then came the pain. His face was bleeding and bludgeoned, lips swollen around broken teeth.

'Smash his legs,' he heard the Queen say happily. 'Cripple him, and convey him to the dungeons.'

'Then, Prince of the Goths,' he heard her breathe softly in his ear through the fog of pain, 'slow and delicious tortures shall be inflicted on you, so that you scream for death before you die. Your men are already in the dungeons, drunk or drugged, where a similar fate awaits them. But you, I promise, shall suffer most.'

His senses reeled from another blow to the head. They were still hitting him, but the pain was receding. The last thing he heard before the darkness and silence was the Queen shrieking, 'His eyes! Let me pluck out his eyes!'

Twenty-four

BEOWULF WAS vaguely conscious of a voice, though the words made little sense. There was a dank smell, as of moss or decaying vegetation. Opening his eyes, he saw a slimy grey wall oozing moisture. At least he had not been blinded, yet.

The voice was male; harsh and uncultured. He was seized with sudden terror that it was that of the demon, Ragnar of Torre, but somehow he would have expected him to be better spoken. He felt a slap across the mouth, and a man's face entered his field of vision A filthy, loathsome face, unshaven but not bearded.

'So, big fellow,' said the gaoler, 'you've come to your senses already. Quicker than I'd expected. That blow on the head would have felled an ox, so they tell me.'

Beowulf shook his head, which was a mistake, for it felt as if his brain was being battered against the inside of his skull. The room blurred and swam. His legs, though sore, were unbroken, but his left ankle was manacled to a huge iron ball. He tried moving his arms, but for some reason they would not respond.

'No good,' said the man with sadistic satisfaction. 'Those bracelets are solid ironwork, and anchored a foot deep. You could stay here till you rot, but will not be that lucky.'

'Where am I?'

'Why, in the lowest, most stinking dungeon in Atrofon, from which escape is impossible. Your henchmen are in similar case, strung up by their wrists until the time comes for their despatch.' The man leered at him, his face blotched and ulcerated as with some leprous disease. His breath was foul. 'Would you like to hear how that will be accomplished?'

'No doubt you will tell me.'

'Indeed. You will be killed at the rate of half a dozen or so a day. Any quicker and there would be less pleasure in it. You, being the leader, will be saved till last. The Queen is especially offended with you, and has vowed to make your ordeal particularly hideous. She is still considering the precise means. Our master is content to leave the decision to her.'

'Ragnar of Torre?'

Even in the midst of his gloating the man flinched. 'That name is seldom spoke,' he said eventually, 'even by the Queen, whose lord he is. The Prince of the East, as we prefer to call him, he who is most powerful, bright and terrible, has a use for those who fall into his power, especially warriors.'

'How so?'

'Their souls are sucked out and sent to Hel. Meanwhile their bodies remain available for the creatures of Muspelheim to inhabit.'

'So Breck Bronding ...'

'Right. The real Bronding is in Helheim. The Thing your friend saw last night was not the Bronding, just his shell. Likewise his sister.'

'Are you ... one of them?'

The man laughed coarsely. 'Fuh! Not I. Not until the day of my death, and with luck that should yet be far away. I still inhabit the body I was born in. You would not call me a good-looking man, I dare say.'

Beowulf did not reply.

'You have the sense not to agree with me too readily, or I would have sunk my fist in your gut. But the spectres who stalk the halls of Atrofon have well-proportioned human bodies, like the Things you saw at the banquet last night.'

Beowulf felt obscurely grateful for the muddled state of his wits, which somewhat dulled the horror.

'What we do,' continued the gaoler, who seemed in talkative mood, 'is search for the weaknesses in our captives, those most susceptible to our lord. They are then invited to assist us in some way, avoiding pain themselves by inflicting it on others. Very few refuse, indeed most soon acquire a taste for it. Then they are killed; their souls fly to our lady in Hel, whilst their bodies remain here for their new occupants.'

'What of those who do not submit?'

'In a sense they are our failures, though they are put to death most horribly of all. Some say their souls mount to the abode of the gods in Asgard or Fanagard, but as to that I know not. Their bodies, by the time we have finished with them, are of little use to us or anyone.'

'Appalling.'

'We have already succeeded in our design with one of your colleagues. He took but little persuading to join us. Indeed we found him a most co-operative fellow altogether. He has volunteered to assist me in making your departure from this life as slow and unpleasant as possible.'

Beowulf could not imagine who it could be. Belatedly it dawned. Amongst the Goths there had been but a single malcontent. He should have known.

Beyond the iron gate to his cell a figure emerged from the shadows. Then the man stepped forward to peer at him through the bars. In the dim light it took a moment to recognize him. But it was all wrong. It could not be.

'Gamli!'

The jovial, honest Gamli. Surely not.

His former henchman smiled his ever-ready smile, and nodded slowly. 'Who were you expecting? That imbecile Hersir, I suppose. Indeed I had hopes of him at one time, but it was not to be. Always grumbling about you and his lot in general – he seemed a promising candidate for the service of our lord. A great disappointment, he proved.' Gamli shook his head in mock sorrow. 'A very great disappointment, I fear.'

'What's happened to him?'

Again the smile. 'What do you think? There was no alternative. When I put the proposal to him, do you know what the damned fool said?'

'Tell me.'

'I cannot recall the exact words, but the gist of it was: "The prince is a soft young bastard, and we'll never be the best of friends. But it takes more than a spell of latrine duty to make a Northman betray his lord." ' Gamli shrugged. 'In fact those were his last words. As I say, there was no alternative.'Yet again he smiled. 'I shoved my knife into the idiot's gut, there and then.' The smile became a broad grin. 'I can still see the expression of surprise on his face.'

'But why? For Odin's sake, why?'

'Why? Well, I have always hated you, Beowulf of Slane. That I, a housekarl from one of the oldest families in Gothmark, should have to take orders from a simpleton. A craven, idle, ignorant milksop, brought up in conditions of privilege beyond belief. And that despite being the spawn of a murderer and a whore.' The smiling mask slipped to reveal an expression of cold hatred. 'My father, remember him?'

'I never knew him. Was he not killed on campaign aginst the Great Cassar?'

'Indeed, that was the story. The truth was rather different. A few years after the last Sferian War your father led a force of Northern volunteers to help defend Rothgar, King of the Dan, from invasion by the Great Empire. Your mother accompanied him on the campaign. Unusual, but methinks he must have guessed what had passed between her and Olaf Wylfing, and dared not leave her at home. At any rate, it seems that by then the scandal was widely rumoured in the army.

'Realizing that she was naught but the veriest whore, my father attempted her. The stupid slut resisted, and your father had him hanged for attempted ravishment. The official story was that he had died in battle. But of course the soldiers knew the truth, and some of them talked. Publicly hanged, for the honour of a whore!

But I shall avenge him, never fear. And most approropriately, too. For 'twill mean not only your own death, but that of your little slut. My father might have failed in his attempt upon your father's woman, but I shall help myself to yours. And like you, she shall beg for death, long ere it comes.'

Something gripped Beowulf by the throat. 'Suth? You have her?'

Gamli's gloating face fell momentarily. 'Not yet, I fear. But she cannot hide from us for long. And the longer it takes to find her, the longer shall be her ordeal.'

'You will be dealt with last,' said the gaoler with relish. 'Our lady, being full of the most marvellous vindictiveness toward you, has persuaded the Prince of the East to allow her to deal with you and your men personally, for all that it means wasting some fine physical specimens. She has delayed the gouging of your eyes and breaking your legs, since she would prefer it done in public. Besides, she may wish to enjoy you carnally first. After being blinded and gelded, you will be led back here and prepared for the next day's entertainment. Artistically handled, a man's despatch may take the best part of a week. I am the best executioner in Atrofon, and can guarantee to hold a man that long. Days before the end, you will be begging for death.' With a leer, the man drew back his cloak to reveal a light, strong sword with foreign runes on the hilt. 'Recognize him?'

'Mine,' said Beowulf shortly.

'Wrong. He is now mine, or will be once I have earned him. It is customary to reward an executioner who has done a good job, and if I make you squirm I have been promised the sword. I will earn him bravely, never fear.'

'I'm sure you will.'

'I will help,' said Gamli. 'Let me help, gaoler, I beg you. I must be allowed to help you! I must!'

Spittle was dribbling from a corner of his mouth. Beowulf intercepted a glance from the gaoler which even in the midst of his gloating might have contained something of contempt. 'Well, we shall see about that. Anyway, big fellow, next door is the Chamber of Death, where most of your companions lie. One or two of them will be despatched within earshot, so that you may hear their screams as the guts are torn from their bodies. But you, as I have said, will be made a public show. Word has gone about the city of such a spectacle to be provided within the week.'

'Do all the citizens of this place delight in such things?'

'But of course,' replied the man softly. 'They love a good show. It matters not who the victims are. They are not vindictive, I assure you. It is nothing personal against you.'

'It is for me,' said Gamli softly, licking his lips. 'Oh yes, it is for me.'

'We are the creatures of Hel and Muspelheim,' the gaoler explained. 'Shadron Mor is our vanguard upon Middle Earth. In the last days we shall conquer utterly. Meanwhile, nothing gives us more pleasure than contriving and observing the torture of the helpless. Here is a sample.'

A fist slammed into Beowulf's smashed ribs. After a moment came the spasm of pain, intensifying until something seemed to snap inside his head, and blackness returned.

BEOWULF heard another voice, cracked with age. Whoever it was seemed to be speaking to him. He opened his eyes.

'Ah, the Gothic prince, is it not? What?'

Beowulf turned his head. His blurred vision gradually focused. It was a prisoner in the next cell, from which his own was separated by a metal grille taking the place of a wall. It was odd that he had not noticed him before. The poor wretch was an old man, indescribably filthy, and like Beowulf himself, suspended from handcuffs drilled into the wall. His face was almost completely obscured by his long white hair and beard, which could not have been cut for years. The gods alone knew how he had managed to survive so long.

'You'll be with us for a while, I expect,' said the old man. 'Or maybe not, if you're lucky.'

Beowulf blinked and focussed again. Considering how long he must have been here, the man was in remarkably good condition for his age. That was to say he was not dead yet, though his arms and legs were ulcerated from his gyves, and despite being emaciated he seemed reasonably alert.

'They can't kill me, the rotten bastards,' grunted the old fellow triumphantly. 'They can't kill me.'

Beowulf rather doubted that, but the aged man's wits had evidently deserted him from long years' imprisonment. 'What's your name?' Beowulf asked.

'It be so long ago,' croaked the ancient one, 'that I've forgotten. They only feed me twice a week, you know, but I survive. I wake up every morning and tell myself I've cheated death another day. Mind you, you probably won't last so long.'

'Probably not,' Beowulf agreed.

The old fellow gave a senile chuckle. 'The last one they had in here, he were finished within a week. Died of gaol fever before they had a chance to get to work on him. I didn't get it, though. I never catch nothing. I've been here nigh on twenty years, and never had a day's sickness. Never a day's illness in my life.'

'Really?'

'They reckon they keep me here to demoralize the other prisoners,' continued his garrulous companion. 'But I know better. They can't kill me, you see. They tried hanging me once, and that were no good.'

'Amazing.'

'Aye. I must be the oldest prisoner in Atrofon. Have been these many years. Most of the others, they hardly last any time at all.'

That he had been left alive so as to demoralize his fellow-prisoners Beowulf could well believe. 'You know the secret of survival here?' the mad old man continued. 'Don't let the bastards grind you down. That's all it is. Don't let the bastards get you down, that's my motto.'

An observation of remarkable unoriginality, yet the old fellow seemed to imagine he had coined it. It should have been of little comfort to one who faced the imminent prospect of death by obscene mutilation, yet something about the old man's insane cheerfulness gave him courage. And for all that he had lost his wits, he was the nearest thing in Atrofon to a fellow human being.

Apart from Beowulf's own men. Remembering them had the opposite effect. They were all in the same plight as himself, and he was to blame.

All, that was, apart from Gamli. Beowulf felt himself choked by an unfamiliar emotion, rising in his throat until he felt an overwhelming need to vomit. Then he recognized it. It was hate. In all his life he had never hated anyone before. Yet now he longed to see Gamli dying in great pain.

'We had a little wench in here just now,' burbled the old man. 'Saucy little minx she were, an' all.'

'Just now,' Beowulf judged, could have meant any time during the last ten years. Time was meaningless here. 'Oh, yes?' he said.

'Aye. Naughty little thing. Flirting with the gaoler, she were, then with me. He didn't like that. Didn't like it at all. Not that she were much of a looker, mind. Not her face, any road. Teeth stuck out a bit.' He laughed crudely. 'But you don't look at the mantlepiece when you're poking the fire. That's what I always say. Yes, that's what I always say. You don't look at the mantlepiece when you're poking the fire, heh-heh.'

'Yes. You've already said that.' A thought struck Beowulf. 'Protruding teeth, you said?'

'Aye, protruding, that's the posh word for it.'

'What did she look like otherwise? What colour was her hair?'

'Eh? Oh, very dark. Black. Unusual for a wench round here to have black hair. Mostly they're fairish. In the Northlands, that is. I come from the Northlands myself, you know. Black hair, she had. Her face were dark, an' all. Not black, like an Ethiope, but dark.'

Surely it couldn't be. 'Dark,' Beowulf repeated, half to himself.

'Oh, aye. Darkest wench I've seen for many a year.' The old man cackled again. 'Come to think of it, she's the only wench I've seen for many a year. But when you get to my age, that don't signify so much.'

'I'll take your word for it,' said Beowulf absently. Did she give her name?'

'Now, funny you should say that. She hadn't told the gaoler her name, but she mentioned it to me while he was sulking. Damned if I can remember it now, though.'

'Try.'

'Sue, was it? Nah. Something like that, though.'

'Suth?'

'Aye, that's it.'

What in Helheim could she be doing here? A diabolical possibility struck Beowulf: that she had been corrupted by her former master, and returned to serve him again. Worse still, perhaps her allegiance had been with the forces of darkness all the time. Maybe the whole story of her being an abused slave had been falsehood, and she had been sent to lure him and his men to destruction here ... Perhaps she was the Helqueen herself in different form. Or perhaps his wits were on the turn. Since arriving in this foul place it had been difficult to distinguish truth from fiction.

'She said, ah-hah, it's coming back to me now ... She said, "Tell the big fellow you've seen me. And tell him, don't despair. Good and ill fortune fall equally on good men and on bad. All that matters to the gods is how you cope with it." '

'She said that?'

'Aye. Funny thing to say, weren't it? 'Specially with her being such a cheeky little minx otherwise. Now, when she said "big fellow" I didn't know who she meant at the time, because the gaoler ain't big, he's a right little runt.' The old man broke off to laugh and cough again. 'Or something like that. To put it politely. Runt rhymes with something else, get it?'

'Yes, thank you,' said Beowulf. 'I did get it.' What on earth was it about this crazy old man that made him want to break into laughter, despite the appalling prospect before him? As if even the forces of evil themselves could not defeat a feeble old fellow's crackpot humour. And what Suth had said ... If indeed it had been Suth.

'Anyway, what was I saying, oh yes - big fellow. I never see anyone else, right, except an occasional prisoner in your cell. So, by the big fellow, she must've meant you. You're big enough. I hadn't thought of that. Of course, you weren't actually here then, but she must have knowed you were coming.'

Beowulf shook his head. 'I can't think how.'

'Any road, that were a while ago. What's your name?' demanded his fellow-prisoner, with the sudden change of subject characteristic of children and the very old.

'Beowulf. Beowulf of Slane.'

'Oh, ah. I think I've heard of you.'

'I doubt it. I'm not very well known outside Gothmark.'

'Oh, I've been to Gothmark. Long time ago it were, but I been. Any road, Beowulf of Slane, you don't look too clever to me. Reckon I'll outlast you, like I done all the others. Mind you, you look better now than you did before. I thought you was a goner last night, you know. Just shows how wrong you can be. You done better 'n I expected already.'

'I'm glad to hear it. Now if you don't mind, I'd like to try and get some sleep.'

'It ain't easy to sleep here. The weight falls on your arms, you see, so the pain keeps you awake. And when you do wake, they feel as if they've been pulled out of their sockets. And as for cramp - I'm a martyr to cramp, you know ...'

Beowulf was not listening. He slept.

Twenty-five

THIS TIME he was roused by a woman's voice. 'Your meal, Sir Executioner.'

He opened his eyes. The gaoler was seated at a rough wooden table, eyeing the delicacies before him. The serving wench stood with her back to Beowulf. She was very small and wore a long dark cloak, draped over her head and extending almost to her ankles. It fell open as she leant forward.

'You're a well-breasted little piece,' said the gaoler appreciatively. 'Come here.'

The girl appeared to be unbuttoning her blouse. The gaoler grunted and pawed at her, pushing the cloak from her shoulders whilst she giggled sluttishly. Now he was drooling at her throat. Suddenly she drove her right hand back and forth.

The gaoler made a strange sobbing sound, and his eyes, which had been gleaming piggishly, widened and stared straight ahead. His mouth fell open. A crimson stream began to mingle with the spittle, slowly at first. Then he coughed up a great globule of dark blood. The woman's hand was jerking from side to side as well as up and down. With a thrill of horror Beowulf realized that she had driven a weapon deep into the man's belly, and was moving it about to inflict maximum damage and suffering. Blood gushed from the gaoler's nose and mouth in a torrent; he made an obscene gargling sound and fell.

The woman stepped back. The long knife in her right hand was drenched in blood and filth, with some of the man's entrails still attached to it. Her hand, arm and cloak were soaked in blood, scarlet and crimson, fresh and congealing. Miraculously the gaoler was not yet dead, but wallowing on all fours amidst his blood and spilt guts. In a gesture both futile and hideous, he was trying to push the butchered organs back into his body. He even managed to lay a hand on his precious sword. The woman let him do so, then with slow and calculated cruelty ground his hand under her boot. As the bones splintered he tried to scream, but could only manage a breathless hiss. Beowulf turned away and felt the need to be sick.

'Suffer, Hellian,' came the woman's voice, thick with triumphant cruelty. 'Know a little of the pain you have been wont to inflict on others.'

Finally she deigned to pick up Ljani's sword and end his agony. At a single blow, the gaoler's head bounced across the floor. Half a dozen fountains spurted from the blood-vessels of the neck.

In Beowulf's confused state of mind he could only imagine that this strange, terrible woman was the Queen, come to inflict tortures on him herself rather than leave the pleasure to the executioner. But he could not think why she had killed the man.

She turned and passed a hand across her face. The sluttish cosmetic was wiped away, and he recognized her as Suth. Something of his terror and revulsion must have shown in his face, for she said, 'Fear not, my lord. I am come to rescue you.' She retrieved the keys from the gaoler's headless corpse and moments later the door to Beowulf's cage swung open.

With a mad spasm of hope, he wrenched at the chains. The muscles of his back and shoulders bunched into giant knots as he heaved first on the right one, then the left. 'It is no good, Suth,' he gasped in despair. 'They are sunk in the stone a foot deep.'

Along the far wall stood a rack full of tools of the executioner's craft. Suth selected a two-handed axe as heavy as herself. 'Hold the chain tight against the wall, my lord.'

Beowulf shook his head, in his hysteria half-laughing despite his fear. 'Hopeless, little one. It takes a berserker to lift that thing. You will not even be able to drag it across the floor.'

She braced herself, and with a convulsive effort smashed the chain to fragments as he watched in disbelief. 'Now the other, my lord.'

Again she shattered it with a single blow of demoniacal power, and dealt similarly with the chain on his ankle. 'Are you fit to walk, my lord?'

The bizarrre idea occurred to him that if he said no she would offer to carry him. He moved his feet painfully. 'I think so.'

'Good.' She handed him the sword. He swung it a couple of times, wincing as the pain stabbed his ribs, but felt the strength surge back into his arms and shoulders.

'A splendid weapon, Suth, but you have earned it. I shall take the axe. And this, methinks.' From the gaoler's collection he selected a

210

massive club, with head-spikes four inches long.

'There is no time to lose, my lord. Your men are in the cells nearby.'

'Right. But first let's free the other prisoner.'

'What other prisoner, my lord?'

'Why, the funny old fellow in the cell next to mine.'

'The cell next to yours is empty, my lord.'

Beowulf stared in disbelief. It was as she said. Of his erstwhile companion there was no trace. Nothing but a broken chain hanging from the wall and a semi-literate runic inscription scraped upon the stones. With his new-found skill Beowulf tried to decipher it: '(Illegible) ... was here ...' The sort of thing the mad old man probably would have scrawled if he had had the use of his hands.

Beowulf shook his head. 'I can't understand it. We had quite a long chat. He said he had spoken with you, and ...'

'I have not spoken with anyone. Hurry, my lord, please.'

He shrugged, and shook his head again. 'Funny, I could have sworn ...' It occurred to him that he had never seen the man's face save in profile. And he had said that he had been hanged ...But already the memory was beginning to fade.

They mounted the steps to the passage. A guard from next door, clad in red and black, looked out to see what was happening. Beowulf splattered his brains with the club, and they entered the chamber beyond.

A dozen Goths were chained to the wall in conditions similar to his own. Their two guards, taken by surprise, were cut down instantly. One of them wore a bunch of keys on a chain around his belt. Within seconds Suth was freeing the prisoners, whilst Beowulf helped distribute weapons from the armoury next door.

Further guards, hearing the commotion, were waiting in the passage, but proved no match for their former captives, crazy for revenge. The mutilated bodies of their enemies were kicked aside and trampled underfoot as the Goths poured out.

Last to be freed were the other leaders, who like Beowulf had each been accorded a cell of their own. Ifar's guard, slower-witted than most, turned only as the Goths entered. With a long sweep of her sword, Suth cut him almost in two at the waist, as Beowulf simultaneously pulped his head.

'Well,' said Ifar, a little shaken, 'that seems to be the end of him. Are we all here?'

'Too bad if we're not,' replied Beowulf briskly. 'Let's go.'

'I know the way out, my lord,' said Suth.

He nodded. 'Go ahead. You are our leader now.'

*   *   *

'AH, Gamli,' breathed Dardo softly. 'I am glad our paths have crossed. So very glad.'

A couple of Goths threw the captive on the stones before him. 'Mercy, I beg, Dardo!' screamed the frantic wretch. 'I ever loved you and your lord! I spoke as I did lately under duress. In my heart, I thought nothing of the sort.'

'Well, we shall soon be examining your heart, and while it is still beating too.' Dardo's saturnine face darkened further. 'I knew the truth about your father, Gamli, and suspected it of you. Good old Gamli! Everybody's friend! Imbecile that I was not to tell Lord Ifar of my suspicions!'

'No-one loves a tale-bearer, Dardo,' one of his companions reminded him. You cannot be blamed.'

'Whether I can or not, let us try to put things right now. A good thing the Earl of Slane is not about. I fear he might disapprove of what we plan to do. A good fellow, you understand, but a shade squeamish at times.'

His companions nodded. 'A little squeamish, it's true,' agreed one of them, smiling wryly. 'There's no other criticism I can make of him, but it has to be admitted, the prince is a trifle on the squeamish side for a Northman.'

'Oh, by the blest gods! Let it be quick!'

From without came the sounds of battle. Dardo sighed impatiently. 'A pity we have not more time, but we must do our best. I had been thinking of the blood-eagle, but fear would take too long to inflict, besides leading to too quick a death. Impalement it must be. And unfortunately we shall want the time to witness the end, so let us leave him to wallow in his own guts for an unpleasant hour or two.' He nodded to his henchmen. 'Proceed.'

THE HELLIAN guards were still disorganized, appearing on the scene in twos and threes, to be slaughtered by the furious Goths without the loss of a man. The prisoners emerged blinking into the torchlit palace courtyard, where further carnage was done. For the first time in his life, Beowulf went berserk, wielding axe in one hand, mace in the other, smashing heads right and left. After the rescue, he had expected Suth to leave the fighting to the men, but she was in the thick of the struggle, and demonstrating no mean powers of swordsmanship. Or swordswomanship, thought Beowulf. In his abnormal state of mind this pathetically feeble joke seemed uproariously funny, and he laughed like a madman. The bodies of their adversaries became an obstacle to progress, as the Goths had to clamber over great heaps of dead and dying. Alarms had sounded, and Hellian reinforcements were arriving faster than they could be killed. About this time the first Goth fell, a

Hrosnaberger being unable to parry simultaneous thrusts from two of the enemy. His comrades exacted savage revenge. Amidst the tumult, from the east tower they could hear the Hellian Queen, screeching:

'Call out the Red Guard! Archers! Archers! Cut them to pieces! Finish them with arrows!'

A flight of death sang into the struggling mass, killing friend and foe alike. It seemed like the end for the Goths, but Ifar and Dardo rallied their men and led the Hrosnabergers in a mad charge, storming the turret stairs to the archers' gallery. Meanwhile the Red Guard, evidently elite troops, attacked in flank, but the men of Slane, berserk from fear and rage, drove them back pell-mell and slaughtered ten for one. Two more fell to the arrows before Ifar and his men reached the archers, tore them apart and threw their bodies down on to the cobbles.

Then the hail of death fell on the Hellians as the Hrosnabergers launched their own arrows against them. Amidst jeers from the outnumbered Goths, the guards fell back to defend the palace chambers.

'At least we can die like men, my lord,' said Kjartan, 'instead of animals in the shambles.'

'Courage, man,' urged Suth impatiently. 'You despair too soon.'

''Tis true we have slain twenty for one,' agreed Beowulf, 'but they still outnumber us a hundredfold. The best we can do is sell our lives dear.'

Kjartan pointed to the highest tower, where further archers were taking position. The Hrosnabergers struck first, bringing down several like birds from their perches, but following an exchange of fire were compelled to abandon their stronghold and rejoin their comrades below.

'This way, my lord,' said Suth. 'Follow me.'

Beowulf signalled the survivors to obey, holding off the enemy meanwhile. Suth, with bloodstained sword, led them to a far corner of the courtyard, where fierce fighting resulted in the slaying of a dozen more Hellians for two Goths.

Suth pounced on an iron hatch amidst the cobbles, seized the ring and raised it with a spasmodic heave. 'The palace drain,' she explained, climbing down. 'Be quick.'

It never occurred to him to query her, and the Goths followed one by one. From the large chamber beneath the hatch there led a culvert, not three feet across and jet black within. With an impatient cry of 'Hurry up!' Suth grabbed a firebrand from the wall, plunged into the narrow opening and writhed ahead on her belly. Inside, the culvert was smoothly tiled, but the filth and stench were appalling, far worse than that of the gaol. In sudden panic, Beowulf wondered what would happen if the culvert never became any wider. In the flickering light he could still see the slave, her trim little behind wriggling from side to side.

'Do you know where we're going, Suth?' he called.

'Yes, my lord, don't worry. It soon gets wider. Watch the slope though, it is quite steep.'

Indeed, the passage soon became both steeper and wider, so that it was increasingly difficult to maintain a grip on the tiles. Suth was scrabbling at the walls to delay her descent. So were they all, but to little avavil. The chute became steeper, they slid faster and faster, finally tumbling out one by one, none the worse save for bruises, into a much wider sewer more than the height of a man. Suth had broken Beowulf's fall, and they helped the others as they emerged. Beowulf counted. Fifteen. Amongst those missing were Hort and Ulf.

'This way,' called Suth, splashing ahead. 'No time to lose; they will soon be after us.'

'Not too soon, I trust,' said Ifar, bringing up the rear. 'For I jammed a shield across the entry to the culvert and wedged it with a couple of spears.'

'Well thought on,' said Beowulf, hurrying after her. 'How do you know this place so well, little one?'

'I was a slave here at one time, and recognized it last night, once we got inside. Slaves were not allowed outdoors, or at least I was not. What did they call the city?'

'Atrofon.'

'It was not called that when I was here. I knew it as Mactaray, but these Cities of the Damned have several names. This is the main drain, known as the Cloka. I was brought down here once to watch a drowning.'

'A what?' asked Beowulf, appalled.

'A drowning, my lord. Slaves were drowned in the sewers from time to time for minor misdemeanours, and other slaves compelled to watch.'

'God of the Gallows,' breathed Kjartan. 'What a monstrous place we have left.'

'Indeed we have. All who visit are contaminated. Did you yourselves not delight in slaughter while we were there?'

'Why, so we did,' said Kjartan. 'But killing those evil creatures hardly counts, surely.'

Beowulf understood Suth better. Never before had he felt the blind compulsion to destroy, or taken such monstrous pleasure as when he had smashed skulls and cut the creatures of Helheim to pieces. It was not good to dwell on such things.

The route had become slippery again, and the flow of slime and filthy water deeper. It was continually fed by tributaries. A large drain of clear water joined them from the right, and soon they had to wade again, led by Suth as ever.

'Do we go on?' yelled Beowulf above the torrent.

'We have to, my lord.'

'Where does it lead?'

'The river, I think. But many a mile yet.'

'On, on!' cried Beowulf. 'And quickly. We have no choice.'

Several times he was almost swept from his feet. The current was deep and strong, but less fetid. Ahead, Suth still held the brand aloft, though the water had mounted as high as her breasts. Behind her the panting Goths were slipping and staggering, supporting one another as best they could, gasping for breath in the stuffy unclean air. The flood ran stronger and faster yet.

'We must swim for it, my lord!' cried Suth, finally swept from her feet.

The brand hissed and died. Never had Beowulf known such darkness, darker than the darkest night outside - so black it pressed in on his eyes as if tangible. Like being blinded, he supposed. And there was no question of swimming; his feet were swept from the tiles, and he was borne along helplessly.

All he could do was try to keep his head above water, gasping and spluttering as he let the current do its work. How long they continued like this he could not tell. It might have been an hour, or only a quarter of that time. Around and behind him he could hear his comrades splashing about, swearing and spluttering.

'Are you still there, Suth?' he cried once, seized with sudden panic that she might have perished in the flood.

'I am beside you, my lord, never fear.'

They groped for each other and held hands. He determined that come what may, they would live or die together. At last, so tiny that at first he thought he had imagined it, a point of light pierced the blackness, like a lone star on a winter's night. He felt a surge of elation as the point became bigger - now the size of a pinhead, now a button, finally a barrel-top, and of a sudden light flooded in, blinding him in a painful glare. With aching limbs he sought a grip, but in vain ...

He was falling again, to land with a thump on wet gravel. Scrambling to his feet, eyes screwed up against the light, he found himself ankle-deep in the shallows of a broad river. Beside him, Suth was smiling and jumping up and down with excitement, like a small child.

'We have made it, my lord! We've made it!'

Beowulf kissed her quickly. 'Thanks entirely to you, my love. You have saved us all.'

Roger Butters

℧wenty-six

THE GOTHS were standing in the shallows of a swift-flowing river, banked by wooded hills. The brightness apparent from within the tunnel had been an illusion; the sky was overcast, and it was spitting with rain. Feeble sunlight filtered through to play on the deeps and ripples of the stream. Yet to Beowulf, it seemed he had never seen anything so beautiful.

Behind him, his companions were tumbling out of the culvert into the torrent; blinking, spluttering and gasping. Some were laughing wildly, others cursing, but not a man had been lost.

'Any wounded?' Beowulf enquired.

'No, my lord,' replied Suth. 'The Hellians use poisoned arrows. It is death or nothing.'

'Do you know where we are?'

'Methinks at the edge of the Blood River, or one of its main tributaries.'

The words were music to his ears. 'Why, that runs down to Kreb's Bridge and Slane.'

'It does,' agreed Ifar, 'some dozen leagues hence and more. We are not out of the wood yet. Those Sons of Muspelheim will soon be upon us, no doubt.'

'Escape by water is our best chance,' Beowulf decided. 'What weapons have we that we could use as tools?'

Their store was depleted, but included amongst other things three axes and five swords, besides Ljani's sword, still strapped to Suth's belt.

'Right,' said Beowulf. 'Three big logs should be enough. No time to build a raft, nor have we anything to secure it with. To work at once.'

He selected the trees himself from a nearby copse, and cut a stout trunk in a couple of dozen blows. The pain in his ribs, which in the heat of battle he had hardly noticed, was now agonizing, but he forced himself to ignore it. Two others took slightly longer to fell a dead ash, whilst Suth assisted those with swords to bring down a birch. The branches were trimmed back, but stumps left for handholds.

'To the river, then,' said Beowulf. 'Six men to a log. There are rapids lower down. When they occur, make for the shore as best you can. The current will be strong, so any man lost must be left to fend for himself. Agreed?'

'Aye,' said the Goths to a man.

'Push out, then. You command the first, Ifar. Dardo the second. I'll bring up the rear.'

Ifar and his men pushed out their log. As the water deepened, he gave the word and they mounted, locking legs round the trunk and gripping the stumps like the pommel of a saddle. Two men bore branches for use as punting poles. The current strengthened and bore them away.

The second log likewise gave no trouble. Last was the birch, gnarled and tough. Suth leapt astride and Beowulf followed, putting his arms around her and using the same handholds. She gripped his forearms tightly.

'Concentrate on holding the log,' ordered Beowulf sternly.

She laughed, but her reply was drowned in the tumult as spray splashed all around them. Now they were well adrift, speeding downstream with the current, and none too early for on the left bank a group of armed horsemen in the black and red livery of Atrofon waved weapons and shouted in impotent rage.

The current took still further hold, as they held on with whitening hands and locked knees. 'How fast are we going, my lord?' asked Suth.

Beowulf observed the banks moving swiftly by. 'Hard to say. As fast as a cantering horse, maybe.'

The river narrowed as cliffs jutted out on either side, and the water roared like thunder in the confined space. Rainbows, faint in the twilight, shone ephemerally in the mist and spray. The rate of fall became frightening; rock faces flashed past, seemingly inches away, and the water boiled as if in a cauldron. The Goths shouted and sang in crazy glee, half fear, half exhilaration as the torrent sped them onward to their goal.

'White water ahead!' bawled Kjartan, in leading position. 'Hold tight!'

The rapids were shallow but swift. Beowulf's legs, already bruised and battered, felt as if they were being flayed. He locked his arms around Suth's waist.

'Do not be afraid, little one!' he yelled in her ear.

She turned and laughed at his concern. 'Hold me tighter, my lord; I am not fragile.'

'You are certainly not,' he agreed. 'Hussy.'

Within moments more rapids were upon them. Beowulf felt a blow on his left knee, without pain; the gravel and stone tore at his legs. The log bobbed and rolled, but somehow they kept afloat, though choked and blinded by the spray. Time lost all meaning. Again and again, they entered white water and survived. At last the rocks receded, the widening river flowed more placidly, and straighter. Ahead, Beowulf glimpsed the logs of their companions.

'All there,' he announced in satisfaction.

'Yes, my lord.'

As Suth spoke, the men in the leading log raised their left hands in unison, and turned to look behind.

'Celebrating,' said one of Beowulf's men.

He heard a muted noise, like distant thunder, and understood. 'No!' he yelled, so loud his voice almost broke. 'Warning! Waterfall! Steer left, for the shallows!'

They thrust deep with their poles, but the current was swifter, the sound of water louder.

'Harder! Harder!' Beowulf cried, as the men poled for their lives. Nothing could be seen but mist; at any moment the river might become a bottomless gulf. Desperately they kicked, but their feet met nothing but water. The boom of the falls was louder still, yet at last it seemed to Beowulf that the poles were no longer driven so deep before they struck bottom.

Two giant shapes loomed out of the mist. 'Rocks!' he shouted. 'Our only chance!'

With agonizing slowness they forced the log towards the shallows. The sound of the falls was deafening now. The first sign of the end, he supposed, would be a dreadful falling sensation, as the river supported them no longer.

Blinded, choked and deafened, yet they were suddenly safe. With a splintering crack the log came to rest, wedged skewiff between the rocks, but firm. The Goths disembarked carefully and stiffly, then hopping, stepping and occasionally wading, made their way to the foot of the steep rock face marking the water's edge.

'Wait here till we recover our strength,' Beowulf advised. 'Then make an attempt on the cliff.'

'What of the others, my lord?' asked Kjartan, voicing the question which had occurred to them all.

Beowulf shrugged. 'I could not see what befell them. Did anyone?'

None had, but the exhilaration of their escape began to give way to increasing gloom about the fate of their friends. Beowulf looked down and took stock of his condition. For the first time he realized the state he was in. His hands, arms and legs were skinned, and the manacles had cut deep sores into his wrists and ankles. His left knee was twice its normal size. As for his ribs, the cold, wet and excitement had numbed the pain till now, but no doubt that would soon change. His companions were no better off. Tirl the minstrel had an enormous bruise on his forehead; Kjartan's left wrist was swollen, probably broken. Suth, who alone had avoided capture by the Hellians, seemed to have suffered less than any.

They set to on the assault, Suth and Beowulf first. He laboured slowly, fearful of the drop below. If he fell but ten feet, it would mean death in the torrent. Suth, less than half his weight, climbed like a mountain goat, her lean, muscular legs driving her effortlessly ahead of him. She turned, gripping a thornbush for support, and waved excitedly. He could not hear till third attempt.

'A path, my lord!'

It had been invisible from below, but there was indeed a path along the cliff-face. Refreshed by the knowledge, Beowulf made quicker progress, grabbed the rock to which Suth directed him and hauled himself up beside her. Their companions joined them shortly, collapsing in varying degrees of exhaustion.

'You are tougher than any of us, Suth,' admitted Kjartan.

'I have always been a healthy slave, my lord.'

'Odin's death,' said Beowulf, pointing ahead. 'Look at that!'

Beneath them, the falls were a seething mass of spray and foam, leading to a sheer drop into a rocky vortex far below.

'Five hundred feet, must be,' said Kjartan. 'We should have been smashed to pieces.'

Beowulf nodded dejectedly. 'As our friends have been.'

'Look!' cried Suth, leaning over perilously and pointing to the base of the cliff. 'Look there!'

Clustered amongst the rocks, not fifty yards nearer the falls, was a six-strong party of Goths. 'Dardo and his men,' said Beowulf, after peering intently for a while. 'We might have known they'd make it. Shout! Encourage them!'

This they did, running along the path, waving and yelling until their lungs were sore. And matters were better than they had thought, for the first head to poke itself over the edge of the path was that of Ifar.

'We thought you had all been lost,' said Beowulf delightedly.

Ifar, still gasping for breath, shook his head. 'Not at all. Every man of us is safe, unless any fail to make the climb. We were some way ahead of Dardo's lot, and already on the ascent, which must be why you missed us.'

'This is excellent news indeed. Come, let us urge them on.'

The Gothic survivors had endured too much to let the cliff defeat them in the end. Dardo was last man up, impassive as ever, and scarcely out of breath.

'Anyone any idea where we are?' asked Beowulf. 'We must have travelled many a league.'

'If I am not mistook,' said Ifar, 'These are the Thunder Falls. There can scarcely be another lot like them in the whole of the north.'

'Difficult to be sure from above,' said Dardo, 'but as a rash youth I once accompanied a hunting party several miles beyond Kreb's Bridge, so that we could hear the falls. A couple of us even went further, and glimpsed them; as I say, difficult to be sure, but ...'

'If these are the falls, how far have we to go? Ljani's map is long lost, alas.'

Ifar smiled. 'From Thunder Falls to Kreb's Bridge is scarcely nine miles.'

'Nine miles!' exclaimed Beowulf amidst cheers. 'Why, we are practically home. On, men. The ordeal is nearly over.'

The words 'Kreb's Bridge' were a tonic to them all. The limit of knowledge for most Goths, and a wild, desolate place, but a blessed haven compared with what they had endured. And from Kreb's Bridge to the border of Slane was but a dozen miles.

The Goths marched along the path in single file, Beowulf in the lead, followed by Suth, then Tirl, singing as ever, a newly-composed account of their adventure, then the men of Slane, of Hrosnaberg, and finally Ifar.

Every man had been magnificent, thought Beowulf. Ifar, the Wylfing, an hereditary enemy, had shown nothing but friendship and steadfast loyalty. The men of Hrosnaberg had fought no less heroically than those of Slane. Servants and slaves had acquitted themselves like warriors. For Suth, words failed him. Only for himself was he less than satisfied. Fate had set him at their head, and he had not been worthy of them. He had led them to near-disaster, yet from their depleted ranks had come no word of complaint.

'You seem thoughtful, my lord,' said Suth.

'Indeed I am, little one. I was thinking of those of our number who have fallen; almost exactly half.' For apart from himself and Suth, there now survived but six warriors each from Slane and Hrosnaberg, two churls and one slave.

'The fortunes of war, my lord. You should not blame yourself.' He had not mentioned blaming himself, but she had read his thoughts.

They rounded the next bend. The river widened and became sluggish. Here in bygone days a landslip had made a natural dam, forcing the waters wide but shallow on either side. Beyond, in the far distance, they could see the low stone arches of the bridge which was their goal. With a mighty cheer the Goths pressed on, with no more than a couple of miles to go, and all but safe. Tirl led them in a final chorus of the March of the Wagmundings.

A quarter of an hour later they were less sure. 'There are men lining the bridge, my lord,' said Kjartan, coming alongside.

'I've seen them. How many, would you say?'

Kjartan screwed up his eyes to squint into the setting sun. 'As many as we are. More perhaps. And warriors.'

Warriors they were indeed, for above the sound of the water they could hear the rum-a-dum-dum of swords beaten upon shields. 'Fifty or more,' said Ifar, worried. 'Friend or foe?'

Amongst the men on the bridge flew a banner, fluttering feebly in the light breeze. 'Can you tell, my lord?' enquired Suth.

Beowulf relaxed. 'Argent and sable,' he said with a smile. 'The colours of Wagmunding.'

'Are you sure?'

'Yes, I'm sure.'

'Thanks be to Odin!' cried Suth joyfully. 'And those men who look so grim and warlike, are they yours?'

'Those of my kinsman. They hammer their shields in greeting, not defiance.'

'How can you know, my lord? The hammering began some miles back, while we could hardly see the bridge. They could not have identified us at that range, even in full daylight, let alone at dusk.'

The men were cheering now, clapping each other on the back and laughing madly as they realized they were home at last.

Beowulf had to shout to make himself heard. 'Do you see that man in the middle, upon the bay horse, who wears his sword to the right, as he were left-handed?'

'Indeed, my lord. Who is he?'

'That man,' said Beowulf, 'could have picked us out at five mile, maybe ten. He is my friend and kinsman, Athelstan of Karron Tha, who men call Hawkeye.'

Twenty-seven

BEOWULF'S PARTY camped that evening but five miles from the Slanish border, in conditions luxurious compared with those of the previous week, for Hawkeye and his men had come well equipped. After supper the Gothic survivors sat round the campfire with their hosts. As darkness closed in, the shadows held no terrors; tired but cheerful faces glowed in the firelight. Suth was at Beowulf's side as usual, half-sitting, half-lying in the crook of his arm. Beside Hawkeye, Ljani sat upon a stool formed from a sawn section of tree-stump. On the aftermorrow Hawkeye would rejoin Wanda in the Land of the Sfear, but for the next fifty hours the red maiden could enjoy the company of her hero.

'Well, Hawkeye,' said Beowulf. 'We have told our story, or most of it. What of events in the north?'

'As bad as can be. There is no choice but war.'

'So you said. Wonred's murder was a bitter blow. I fear Ifar has taken it hard.'

The new Earl of Hrosnaberg had retired early, to ponder the irony that after all the perils he had surmounted, it had been his father, safe at home, who had died by violence.

Hawkeye nodded. 'To lose both father and grandfather at a stroke, and find oneself the Earl, must take some getting used to. But your friend's absence gives us the chance to broach a subject which might have been unwelcome to him.'

'Hyglack's treachery?' For the Earls of Hrosnaberg and their followers were all Hyglack's men.

'Alleged treachery.' Hawkeye corrected. 'For although I was the victim, and most of my countrymen blamed him, I cannot say that I was entirely satisfied as to his guilt.'

Beowulf nodded thoughtfully. 'What say you, Ljani? You can divine most things. Had it not been for you, our men tonight would be content to shiver with cold at Kreb's Bridge, instead of dining in comfort seven miles nearer home.'

Ljani's red mane tumbled as she shook her head. 'Guessing the whereabouts of Brother Bear is one thing. To know the heart of a man is another. Yet ...'

'Well?'

'Prince Hyglack certainly behaved intemperately, but of course that is his way. It might even be a sign of innocence.'

'If he were innocent,' said Hawkeye, 'one would have expected him to tell the difference in the weight of his lance. I'm sure I would have done.'

'Hyglack is an exceptionally strong man, my lord. He may have lacked your sensitivity of touch.'

'It is possible. As I said, I'm not convinced either way. But if not him, who? And why?'

'Let's try to puzzle it out,' suggested Beowulf. 'I am a numbskull, of course, but talking it over we might come across a few ideas. Suppose, for argument's sake, that Hyglack is guilty. He would have required an accomplice amongst the ranks of the Sfear, for he took his lance from the Sferian end of the lists.'

'Both lances broke at the first passage of arms,' Hawkeye confirmed. 'An unusual event in itself.'

'Excessively unusual,' contributed Ljani. 'How often would you say a lance breaks in combat, Brother Bear?'

Beowulf shrugged. 'Once in twenty times?'

'Not so often,' said Hawkeye. 'And then only one lance out of the two.'

'Well then,' said Ljani, 'for both to break must be unique, or nearly so. Surely no-one would found a plot upon so slim a chance.'

'True,' agreed Beowulf. 'It was evidently arranged that Hyglack's lance broke at the first passage of arms, so that he could rearm with the guilty weapon. Yours had to break too, to prevent your unhorsing him at first attempt.'

'So both original lances were tampered with,' said Hawkeye. 'But why not just give me a flawed, Hyglack a normal lance? Then he could have knocked me over straight away, and no-one would have suspected anything.'

There was a long silence. 'I cannot think of an answer to that,' Beowulf admitted. 'You were damned lucky, anyway. You could have been killed.'

'Brother Bear,' said Ljani, 'you have spoken truer than you think. Lord Hawkeye could have been killed.'

Hawkeye snapped his fingers. 'Imbecile that I am! Of course. I did not mention it before, but an attempt was made upon my life the previous day.'

'You mean the chariot accident?' asked Ljani.

'If it was an accident; I begin to wonder now. But I was referring to the archer who took a shot at me in Castletown as I was shopping with Wanda. The slave died before he could talk.'

'Who might have wished to do such a thing? Do you know?'

Hawkeye hesitated. 'Yes,' he admitted. 'I know. Do not let what I say go further.'

'Of course not, if you forbid it.' Ljani and Suth nodded.

'The rogue was servant to my wife. As he lay dying, he confessed his guilt, and her involvement.'

'Are you certain, my lord?' asked Ljani. 'What words were used?'

'I asked if his mistress had put him up to it. He replied, "Yes, it was she." Then he died.'

'That seems to put the matter beyond doubt,' Beowulf agreed. 'They say the dying always speak the truth.'

Ljani, who detested Roslindis, said nothing, but shrugged. 'Anyway,' continued Beowulf slowly, 'if the object were to kill you, rather than just unhorse you, I should say Hyglack is probably guiltless.'

'Yes,' agreed Hawkeye. 'So should I. He seems to have no motive for my death; indeed I seem to get on with him better than most, if anything.'

Beowulf nodded. 'And to speak frankly, Hawkeye, the reputation of several jousters exceeded yours. Not only Hyglack himself, but Ottar, even Ali. Yet he bested them fair and square. What need had he to resort to villainy against you? Hyglack is not a modest man; I have no doubt he reckoned he could beat you anyway. There was no need for him to do it.'

'Many men steal,' Ljani pointed out, 'who have no need to steal. A better argument is that he was sure to be found out. And why bother with the flawed lances at all? Why not just give Hyglack the heavy weapon at once?'

'He would have spotted it at that stage,' said Hawkeye. 'Later, with a passage of arms behind him, in a state of physical excitement, he could have missed it.'

'So Hyglack is guiltless,' said Beowulf, 'unless someone can think of a flaw in our reasoning.' No-one could. 'And evidently the first pair of lances were tampered with before the fight. How could that have been achieved?'

'It would not have been difficult,' said Hawkeye. 'All lances were kept in the armourer's tent, to which everyone who rode that day had access. Jousting lances are insubstantial. A sharp tap in the right place with a hammer will cause them to flaw and crack. After that they break at the first encounter.'

'Apart from Hyglack, whom would you suspect?'

'The black knight,' said Hawkeye firmly. 'He came from - wait for it - Shadron Mor.'

Beowulf broke the silence that followed. 'The land of evil,' he said unnecessarily. 'And methinks I saw him again, in Atrofon. Though I am not sure ...' He shook his head. 'It's strange, very strange ...' Already the memory was beginning to fade. 'Well,' he continued briskly, 'though we cannot be certain, he seems to be the best bet. The scheme may well have been to kill you, Hawkeye. Alternatively, or in addition, it may have been decided to set Goth and Sferian at each other's throats.'

'They seem to have succeeded,' said Hawkeye sadly. 'War cannot in honour be prevented now. Angantyr called Hyglack nything, and a blow was struck. Besides, both parties are sworn to war by the Ninefold Oath.'

Beowulf nodded grimly. 'What is sworn cannot be unsworn. Yet after meeting with real evil, I have little stomach for fighting other Northmen.'

'Nor I, believe me, Beowulf. Yet fight we must. No doubt the Lord of Shadron will be delighted. What did you say his name was?'

'Ragnar of Torre. I had not heard of him previously. What of you, Ljani?'

Her pale face was grave in the firelight. 'One of the Sons of Muspelheim, with Fenrir and Jormungand, Garm and Hrym, Dmitri the Damned and Bogdan Half-face. Some say that Ragnar is the fiend Loki come in human form. Others, that he is the Queen of Hel, and can assume the shape of man or woman as he pleases.'

'That is mere superstition,' said Hawkeye uncomfortably. 'Old women's talk.'

'Think so if you wish, Lord Hawkeye,' said Ljani quietly. 'Till experience change your mind.'

'YOU seem preoccupied this evening, Brother Bear.'

Beowulf had arranged it so that their paths crossed, for he felt the need to speak to Ljani tonight. A little. I have been thinking; I did not perform well on the journey. Several of my decisions were wrong. Especially that which led us to Shadron Mor. I should have chosen the valley.'

'They say, the man who never made a mistake never made anything, Brother Bear.'

'But my mistakes cost men's lives. I took four-and-thirty men with me on that trip, Ljani, and brought sixteen back. Less than half. And every time I was at fault, men died who would now be alive. They fell victim to my inexperience and folly. I was so anxious to get everything right for once, too.'

'You do yourself scant justice, brother. I have overheard several of the men talking. All speak highly of your courage and resolve.'

'Courage?' Beowulf shrugged. 'Courage is not so great a thing; few men lack it. Even there at times, expecially in the gaol at Atrofon ...' He shook his head. 'No, Ljani, I did not do well.'

His sister was not one to offer glib words of comfort, and they walked a few steps in silence. Then she said, 'Such doubts are the price you pay for leadership, Brother Bear. You were born to greatness. It follows that your mistakes will be costly, even to the extent of men's lives.'

'That is a very heavy burden,' he said after another long pause.

'Methinks your shoulders are broad enough.'

Again he shook his head. 'I'm not sure they are.'

'You cannot have it otherwise. Will you enjoy the lands and titles of Slane without the responsibilities? Either take up the burden, or go and live in a cave somewhere as a hermit. There is no other honest choice.'

'You help me, Ljani.' He sighed. 'But a man like me - son of a murderer and a whore. Am I worthy to command men's lives?'

'Is anyone? Do you think Bjorn Longspear never made a mistake, or lost men needlessly? Did he never doubt himself? Two kinds of men, Prince of the Lake, are unfitted for power: those who have no doubts, and those who cannot live with them. You will never be a man of the first sort; you must take good care not to become a man of the second.'

As occasionally the case with Ljani, he had the curious feeling that it was not his nineteen-year-old sister speaking, but someone he had known long ago; long, long ago, before he could remember. And why had she called him Prince of the Lake, instead of Brother Bear as usual?

'I will think further on it,' he said slowly.

'Do so, Brother Bear. Think on.'

'IFAR,' said Beowulf uncertainly, 'I hope I do not disturb you.'

The new Earl of Hrosnaberg drew back his tent-flap. 'Of course not, my friend, come in. What is it?'

'I had not known what to say earlier on. It is hard to lose one's father, but remember, you have known yours until almost middle age. I can scarcely remember mine.'

Ifar smiled sadly. 'For one who claims to be a fool, Beowulf, you have a gift for choosing the right thing to say. I had been thinking upon similar lines myself. Rather than bemoan my fate, I should accept it, and reflect that many are less fortunate.'

'I am pleased you have taken it so well. Anyway, to business. I thought we should discuss rewards for our henchmen. Though the mission was a failure, they acquitted themselves nobly. Neither of us is a poor man. In my view they deserve more than thanks.'

'Again, you think for me. It would be best, I'm sure, for us each to reward our own men, but equally. What amount had you in mind?'

Beowulf had been afraid Ifar would pose the question first. Whatever he suggested, as a matter of honour Ifar could hardly offer less. The figure he had thought of was sixty thalers, or a quarter of a gold piece, per man. But outside the royal house, Beowulf was by far the richest man in Gothmark. Ifar, though wealthy, might have difficulty in matching it.

'For myself,' Ifar continued, noticing his hesitation, 'I was thinking of a quarter of a gold piece per man, that is three score thalers of silver, for the housekarls. What say you?'

'Exactly the figure I was about to propose,' said Beowulf in relief. 'To the churls, thirty thalers, and the slave, ten and his freedom. Families of the dead to take their share. Agreed?'

'Agreed.' Ifar smiled. 'Suth of course is rather a special case. Her reward should indeed be princely, but I imagine I can leave that up to you.'

BY the time Beowulf reached his tent, Suth had retired and was lying under one of his cloaks. She was not asleep.

'We need to talk, little one,' he said.

She sat up. 'As you wish, my lord. And my name is Suth.'

'Now Suth, do not be so standoffish. I thought we were friends, but you have hardly had a word to say all evening. I fear I have offended you.'

'Not at all, my lord. I am just tired.'

'Nonsense. You are indefatigable, certainly not as tired as me. I am out on my feet, but not nearly as surly as you.'

'I am not in the least surly, my lord.'

'Well, you seem so to me.' He hesitated. 'I am not sure what to say to one who has saved my life, and those of all my henchman, besides sparing me an ordeal which I am not sure I could have endured as a warrior should.'

' "Thank you" will suffice, my lord.'

'I hardly think so. First, it goes without saying that you have your freedom.'

'I see.'

'Second,' he continued imperturbably, 'I think ten gold marks, the price I paid for you, should be quite sufficient to make you the richest freedwoman in Gothmark. You could afford a house in the fashionable quarter of Geatburg, and have enough left over to live in comfort for the rest of your life.' He paused for her reaction. 'You seem less than thrilled by the prospect. Is it possible that you are dissatisfied?'

'Yes, my lord,' said Suth. 'I am very much dissatisfied.'

'Well, well.' He smiled. 'What other sign of favour could a freed slave want from her lord?'

Suth scowled. 'You are making fun of me.'

'Maybe just a little. Are we friends again?'

She gazed at him through narrowed eyes. 'I'm not sure that we are, my lord. I would remind you that you have another favourite slave back home, with whom you will no doubt soon be reunited. What is she like?'

'Starlight? Fair as the dawn. Incredibly beautiful.'

'More beautiful than me?.'

'Far more. You are not very beautiful; you said so yourself. You even went so far as to use the word ugly.'

'You really are hateful tonight. I suppose she is gentle and submissive too.'

'Er, well, no. Actually she is almost as much of a handful as you are. I seem to be attracted to temperamental women. And she is several years your senior.'

'I see. She is losing her looks, so you seek a younger slave to replace her. That is the way of men, so I suppose I cannot blame you.'

'You are in the funniest mood tonight, Suth. There is no reasoning with you. Have I said anything about seeking to replace her?'

'So, you expect us to be content to let you share our favours. I might have known.'

'Oh, I don't know about that. One temperamental woman in my life is more than enough.'

Suth was silent for a moment. 'I wish I knew if you were serious, you cruel pig. And what of the Queen of Atrofon? Did you not find her beautiful too? Did she give you good sport?'

Beowulf frowned and shook his head. 'I must admit that at first she seemed most beautiful to me. But I did not have any sport, as you put it, for I soon realized what a vicious, monstrous creature she was. Does that answer your question?'

'Yes, my lord,' said Suth, somewhat mollified. 'It answers one question.'

'Also, to my intense irritation, I found I could not get a certain rebellious little slave out of my mind. Not beautiful, you understand, but a shipshape little craft, both prow and stern.'

'How dare you,' Suth protested, looking pleased.

'Unfortunately, with several cracked ribs and manacles on my wrists and ankles, I am in no position to take matters much further with her at the moment. A visit to the blacksmith's tomorrow and some of Ljani's potion should soon cure things, however.'

'I suppose you can tumble me any time you like, and continue to enjoy Starlight too. Well, let me tell you this, Beowulf of Slane: it is her or me, and you will have to decide which.'

'That seems reasonable. Anyway, we will talk further tomorrow, little one, when I am in better shape and you in better temper.'

'That is another thing. You will stop calling me "little one." I have often told you about it before. I find it unbearably condescending.'

He climbed into bed and rolled over. 'Goodnight, Suth.'

Twenty-eight

THE SKY was paling with the earliest hint of dawn as the warrior lords, one old, one young, descended the hill at Leontarda. On the summit, the royal standard of the Goths fluttered above the tent they had just left. Both men wore the Emunding surcoat of emerald green, charged with three gold acorns. From the camp below a youth of about eighteen, similarly clad, approached on horseback.

'What news, father?'

'Not good,' replied the Old Emunding. 'Exceeding ill. The King will ride forth tomorrow.'

'Why,' enquired the youth, 'is Hyglack nearer than we thought?'

'No. But the King will forth, with or without his brother.'

'But that is out of all reason. We number scarce a thousand, the enemy four times as many.'

His brother, Artur, spoke for the first time. He might have been five-and-twenty, or even forty - a man of middle years who had aged slowly, or one still young but already wise. He shook his head. 'It was urged on him from all sides: by the marshal of his guard, ourselves, and warriors of lesser rank, but to no avail. He will not yield a foot of Gothic land. Tomorrow he rides with small force against the whole might of the Sfear.'

'Has he explained himself further?'

'The King need not explain himself,' said the old man sadly. 'He decides, and we obey.'

'Surely he is not himself. His recent illness ...'

'Something of that, brother,' agreed Artur. 'Yet to my mind the king has ever been a moody and suspicious man. 'Tis thought Prince Hyglack plots his overthrow.'

'There were many thought that when he became King. And were it not for Hyglack, we should not have become embroiled in this damned war.'

'No more of that, lads,' said the old man severely. 'The King is our lord, and as for Hyglack, whatever he may be, it seems that we have no choice but to trust him.'

'What of the Earl of Slane?'

The Old Emunding smiled. 'The King has small opinion of his loyalty either. The Wagmundings have ever looked after themselves.'

'True, father,' the youth agreed. 'And Beowulf is deemed as slight in valour as he is mighty in stature.'

'There methinks you do him wrong,' said his brother. 'I spoke with Ifar of Hrosnaberg the other day. He tells me Beowulf has been much abused, and throughout the disastrous venture to the Isles conducted himself as a valiant warrior and honourable man.'

'So you argued before the king,' said the old man, 'and I was glad to hear it. Yet Slane is still great friends with his kinsman of Karron Tha; therefore I do not think his loyalty can be relied upon absolutely. However that may be, the King rides out tomorrow with a thousand men against an army.'

'Courage is one thing,' said the youngster impulsively, 'suicide another. Let us leave him and join with Hyglack.'

'What!' cried the old man in horror. 'The Emundings desert their lord in need? Would you have us known as cowards and nythings?'

'It would not be treason exactly,' said Artur. 'For the King is bent on death. If we fall with him, so much the worse for Gothmark. With Hyglack there is still hope. And he would be our king.'

'That is politician's talk,' said the Old Emunding angrily, 'such as I never thought to hear from a son of mine. Remember, we are the heirs of Bor, not Slane. Our house is the oldest in all Gothmark - an Emunding fought with Longspear - and not merely the oldest, but the most honoured too. Every house but ours, aye, even that of royalty, has numbered traitors amongst it, as well as patriots. We alone have kept our honour bright these dozen generations and more. Would you have us be the first to dishonour our name?'

'There is truth in what you say, father,' agreed Artur. 'I know that when the great families of Gothmark talk amongst themselves, they will complain of one another - Wylf of Wagmund, Numa about Falgard and vice versa, some, as you say, even of royalty. We alone are universally respected. But to join Hyglack would not be such a heinous crime. I cannot think our sister would have stayed with him if he were nything.'

'Elfryth is an Emunding,' said the old man calmly, 'and will make her own decision, as must we all. To join with Hyglack could indeed in some sense be justified, but would it not, be honest, have something of the stench of cowardice about it?'

'If we do not,' said young Ranulf, 'we shall all die, and that will be the finish of our house, honour and all.'

The old man shook his head. 'Honour lasts beyond the grave. The honoured dead live for all time in men's memories. And as for a man, so for his house. When the Norns decide it's time, it is time. Let us put our trust in Longspear, and prepare ourselves for the morrow.'

A SMALL slave entered the tent of the Earl of Slane stood before him. She was very slim and fair, and it had to be admitted, far more beautiful than Suth. For a moment Beowulf felt a twinge of regret.

'Ah, Starlight.'

She inclined her head. 'My lord.'

One is fair and fickle ... The phrase came into Beowulf's mind, but whence he could not recall. In the circumstances, perhaps the more fickle the better. He cleared his throat. 'I dare say you will have heard of my friendship with Suth.'

Starlight drew her upper lip back from her perfect teeth. ' "Friendship" is a nice choice of word. I am told she is your latest whore.'

Beowulf's face darkened. 'She is not. And neither you nor anyone else will ever use that word of her again.'

'Well, whatever she is, I am a slave, my lord. I have no rights over you.'

He sighed. 'You are making this difficult for me, Starlight. You are well aware that I do not regard slaves as in any way different from other people.'

'In other words, you would have treated a free woman similarly. I do not doubt it.'

'You are a free woman. I meant to tell you. As from today, your slavery is at an end.'

'So that is supposed to placate me. My reward for being a royal whore.' Starlight pursed her lips and tightened her shoulders. 'I suppose I can have no complaint.'

'But of course you have, and I wish you would be frank about it, instead of adopting that cold, hard veneer, which does not suit a passionate woman like you at all..'

Starlight drew a deep breath, but spoke unsteadily. 'Very well. I have always known that this day would come, but tried to persuade myself that it would not. I am very much angered and hurt, but if you expect me to spit and throw things you will be disappointed. I do not intend to give you that satisfaction.'

She was shaking with suppressed rage, and as he had dreaded, not far from tears. No man had the slightest idea how to react when a woman used tears as a weapon. Besides which he could not pretend that he did not feel guilty.

'Come, Starlight, neither of us ever pretended that mutual faithfulness was part of our arrangement. For instance, I have heard one or two rumours about your behaviour during my absence which might worry a less easy-going man. Be that as it may, I have still considered it my duty to make reasonable provision for you; to ensure that you do not suffer overmuch as a result of my bringing matters to an end.'

'So, you are going to pay me off. Thank you very much. I never really felt like a whore till now.'

'Pay you off? No, not exactly.' Beowulf paused. 'You'll be aware, I'm sure, that all those accompanying me on the recent trip, having given me loyal service, are entitled to reasonable, indeed generous remuneration as a result.'

'No doubt, my lord. But I hardly see that it concerns me.'

'Not directly, perhaps. I was however about to add that young Kjartan performed particularly well.'

Starlight swllowed. 'Er ... Kjartan, my lord?'

'Yes. You may have heard that I appointed him second-in-command of the Slanish contingent after the death of Saward. He was not next in seniority, but as I told him at the time, in my view the best man for the job. I'm pleased to say that in that respect at least my judgment proved correct. He displayed courage, competence and loyalty in the highest degree. And I have naturally felt obligated to reward him in an amount which, however inadequate in comparison to his deserts, nevertheless goes some way towards expressing my appreciation of his services.'

Beowulf observed with relief that throughout this panegyric Starlight had been unable to prevent herself quivering with pride. Her voice shook. 'Er ... you speak of Kjartan, my lord?'

'Yes, Starlight. At the risk of repeating myself, Kjartan. He will deservedly become one of the richest housekarls inGothmark. I understand he has already decided to extend his estate by a further two hundred hides of land, and convert his comparatively humble dwelling into a mansion more befitting his rank.'

Starlight spoke briskly. 'I am very pleased to hear it, my lord. I have always thought Kjartan a very admirable young man. But what has this to do with me?'

'I am coming to that. His extended household will naturally mean that he is looking to increase his staff. I therefore took the liberty of suggesting to him that he might care to offer you employment, possibly as stewardess in charge of the female slaves.'

'I see.'

'Upon which, the fellow's face lit up in the most extraordinary

234

manner. But then, I'm sure you are well aware of his feelings for you.'

Starlight gaped. 'M-my lord?'

'Whenever your name is mentioned it seems to have the same effect on him. During our journey I observed that one way of ensuring his happiness was to introduce your name into the conversation. Ask anyone who was on the trip and they will tell you that he became a perfect bore on the subject.'

'So. I have been the subject of soldiers' talk. I suppose I ought not to be surprised.'

'Oh, nonsense, Starlight, you are determined to be difficult. I can assure you that his references to you were always most respectful. Not that "respectful" is quite the word I should choose to describe his feelings for you. "Besotted" would be nearer the mark.'

'Is this true, my lord?'

'Ask anyone you like. You seem to be the only one unaware of it.'

'Indeed. I ... er ... was not aware of it, my lord. No, really I was not aware.'

For once Beowulf was sure she was speaking the truth. The lovely face had become almost comical, so complete was her surprise. Amazing how blind people could be when their emotions were involved.

'That surprises me,' he said truthfully. 'as does the fact that he appears to have been similarly unaware of your feelings for him. I did not consider it my business to enlighten him. However, I would suggest that you wipe that vacant look off your face before speaking to him. Even the loveliest face needs some expression if it is not to appear feeble-minded.'

Starlight gulped and made an effort to recover her composure. 'So, it would seem that you have been as fortunate as ever, my lord. You think you can dispose of your cast-off mistress upon one of your henchmen.'

'You are wrong in several respects, Starlight. For a start, Kjartan is not "one of my henchmen," but, saving only Hawkeye of Karron Tha, my best friend. Second, the phrase "cast-off mistress," suggesting as it does an ageing relic, does the most beautiful woman in Gothmark far less than justice. Thirdly, neither of us expected our affair to last for ever. If I had not brought things to an end I doubt not that you would soon have done so. Finally,' he grinned, 'we are both aware that from time to time there were lapses from absolute fidelity on both sides. In fact the ungenerous might be tempted to describe our affair as little short of disreputable.'

Starlight had tried to remain angry, but despite her best efforts was unable to restrain a smile. 'Damn you, Beowulf, you always were a lucky bastard. And I'm a vain bitch, as well you know. I'm piqued because you're the first man ever to have dumped me. It's always been me to bring things to an end before.'

Beowulf relaxed and smiled broadly. 'You're not such a bitch. And don't think that there are no regrets on my part. You'll always be part of my past. And a very eventful part. How about a goodbye kiss?'

She shrugged. 'Why not?'

'Come here, then.'

'By Odin's death, Beowulf,' she said breathlessly, extracting herself a few seconds later. 'I didn't expect that sort of a kiss. We're supposed to be breaking up, remember?'

Beowulf laughed. 'It was our last kiss. I thought I should make it worthy of the occasion. There was never anything platonic about our feelings for one another.'

She laughed rather shakily. 'No. No, that's true.'

'Now be off with you. If I'm not mistaken, young Kjartan is likely to be waiting outside. And if you're looking for something permanent and respectable I think you'll find him a far better prospect than me.'

ANGANTYR, King of the Sfear, rode between Gerd and Hakon, his chief advisers in the business of war. Ahead and around him were borne the banners and panoply of royalty: the Northern Cross, and the Boar of Frey, and his personal standard, the Fighting Lady of Syrdan. Though white-haired and over sixty years of age, the king remained a vigorous and active man, ready to play his full part in the battle.

'The Goths have taken possession of the hill at Ravenswood, my liege,' said Hakon. 'It is confirmed by our scouts.'

Angantyr nodded. 'Yet they number scarcely a thousand men. Their main force under Hyglack lags some hours behind. Is this some deep-laid trap? Or has the King of Gothmark taken leave of his senses?'

'You met him at Castletown, my lord,' Gerd reminded him. 'And must know he is not the most rational of men. The wonder is that the Goths still follow him. 'tis certain, anyway, that there is no supporting force within twenty mile.'

'Send orders to the Princes Ottar and Ali to bring up their forces. Ottar on our left, Ali to the right. We shall command the centre.'

'Will you await the Earl of Karron Tha, my liege?'

'Nay. The arrangement was to join with him tomorrow, but the main Gothic force will be here by then. Let us attack without delay.'

NEXT morning Beowulf woke early and looked down at the dark little face beside him. The previous night Suth had shared his bed for the first time, not without a further passage of verbal arms between them over his relationship with Starlight. Fortunately the state of affairs between the latter and Kjartan had been so apparent that the misunderstanding had soon been smoothed over. So everything had ended happily for all concerned, he told himself. Undoubtedly the Earl of Slane was in some ways a very fortunate young man.

He enjoyed deciding where to kiss the sleeping Suth, finally opting for the tip of her left breast. She awoke, blinking and making happy little grumbling noises. 'Good morning, my lord.'

'Good morning, hussy. I am glad you have remembered to show me some respect. Last night you never called me my lord. It was always darling, lover, even your warrior, or great bear ...'

'Really, my lord? What insolence. Am I to be beaten?'

'I'm afraid not. Since you are free I am no longer entitled to beat you, however provoking you are.'

'I do not have to be free, my lord.'

'Of course you do, we have been through all that before. Anyway, we have more important matters to discuss, and plans to make. You may remember that the other day, when I offered you your freedom, and a modest reward to boot, you flew instantly into the most violent temper, and refused absolutely to discuss the matter. Last night, though in some ways, shall we say, more amenable, you nevertheless persisted in your refusal.'

He had never known anyone who could scowl as blackly as Suth when she chose. 'I certainly did.'

He kissed her gently. 'Now wipe that expression off your face at once, or if the wind changes you will stick like it. Anyway, since independence apparently does not suit you, you may prefer instead to become head of my household. You are obviously very brainy and learned - keeping accounts, organizing things and controlling servants should be child's play for you.'

She looked doubtful. 'Does not Ljani do that at present, my lord?'

'Yes, but it bores her senseless, so half the time it does not get done. She would be delighted for you to take the work from her.'

'In that case, my lord, I should be very pleased. But I have never given anyone an order in my life. Your servants might not take kindly to being told what to do by a former slave.'

'I am glad to hear you say "former." At least you have conceded that you can no longer remain as a slave. As for their taking orders from you, I cannot see any difficulty. You are already something of a heroine to the Goths, and will become more so as the story of your exploits becomes better known.'

Suth was no longer paying much attention, but was running her tongue greedily around her lips, whilst digging her fingers deep into the huge muscles of his shoulders. 'You are a magnificent physical specimen, my lord.'

He kissed her breasts again. 'And you the most brazen baggage in Gothmark. Quite apart from having the finest pair of pumpkins I have seen for some time.'

'Beast. Anyway, it's not true. They sag.'

'Just a fraction. That comes from their being decidedly on the large side for such a small girl. Anyway, do you want to hear the rest of my plans for you?'

'Later, my lord. Just at the moment I should like other things ...'

'Now do you want to hear my plans for you?' he demanded about half an hour later.

She cuddled close to him. 'Mm, yes please, my lord. I feel much more comfortable now.'

'Well, for a start, it goes without saying that you will share my bed every night from now on.' Suth made lecherous noises of assent. 'Secondly, I observed that yesterday you drank some of the juice from the mutango fruit.'

'Yes, my lord, you need have no worries there. I am perfectly safe.'

'My meaning was precisely opposite. You will prepare yourself for some bearcubs.'

She gave a little squeal of joy. 'B-but, my lord, I am only a freedwoman ... Surely you do mean that you want ...'

'Babies, to speak plainly. Half a dozen at least. More might be excessive; I do not want you looking like a melon all the time.'

'Oh. H-have you had many bastards, my lord?'

'I have done many foolish things, Suth, but getting unwanted children is not one of them. Yours will be the first.'

She shook her head helplessly. 'I cannot believe this, my lord. I wonder if it possible to go mad with joy. But there, nothing is ever perfect. No doubt my lord will wish to marry a fine lady one day to preserve the family line, and then it will be goodbye to his little slave.'

'You are a very silly slave,' said Beowulf, kissing her again, 'to worry about the end of an affair before it has hardly started. Or silly freedwoman, to be more accurate. However, to put your mind at rest, under the laws of Gothmark, any man with no legitimate son may be succeeded in his title by an acknowledged bastard, if he so elects. So although the law may prevent our marriage, as I fear it does, our eldest son, Odin willing, will one day be Earl of Slane. No, stay where you are. I owe you a meal, if you remember, from our little wager about the oar, so without creating any sort of precedent, you understand, I shall get you breakfast in bed.'

'Oh, my lord. I have never had breakfast in bed before.'

'Well, you can start now. Mind you, I shall expect a reward.'

Suth squirmed ecstatically. 'Of course, my lord, that is only reasonable.'

* * *

THE SUN was piercing the horizon as the royal messenger galloped into the village at Dannen Ford. Clattering into the market place, he flung his reins over the hitching-post and required direction to the Earl of Slane. Beowulf had his quarters at the village tavern, where he had left Suth safely tucked up in bed for the night. He hoped shortly to join her. Hearing the commotion, he strolled out into the inn yard.

'What news?'

'Royal message for Beowulf, Earl of Slane.'

'I am Beowulf.'

'Forgive me, my lord. News is, the King rode forth today against the Sfear, and bids you join him at Ravenswood without delay.'

'Why, that is twenty miles hence. My men have marched all day, and are tired.'

'It is his order, my lord,' repeated the man uncertainly. 'There is no time to lose.'

'What of Prince Hyglack's force?'

'The last I heard, approaching Leontarda.'

'Then he is as far from the King as we are.' Beowulf sighed in exasperation. 'What means the King by this folly, anyway? Is he mad?'

'Yes, my lord,' said the messenger bluntly. 'The King is mad.'

'IS the King not here?' demanded Hyglack.

The village headman came forward, fiddling with the buttons on his jerkin and avoiding Hyglack's eye. Yesterday he had spoken with the king, but his mighty brother somehow seemed an altogether more intimidating proposition. A massive figure in black armour, surrounded by his henchmen and the southern lords, Hyglack was known for his fierce temper and impatience with fools and those who might disagree with him.

'He was till yesternight, my lord, then announced he would ride against the Sfear this very day, with or without you.'

'Hyglack and his men exchanged bewildered glances.

'Why, this is madness, my lord,' said the Earl of Rigel. 'What strength had he?'

'Some three score horse, a hundred archers, and five hundred men at arms. The Earl of Bor and his sons rode with him, their number perhaps half as many. Er ...' The man paused and cleared his throat.

'What is it, fellow?'

'I believe, my lord, that the King's henchmen urged caution upon him, but he overruled them.'

'Hm, well,' said Hyglack sourly, as if recognizing that discussion of his brother's failings before the lower orders might be uncalled for, 'courage is an admirable thing; no doubt he had reasons for his action, extraordinary as it seems. When did he set out?'

'At the earliest hint of dawn, my lord, as the stars began to fade.'

'Never mind the poetry,' said Hyglack. 'Whence did he go?'

'Ravenswood, my lord, or so he said.'

'Where the Sfear await him in almost full force,' provided the Earl unnecessarily, 'at least if reports are to be believed. And he has over eight hours start on us.'

Hyglack frowned. 'How many of our cavalry are brought up, Hrosnaberg?'

'Some three hundred, my lord,' replied Ifar. 'Practically our entire force.'

'Send half ahead to intercept the King, and try to reason with him. If he has not reached the Ravenswood by then, all may not be lost. If he has, extra cavalry might help delay the worst.'

'Is it prudent, my lord,' asked Rigel boldly, 'to risk half our cavalry on such a venture?'

'No,' said Hyglack, 'it is not prudent, but I can do no other. I would send all, but we have a duty to ourselves as well. By Odin's balls, I had thought to have joined forces by now, and ride in good order against the Sfear after a night's rest. Slane should be here as well. What of him?' he barked at the unfortunate headman.

'I was about to mention it, my lord. His messenger has been awaiting you this last hour.'

'By day and night, man, bring him forth, then. What news?' he enquired, scowling at the Wagmunding herald, a youngish man, light-armoured, on a speedy horse.

'My lord,' replied the herald undaunted, 'the Earl of Slane sends greeting. When I left him, he was at the Dannen Ford, ten miles east of here.'

'His power?'

'Six score cavalry, three hundred archers, and five hundred men.'

'Almost as great as the King and the Emundings together,' observed Hyglack, somewhat appeased by the news. 'Yet we shall need every man.'

'Indeed we shall, my lord. Where shall I tell the Earl to join you?'

'Let him head straight for Ravenswood. It is the best chance for the King. We shall do likewise, and hope to join you there. Press on, my lords, full speed, and trust we come not too late.'

Twenty-nine

FROM THE HILL at Ravenswood, Athkyn and his henchmen watched the tide of Sferian armour flood around their island stronghold. The young Emundings supervised construction of fortifications from logs and brushwood.

'We shall soon be surrounded, my lord,' said their father to the King. 'I have thrown out a screen of archers and cavalry to delay the enemy advance. The gods willing, we may hold out until the arrival of Prince Hyglack.'

'Never!' cried the King, rising in his stirrups. 'We ride against the Sfear this very hour.'

He pointed with his sword to the enemy camp on the plain below, and the knot of horsemen around the tent flying the banner of the Fighting Lady. From every direction came the dull rum-a-dum-dum of the Sferian wardrums.

'My lord, we thus abandon the advantage of high ground. Were it not better ...'

'No!' shrieked Athkyn, and slammed the visor shut over his pale face. 'Summon all cavalry for the charge. We ride against our enemy, Angantyr of the Sfear. When he is slain, the Sferians will flee the field.'

The Emundings exchanged glances with those of the royal guard. Raud, the King's marshal, who as chief of the lists had been known as Bluemantle, gave the tiniest shrug. No longer was there any doubt that the King was mad; what little grasp he had on reality had finally slipped, yet he was still their King.

The Old Emunding bowed his head. 'Pass the order,' he confirmed to his chief of guard.

Athkyn rode briskly, sword extended, downhill towards the host. Around him, old warriors who had served the royal house a lifetime, youngsters in their first taste of battle, thanes, housekarls and yeomen, elite and humble, all rode to death along with their king.

The man who led them, confused and deranged, was yet not completely mad. In the eight months since he had succeeded to the throne of Gothmark, Athkyn had realised that the price paid had been too high. The ghost of Herbald, slain that late spring evening eleven years ago, was coming up the hill to meet him. At the time Athkyn had told himself it was the stag that had caused the sudden shaking of the bushes in that forest glade. The flight of an arrow later, Athkyn had become heir to the Gothic throne. It had been the stag, he had told himself. Would that he had believed it.

If he died now, sword in hand, against his country's enemy, might he escape the fate of kinslayer, and sup with Odin after all? Two centuries before, Kjartan Knuting, called the Kinslayer, had proved a good king, valiant in battle against the evil hordes from the east, so that his countrymen had forgiven the way he had achieved the throne, and called him Son of Longspear. And they had known of his guilt. Of Athkyn, no man had ever known, or would know, if it died with him. Odin himself, they said, knew not the hearts of men. Of Finbar the Craven, had it not been said that if he had not lived like a king, at least he had died like one? So it could be with himself - remembered for one last mad charge before the end.

Perhaps Hyglack suspected. Athkyn had never been sure of his loyalty, despite the Ninefold Oath. Nor that of Slane - none ever trusted the Wagmunding lords. The future boded ill for his countrymen; maybe Gothmark was doomed, as he was himself.

But no-one, god or man, positively knew the truth. Or rather, one man knew: one who mattered more than all the rest. Athkyn Rathlecking knew - knew himself a traitor, murderer and nything - a man without honour. And when he died, his secret would be safe.

He turned in the saddle, drew back his arm and extended it again in the order for the charge. The horsemen behind urged their mounts into a trot, a canter, and finally the gallop.

THE OLD Emunding watched from the hill. Maybe the King would die gallantly if needlessly, as Finbar the Craven had done at the Hrosnaberg Gap. Yet even this was to be denied him. From the Sferian archers on their flanks, a hail of arrows split the rash horsemen into a struggling mass of armoured, swearing men and squealing horses. Their comrades behind were brought down to form a second wave of death on top of the first. The king, one of the few who still stood, made a perfect target, and toppled from the saddle with half a dozen arrows in his breast. Then the Sferian horse moved in, cutting and spearing the grounded men. A few were dragged from the saddle and slain by the desperate Goths before they themselves were slaughtered. Raud Bluemantle was down, unhorsed and hacked to pieces by Sferian men-at-arms moving in on foot to despatch the survivors. The banner of the Lone Star remained aloft almost to the last, before being trampled in the dust with its defenders.

'Do we move, my lord?' enquired the Emunding's captain of guard.

The old man shook his head. 'Nay, lad, we cannot save them now. The King is dead; we must defend ourselves and await the advent of King Hyglack.' It was the first time any had referred to him by that title.

A remnant of the Gothic horse had rallied to cut their way back uphill, first harried by enemy cavalry, then brought down by archers. Below, amidst the riderless horses, broken banners and discarded armour, wounded men and animals were slaughtered by Angantyr's men in an orgy of bloodlust.

Artur led the survivors back to Ravenswood. Amongst the dead he left behind were his king, Raud Bluemantle, and seventy housekarls of Geatburg and Bor, including his younger brother.

'Did he make a good death?' asked the old man.

'Aye, father, fighting in the thickest press of the enemy. He slew one Sferian that I saw.'

The old warrior nodded, satisfied.

'We will go again, my lord,' said one of the survivors.

'Nay, man, you have done enough, and more.' The Old Emunding pointed out to the west. A bank of fog lay on the horizon, near the Great Lake. 'The mist will have come down in an hour. Let the remaining cavalry form a screen. Collect all enemy arrows to fire back, and conserve our strength for the morrow. The gods grant we hold out till then.'

They did hold out till then, for not all the confusion was on the Gothic side. The mighty Sferian force, with triple leadership, had difficulty in co-ordinating its efforts. There was hard fighting none the less, but as the mist descended that evening, the Lone Star and the acorn-banners still fluttered over the hill at Ravenswood. Thereafter the Sferian war-drums kept up a constant beat, as Angantyr's herald moved back and forth within earshot of the beleagured Goths, threatening them with slaughter upon the morrow, when their corpses would be strung up for the crows. Yet they did not dare press the attack further, lest the three divisions of their army blunder into one another in the fog and mistake friend for foe.

Soon after the Sferian king reluctantly called off the assault for the night, the vanguard of Hyglack's cavalry made their first contact with the enemy, skirmishing briefly in the mist with outposts of Prince Ottar.

Hearing the fate of their King from a fleeing Goth, they advanced no further, but rode back to their leader with the news.

Last of the participants in the drama to hear news of the day's events was Athelstan Hawkeye, at his summer quarters at Bettany. As the mist fell he was alerted by a messenger advising him of the battle, and requiring his immediate march on Ravenswood. He departed within the hour, at the head of four score cavalry, a hundred and fifty archers and six hundred men-at-arms. Out east he could hear the wardrums of his countrymen as they closed on Ravenswood.

MIST spread from the lakes that chilly autumn day, first blurring, then obscuring, the westering sun. On the shore of Lake Fanora, a ghostly army flitted amongst the broken wood of ash and birch, bearing before them the black and silver banners of the Earl of Slane. Men-at-arms in full mail: yeomen with pikes: heavy and light horse, thin spectral archers, and giant, helmeted berserks. At their head rode an even huger man on a heavy warhorse, and beside him, mounted on a chestnut mare, a slim girl in light armour. Even in the dim light, her uncovered hair glowed fiery red.

'War is no business for a maid, Ljani,' advised Beowulf sternly. 'Leave us here.'

'Another time I should dispute it with you, Brother Bear. But now I have other business.'

'Where?' he asked, puzzled.

'Bettany.'

Beowulf raised his brows in silent query.

'I have seen it in a dream. I shall be needed at Bettany on the morrow.'

'A dangerous trip, with the countryside full of armed men. Make sure you pass behind the Gothic lines.'

'Farewell, Brother Bear. We shall meet again, never fear.'

She rode into the mist; her outline grew faint, and she was lost amongst the trees. Beowulf shook his head slowly, and turned his attention back to the march. Ahead and to the west he could hear the constant, threatening beat of the Sferian drums. A-rum-a-dum-dum. A-rum-a-dum-dum.

At sunset, they fell suddenly silent. The effect was eerie and unnerving. Behind him he could hear the clank of harness and armour, and subdued conversation; in the background, the constant soft lapping of the lake. Trees emerged from the mist like ghostly sentinels. Once, a small pack of wolves, living symbols of his house, trotted silently away into the forest.

Until the mist lifted it would be impossible to tell the enemy's position, but in any case he must not get trapped beside the lake. The useful landmark must be abandoned. He gave orders; his company wheeled left, each man keeping those ahead in view. A sharp lookout was essential; the ultimate folly would be to blunder into the enemy unawares. Eyes like those of his kinsman would have helped.

Where was his valiant cousin, now his foe? By luck and judgment, Edgtyr and his brother had managed to keep their armies apart during the Fifth War. Surely he and Hawkeye could do as much for a single day. The Wagmunding lords should not have been enemies. They ought to have been fighting alongside.

Indeed they should. Whether it was the spectral surroundings, the silence, or the thought of his kinsman, a strange idea began to form in the mind of Beowulf of Slane. His cousin was not merely his kinsman, but his friend. Their common ancestor, Eymor, had been a henchman of the Sferian king. The Sfear, not the Goths, had been the first to help a penniless exile. Wagmund himself, some said, had intended to support the Sfear in the Fifth War, and his younger son, Alfar, had actually done so. Only Beowulf's father, the disgraced Edgtyr, had fought on the Gothic side throughout. Their present king, Athkyn, was a crazed weakling, unworthy of the crown; his heir, Hyglack the Dark, no friend of Beowulf or his house.

Who had put this idea into his head? The High One, perhaps, upon his invariable visit on the eve of battle? Many were the times he had changed allegiance at the last moment. Truly it must be Odin, Lord of the Gallows, Chooser of the Slain.

'Chooser of the Slain.' The motto adopted by Wagmund, First Earl, a punning adaptation of the original 'I Choose,' still borne by the cadet branch of their house under Hawkeye.

'I choose.' Most Gothic warriors followed their immediate lord rather than the King, and since the fiasco at Castletown neither Athkyn nor Hyglack was popular in Slane. Hyglack himself might well be traitor. And Ifar, Earl of Hrosnaberg, now his friend. - he had said the feud was over, but was it? His younger brother, Wulfgar, was said to be less forgiving.

How would those he valued most view the question? If he changed sides, would they understand, or think him traitor? Their faces presented themselves to his mind's eye: Ljani, with that cool, half-mocking expression as she called him 'Brother Bear,' and told him to be a leader. Suth, when she spoke of Hyglack: 'You always think the best of people, don't you, my lord?' His father, whom he had never known, indeed had any man? Bjorn Longspear, living and dead long before the Sferian feud. And Hawkeye himself; would he be grateful for his kinsman's change of heart, or secretly despise him as a turncoat?

So Beowulf's mind raced, but came to no conclusion. Within the hour, the Sferian drums started up again, closer this time. Folly to advance further. He ordered a halt, and they bivouacked for the night. A damp and miserable few hours, with moisture dripping from the sodden branches, and clammy mist shrouding the figures of the sentries. Yet he was grateful for the respite. In another mile or two, his foremost warriors would have started to engage the outposts of the Sfear, and the decision would have been made for him. That would not do either. He must choose for himself.

Of that, he was sure, his grandfather would have approved. I choose. Of all those to whom Beowulf had mentally appealed for help, he would best have understood. Bjorn Longspear had been perfect, or nearly so; he could never have been tormented by doubts of this kind. The right course for him had been obvious.

As a boy, Beowulf had often paused before the great portrait of his grandfather in the hall of Wagmunding Castle. The likeness, according to those who had known him, was a good one, yet the expression in the eyes had eluded the painter, and as a result his countenance had seemed rigid and over-formal. Young Beowulf, that dreamy, idle youth, had often wondered what sort of a man his grandfather had been. A patriot, or a traitor? Was there, in a sense, any difference? An opportunist, or one true to himself? A man with honour, or without?

The last thing Beowulf saw before drifting into uneasy slumber was the face of his grandfather; not fixed in the wooden stare of the painting, but as it had been in life - that of the devious, subtle, unmalicious man, who had held the balance between two enemy kings, and been the friend of both. The calm, inscrutable, yet strangely compassionate gaze of Wagmund of Slane, the greatest nything of them all.

Thirty

AT RAVENSWOOD Hill, the beleaguered Goths were on the move, tramping about to keep warm in the damp air. Steam rose from the bodies of their horses and puffed from their nostrils in dragon's breath. Men were polishing armour, testing sword and axe in their hands, more for something to do than with any real object. Two hours were left until sunrise. On the wooded slopes below they could hear the sounds of the Sferian host preparing to move. Old Garth Emunding walked stiffly over to his son and embraced him.

'We are the last of the Emundings, lad,' he reminded him. 'Today we write a glorious last chapter in the history of our house.' Artur, sparing of speech as ever, nodded and untethered his mount. Talk amongst the rest was spasmodic and subdued. This for most of them would be their last day on earth.

THREE miles south, Hyglack and the leaders of the main Gothic force drew rein to consult. 'According to report,' said Ifar, 'our countrymen still hold out, though surrounded on all sides by the forces of the Sferian king and his sons.'

'What of the Earl of Karron Tha?'

'Of him, my lord, there is no positive news. 'Tis thought he planned to join the Sferian force from the west, but may not yet have done so. Probably not, in this fog. It will have cost him time, as well as us.'

'Then this shall be our battle plan,' said Hyglack. 'You and I, Hrosnaberg, will lead our main cavalry assault upon the Sferian host south of Ravenswood Hill. The infantry will advance in support at full speed. Meanwhile you, my lords of Feldmark and Rigel, will advance to the left to hold off any flank attack from Karron Tha, and if possible prevent him from joining the main Sferian host.'

'What of the right, my lord?'

'The Earl of Slane advances there, as I understand. He will engage the enemy from flank and rear.' Some of his henchmen looked doubtful. 'And if he arrives not in time,' continued the prince boldly, 'why then, we trust to our own valour, and the will of the High One. Forward, my lords, there is no time to lose.'

ON the hill the battle was all but over. Half a dozen times the cavalry and skirmishers of Prince Ali had advanced against the Emundings and their handful of men; half a dozen times the desperate defenders had hurled them back. But each time, not so far back, and fewer men remained. The eastern slopes already lay in Sferian hands, whilst to the south Angantyr's infantry had breached the outer line of Gothic defence and were forcing their way through the tangled brushwood toward the heart of the defenders' position, a small clearing stockaded by logs, piled branches and felled trees, where the Goths would make their last stand. From the north, the Sferian reserve under Ottar looked on unmoved.

The last Gothic men-at-arms drew themselves up square behind their long shields. Pikemen drove staves into the gound. Artur and the handful of remaining cavalry trotted restlessly to and fro as they awaited the final onslaught.

And now it came, preceded by a flight of arrows, as Angantyr's men broke cover and hurled themselves against the Gothic shields. The defenders fought in silence; as each man dropped those on either side closed ranks with axe and broadsword against the waves of lumbering cavalry and heavy combat troops, the mad berserkers and the swordsmen of Syrdan and Janfar Delee. In the centre of the Gothic square the green acorn-banner still waved defiantly above their hopeless cause. The end, when it came, would be sudden. Once two or three determined horsemen forced a gap in the defenders' ranks, all order would be lost, and they would be ridden down and slaughtered to a man.

Yet, as time passed, there came no sign of the end. At first the Old Emunding thought he had imagined it, but he had not. Sferian cavalry were withdrawn piecemeal until none remained, and even the infantry began to waver.

It was Artur who first realized the truth, as he glimpsed the turmoil in the plain below, around a thin wedge of horsemen bearing the Lone Star. 'Hyglack!' he cried madly. 'Hyglack is come!'

A mighty cheer broke from the depleted ranks. 'Hyglack is come!'

'Nay, the King!'

'Hyglack!'

'Long live the King!'

And with insane courage, some men broke ranks and put the Sferian infantry to flight, back down the hill and on to the plain below.

'Aye, Hyglack,' said the Old Emunding, 'but there will be hard fighting yet.'

And so it proved, for the relieving force was outnumbered ten for one. The impetus of their first charge was spent, but the Lone Star and the Red Chevron of Hrosnaberg struggled on yard by yard, as their leaders hewed a path to the foot of Ravenswood Hill. The wedge became an arrowhead, then a spear, as the Gothic cavalry were squeezed from both sides. At any moment their line could break, and the horsemen be swept to defeat.

Less than a mile to the south, three thousand men-at-arms from Geatburg, Numa and Hrosnaberg advanced at the trot, as their leaders strove desperately to combine speed with good order. And further south still, Ljani the Red on her chestnut mare trotted calmly towards Bettany.

BEOWULF and his men set off at dawn, guided by the Sferian drums. He rode ahead, light of heart. Morbid fancies of the night had clouded his judgment, but now he knew.

The forest thinned; he called a halt to marshal forces. On the right flank, archers took up position under cover of the trees. Kjartan's infantry were drawn up in shallow echelon. Beowulf, who would lead the cavalry assault, rode before his men in full armour, black and silver, the Chevron of Slane on his shield and surcoat. In part to be satisfied of their formation; in part to show himself, for men needed to see their leader before battle.

'The scouts report we have o'er-run our position, my lord,' said Kjartan, worried. 'We now stand on the extreme flank of the field, somewhat indeed behind the Sferian lines.'

'Aye,' agreed Beowulf, 'that we do. All the better, methinks.' He raised an arm. 'Forward. Delay the assault till the trumpet sound.'

Their force broke cover not two hundred yards from the Sferian flank. The mist had lifted; to their left, the Northern Cross and the Fighting Queen fluttered over Sferian men-at-arms moving solidly forward to crush the thin line of Hyglack's cavalry. Further north, the lances and mailcoats of Ali's light cavalry glittered in the morning sun as they rode against the hill at Ravenswood.

'Sound advance!' cried Beowulf to the buglers. He turned in the saddle. 'For Gothmark, and Longspear!'

From his right, a thousand arrows took the air, poised momentarily at the top of their flight, and fell upon the splendid cavalry of Prince Ali, toppling men and horses to the ground in colourful confusion. Kjartan's men pressed forward with a cheer.

On the left, Beowulf rode in the van, slowly at first to maintain formation. A hundred yards to go, and still the men of Angantyr pushed forward against Hyglack, oblivious of the destruction thundering down on them from the rear. Three score yards, and the Gothic cavalry were at full gallop, with berserker yells and cries of 'Gothmark!' and 'Longspear!' At thirty yards, the infantry began to turn, too late. Beowulf and his men crashed through, beating down helm and shield, hacking, clubbing and forcing their way on in a great wave of death.

Angantyr's men were in turmoil; some still advancing with their king up the hill, others pressing the attack upon Hyglack's cavalry, yet others trying desperately to fend off the new assault. Ali's men, hard-pressed by Kjartan's infantry and the persistent hail of arrows from the wood, were unable to assist.

A quarter of an hour later the battle was decided, as the Gothic infantry reserve arrived, and Dardo's Hrosnabergers fell upon Angantyr's men from the south. The old king himself was down, beaten to his knees in single combat by Wulfgar of Hrosnaberg. Before his squires could come to his aid, Ifar was upon him, and with a furious hammer-blow stretched him lifeless on the ground.

The Sfear were not beaten yet. In particular, the reserve infantry of Prince Ottar still stood unbroken, as they had throughout. But Angantyr's men were cut off and crushed before his son's force could arrive, some flinging down their arms and pleading for quarter, others fighting to the last. Amid mad shouts of Gothic triumph, the Fighting Lady was seized and the Northern Cross trampled underfoot. Only a handful of determined men managed to hack their way out and join with the forces of Prince Ottar.

When they learnt that their King was slain and his force destroyed, the outnumbered Sfear began their retreat. Slowly and inexorably the Goths pushed them back down the slope, not in panic flight, but in good order, disciplined, and fighting all the time.

And so the princes of the Sfear, defeated but not disgraced, made good their retreat to the north. Meanwhile atop the hill at Ravenswood, Hyglack, Beowulf and Ifar joined forces and clasped hands with one another and the gallant defenders.

The Old Emunding was the last man to fall, killed by a stray arrow loosed by the retreating Sfear.

NEAR the Great Lake west of Slane, Hawkeye had his force wheel left to engage the exposed flank of the Gothic army. By an hour after dawn, the wooded slopes beside the lake were the scene of light skirmishing with the ourtposts of the southern lords, Falgard and Rigel.

The broken, wooded country was unsuited either to cavalry or the deployment of massed infantry. Amidst the trees and undergrowth, Goth and Sfear laid ambushes, crossed swords and fired arrows in confused melee. Hawkeye, on foot, moved amongst his men, urging them on and wielding sword himself. Left-handedness, so often a curse, was for once a boon, for the wound in his right shoulder, though stiff and sore, showed no sign of reopening. With some advantage in numbers, he and his men gradually obtained the upper hand. Here and there, the Goths made a brief stand, fired off arrows and fled, but little by little they were pushed back towards the site of the main battle. As woodland gave way to scrub, they began to falter, and finally broke and fled, pursued by Hawkeye and his skirmishers.

The hill at Ravenswood, not half a mile distant, was clearly visible in the morning sun. Its slopes were alive with horsemen and men-at-arms, archers and standard-bearers pressing on to the north. Banners flooded down the hill and around its foot in a riot of colour: scarlet, purple, blue and gold of the Chariot, red and silver of Hrosnaberg, black and silver of Slane, and the green and gold of Bor.

Hawkeye stood aghast. The battle was lost, and his countrymen were in full retreat. Between him and them stood the whole might of the Gothic army.

Roger Butters

Thirty-one

'SOUND THE RETREAT!' yelled Hawkeye wildly.

'My lord,' protested his young squire, 'the enemy give way before us.'

'The battle is lost, and so are we, if we advance further. The whole Gothic army lies between us and our countrymen.'

Bragi, Hawkeye's chief of guard, required no such explanation, and had already passed the order. Within seconds, the thousand men of Karron Tha were in full flight between the trees.

'Take horse, my lord,' gasped Bragi. 'You may then escape.'

'Nay, I chose to fight on foot and will take my chance with the rest. Do you think I would desert them now? On, on, brook no delay.'

Through the Slanish forest, the men of Karron Tha hastened pell-mell, some tripping over tree-roots, others pausing to help comrades in difficulty, yet others turning to fire arrows at their pursuers, but making good speed. The pursuit lagged, for the lords of Feldmark and Rigel were both wounded, and their outnumbered forces dared not press too hard.

'The southern lords fall behind,' said Bragi.

'Hyglack's cavalry are the danger. Once they learn of our whereabouts, they can close the Bethan gap and cut us off. On, on!'

Later he remembered little of that mad retreat - the men around him stumbling and cursing, throwing off armour to ease their flight, as behind them the light cavalry of Karron Tha crashed through the undergrowth, skirmishing occasionally with the van of their pursuers.

The mist, descending again in late afternoon, was now their friend, though adding to the nightmarish quality of the chase. Confused noise was all around, whether friend or foe Hawkeye knew not. Figures loomed through the mist, to disappear again amidst the gaunt leafless trees. Though he knew the forest as well as any, he lost all sense of direction.

'What ails you, my lord?' asked Bragi in concern. 'Are you ill?'

The shoulder wound had reopened, and hot sticky blood was gluing his tunic to him. 'Nothing, a scratch. On!' he cried feverishly, as man and horse plunged through the brush beside him.

'Move it, you lazy buggers!' Bragi yelled. 'To Bettany!'

Bettany was their only hope. The southernmost point of Karron Tha, it lay at the tip of the thin spear of land thrusting deep into Gothic territory. For which reason, the castle was the most strongly fortified in Sfearland, an edifice of solid rock surrounded on three sides by the Western Lake. Fortunately the harvest had been good; a thousand men could hold out there for months, and long ere then the bleak northern winter would force the enemy to abandon any siege.

At last they reached the shore, and Hawkeye took bearings. Three miles, no more, to Bettany Castle; he could see the torch-light gleaming out in the middle of the lake. Three miles to safety, but his wound was hot and gaping. The scene began to blur.

'Steady, my lord, steady! We must hurry. The enemy are close behind.'

'Nay, I cannot make it. Go on, with the men. You will be in Bettany well within the hour.'

'Never, my lord.'

'I shall be all right. I know this place well. Not half a mile distant is Forest Manor. It had been my intent to meet the Lady Wanda there after the battle, had we been victorious. The Goths will not realize I am there.'

'Suppose raiding parties visit?'

'I can hide. Besides, I doubt whether the Goths will plunder Wagmunding lands. They know the power of our house.'

'My lord, I'll come with you.'

'No, Bragi, the men need you to organize the defence. Go now, for the Goths advance on all sides.' Bragi still shook his head uncertainly. 'An order, Bragi. I promise you I shall be all right. Quick, ride on!'

The guardsman clasped him quickly. 'The High One protect you, my lord.'

'And you, my good chap. Now go!'

FOREST Manor lay on the border between Slane and Karron Tha. Despite his confident talk, Hawkeye had feared that it might already have fallen to the Goths, but as he approached there was no sign of activity. The sounds of battle were receding as he staggered from the trees and saw it there before him, half-timbered gables wreathed in the mist of the dying sun. Forest Manor, his favourite home, country residence of the Earls of Karron Tha. Here, that summer, he had spent many a pleasant hour with Wanda, strolling on the lawns and in the flower gardens, and feeding the fish in the glistening ornamental lakes.

From the gardens to the rear, a plume of smoke rose from an evening bonfire. He could have called upon the gardeners for help, but preferred to make it unaided if he could. The elm-lined drive was a hundred yards long, and a couple of times he thought he might pass out, as pain flooded through his shoulder and his senses reeled. Yet finally he gained the rustic bridge before the main entrance to the lodge. He practically crawled the last few yards, straightened himself in the porch, and tugged on the bellrope.

'Why, my Lord Athelstan,' said his old servant Rolf. 'You are sore wounded. Went the day ill?'

'Not well, but we have avoided the worst. The men of Karron Tha have retreated to Bettany Castle. We lost a handful of men, no more.'

'But you yourself, my lord,' said the old man, helping him to his feet. 'Did they desert you? Cowards and nythings if they did.'

'Nay, I ordered them to leave me. I can hide here.'

'Let us call a physician to attend you, my lord.'

'No, no, my being here must be kept secret. Is my lady here? She can see to it.'

'Aye, my lord, that she is.'

He had meant Wanda, but in fact it was Roslindis who entered the hall, standing at the foot of the great oaken staircase and peering at them suspiciously.

'What is it, Rolf? A vagrant?'

'No, my lady, your lord Athelstan. Wounded in the battle.'

'Is no man with him?'

'My men are safe in Bettany Castle by now, Odin willing. I will explain later if you are interested. Is Wanda here?'

Roslindis's plump features twisted in distaste, as they always did at mention of her cousin's name. 'Leave us, Rolf,' she ordered coldly. At a nod from Hawkeye the old man withdrew. 'No, Hawkeye, your slut is not here. Were you expecting her?'

'Later, perhaps. Anyway, you need not trouble yourself on my behalf. I will find somewhere to hide should the Goths arrive.'

'Take him to his room,' she said to some servants as if he had not spoken. 'See that his wound is dressed.'

He hated the idea of being under any obligation to her, however slight. 'I had thought you might be awaiting Prince Ali at Scarlettown.'

'No,' she said shortly. 'Anyway, I expect he plans to remain with his men.'

Evidently she thought Hawkeye had turned coward and fled the field. She could think so for all he cared.

'Did he fight well?'

He would have liked to tell her that Ali had performed ignominiously, but would not lie. 'I have no idea. Our paths did not cross. Everyone fought well, so far as I know. The gods favoured the Goths. Another time they will look kindly upon us.'

'Yes, well, politics are no concern of mine. You may stay here until you are recovered.'

'Thank you,' he said with heavy sarcasm. 'May I have the attention of my own servants?'

'You are in no condition to attend to anything. I will send them to clean up your wound. Meanwhile I shall withdraw, as I am sure my presence is as unwelcome to you as yours to me.'

After some hours rest and even a little sleep, Hawkeye felt better. The shoulder wound was sore but tolerable. From the turret window of the west tower he gazed out over Gothmark, the beautiful, dangerous land of his enemies. All was yet well; the Emerald Forest lay black and silent in the moonlight. He made his way downstairs.

Roslindis was in the banqueting suite, where a light meal had been laid out for him. She was dressed more simply than usual, in a white gown gathered tightly at the waist, with a buckle beneath her plump breasts. She looked at him coldly.

'Have you thought further of our divorce?' he asked.

She shrugged. 'Have it as you will.'

'I told you I desired to marry the Lady Wanda. You will not find me ungenerous if you agree. And no doubt you have ambitions to regularize your liaison with Prince Ali.'

'Regularize my liaison?' she repeated witheringly. 'Yes, indeed I would have liked to "regularize my liaison," but for the fact that Prince Ali, it seems, has other plans. He told me the night before last. To put it in your sort of language, it seems he has been trifling with my affections.'

'I don't understand you.'

'He is to marry Ursa, Princess of the Dan. Apparently she is considered by the royal family a more suitable match than the best-known whore in Sfearland.'

For the first time he noticed that her eyes were puffy from tears. 'I'm sorry,' he said lamely.

'I'm sure you are. It may mean you will have to make more provision for me. I do not know the legal details, but imagine it may be so. If it is any consolation to you' - her voice faltered before she recovered herself and continued - 'I can assure you it would have given you much amusement to see your proud wife begging Prince Ali to reconsider, whilst swearing her eternal love for him. Indeed I made a complete fool of myself; the first time I can remember doing so over a man. Never again.'

Hawkeye had never seen his wife in tears, and felt an unfamiliar stab of sympathy. Then he remembered the attempt on his life at Castletown, and hardened his heart. 'It does not strike me as particularly comical.'

'Well, there you are.' There was a defeated note in her voice. 'Things are different now, but you may still have your divorce if you wish.'

'No doubt you will soon find someone else.'

She looked at him bleakly. 'I don't think you can ever have been in love, Hawkeye.' Her face began to crumple. 'I don't want anyone else.'

For his part, it had never occurred to him that his wife was capable of any feelings other than the most physical. He was just considering what to do in the embarrassing event that she burst into tears, when she stiffened suddenly and said, 'Goths.'

He abandoned the meal and sprang to his feet. 'Where?'

'Emerging from the forest yonder. The cellar, quickly.'

'What of you? Can you cope?'

'I shall have to. I imagine pillage is their purpose, in which case they should soon be disposed of.'

'No doubt you will be glad to accomodate them if they are interested in rape.'

She struck him hard across the face. Whenever she had hit him before he had retaliated, but not this time, for he had deserved it. 'I will find my own way,' he mumbled, making for the cellar steps.

A QUARTER of an hour later, Hawkeye, crouching on hands and knees in the darkest corner of the wine cellar, heard men pushing their way through the racks towards him. There was no sense in delaying things. He stood. 'I am here, Goths, alone and unarmed.'

'Seize him,' said their leader brusquely. 'Are you Athelstan Wagmunding, called Hawkeye? Come, no denying it. We knew you would be here.'

'I am. How did you know?'

The man laughed crudely. 'Your female, of course. Any man is a fool if he puts his trust in a skirt. She has done us some good anyway, for methinks there should be a tidy reward in this for us. Hyglack of Ironside, King of Gothmark, has given orders for your capture. Come, let's convey him to the king.'

'THE Lady Wanda of Bronding, my lady.'

Roslindis entered the hall and indicated that the servant should leave. 'So, Wanda,' she said. 'Are you come to seek Lord Hawkeye? He is not

257

here.'

'I had arranged to meet him.'

'So he said. You will excuse me if I do not greet you with much courtesy. I have other things on my mind.'

'It is rumoured that he was taken by the Goths,' said Wanda. 'And that it was you betrayed him to them.'

'I need not justify myself to you. Your lover is not here - go seek him at the court of King Hyglack. Now get out before I tell the servants to set the dogs on you.'

'I believe you would.'

'Believe it, Wanda. Sigurd! Rolf!'

'You waste your breath, Roslindis. They will not obey you.'

'They will! They will! Get out!'

Wanda stood calm and proud. 'When I am ready.'

Roslindis' lunge took Wanda by surprise, and tumbled her to the flagstones of the great hall. As her head hit the stone, Roslindis was astride her, clawing wildly at her face and breasts. Wanda writhed free and grappled with her assailant. On the floor of the entrance hall of Forest Manor, the two women fought like wildcats.

HYGLACK held temporary court at Wagmunding Castle. Dressed in black for his brother, he sat at the table of justice in the Chevron Chamber. Beside him stood Beowulf, also in black, and the Hrosnaberg lords, Ifar and Wulfgar, together with a few Wagmunding courtiers, amongst whom Hawkeye recognized Hrothgar, his erstwhile envoy to the royal court.

'Stand aside,' said Hyglack to the guards.

As they released him, Hawkeye staggered and almost fell.

'Let him be seated.'

'I prefer to stand, my lord.'

'As you wish. Well, Karron Tha, the God of War has turned against you, it seems.'

'It would appear so,' Hawkeye turned his gaze on Beowulf. 'Greetings, cousin.'

'Hello, Hawkeye,' replied Beowulf, in his usual friendly tone.

'You fought well, Karron Tha,' said Hyglack. 'As for the episode which brought our countries to war, believe me, it was none of my making.'

'I believe you, my lord.'.

'The matter has been investigated,' Hyglack continued, 'and resolved in a way which makes it clear that neither Goth nor Sferian was in any way to blame. The black knight of Shadron Mor - cursed be that name! - must have switched lances in an attempt on your life. Beowulf has convinced me of it.'

'It is true, Hawkeye,' Beowulf assured him. 'To my shame, I was at one time suspicious of my friend the King, but now know that my fears were groundless.'

'We mourn our brother,' said Hyglack, 'as your countrymen do your King.'

Hawkeye had not known. 'Is Angantyr then dead?'

'Aye. Slain in fair fight by Ifar of Hrosnaberg. No doubt Ottar Wendelcrow will shortly be your King. Well, we came out better yesterday, though the Sfear fought valiantly. Methinks our peoples should no longer be foes.'

'My lord,' said Hawkeye fervently, 'I am right glad to hear you say so.'

'Honour is satisfied,' said Beowulf, 'on both sides. It has been agreed by the Wittan in council. We trust to obtain a similar response from the Sfear.'

'And greatly hope,' said Hyglack, smiling, 'that you will convey our peace offer to your king, Ottar - peace with honour, upon both sides. Whether you will or no, you are free without ransom.'

Hawkeye looked to Beowulf in bewilderment.

'Do not thank me, Hawkeye,' said his cousin. 'My intercession was not needed. King Hyglack suggested it himself.'

Hawkeye stepped forward, and on impulse seized the Gothic king's arm in both hands in the traditional northern gesture of eternal friendship. 'Prince Ottar is an honest and generous man. He will not be forgetful that you have freed his greatest servant without ransom. For myself, I grieve that I ever thought you my enemy.'

'I never was your enemy, Karron Tha,' replied Hyglack. 'For between men of honour, though there may be conflict, enmity there can never be. Go, and may Longspear ride with you.'

'Well said, my lord,' agreed Beowulf. 'But, Hawkeye, one other thing. It grieves us both, but we must tell you. We should not have known that you were in the manor, but you were betrayed.'

'By whom?' asked Hawkeye wryly. 'As if I didn't know.'

Hyglack - the forceful, confident Hyglack - hesitated a moment. Then he said, quite delicately, 'It's not a name you'll care to hear, Wagmunding.'

'I know anyway,' said Hawkeye. 'My wife, is it not?'

'No, Hawkeye,' said Beowulf sadly. 'Not your wife.'

Roger Butters

Thirty-two

'PINION HER,' ordered Wanda harshly.

Roslindis was seized by the arms and hair and dragged to her feet, still struggling. Her new assailants, three brawny retainers in red and black livery, had taken good care to expose and bruise her body.

'Had it not been for these fine fellows,' said Wanda breathlessly, 'you really might have escaped me.'

Roslindis's eyes were bright with loathing. 'Devil! I always knew you for what you were.'

'Aye, so you did, Roslindis. Fortunately your fool of a husband was less observant. What arrogance, to imagine I could forgive his jilting me for a slut like you. Well, he shall pay for it. King Hyglack is no friend of his, or his house. The joke is that he believes 'twas you betrayed him. He will die cursing you for the most treacherous whore that ever lived.'

Roslindis spat at her.

'Thank you for that, Wagmunding bitch,' Wanda continued. 'And for my bruised face and cut lips. You shall be repaid for them a thousandfold ere you die.' She turned to her followers. 'Drag the slut outside and tie her to a tree.

'These stout fellows of mine,' said Wanda walking alongside the stumbling Roslindis as they marched her off, 'have already slain your servants, every one.'

Roslindis sobbed, 'No, no.'

'Yes, every one, Roslindis, not excepting young Sigurd, who was your lover, and Alfgifu, your nurse since childhood. Before leaving, they will pillage your belongings, and fire the house. The blame will fall upon marauding Goths. A neat scheme, is it not?'

261

'Oh, by the gods,' groaned Roslindis as they wrenched her hands behind her and tied her to an ash. 'Am I to be spared nothing?'

'Nothing, bitch,' whispered Wanda. She gestured to her men. 'Tear her dress to the waist.'

The men did so, feasting their eyes on the upper half of Roslindis' body.

'These fellows,' Wanda continued, 'have not had a woman for some time. I have always hated you, Roslindis, far more than your husband. For him, death will be sufficient. But a quick death is far too good for you. After they have had their sport, and your humiliation is complete, I shall take over, and what they have done to you shall be as nothing.'

'You are insane.'

'Oh no, Roslindis, not insane.' Wanda smiled and passed her tongue around her lips. 'But I delight in vengeance, and have much to repay you.'

About eighty yards away, atop a small hillock on the edge of the forest park, a chestnut mare was reined in by her rider, a slim girl with red hair.

'It shall fall not only on you, but your husband, and on the Wagmunding of Slane, who has escaped us once, but shall not a second time ... Yet most of all, Roslindis, on you.'

'Fiend!'

'That is nearer the mark.' A vague look flitted across the face of Wanda of the Isles. 'The Lord of the East is good to those who serve him.'

'I know him not.'

'Not heard of the Count of Torre? Perhaps not, by name, but all are acquainted with him, whether they know it or not. He has many names.'

From the brow of the hill, Ljani looked down and narrowed her eyes to pierce the darkness.

'He is one of those who will ride on the last day - Fenrir and Jormungand, Loki and Gimli, Grendel, Garm, Dmitri and Mircon, led by Surtur, Lord of the Fire. Methinks burning would be a fitting way to finish you. A sacrifice to our lord, besides being, as I understand, most exquisitely painful. Meanwhile these fellows grow impatient for your body.' Wanda nodded to her henchmen. 'Ravish her.'

Roslindis had nothing left but a sick, numb terror. She bowed her head and willed herself to die upon the instant; anything to avoid the fate she must now endure. But she could not die ...

There was a curious vibrating sound in her head, like the breaking of harpstrings. Perhaps she had gone mad with fear, and something inside her had snapped. She waited for the sensation of the men's hands on her body, pawing, bruising and tearing, but it did not come. And all the time she could hear the strangely musical ringing, singing sound, like

the whisper of approaching death, and a soft, heavy pattering, like drops
of thundery rain.

She forced herself to raise her head. The air was dark with arrows,
like a flock of deadly birds. To her confused mind it seemed a score
were on the wing at once. They fell on their target softly but powerfully,
with a dull thump, thump, thumping sound as they struck home.

Two men were already dead, a third writhing on the ground with a
couple of arrows in his gut. Two more ended his agony. Yet the arrows
still took flight, falling with terrible accuracy upon dead and living alike.

Wanda, only slightly wounded but unhinged by the sudden hail of
death, was running round blindly, making animal-like noises of rage and
impotent fear. She stumbled as an arrow took her in the thigh. In the
end, her hate for Roslindis overcame even the desire for self-
preservation. She seized one of her henchmen's swords and stumbled
toward her captive, teeth bared.

Roslindis turned her head away.

There came another soft thud, and another. Again Roslindis steeled
herself to look. Wanda's grey eyes had opened wide, their gaze fixed.
Blood was trickling from a corner of her mouth. A barbed arrowhead
had torn open the smooth whiteness of her throat. Another protruded
from the red-stained lace above her left breast. She fell against Roslindis,
who flinched from the unnatural embrace as two more arrows impaled
the servant of the Count of Torre.

On the hilltop, Ljani the Red lowered her bow and turned the head
of her chestnut mare back whence she had come.

IT was evening by the time Hawkeye returned to the charnel-house
which had been his home. Roslindis was sitting in the banqueting-hall, a
half-eaten meal in front of her. She stared at him, dead-eyed.

'By day and night,' he said, shaking his head helplessly, 'you have
suffered much. We met Ljani the Red on the road, and learnt from her
what had happened. My men are clearing things up. Leave it to them - it
is not fit for a woman to see.'

'Ljani?' Roslindis had not followed half he had said, and shook her
head dumbly. 'How could she know? Your slut and her men were struck
down from heaven.'

'Not from heaven, Roslindis. Well, never mind. I have been most
wrong, and misjudged you cruelly. That slave of yours, Karl, who tried
to kill me in Castletown. I asked who ordered him to do it. I said, "Was
it thy mistress?" and he replied, "Yes, it was she." He must have thought
I said "my mistress." '

'So you thought ... well, no matter.'

'It does matter.' Hawkeye paused awkwardly. 'I have never loved
you, Roslindis, but today for the first time I begin to feel that I should

like to know you better.' He gave a short bitter laugh. 'What a ridiculous thing to say to one's wife.'

It was several seconds before Roslindis responded. 'I never hated you, Hawkeye, till you took up with her. She was a vicious creature, even as a child. She took delight in breaking other children's toys, and causing pain to animals. I wonder she managed to disguise her nature when she was with you. I tried to warn you.'

He nodded. 'So you did. Now I think of it, there were incidents with her ... I tried to ignore them as of no moment ... They say love is blind. I certainly was.'

'No more blind than I. You warned me that Prince Ali regarded me as a plaything, not a wife.'

'Let's call an end to recriminations, Roslindis. Could we not declare a truce?'

She laughed shortly. 'Truces seem to be in fashion. But even at the height of the war, the Goths and Sfear were the best of friends compared with us.'

Hawkeye said nothing.

'I used to love you, Hawkeye, at first. I had always been a fat, plain thing - when I thought you preferred me to my beautiful, vicious cousin, I was the happiest woman in the world. It did not take long for you to disillusion me, with your coldness and constant talk of her. You never knew how much that hurt. So I had to prove to myself that other men wanted me, if you did not. As it is, no doubt you think that you can just return to my bed and use me to soothe your injured feelings.'

'No,' said Hawkeye slowly. 'I don't think that would work.'

'For once you are right. I have feelings too, and Prince Ali has trampled them as brutally as you did.'

Hawkeye was silent for a while, then ventured to place a hand on hers. She did not withdraw it. 'Suppose, Roslindis, that for a start we delay the divorce, and see a little more of each other than of late. We could talk, and try to understand one another better...'

'You mean you should pay court to your own wife?' Roslindis looked away. 'Wh-what a bizarre idea. I never ...' - and now she was laughing and crying at the same time - 'I never heard of anything so damned stupid ...'

Epilogue

Message from the East

THE GREAT hall of Castle Longspear rang with music, cheerful toasts and the sounds of good fellowship. Eight weeks had elapsed since Ravenswood, and tomorrow, first day of the new year, Hyglack would be crowned. The Gothic lords and housekarls were in high spirits, for at last the right man was King.

Hyglack, at the head of the table, clapped Beowulf on the shoulder. 'Drink up. The war lost me a brother, but gained me a friend, nay, more than one. I cannot be sad.'

'Right indeed, Hyglack. We shall understand one another better in future.'

Ljani, to Beowulf's right, was pale and thoughtful. 'Cheer up, little sister,' he said. 'You have saved the woman of the man you love, but 'tis thought their reconciliation may not last. Anyway, there will be other men, other loves.'

Ljani smiled sadly and shook her fiery mane. 'I think not, Brother Bear. For me, the Lord of Karron Tha is a man incomparable. I shall not fall in love again.'

Suth, sitting on the bench beside Beowulf, clung to him even closer than usual and smiled. 'It took me many years to find happiness, my lady. You are yet young. There will be others.'

'Hear that, Ljani,' said Beowulf heartily. 'Suth always speaks the truth. One day there will be a warrior to share your bed and give you babies.'

Both Suth and Ljani coloured at this blunt talk. 'I am not absolutely sure yet, my lord,' protested Suth, but hugged herself in happiness.

'I must say,' contributed Hyglack's wife Elfryth, 'you are looking

265

positively maternal, Suth.'

'So much joy is infectious,' said Hyglack. 'We are all grateful to you, Suth.'

'Not only that,' said his wife, 'but for bringing Beowulf back safe and sound from Shadron Mor. We understand you were the heroine of the whole exploit.'

This praise from the mighty was too much for Suth, who seemed grateful for the distraction provided by a sudden clamour outside the great door. It burst open and a guard strode in, carrying a spear.

'What means this?' demanded Hyglack, rising.

'Pardon the interruption, my liege,' said the man, 'but a strange rider approached the castle just now. When challenged, he threw this war-spear into the main gate, and rode off at high speed without a word. The archers fired on him, but he made good his escape.'

'A defiance from our northern cousins? I thought Ottar Wendelcrow had now confirmed the peace.'

Beowulf pointed to the neck of the weapon, which bore a circlet in red and black. 'Those are not the Sferian colours, my lord.'

'Indeed not. Is there a message? Then let it be read.'

The guard broke the seal and opened it. 'It is to the Earl of Slane, my liege.'

Hyglack and Beowulf exchanged puzzled glances. 'If it be for you, nephew,' said the king, 'By all means read it. No doubt you will tell us if it concerns me.'

Beowulf laughed. 'My lord, I can now read, but since we have not two or three days to spare, you, Suth will have to read it for me.'

'My lord,' she said, 'you are not that slow - much improved lately, in fact.'

'Not so quick as you. Read it, please.'

Suth recognized the seal, and winced. She had to be prompted to start, but finally read it aloud, in a clear voice of forced calm.

' "To Beowulf Wagmunding, Earl of Slane. The vengeance of the East fall upon you and your house. Henceforward know the curse of a son of Muspelheim, Prince of the Light, Scion of Surtur. You are observed in all you do. My creatures are everywhere, by day and night, in the four corners of Middle Earth, amongst those closest to you, in all you trust and know and love. In future, never know a moment's peace; see my shadow in the face of every man, in the smile of every friend, in the touch of every woman's love. Doubt and despair in all you do. Live in fear, die without hope." '

Beowulf asked quietly, 'Is it signed?'

Suth pointed to the end, which bore the Twisted Cross of Torre.

Hyglack blew through his lips contemptuously. 'A trifle.'

'Aye,' agreed Beowulf, 'that it is. Yet methinks we may have yet a joust or two to ride against the Lord of Torre.'

'Well, time enough for that. Tomorrow we are crowned, tonight we make merry with our friends. Let Tirl and his minstrels write our names in their legends, that men as yet unborn may know of our exploits and learn from our mistakes. As for these vapourings from the Count of Torre, why, we defy them, and we laugh at him. For evil never yet did triumph over good, if men defend the right with goodly courage and stout hearts. Come, let's hear the minstrels play.'

The Minstrels' Song

HARK! A song of Hyglack's triumph;
Rathleck's son at Raven's Wood.
Avenger of King Athkyn's slaughter,
Shame wiped out in Sferian blood.
King of Gothmark, great and valiant,
Liege of his sister's son, who bore
Arms 'gainst the puissant Prince of Evil,
Stormed his stronghold, Shadron Mor.
Minstrels sing of mighty heroes,
Deathless names which never pall;
Bolferk, Ranulf, Bastard Swertan -
Heirs to the greatest Goth of all.
Sons of Longspear, Lords of Gothmark,
Shields against the Sferian foe;
Evil trolls from Northern badlands
Ne'er shall lay the Northmen low.
Brave Hyglack and his bearcub nephew
Long in the hearts of men shall reign
Sons of Longspear, Sons of Geat,
Sons of the Chooser of the Slain –
Odin ... HARK!
A tale of timeless glory - Hark ...
Hark ... Hark ...

Roger Butters

Appendix A

Important Dates in Gothic and Sferian History

1000	Foundation of Geatburg by Geat the Mighty, first King of Gothmark.
1188	Defeat and death of Styr the Left-handed, last of the Eight Good Kings, at the Battle of the Sands. End of the Golden Age. Draco the Destroyer, first of the evil Drakonian rulers, becomes king. The Goths secretly elect Bjorn the Elder, 'Ironside,' their King de jure.
1203	Birth of Bjorn Longspear, son of Bjorn the Elder.
1221	Death of Bjorn the Elder. Bjorn Longspear elected King.
1225	Battle of the Doomed. Defeat and death of Dmitri the Damned, last of the evil Drakonian kings. Bjorn Longspear becomes king de facto and de jure.
1232	Death of Bjorn Longspear.
1258	Foundation of Bakir, capital of the land of the Sfear, by Shylf, first King of the Sfear.
1307	Second invasion by kings from the east. Defeat of the Goths at Blood Valley by Bogdan Half-face, who becomes king. The Goths secretly elect 14-year-old Ranulf Ironside (later called Ranulf Redbeard) their king.
1326	Battle of the Northmen. Defeat and death of Igor the Venomous, last of the evil Slavonian Kings, by Ranulf Redbeard and Rolf Snorring, Regent of the Sfear.
1379	Outbreak of the Sferian Civil War.
1382	Deposition of Guthmund the Vile by Finn the Valiant, who becomes King of the Goths.

1401	End of Sferian Civil War. Saur Silverspur becomes King of the Sfear.
1402	First Sferian War ends in victory for the Goths. Deaths in battle of Finn the Valiant and Saur Silverspur.
1408-10	Second Sferian War ends in defeat and subjugation of the Goths by Ulf the Avenger. Death of Finbar the Craven, King of Gothmark. Asmund the Simple becomes puppet king.
1414	Unsuccessful rebellion (Third Sferian War) by Asmund's son, Sigmund the Exile, who flees to the Isle of the Goths.
1425	Death of Asmund. Ulf the Avenger becomes King of the Goths and Sfear. Gothic exiles proclaim Sigmund their king.
1432	Death of Sigmund the Exile. Succeeded by his daughter, Fanora the Fey, First Queen of the Goths.
1435	Swertan the Bastard, illegitimate son of Saur Silverspur, rebels against Ulf and marries Fanora the Fey. Outbreak of the Fourth Sferian War.
1438	Death of Ulf the Avenger. End of Fourth Sferian War. Goths achieve independence under Swertan and Fanora.
1462	Death of Fanora the Fey.
1466	Swertan killed in border skirmish. His son, Rathleck the Wild, defeats the Sfear in the Fifth Sferian War. The Treaty of Bettany agrees truce for a further 27 years.
1485	Death of Herbald, Crown Prince of the Goths, killed by his brother Athkyn in hunting accident.
1495	Outbreak of further skirmishing between the Goths and Sfear.
1496	Death of Rathleck the Wild, succeeded by his elder surviving son Athkyn.

Appendix B

Kings of Gothmark

House of Geat
1000	Geat the Mighty
1050	Sigmund I, the Reckless
1058	Samund the Pious

House of Gothmark
1095	Hrauding of Gothmark
1097	Gerriod the Generous
1123	Agnar the Young

House of the Harlot
1132	Sigmund II, Whoreson
1175	Styr the Left-Handed

House of Draco (de facto only)
1188	Draco the Destroyer
1212	Dragoslav Redsword
1222	Dmitri the Damned

House of Ironside
1188	Bjorn I, the Elder (de jure only, never reigned)
1221	Bjorn II, Longspear (de jure only until 1225)

House of Knut
1232	Knut the Usurper

1232   Kodran the Dwarf
1233   Kjartan Kinslayer, 'Son of Longspear'
1257   Eric the Pervert

House of Ironside
1259   Bolferk the Mad, 'Son of Longspear'
1289   Ifar the Hapless

House of Slavonia (de facto only)
1307   Bogdan Half-face
1320   Igor the Venomous

House of Ironside
1307   Ingfor the Traitor
1307   Ranulf I, Redbeard, 'Son of Longspear' (de jure only until 1326)
1353   Ranulf II, the Cripple
1364   Gormbald Gutspiller
1377   Guthmund the Vile

House of Falgard
1382   Finn the Valiant, 'Son of Longspear'
1402   Finbar the Craven

House of Ironside
1410   Asmund the Simple

House of the Chariot
1425   Ulf the Avenger, King of the Sfear (de facto only)

House of Ironside
1425   Sigmund III, the Exile (de jure only, never reigned)
1432   Fanora the Fey, Queen of the Goths (de jure only until 1438)

House of Silverspur
1438   Swertan the Bastard, 'Son of Longspear' and Fanora the Fey
1462   Swertan the Bastard
1466   Rathleck the Wild, 'Son of Longspear'
1496   Athkyn the Scholar

APPENDIX C
Genealogies
I. Kings of Gothmark
(Kings' names capitalized)

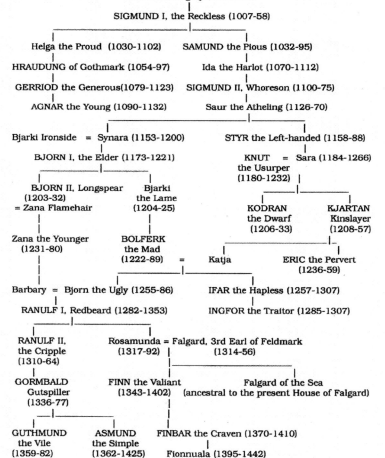

GEAT the Mighty (975-1050)

SIGMUND I, the Reckless (1007-58)

Helga the Proud (1030-1102)   SAMUND the Pious (1032-95)

HRAUDUNG of Gothmark (1054-97)   Ida the Harlot (1070-1112)

GERRIOD the Generous(1079-1123)   SIGMUND II, Whoreson (1100-75)

AGNAR the Young (1090-1132)   Saur the Atheling (1126-70)

Bjarki Ironside = Synara (1153-1200)   STYR the Left-handed (1158-88)

BJORN I, the Elder (1173-1221)   KNUT   = Sara (1184-1266)
                                        the Usurper
                                        (1180-1232)

BJORN II, Longspear   Bjarki   KODRAN   KJARTAN
(1203-32)   the Lame   the Dwarf   Kinslayer
= Zana Flamehair   (1204-25)   (1206-33)   (1208-57)

Zana the Younger   BOLFERK
(1231-80)   the Mad
                        (1222-89)   =   Katja   ERIC the Pervert
                                                         (1236-59)

Barbary = Bjorn the Ugly (1255-86)   IFAR the Hapless (1257-1307)

RANULF I, Redbeard (1282-1353)   INGFOR the Traitor (1285-1307)

RANULF II,   Rosamunda = Falgard, 3rd Earl of Feldmark
the Cripple   (1317-92) | (1314-56)
(1310-64)

GORMBALD   FINN the Valiant   Falgard of the Sea
Gutspiller   (1343-1402)   (ancestral to the present House of Falgard)
(1336-77)

GUTHMUND   ASMUND   FINBAR the Craven (1370-1410)
the Vile   the Simple
(1359-82)   (1362-1425)   Fionnuala (1395-1442)

273

Roger Butters

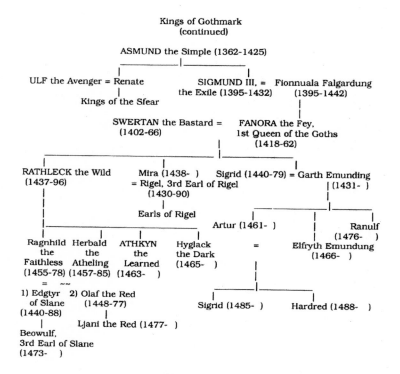

Kings of Gothmark
(continued)

ASMUND the Simple (1362-1425)

ULF the Avenger = Renate
Kings of the Sfear

SIGMUND III, = Fionnuala Falgardung
the Exile (1395-1432) (1395-1442)

SWERTAN the Bastard =
(1402-66)

FANORA the Fey,
1st Queen of the Goths
(1418-62)

RATHLECK the Wild
(1437-96)

Mira (1438-)
= Rigel, 3rd Earl of Rigel
(1430-90)

Earls of Rigel

Sigrid (1440-79) = Garth Emunding
| (1431-)

Artur (1461-)

Ranulf
(1476-)

Ragnhild
the
Faithless
(1455-78)
=
1) Edgtyr
of Slane
(1440-88)
|
Beowulf,
3rd Earl of Slane
(1473-)

Herbald
the
Atheling
(1457-85)

ATHKYN
the
Learned
(1463-)

Hyglack
the Dark
(1465-)

=

Elfryth Emundung
(1466-)

2) Olaf the Red
(1448-77)
Ljani the Red (1477-)

Sigrid (1485-)

Hardred (1488-)

274

II. House of the Chariot
(Kings of the Sfear are Capitalized)

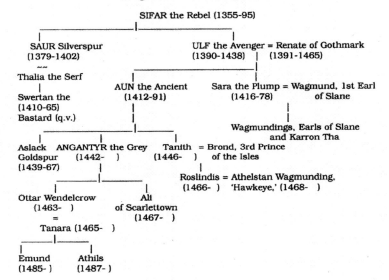

SIFAR the Rebel (1355-95)

SAUR Silverspur
(1379-1402)

~~

Thalia the Serf

Swertan the
(1410-65)
Bastard (q.v.)

ULF the Avenger = Renate of Gothmark
(1390-1438) | (1391-1465)

AUN the Ancient
(1412-91)

Sara the Plump = Wagmund, 1st Earl
(1416-78) of Slane

Wagmundings, Earls of Slane
and Karron Tha

Aslack   ANGANTYR the Grey
Goldspur   (1442-)
(1439-67)

Tanith   = Brond, 3rd Prince
(1446-)   of the Isles

Roslindis = Athelstan Wagmunding,
(1466-) 'Hawkeye,' (1468-)

Ottar Wendelcrow
(1463-)
=
Tanara (1465-)

Ali
of Scarlettown
(1467-)

Emund   Athils
(1485-)   (1487-)

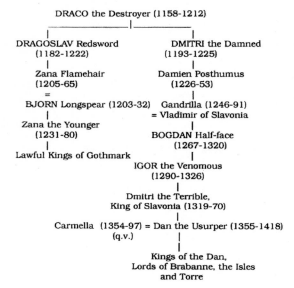

III. The Kings from the East
(*de facto* Kings of Gothmark capitalized)

DRACO the Destroyer (1158-1212)

DRAGOSLAV Redsword
(1182-1222)

DMITRI the Damned
(1193-1225)

Zana Flamehair
(1205-65)
=
BJORN Longspear (1203-32)

Damien Posthumus
(1226-53)

Gandrilla (1246-91)
= Vladimir of Slavonia

Zana the Younger
(1231-80)

BOGDAN Half-face
(1267-1320)

Lawful Kings of Gothmark

IGOR the Venomous
(1290-1326)

Dmitri the Terrible,
King of Slavonia (1319-70)

Carmella (1354-97) = Dan the Usurper (1355-1418)
(q.v.)

Kings of the Dan,
Lords of Brabanne, the Isles
and Torre

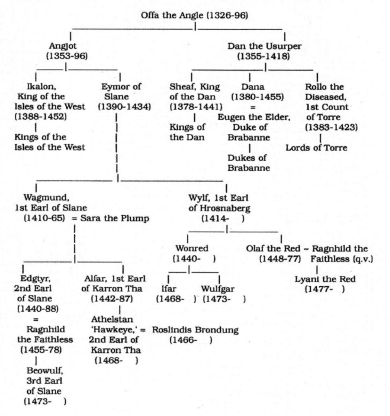

IV. Houses of Offa, Dan, Wagmund and Wylf

Offa the Angle (1326-96)

Angjot
(1353-96)

Dan the Usurper
(1355-1418)

Ikalon,
King of the
Isles of the West
(1388-1452)

Kings of the
Isles of the West

Eymor of
Slane
(1390-1434)

Sheaf, King
of the Dan
(1378-1441)

Kings of
the Dan

Dana
(1380-1455)
=
Eugen the Elder,
Duke of
Brabanne

Dukes of
Brabanne

Rollo the
Diseased,
1st Count
of Torre
(1383-1423)

Lords of Torre

Wagmund,
1st Earl of Slane
(1410-65) = Sara the Plump

Wylf, 1st Earl
of Hrosnaberg
(1414-   )

Wonred
(1440-   )

Olaf the Red ~ Ragnhild the
(1448-77) Faithless (q.v.)

Lyani the Red
(1477-   )

Edgtyr,
2nd Earl
of Slane
(1440-88)
=
Ragnhild
the Faithless
(1455-78)

Beowulf,
3rd Earl
of Slane
(1473-   )

Alfar, 1st Earl
of Karron Tha
(1442-87)

Athelstan
'Hawkeye,' =
2nd Earl of
Karron Tha
(1468-   )

Ifar
(1468-   )

Wulfgar
(1473-   )

Roslindis Brondung
(1466-   )

Roger Butters

Appendix D

Gothic Language and Alphabet

THE FUTHARK, or Gothic Alphabet, ran as follows (English equivalents in brackets):

1. fehu (f or v)
2. uruz (u)
3. thurizaz (th)
4. anzus (a)
5. raido (r)
6. kano (k or hard c)
7. gebo (hard g)
8. wunjo (w)
9. hagalaz (h)
10. nauthiz (n)
11. isa (i)
12. jera (j or soft g)
13. perth (p)
14. ywaz (y as a vowel)
15. algiz (z)
16. sowelu (s)
17. teiwaz (t)
18. berkana (b)
19. ehwaz (e)
20. mannaz (m)
21. laguz (l)
22. inguz (ng)
23. othila (o)
24. daguz (d)

Notes on transliteration into English:

Where there is a clear English equivalent of a Gothic name, it has usually been translated, e.g. Castletown, Ravenswood. Names resembling English words have been spelt as in English, e.g. Wanda, Slane, Breck, Rigel (hard g). Otherwise the following guide to pronunciation may assist:

Consonants: Generally as in English. The letter g was always pronounced hard, unless preceded by d, when pronounced as j. (The

Roger Butters

Gothic spelling of the latter sound was j, or jera. No Gothic word began with it.) The sound represented in English by the consonantal y has been spelt j, as in German, e.g. Ljani.

Vowels: Short vowels as in English, save that short u was always pronounced as in German, viz. as in 'put,' not as in 'cut.' The long e was pronounced rather like 'ay,' but pure, not a diphthong. The long vowel in the English 'see' has been spelt as in English when stressed, (e.g. Janfar Delee,) otherwise as 'i.' The only sound without a close English equivalent was that in the French word lune. This has been spelt 'y.'

Diphthongs differing from English prononciation were:
1. 'Ai' (or 'ay' at the end of a word) was pronounced as in 'Saigon.'
2. 'Ei' (or 'ey' at the end of a word) was pronounced as in 'eight.'
3. 'Au' was pronounced as in German, viz. as in 'Saudi.'
4. 'Eu' was pronounced as in German, viz., as 'oy.'

Stress in a Gothic word usually fell as in English.
    Exceptions to the above rules were few, Gothic being spelt phonetically. The final 'e' in most words was pronounced, as in German, save in a few words of foreign origin, e.g. Torre, Brabanne, where it was silent. The suffix 'heim' was pronounced anomalously as 'hime.'

Appendix E

The Gothic Calendar

THERE WERE twelve months in the Gothic year, each of thirty days. The days of the week were Sunday, Moonday, Tyrsday, Odinsday, Thorsday and Freyasday. There being only six weekdays altogether, each month consisted of exactly five weeks. In addition there were five days in the year not designated as weekdays, nor forming part of any month. These were New Year's Day, and the quarter days Midspring, Midsummer, Midfall and Midwinter. In leap years the extra day was added immediately after Midsummer Day. New Year's Day fell on the day following Midwinter, after which the months were named according to the stars most prominent at the time, viz:

1. The Month when the Stars Shine Brightest.
2. The Month of the Diamond Star.
3. The Month without a Star.
4. The Month when the Stars are like a Wolf.
5. The Month of the Bear.
6. The Month of the Golden Star.
7. The Month of the Silver Star.
8. The Month of Ten Thousand Stars.
9. The Month when the Stars are like a Sword.
10. The Month when the stars are like a Shield.
11. The Month when the Stars are like a Spear.
12. The Month when the Stars are like a Bow.

Years were counted from the foundation of Geatburg, which was given the arbitrary date 1000, thereby avoiding the inconvenience associated

Roger Butters

with our 'BC.' The Goths also operated a twelve-year cycle consisting of the Years of the Rat, Ox, Tiger, Hare, Dragon, Serpent, Horse, Goat, Elk, Eagle, Wolf and Boar. The year 1000 had been the Year of the Boar.

Appendix F

Gothic Weights, Measures and Currency

THE GOTHIC inch, foot and yard were each about 4% shorter than their Imperial equivalent. Beowulf therefore, nearly 7 feet tall in Gothic units, would have been 6 feet 8 inches in ours: Suth, at nearly 5 feet 4, just over 5 feet one inch.

Longer measurements were:
      200 Yards = one Furlong, or (nautically) Cable Length
      10 Furlongs = one Gothic Mile
      4 Miles = one League.

Distances up to 20 miles were usually expressed in miles, beyond that in leagues. A Hundred was a square Furlong, (or one hundredth of a square Mile), and a Hide was a tenth of a Hundred, or about three-quarters of an acre.

Weights and measures approximated closely to their imperial equivalent. A Flagon was half a gallon.

The smallest unit of currency was the Penny, or copper piece; the smallest coin one quarter of that amount. 240 Pennies made a silver piece, or Thaler, and 240 Thalers made a gold piece, or Mark. The word 'Mark' alone meant a gold piece, but a penny was sometimes referred to as a Copper Mark, and a thaler as a Silver Mark. Similarly the word 'thaler' on its own meant a silver piece, but a 'Gold Thaler' was the Mark, or gold piece. This usage could lead to confusion.

Very roughly a copper mark might have been considered equivalent to a 20p piece, a silver mark to the sum of about £50, and the gold mark therefore about £12,000.

Roger Butters

Glossary

**Names, places and expressions used in the Chronicle
(important characters are capitalized)**

Aftermorrow.	The day after tomorrow.
Alfar Wagmunding,	1st Earl of Karron Tha (1442-87). Hawkeye's father, who fought for the Sfear in the Fifth War.
Alfgifu.	Roslindis' aged nurse.
ALI, Prince of Scarlettown (1466-)	Younger son of the Sferian king, Angantyr; Roslindis' cousin and lover.
ANGANTYR Auning (1442-).	King of the Sfear since 1491. Father of the princes Ottar and Ali.
Angjot Offing (1353-96)	Elder son of Offa the Angle. Ancestor of Beowulf, Hawkeye and Ifar.
Anselm.	One of Beowulf's housekarls. No relation to:
Anselm of Ghul.	A minor Sferian aristocrat, competitor in the archery tournament at Castletown, and former lover of Roslindis.
ARTUR Emunding (1461-)	Elder son of Garth Emunding, Earl of Bor. Nephew of Rathleck, and brother of Hyglack's wife Elfryth.
Asgard	The abode of most of the Gods, including Odin and Thor. One of the Nine Worlds.
Ashen Tarn, Slane.	A small lake south-east of Sleinau.

Aslack Goldspur (1439-67).

Crown Prince of the Sfear, killed by Rathleck in the Fifth Sferian War. Elder brother of Angantyr.

Asmund the Simple (1363-1425)

Younger brother of Guthmund the Vile, King of Gothmark 1410-25, as a puppet of the Sferian King, Ulf.

ATHELSTAN Alfarring or Wagmunding (1468-)

See HAWKEYE.

ATHKYN Rathlecking (1463-)

Succeeded his father, Rathleck the Wild, as King of Gothmark in 1496, having killed his eldest brother Herbald in a hunting accident eleven years before. Elder brother of Hyglack.

Atrofon   One of the Seven Cities of Shadron Mor.

Aun the Ancient (1412-91)

King of the Sfear 1438-91. Father of Aslack Goldspur and Angantyr.

Bakir, Shylf.   Capital and largest city in the Land of the Sfear.

B., Battle of (1402). Last battle of the First Sferian War, at which both Saur Silverspur and Finn the Valiant were killed. A victory for the Goths.

B., Treaty of (1402). Treaty imposed on the Sfear after their defeat in the First War.

Bat-lizards.   Reptilian flying creatures with bat-like wings, common in the Lost Land of Fanora. Also called Leatherwings.

Battles, God of.   One of Odin's titles.

Bay Horse.   Badge of the Earls of Hrosnaberg.

Berserk(er)s.   Giant infantrymen who fought in a frenzy of rage. Originally they despised the use of armour, but by Beowulf's time most had begun to use it to some extent.

B. yell   A loud shout, not exclusive to berserks, used to intimidate the enemy.

BEOWULF Edgtyring, 3rd Earl of Slane (1473-)

Also called Beowulf Wagmunding. Son of Edgtyr Wagmunding and Ragnhild, only daughter of Rathleck the Wild. According to his half-sister, Ljani the Red, Beowulf was a reincarnation of the greatest Gothic king of all, Bjorn Longspear, Prince of the Lake.

Bethan Gap,   Slane. A narrow strip of land near Bettany, between the high ground of Ravenswood and the Western Lake.

Bettany, Karron Tha.   Most southerly town in the Land of the Sfear.

B., Treaty of (1468).   The Treaty bringing to an end the Fifth Sferian War.

Bifrost.   The rainbow bridge between heaven and Midgard. On the last day the Sons of Muspelheim will ride over it and shatter it to pieces.

Bjarki the Lame (1204-25)
    Younger brother of Bjorn Longspear and father of Bolferk the Mad. Killed at the Battle of the Doomed. Ancestor of the present Gothic royal house.

Bjorn the Elder (1173-1221)
    King of Gothmark de jure 1188-21. First King of the House of Ironside, and one of the only two Gothic kings who never reigned. Father of Bjorn Longspear and Bjarki the Lame.

BJORN Longspear (1203-32)
    King of Gothmark de jure 1221-32, de facto 1225-32. The greatest of all Gothic kings, who freed his country from the tyranny of the evil Drakonian rulers. With his brother, Bjarki the Lame, he won the Battle of the Doomed (1225), defeating Dmitri the Damned. Many legends were told of Longspear, who by Beowulf's time had become a semi-divine figure. Great-grandfather of Ranulf Redbeard, and ancestral to the present Gothic royal house.

Black Bear.   Beowulf's personal standard and badge.

Black Chevron.   The standard of the Wagmundings, used by both Beowulf and Hawkeye.

Black Fever.   The illness known to us as bubonic plague.

Blood River.   A river in the east Northlands, rising in Fanora and joining the Wolf River south of Cstletown.

B. Valley.   The valley of the Blood River. Site of a

battle in 1307, at which the Goths were defeated by the evil Slavonian king Bogdan Half-face.

Bluemantle.   See Raud Bluemantle.

Bogdan Half-face (1267-1320)

One of the evil Slavonian kings, de facto King of Gothmark 1307-1320. Reputedly one of the Sons of Muspelheim.

Bolferk the Mad (1222-89)

King of Gothmark 1259-89. Son of Bjarki the Lame and nephew of Bjorn Longspear. One of the greatest Gothic kings. Ancestral to the present royal house.

Bolferk's Cross, Rigel.   A hamlet on the border of Rigel and Silvermount, on the main overland trade route from Rigel to Port Targon.

Bor, province and river.

The north-western province of Gothmark, and its river, the Sferian frontier.

B., Earls of.   See Emundings.

Brabanne.   A Teutonic land, formerly part of the empire of Offa the Angle.

B., Dukes of.   See Eugen and Rikhard.

B. and Torre,   Count of. One of the titles claimed by Ragnar of Torre.

Bragi Haralding (1465-   )

Hawkeye's captain of guard at the Battle of Ravenswood.

Breck Bronding, Prince of the Isles (1472-95)

Ruler of the Isle of the Goths. A boyhood friend of Beowulf.

Brond of the Eastern Sea (1404-58)

First Prince of the Isles, ally of Swertan the Bastard in the Fourth Sferian War. Breck's great-grandfather.

Brondings.   Tail-male descendants of Brond. Breck was the last.

Cadmon of Thorn.   An archer competing in the Great Tournament at Castletown.

Cassar.   See Great Cassar or Kassar.

Castle Longspear.   See Longspear, Castle.

Castletown, Slane.   Most easterly town in Gothmark, on Lake Fanora. Site of the Great Tournament of 1496.

C., Treaty of.	The treaty securing Gothic independence after the Fourth Sferian War.
Chariot, House of.	The royal house of the Sfear.
Chief among the Mighty.	A title of Bjorn Longspear.
Chooser of the Slain.	A title applied to any of the deities who visited on the eve of battle to decide which men would fall next day. Used especially of Odin, occasionally of Freya. Also Beowulf's motto, originally adopted by his grandfather, Wagmund of Slane, as a pun on the name of his province.
Churl.	A free man other than an aristocrat or housekarl. Over 80 per cent of Northmen fell into this category, most of the rest being slaves.
Cloka.	The great drain leading from the city of Atrofon.
Count.	A title not used by the Northmen, but corresponding to their Earl.
Crypt of the Kings.	The burial vault of most Kings of Gothmark.
Cunning. Clever; skilled.	To the Goths the word bore no pejorative sense.
Dan the Usurper (1355-1418)	King of the Teutonic Empire 1396-1418. Son of Offa the Angle. He usurped the throne from his brother's sons, but eventually lost most of the empire. Ancestral to the Kings of the Dan.
Dan, Land of.	The only part of the Teutonic Empire controlled by Dan until his death, and named after him. Place of exile of Beowulf's father, Edgtyr.
Dandy.	Hawkeye's favourite horse, a bay stallion.
Dannen Ford, Slane.	A village in east Slane.
Dannenberg.	A hill in the Land of the Dan, site of an indecisive battle (1476) between the Dan and the Great Empire.
Dapple Heath, Karron	Tha. Site of the bloodiest of all battles between the Goths and Sfear, during the Fourth War (1437). A victory for neither side.

DARDO Sigurding (1458-   )

> Ifar's captain of guard, accompanying him on the journey to the Isles. Fought for the Teutons against the Empire of the South, 1481-4.

Dead, Prince of the.   One of Odin's titles.

Deathless Ones.   Those stars of the northern sky which never set. Believed by Ljani to be the souls of heroes.

Dmitri the Damned (1193-1225)

> Last and worst of the evil Drakonian Kings of Gothmark, ruler de facto 1222-25. Defeated and killed by the forces of Bjorn Longspear at the Battle of the Doomed. A Son of Muspelheim.

Doomed, Battle of the (1225)

> The greatest battle in the history of the Northmen, at which Bjorn Longspear and his brother Bjarki the Lame defeated the host of Dmitri the Damned. Also called the Battle of the Lake.

Draco the Destroyer (1158-1212)

> First of the evil Drakonian Kings of Gothmark, ruler de facto 1188-1212. Father of Dmitri the Damned.

Dragon   A rather vague term applied by the Goths to any large or fierce reptile.

Dragoslav Redsword (1182-1222)

> Second of the Drakonian kings, elder son of Draco the Destroyer and brother of Dmitri the Damned. Alone of the Drakonian kings, Dragoslav was conceded by the Goths to have had redeeming features, possibly because his daughter, Zana Flamehair, became the wife of Bjorn Longspear.

Drakonia.   A land far to the east of Gothmark, home of the evil Drakonian kings, who ruled Gothmark 1188-1225.

Draw (in personal combat, especially sport)

> To give less than one's best; to flinch from whole-hearted contact.

Duke.   A title not used by the Northmen, supposedly more eminent than that of Earl.

East Current.   The south-westerly current between the

290

Gothic mainland and the Isle of the Goths.

East, Lord (or Prince) of the.
    A title of Ragnar of Torre.

Eastern Lake, Slane.   Largest Lake in the Northlands, east of Slane and notionally forming part of it. Also called Lake Fanora.

E. Sea   The sea separating the Northlands from Teutonia and the eastern lands. Large areas of it were uncharted.

E. S., League of the.   A trading organization consisting of seven ports, chief of which was Targon.

Earl.   The only aristocratic title recognized by the Northmen. Equivalent to the Teutonic Count.

EDGTYR Wagmunding, 2nd Earl of Slane (1440-88)
    Beowulf's father. Fell from royal favour after his murder of Olaf the Red, as a result of which he was exiled to the Land of the Dan, where he died.

Edric.   A young housekarl of Hrosnaberg.

Eight Good Kings, the.   The first eight Kings of Gothmark, from Geat the Mighty to Styr the Left-handed.

E.G.K., Age of the (1000-1188)
    See Golden Age.

Egbert (1485-).   A boy spectator at the Great Tournament.

Elfryth Emundung (1466-)
    Hyglack's wife and cousin.

Emerald Forest, Slane. Largest forest in the Northlands, apart from the far-northern Taiga. Mostly deciduous.

Empire of the South.   The Great Empire of the Cassars, who were believed to rule the whole world south of Teutonia.

Emundings. Earls of Bor.
    The oldest noble house in Gothmark.

EUGEN of Brabanne (1459-
    Younger brother of Rikhard, also a Duke of Brabanne. Invaded and occupied Port Targon in 1494.

Eusebius.   Architect from the Empire of the South. One of the designers of Fanora City.

Evergreen King, the.   A title of Bjorn Longspear.

Evil, Lord of.   Surtur, the Fire Demon who rules Muspelheim, and will destroy the gods at Ragnarok.

Eymor of Slane (1390-1434)

    Grandson of Offa the Angle, exiled by his uncle, Dan the Usurper. Great-grandfather of Beowulf, Hawkeye and Ifar.

Faldo (1456-)

    One of Hawkeye's grooms at the Great Tournament.

Falgardings.

    Earls of Feldmark, including two former Kings of Gothmark, Finn the Valiant and his son Finbar the Craven.

Falhal.

    Hall of the Slain in Asgard, to which warriors who fell sword in hand were admitted to dine with Odin.

Fanagard.

    Home of several northern deities, including Freya and her brother Frey, and their father, Njord.

FANORA the Fey,

    First Queen of the Goths (1418-62). Last of the Ironside rulers of Gothmark, and the only queen to rule Gothmark in her own right. Queen de jure 1432-62, de facto (jointly with her husband, Swertan the Bastard) 1438-62. A famous seer and sorceress.

F. City

    A city on the east coast of the Northlands, founded by Swertan the Bastard as a tribute to his wife, Fanora the Fey. By Beowulf's time it had been abandoned.

F., Earl of.

    A subsidiary title of the Kings of Gothmark since Swertan.

F., Isle of.

    A small island near to the Isle of the Goths.

F., Lake.

    Another name for the Eastern Lake.

F., Lost Land of.

    A large area in the east of the Northlands, formerly known as the Land of Yflon.

F., River.

    The river on which stood Fanora City.

Fanoran Hills.

    A low range of hills west of Fanora City.

Fasling.

    Sword belonging to Bjorn Longspear.

Fates.

    See Norns.

Feldmark.

    A coastal province of south-west Gothmark, ruled by the Falgardings.

Fenrir.

    The giant wolf who will devour Odin at Ragnarok. A son of Muspelheim.

Finbar the Craven (1370-1410)

    Last Falgarding King of Gothmark, reigned 1402-10. Son of Finn the Valiant. Killed at the Battle of Hrosnaberg Gap, thus ending the Second Sferian War.

Finn the Valiant (1343-1402)	First Falgarding King of Gothmark, who usurped the throne from Guthmund the Vile in 1382. Victor of the First Sferian War, killed at the Battle of Bakir. Father of Finbar the Craven.
Fire, Land of the.	Muspelheim, the land of evil, ruled by Surtur.
F., Lord (or Prince) of the.	Surtur, Ruler of Muspelheim.
Five Great Kings, the.	The greatest Kings of the Sfear, beginning with their founder, Shylf. Ulf the Avenger was the third.
Flagon.	Half a gallon.
Forest Manor.	Hawkeye's summer home near Bettany.
Forest, Prince of the.	One of Hawkeye's titles.
Forestmount, Slaughter of (1483)	A massive disaster sustained by the Empire of the South in one of their Teutonic wars. Dardo took part on the Teutonic side.
Foryesterday.	The day before yesterday.
Fourash, Rigel.	Site of one of the seven great battles of the Fourth Sferian War (1436). Both sides claimed the victory.
Fourth Prophesy, the.	One of the prophesies of Fanora the Fey. According to Ljani it foretold that Beowulf would become King of Gothmark.
Free man.	Any man other than a slave, whether noble or churl.
Freedman.	A former slave, now free.
Freja.	Most important goddess of the Northmen, associated with fertility, sexual love and death. Sister of Frey, and thought to be Odin's wife.
Freja.	The longship in which Beowulf and his men set out for the Isles.
Frey	Northern god of fertility, twin brother of Freja. His symbol was the boar.
Futhark.	The Northmen's alphabet, consisting of 24 runes. Also used for divination.
Gallows, Lord of the.	A title of Odin.
Gamli (1468-)	One of Beowulf's housekarls.
Garm.	A giant hound who will devour the god Tyr

	at Ragnarok. A son of Muspelheim.
Garmund.	Father of Offa the Angle.
GARTH Emunding (1431-)	
	Earl of Bor, father of Hyglack's wife Elfryth, Artur and Ranulf. Also called the Old Emunding.
Geat the Mighty (975-1050)	
	Founder of Gothmark, ancestral to all its subsequent
legitimate kings.	Possibly legendary.
Geatburg, Geatland.	Capital and largest city of Gothmark, on the River Bor.
G., Earl of.	A title of all Gothic kings.
G., Treaty of (1410).	The treaty imposed on the Goths by Ulf the Avenger after their defeat in the Second Sferian War.
Geatland, Royal.	A western coastal province of Gothmark, containing its capital, Geatburg.
G., Greater.	All of Gothmark west of the River Slane, viz. Royal Geatland, Numa, Feldmark, Rigel and part of Hrosnaberg; also known as Old Gothmark.
Gerd (1448-).	A Sferian general at the Battle of Ravenswood.
Ghul.	A province in north Sfearland, ruled by the Earls of Redcape.
Golden Age.	The earliest period of Gothic history, from the Foundation of Geatburg in 1000 until the defeat and death of Styr the Left-handed at the Battle of the Sands in 1188. Also known as the Age of the Eight Good Kings.
Golden Chalice,	Lance, Arrow and Whip. Traditional prizes awarded at the Great Tournament to the overall Champion, Champion of the Joust, Archery and Chariot respectively.
Goldspur,	Aslack. See Aslack Goldspur.
Good and Evil,	God of. One of Odin's titles.
Gothic Isle.	See Isle of the Goths.
G. I., Lord of the.	A title of the Kings of Gothmark since Sigmund the Exile.
G. Strait.	The narrow sea between Port Targon and the Isle of the Goths.
G. Wars.	The Sferian term for the Sferian Wars.
Gothmark, Goths.	Beowulf's land and people, probably the

oldest inhabitants of the Northlands, whose history dated back at least 500 years.

G., New.   All the lands claimed by the Goths outside Greater Geatland, including Slane, most of Hrosnaberg, Silvermount, Fanora and the Isles. Only Slane and Hrosnaberg were under effective Gothic control.

G., Old   See Greater Geatland.

Goths, Lord of the.   One of the titles of Bjorn Longspear.

G. and Sfear,   King of the. Since the beginning of the Sferian Wars, a title claimed by the Kings both of Gothmark and the Sfear.

Great Ash.   See Yggdrasill.

G. Lake, Slane.   In fact only the second largest lake in the Northlands, in west Slane. Also called Lake Longspear, and the WesternLake.

G. Cassar or Kassar.   Ruler of the Empire of the South. The Goths were not sure whether he was still alive.

G. Tournament. A   periodical trial of martial prowess held between the Goths and Sfear in olden days. Revived by Hawkeye in 1496.

G. War   The fourth Sferian War, also called the War of Liberation (though not by the Sfear).

Green divers.   Large marine birds with hooked beaks, who lived on fish. Common throughout west Gothmark.

Grendel.   A half-human fiend; a son of Muspelheim.

Greyshadow Pass,   Silvermount. A high pass through the mountains of south-east Gothmark, on the trade route from Rigel to Targon.

Guthmund the Vile (1359-82)
                  A depraved mediaeval King of Gothmark, deposed and murdered by Finn the Valiant. The end of his reign was considered by Goths to be the beginning of modern times.

Haggar's Cross, Shylf.   Site of one of the seven great battles of the fourth Sferian War (1436). A victory for the Goths.

Hakon (1452-).   A Sferian general at the Battle of Ravenswood.

Handshake, Treaty of the (1491?)
                  A verbal agreement of uncertain date between Beowulf and Hawkeye that neither

would allow Wagmunding land to be used for vicking raids.

HAWKEYE (1468-   )   Also called Althelstan Alfarring, or Wagmunding. 2nd Earl of Karron Tha; Beowulf's cousin and greatest friend. Husband of Roslindis.

Helheim.   The abode of the dead. A dark and cheerless place.

H., Queen of.   A hideous female monster who rules Helheim.

HELGA Bronding (1471-   )
Princess of the Isles, sister of Breck Bronding. Later Queen of Shadron Mor.

Hellian.   An inhabitant of Hel or Muspelheim; an evil warrior.

Helm.   A remote ancestor of Beowulf.

Herbald Rathlecking (1457-85)
Eldest son of Rathleck the Wild, killed by his brother Athkyn whilst hunting.

Hersir. (1467-   )   One of Beowulf's housekarls.

High One, the.   A title of Odin.

Horsemount, Hrosnaberg.
The hill from which Hrosnaberg derived its name.

Hort (1460-   )   Beowulf's storekeeper during his trip to the Isles.

Houndstooth. Sferian   Earls of the Taiga.

Housekarls.   Warriors of distinction, serving a king or earl.

Hronesness, Geatland.   A headland on the west coast of Gothmark, site of the tomb of Bjorn Longspear.

Hrosnaberg, town and province.
A region in central Gothmark, ruled by the Wylfings.

H. Gap, Hrosnaberg.   Site of the last battle of the Second Sferian War (1410), at which Finbar the Craven was killed. A victory for the Sfear under Ulf the Avenger.

Hrym.   A frost giant; one of the sons of Muspelheim.

Hugo (1461-   )   One of Beowulf's housekarls.

HYGLACK Rathlecking, Prince Ironside (1465-   )
Younger brother of King Athkyn, and Beowulf's maternal uncle.

IFAR Wonredding or Wylfing (1468-   )

    Eldest grandson of Wylf, Earl of Hrosnaberg. Beowulf's second cousin.

Igor the Venomous (1290-1326)

    Last of the evil kings of Slavonia, de facto King of Gothmark 1320-26. Defeated and killed by Ranulf Redbeard at the Battle of the Northmen.

Ikalon Angjotting (1388-1452)

    Rightful heir to the Teutonic Empire, deprived of the throne by his uncle, Dan the usurper. King of the Isles of the West.

-ing and -ung

    Suffixes denoting descent. -ing was masculine, -ung feminine.

Ingeld (1472-).

    Beowulf's farrier during his trip to the Isles.

Ironside, House of.

    The mediaeval royal house of Gothmark, extinct in tail male by Beowulf's time, but ancestral to the present royal house of Silverspur through Fanora the Fey.

I., Port.

    The port of Geatburg.

I., Lord, (or Prince) of.

    A courtesy title usually bestowed on a younger son of the Gothic king.

Isle of the Goths.

    Larger of the two isles ruled by the Prince of the Isles. (The other was Isle Fanora). Place of exile of Sigmund III after his unsuccessful rebellion against Ulf the Avenger. Also sometimes called the Gothic Isle.

Is. of the West.

    A group of islands across the Western Sea, ruled by Ikalon and his descendants.

Is., Prince of the.

    A title first bestowed on Swertan's ally, Brond of the Eastern Sea. Breck Bronding was the last.

Janfar Delee, Shylf.

    A port in northern Sfearland.

Jewelbirds.

    A term used by the Goths for any small, brightly-coloured bird.

Jormungand. A

    giant sea-serpent who will kill the god Thor at Ragnarok. A son of Muspelheim.

Jotunheim.

    Land of the giants; one of the Nine Worlds.

Karl (1473-)

    A servant of Hawkeye's wife, Roslindis.

Karron Tha.

    Hawkeye's province, in south-east Sfearland, bordering Beowulf's province of Slane.

Kassar, Great, the.

    See Great Cassar or Kassar.

Keys to Heaven, the.

    A dangerous group of rocks off the coast of Silvermount.

KJARTAN Tosting (1474-)
A housekarl and friend of Beowulf. No relation to:

Kjartan Kinslayer (1208-57)
King of Gothmark 1233-57. He acquired the throne by murdering his father and brother, but made amends by defending Gothmark valiantly against the evil kings from the east.

Kovack (1456-)   A bandit leader in Silvermount.
Kranting.   Rathleck's sword.
Kreb's Bridge, Fanora.   A Bridge over Blood River, a few miles outside Slane. The limit of knowledge for most Goths.

Lake, Battle of the.   See Battle of the Doomed.
L. Fanora.   See Eastern lake.
L. Longspear.   See Western Lake, or Great Lake.
L., Prince of the.   One of Bjorn Longspear's subsidiary titles. The Wagmundings of Slane were also sometimes known by this title.

Land of the Fire.   See Fire, Land of the.
Ls. between the Lakes.   The Wagmunding lands, Slane and Karron Tha.

Lands Between the Seas.   The Northlands generally.
L. B. t. S., Lords of the.   The Kings of Gothmark.
Lars (1468-)   One of Beowulf's slaves, accompanying him on the trip to the Isles.

Last Day.   ee Ragnarok.
Leatherwings.   See Bat-lizards.
Lendrol trees.   Medium-sized trees with bright yellow flowers, common in the warmer parts of Gothmark.

Leofric (1465-).   Hawkeye's squire and chief groom at the Great Tournament.

Leontarda, Slane.   A village south of Ravenswood.
Liberation, Wars of.   According to the Goths, there had been three of these. The First was waged by Bjorn Longspear against the Drakonian Kings, 1222-25. The Second was waged by Ranulf Redbeard with Sferian aid, against the Kings of Slavonia, 1321-26. The third was the Great War, sometimes just called the War of Liberation, under Swertan the Bastard against the Sfear, 1435-38. All three resulted in the Goths regaining their freedom.

LJANI the Red (1477-   )

Beowulf's bastard half-sister, daughter of his mother,

Ragnhild the Faithless, and Olaf Wylfing.

The most learned woman in Gothmark, with obscure magical powers.

Loki.

A northern god who turned traitor and fought against the other gods at Ragnarok. A son of Muspelheim.

Lone Pine, Silvermount. A hamlet in Greyshadow Pass.

Lone Star.

The standard of the house of Ironside, also adopted by their successors, the House of Silverspur.

LONGSPEAR, Bjorn. See Bjorn Longspear.

L., Castle, Geatburg. The royal residence at Geatburg.

L., Lake. See Lake Longspear.

L., Son of.

A title awarded to those Kings of Gothmark who had triumphed in battle over their country's enemies. Rathleck the Wild was the sixth.

Magavell. A steward at the court of Atrofon.

Magnus of Syrdan (1473-)

An archer in the Great Tournament.

Manfred (1470-). Another archer in the tournament.

March, Earl of. One of Beowulf's titles.

Margrave. Border lord.

Not a formal Gothic title, but occasionally applied to those earls whose lands marched with those of the Sfear, e.g. Beowulf and the Emundings.

Mediaeval period.

The period in Gothic history from the first invasion from the east in 1188 until the accession of Finn the Valiant in 1382.

Merchants' Council.

Governing body of Port Targon, abolished by Eugen in 1495.

Midgard, or Middle Earth.

The World of Men; one of the Nine Worlds.

Mintaka (c.1380-1488). A Gothic wizard; Ljani's tutor.

Mircalla.

A beautiful courtesan of the King of Parthia, according to Suth purchased by the King of Drakonia for an enormous sum.

Mircon. A Son of Muspelheim.

Mist, Isle of.

The Larger of the two small islands in the Western Lake.

Modern period.

The period of Gothic history dating from

	the accession of Finn the Valiant in 1382.
Most High.	One of Odin's titles.
Mountain City, the.	Another name for Atrofon.
Muspelheim.	Land of the Fire, ruled by Surtur, Lord of Evil.
Muspelheim, Sons of.	The demons and monsters who will destroy the gods at Ragnarok.
Mutango.	A Gothic shrub, the juice from whose roots was used as a contraceptive.
Naur (1422-)	The aged priest attending Rathleck the Wild on his deathbed.
Nayling.	Beowulf's sword, given to him by Ljani.
Nine Worlds, the.	Asgard and Fanagard, the worlds of the gods: Alfheim, the world of the elves: Swartalfheim, the world of the dwarfs: Midgard, the world of men: Jotunheim, the world of giants: Niflheim, land of mist: Helheim, land of the dead: and Muspelheim, land of the fire.
Njord.	God of the sea and ships; father of Frey and Freja.
Non-pareil, the.	One of Longspear's titles.
Norns.	The Fates who sit at the foot of the giant ash, Yggdrasill, and decide the course of men's lives. Their names are Urd (Fate), Skuld (Being), and Verdandi (Necessity).
North, Lord (or Prince) of the.	
	A title of Longspear, also accorded to those named as his sons.
Northlands.	The large island including Gothmark, the Land of the Sfear, Fanora,
Targon, Shadron	Mor and possibly Torre.
Northmen.	The Goths and Sfear. Occasionally also applied to the men of Targon and the Isles.
Numa, Earls of.	Rulers of the province of that name. Like the Earls of Rigel, their own name was also that of their province, viz. Numa of Numa.
N., town and province.	A port in south-west Gothmark, and the surrounding province.
N., Young (1477-)	The Earl of Numa's younger son, who competed in the joust at Castletown.
Nything.	A coward or traitor; literally 'a man without honour.'
Odin.	Chief god of the Northmen; god of wisdom,

	battle and death. He had many other names and titles.
O., Son of.	A title of all Gothic kings.
Offa the Angle (1326-96)	
	Greatest of all the Teutonic kings; ancestor of Beowulf,
Hawkeye and Ifar.	
Olaf Wylfing, the Red (1448-77)	
	Natural father of Ljani by his adultery with Rathleck's daughter, Ragnhild. Killed by Beowulf's father, Edgtyr.
Old Emunding, the.	See Garth Emunding.
Old Gothmark.	See Geatland.
One-eyed Lord.	Another name for Odin.
OTTAR Wendelcrow, Prince of Wendel (1463-)	
	Crown Prince of the Sfear. Angantyr's elder son, and brother of Ali.
Parthia.	A remote eastern land of which the Goths knew little.
Port Ironside.	See Ironside, Port.
Port Targon.	See Targon, Port.
Practice	Treachery; sharp practice.
Prince.	Strictly, an earl of royal blood, but often used of any distinguished warrior of noble descent. Occasionally specifically bestowed, e.g. upon the First Prince of the Isles.
P. of the Dead.	One of Odin's names.
P. of the East.	Ragnar of Torre.
P. of Evil.	Surtur, the fire demon who rules Muspelheim.
P. of the Forest.	See Forest, Prince of the.
P. of the Isles.	See Isles, Prince of the.
P. of the Lake.	See Lake, Prince of the.
P. of the Light.	Ragnar of Torre.
P. of the North.	See North, Prince of the.
Purple Mountains, Karron Tha.	
	The range of mountains separating Karron Tha from Syrdan, and marking the northern extremity of Wagmunding lands.
Queen of the Goths.	See Fanora the Fey.
Q. of Shadron Mor.	See Helga Brondung.
RAGNAR, Count of Torre (1471-)	
	A savage warlord ruling not only Torre but Shadron Mor and parts of Fanora.

	Reputedly the worst man in the world, and a Son of Muspelheim.
Ragnarok.	Doomsday, when the gods will be overthrown by Surtur and the Sons of Muspelheim, and heaven and earth will come to an end, to be reborn later.
RAGNHILD the Faithless (1455-78)	
	Mother of Beowulf and Ljani, wife of Edgtyr of Slane. Daughter of Rathleck the Wild. Killed herself as a result of her disgrace and the death of her lover, Prince Olaf.
Rainbow Falls, Karron Tha.	
	Falls at the northern tip of Lake Longspear, where Ulf the Avenger died in 1438.
Ranulf Emunding (1476-)	
	Younger son of Garth Emunding, and brother to Artur.
R. Redbeard (1282-1353)	King of Gothmark de jure 1307-1353, de facto 1326-1353. Great-grandson of Bjorn Longspear, and apart from him probably the greatest of the Gothic kings. Victor of the Battle of the Northmen, when Igor the Venomous was defeated and slain. The first King of Gothmark to be both descended from Bjorn Longspear and ancestral to the present Gothic royal house.
R. of Torre (1454-73)	According to some, the father of Ragnar of Torre.
RATHLECK the Wild (1437-96)	
	Son of Swertan the Bastard and Fanora the Fey. King of Gothmark 1466-96. Victor of the fifth Sferian War. Beowulf's maternal grandfather.
Ravenswood, Slane.	A hill on the northern fringe of the Emerald Forest, site of a battle between the Goths and Sfear in 1496.
Raud Bluemantle (1441-)	
	Gothic Marshal of the Royal Guard, and Marshal of the Lists at the Great Tournament.
Red Horse.	See Bay Horse.
Red Chevron.	The standard of the Earls of Hrosnaberg.
Redcape	Name of the Earls of Ghul, in the Land of the Sfear.

Red Fever.	The Gothic name for various fevers, including typhus.
Regin the Mad (1454-73)	Reputedly the mother of Ragnar of Torre, by her incest with her twin brother, Ranulf.
Renate of Gothmark (1391-1465)	Daughter of Asmund the Simple and wife of the
Sferian king,	Ulf the Avenger.
RIGEL, Earl of (1453-)	Earl of Rigel in Beowulf's time. Called after his province, viz., Rigel of Rigel.
R., town and province.	A large port in south Gothmark, at the mouth of the River Slane, and its province. The only port in the Northlands to be free of ice throughout the year. Pronounced 'Rye-gel' with a hard g.
R. Bay.	The large bay at the mouth of the River Slane, containing the port of Rigel.
R. Mount, Rigel.	A hill east of Rigel, site of one of the seven great battles of the fourth Sferian War (1435). A victory for the Sfear under Ulf the Avenger.
Rikhard, Duke of Brabanne (1452-)	Elder brother of Eugen of Brabanne.
Rockenwolves.	Gigantic demonic wolves believed by the Goths to haunt ryefields at night.
Rollo of Bakir (1468-)	A competitor in the great archery tournament at Castletown.
Rolf (1436-).	An elderly servant of Hawkeye and Roslindis. Not related to:
R. Snorring (1275-1331)	Regent of the Land of the Sfear at the time of the Battle of the Northmen (1326), who assisted Ranulf Redbeard in his victory over Igor the Venomous. Ancestor of the Sferian royal house.
Romberg.	Capital of the Great Empire of the South, ruled by the Cassars. Said by some to be the largest city in the world.
ROSLINDIS Brondung (1466-)	Hawkeye's wife. Niece of King Angantyr, and daughter of Brond Bronding, 3rd Prince of the Isles. Cousin of Wanda and Helga.

Roger Butters

Rothgar of Castletown (1471-   )
> Beowulf's envoy at the Gothic court. No relation to:

R. Halfdanning (1430-   )
> King of the Dan since 1453, Befriended Beowulf's father, Edgtyr, and offered him sanctuary after his exile.

Royal Geatland. See Geatland.

Runes. Letters of the Gothic alphabet, used for communication and divination. Cf. Futhark.

Sailbacks. Large savage reptiles inhabiting parts of Fanora, so called from the sail-like structure along their spine.

Sands, Battle of the (1188)
> The Battle at which Styr the Left-handed, last of the Eight Good Kings, was defeated and slain by the invaders from Drakonia, thereby bringing the Golden Age to an end.

Saur Silverspur (1379-1402)
> Sferian king defeated and slain by Finn the Valiant at the Battle of Bakir. Natural father of Swertan the Bastard, founder of the Gothic royal house.

Saviour of the Goths. A title of Bjorn Longspear.

Saward Sawarding (1441-   )
> Beowulf's captain of guard.

Scarlettown, Shylf. A town in north-western Sfearland, home of Prince Ali.

Sea and Sky, God of the.
> Another name for Thor.

Serf The lowest rank of slave.

Seven Cities of Shadron Mor.
> Mysterious cities in the mountain kingdom of Shadron Mor. Atrofon was the only one identified to Beowulf. Even Ljani was uncertain of the others.

Sfear, Sferians. The northern people, related to the Goths, whose lands bordered on theirs. Language: Sferian, a Gothic dialect considered a separate tongue only for political reasons. Land: Sfearland, or Land of the Sfear.

Sferian Civil War (1379-1401)
> A war of disputed succession between the house of

304

Harald and the House of the Chariot.

It ended in victory for the latter under Saur Silverspur.

S. Wars.

There had been five of these before Beowulf's time, dated 1402, 1408-10, 1414, 1435-38 and 1466-7. The First and Fifth had been victories for the Goths, the Second and Third for the Sfear. The Fourth War, or War of Liberation, had been effectively a Gothic victory, since it resulted in restoration of their independence. To the Sfear known as the Gothic Wars.

Shadron Mor, Fanora.

A mountain land east of Lake Fanora, of which the Goths knew little.

Shylf the Founder (1232-76)

First King of the Sfear, and founder of their capital, Bakir.

S. province.

A province of west-central Sfearland, containing the capital, Bakir.

Sigmund III, the Exile (1395-1432)

Last of the Ironside Kings of Gothmark, king de jure 1425-32, but never reigned. Father of Fanora the Fey.

S. Rebellion.

Another name for the Third Sferian War (1414).

Sigurd (1469-).

A servant and former lover of Roslindis.

Silvermount.

A mountainous region in south-east Gothmark, over which the Goths claimed a rather tenuous sovereignty.

Silverspur, Saur.

See Saur Silverspur.

S., House of.

The royal house of Gothmark, descended from Saur Silverspur through his natural son Swertan the Bastard.

Slane.

The largest and probably richest province in Gothmark, comprising not only most of the land between the Lakes Longspear and Fanora, but the lakes themselves. Ruled by the senior branch of the Wagmundings, currently by Beowulf, the 3rd Earl.

S., Castle.

The Wagmunding residence at Sleinau.

S., Earls of.

The senior branch of the Wagmundings.

S., Forest of.

The northern part of the Emerald Forest, mainly deciduous.

S., River.

One of the main rivers of Gothmark, rising

	in Lake Longspear and reaching the sea at Rigel. The northern reaches defined the southern boundary of Wagmunding lands.
Slaughter Hill, Bor.	Site of the last great battle of the fifth Sferian War (1467), in which Aslack, Crown Prince of the Sfear, was killed. A victory for the Goths under Rathleck the Wild.
Slave.	A general term for the unfree, who comprised almost a fifth of the population of the Northlands. The term was also used as an insult.
Slavonia.	A land far to the east, home of the evil Slavonian kings. Cf. Drakonia.
Sleinau, Slane.	Capital of Slane province. On Lake Longspear.
S., Lord of.	One of Beowulf's subsidiary titles.
Sleinau, Siege of (1438)	One of the seven great battles of the Fourth Sferian War. A victory for neither side.
Sleipnir.	Odin's legendary eight-legged horse.
Snake-fish.	Long thin fish without fins, common off the coasts of Gothmark.
South Rock, Rigel.	A coast-guard station on the Southern Shore.
Southern Empire.	See Empire of the South.
S. lords.	A collectivel term for the Earls of Feldmark, Rigel, and Numa.
S. Shore, Rigel.	The coastal strip of land forming the eastern extremity of Rigel province.
S. Shore, Lord of the.	A subsidiary title of the Earls of Rigel.
Spearbills.	Tall wading birds with long beaks, who lived on fish.
Squire.	An earl's personal attendant. Sometimes a housekarl, usually a churl.
Starlight (1464-)	Beowulf's mistress and favourite slave until he met Suth.
Styr the left-handed (1158-88)	
	King of Gothmark 1175-88. Last of the Eight Good Kings, defeated and slain by Draco the Destroyer at the Battle of the Sands.
Sunset Castle, Slane.	The southernmost tip of Wagmunding lands, at the junction of the Slane and Wolf Rivers. The most northerly point at which the sun rose in midwinter.

Surtur. Ruler of Muspelheim

> The fire demon who will destroy the gods at Ragnarok.

SUTH (1473-   )

> Beowulf's name for the female slave he rescued from the servants of Ragnar of Torre.

Swamp lizards, or toads.

> Giant amphibious creatures found in Fanora and south Gothmark.

SWERTAN the Bastard (1402-66)

> Natural son of Saur Silverspur, King of the Sfear. Restorer of Gothic freedom in the Fourth Sferian War (1435-38). Reigned as King of Gothmark jointly with his wife Fanora the Fey until her death in 1462, thereafter alone. Killed at the outbreak of the Fifth Sferian War, and succeeded by his son, Rathleck the Wild.

Swertan's Road or Way.

> An unfinished road from Castletown in the west to Fanora City in the east. Only the extremities were ever completed.

Sword, Song of the.

> A traditional Gothic martial tune.

Sylthings.

> Former Earls of Karron Tha. The last of them was killed at Slaughter Hill (1467), and their lands and title were then bestowed upon Hawkeye's father, Alfar Wagmunding.

Syrdan, town and province.

> A region in east Sfearland, site of one of the seven great battles of the Fourth Sferian War (1437). A victory for the Sfear.

S., Earls of.

> The Magnussings, one of the noble houses of the Sfear.

Taiga.

> The remote Sferian province forming the north-western peninsula of the north lands. Mostly coniferous forest and mountain.

Tan (1471-87).

> Beowulf's old terrier.

Tanara Egbertung (1464-   )

> Wife of Ottar, Prince of Wendel.

Targ River, Silvermount.

> A river rising in Silvermount and reaching the sea at Port Targon.

T. Bridge.

> Site of a great Gothic victory in the fifth Sferian War (1467). Saward fought there.

Targon, Port.

> Largest city in the Northlands, with a population estimated at over 100,000.

	Governed by the Merchants' Council until their deposition by Eugen of Brabanne in 1495. A huge centre of trade and commerce, chief port of the League of the Eastern Sea.
T. Province.	The region in the Targ Valley over which Port Targon exercised nominal jurisdiction. Language: Gothic. People and adj: Tarragonian.
Tears, Song of, the.	A traditional Gothic air.
Teutonia.	A term applied to all lands formerly part of the empire of Offa the Angle, excluding the Isles of the West and the Land of the Dan. By Beowulf's time the various Teutonic lands had little in common but the Teutonic language, spoken in a variety of dialects.
Teutonic Wars.	A series of wars fought between the Great Empire of the South and various Teutonic peoples since about 1400. Swertan and Dardo both fought on the Teutonic side at various times.
Thalia the Serf (1380-1435)	
	Favourite slave of Saur Silverspur, and mother of his son, Swertan the Bastard.
Thane.	A term variously used. Often applied to the head of a family of housekarls, confirming the tendency for housekarls to form a minor aristocracy.
Third Kingdom, the.	An informal term for the Wagmunding lands, Slane and Karron Tha.
Thor.	God of the sea, sky, storm and thunder. Son of Odin.
Thorn, Feldmark.	Capital and largest town in Feldmark province.
Thrall.	Another term for slave. Pronounced to rhyme with 'shall,' except in the expression 'in thrall.'
Thunder Falls, Fanora.	Falls on the Blood River, north of Kreb's Bridge.
Tirl (1475-)	Beowulf's minstrel.
Torre.	The Goths had little idea where Torre was, save that it was some way north-east of Fanora. Governed by a succession of depraved warlords, of whom the latest,

	Ragnar, was the worst.
Treppian Way, Targon.	The great road into Targon from the south-west.
Triple Anchor.	The banner and badge of Port Targon.
Triumph and Disaster, Bringer of.	
	Another of Odin's titles.
Trolls.	Grotesque half-human creatures like overgrown dwarfs. Some were reputed to have fought alongside the Sons of Muspelheim at the Battle of the Doomed.
Tubers.	Common Gothic vegetables with swollen roots, which were good to eat.
Twisted Cross.	The badge of Torre.
Tyr.	A god of battle, after whom Tyrsday was named.
Ulf (1463-)	One of Beowulf's housekarls. No relation to:
Ulf the Avenger (1390-1438)	
	Younger brother and avenger of Saur Silverspur. King of the Sfear 1402-38. victor of the Second and Third Sferian Wars. Reigned as King of Gothmark de facto after the death of the puppet king Asmund the Simple in 1425 His death brought the Fourth Sferian War to an end and ensured Gothic independence.
Vannius.	A famous architect from the Southern Empire, employed by Swertan to design Fanora City.
Vicking raid.	A minor raid on the territory of another nation, without formal declaration of war.
WAGMUND of Slane (1410-65)	
	First Earl of Slane, and paternal grandfather of Beowulf and Hawkeye. Supporter of Swertan the Bastard in the Fourth Sferian War, and founder of the house bearing his name.
Wagmunding Castle, Slane.	
	Beowulf's official residence at Castletown.
Ws.	Tail-male descendants of Wagmund of Slane, viz. his sons Edgtyr and Alfar, and their respective sons Beowulf and Hawkeye.
Ws., March of the.	The Wagmunding anthem.
WANDA Beanstannung (1473-)	
	Hawkeye's mistress, supposedly the most

	beautiful woman in the Northlands. Cousin of Hawkeye's wife Roslindis. Sister of Breck Bronding and Helga of Shadron Mor.
War of Liberation.	A Gothic term for the Fourth Sferian War (1435-38).
Wendel, town and province.	
	A town in central Sfearland and its surrounding province. Home of the Sferian Crown Prince, Ottar Wendelcrow.
Wergeld or Wergild.	Blood-money, paid as compensation for a homicide.
Western Lake.	See Great Lake.
W. Sea.	The sea west of the Northlands.
Weyland Smith.	The legendary blacksmith of the gods.
Whale's Ness.	See Hronesness.
Whale-serpents.	Huge animals like reptilian whales, found in the Eastern Sea, off the coast of Fanora.
What is and What is Not, God of.	
	Another of Odin's titles.
Witlag.	A remote ancestor of Beowulf.
Wittan.	The Gothic council of elders, responsible for advising a king on policy, and electing a successor after his death.
Winter Star, King of the.	
	According to Ljani, a great King of Gothmark, yet to come. Beowulf's successor, not yet born.
Wolf.	Traditional badge and symbol of the Wagmundings, borne by Hawkeye on his banner and shield.
W. River, Fanora and Slane.	
	A river of south-east Gothmark, rising in Fanora and joining the Slane at Sunset Castle.
W. Valley, Slane.	Site of one of the seven great battles of the Fourth Sferian War (1438). A victory for the Goths.
Wonred Wylfing (1440-)	
	Son of Wylf, 1st Earl of Hrosnaberg, and elder brother of Ljani's father, Olaf the Red. Father of Ifar and Wulfgar.
World Ocean.	The great sea surrounding the whole of Midgard. According to Ljani the edges of it were iced over to prevent it draining off into

the void.

Wulfgar Wonredding or Wylfing (1473-)

Son of Wonred and younger brother of Ifar.

Wylf of Hrosnaberg (1414-)

Younger brother of Wagmund of Slane. Founder of the house bearing his name. Father of Wonred and Olaf; grandfather of Ifar, Wulfgar and Ljani.

Wylfings.

Tail-male descendants of Wylf of Hrosnaberg, Since the murder of Olaf the Red by Edgtyr of Slane, there had been a blood-feud between them and their cousins, Beowulf's family, the Wagmundings.

Yflon.

The former name for the Lost Land of Fanora.

Yggdrasill.

The giant ash at the centre of the Midgard, whose branches extend up into Asgard, and whose roots descend into Helheim. It will survive Ragnarok.

Zana Flamehair (1205-65)

Daughter of Dragoslav Redsword. Wife of Bjorn Longspear, and thus ancestral to Ranulf Redbeard and all subsequent Kings of Gothmark.

Immanion Press Books That Might Interest You

Oliphan Oracus - By Neil Robinson

Everyone is curious about the future. It would be a nice place to visit - but would you want to live there?...

In 2257 Keef is a television, a dishevelled, shamanic figure roaming a vast autumnal forest where big cats hunt, squirrels and monkeys teem in the canopy, and boar root in centuries of leaf litter.
In 1995 Kate Wallis is a junior research assistant at a leading pharmaceutical company's laboratory complex, and she has no idea that she will soon find herself living the plot of a science fiction soap opera.
Kate is accidentally exposed to an experimental longevity virus that causes a 262-year coma. She wakes in Keef's world and they begin a love affair that has profound repercussions for his community.

...Be warned: the resourceful heroes of science fiction stories are mythological figures, and technology might as well be magic.

Available Now
ISBN 1-9048-5300-5

Printed in the United Kingdom
by Lightning Source UK Ltd.
125107UK00002BA/46/A